UNSTEADY

UNSTEADY

A Novel

PEYTON CORINNE

ATRIA PAPERBACK

NEW YORK LONDON TORONTO SYDNEY NEW DELHI

ATRIA
PAPERBACK

An Imprint of Simon & Schuster, LLC
1230 Avenue of the Americas
New York, NY 10020

First Atria Paperback edition March 2024

ATRIA PAPERBACK and colophon are trademarks of Simon & Schuster, LLC

Simon & Schuster: Celebrating 100 Years of Publishing in 2024

For information about special discounts for bulk purchases, please contact Simon & Schuster Special Sales at 1-866-506-1949 or business@simonandschuster.com.

The Simon & Schuster Speakers Bureau can bring authors to your live event. For more information or to book an event, contact the Simon & Schuster Speakers Bureau at 1-866-248-3049 or visit our website at www.simonspeakers.com.

Interior design by Dana Sloan

Manufactured in the United States of America

1 3 5 7 9 10 8 6 4 2

Library of Congress Cataloging-in-Publication Data has been applied for.

ISBN 978-1-6680-6698-0
ISBN 978-1-6680-6700-0 (ebook)

For my dad,
who spent his life with a book in one
hand, and my hand in the other.

It never mattered what the book was
going to be about, it was always going
to be for you.

PLAYLIST

It's Called: Freefall • *Rainbow Kitten Surprise*

Little Dark Age • *MGMT*

American Teenager • *Ethel Cain*

Cherry Waves • *Deftones*

this is me trying • *Taylor Swift*

Heartbeats • *José González*

Sleep Alone • *Two Door Cinema Club*

Juliet • *Cavetown*

No Sleep Till Brooklyn • *Beastie Boys*

Waterloo • *ABBA*

Fast Car • *Tracy Chapman*

The Difference • *Flume ft. Toro y Moi*

Make This Go On Forever • *Snow Patrol*

Uncomfortably Numb • *American Football ft. Hayley Williams*

The Hills • *The Weeknd*

Getaway Car • *Taylor Swift*

Losing My Religion • *R.E.M.*

Barely Breathing • *Duncan Sheik*

Let's Get Lost • *Beck and Bat for Lashes*

Gilded Lily • *Cults*

Meddle About • *Chase Atlantic*

Asphalt Meadows • *Death Cab for Cutie*

The Kids Aren't Alright • *The Offspring*

Sex • *The 1975*

A Little Death • *The Neighbourhood*

Cupid's Chokehold • *Gym Class Heroes ft. Patrick Stump*

Cherry Flavoured • *The Neighbourhood*

peace • *Taylor Swift*

Yippie Ki Yay • *Hippo Campus*

Killer • *Phoebe Bridgers*

Revolution 0 • *boygenius*

Don't Look Back in Anger • *Oasis*

Savior Complex • *Phoebe Bridgers*

Sparks • *Coldplay*

California • *Lana Del Rey*

Your Best American Girl • *Mitski*

R U Mine? • *Arctic Monkeys*

When I Get My Hands On You • *The New Basement Tapes*

Matilda • *Harry Styles*

Family Line • *Conan Gray*

Boy With The Blues • *Delacey*

Heaven • *Brandi Carlile*

Love song • *Lana Del Rey*

Bite the Hand • *boygenius*

Delicate • *Damien Rice*

Enter Sandman • *Metallica*

Repeat Until Death • *Novo Amor*

Wish You Were Here • *Pink Floyd*

Jackie And Wilson • *Hozier*

Space Song • *Beach House*

PROLOGUE

Three Months Ago

Rhys

I can't breathe.

The icy cold seeps in through my jersey. I can feel it on my stomach—*fuck*, I'm on my stomach on the fucking ice. *Did I pass out?*

"Son, you're doing fine—can you lift your head for me?"

Everything is black. I shut my eyes and open them again. Nothing. I keep blinking; at least, I think I am . . . Fuck, how long was I out?

"Koteskiy, I need you to breathe," another voice says, before there's a hand gripping my arm. "Don't move him, Reiner, not yet."

A scrape of a blade against the ice, then my best friend Bennett's voice: "What's wrong? What happened?"

I want to call for him. I try desperately to push his name through my mouth, but it feels like my lips have been fused together.

"Back up, everyone. Back up!"

"I can't see," I manage to wrangle out. "I can't see." The second one comes out like a choked sob.

"Calm down," Ben offers, his voice soft, soothing the fear and adrenaline coursing through me. "Take it easy, Rhys—just breathe."

"Where's my dad? I can't see anything."

1

My voice is like this foreign thing echoing in a cavern. Am I speaking or is it in my head? *Why can't I see?*

Everything starts to muddle together again, and the pain throbs in my head even harder. I want to open my eyes. I want to push my tongue against my teeth to check that they're all there, and swear I'll wear a mouth guard next time. I want to go back and pay attention, keep my fucking head up against that hit. I don't want to be here.

I don't want to be here.

I don't want to be here.

The voices around me start to muddle to nothing as I slump into the thick darkness entrapping me.

CHAPTER ONE

Present

Rhys

"Just try it today, and if you still feel like shit, I won't ask you to do it again. Okay?"

Even with the volume on my phone turned so low it should be silent, my father's voice is a booming echo through the speaker. I wince lightly, using muscle memory to pull the black joggers over my legs in the darkness of my bedroom. After gently shrugging a hoodie over my head, I swipe the phone from where it lies on the dresser.

"I'm fine," I say. It's not really an answer, but I know what he's really asking beneath his command.

We're cut from the same cloth, my father and I—both calm under pressure, both "dipped like Achilles into a pool of confidence" as my mother so often puts it. I've been compared to him all my life—for the way I look, the way I skate, the way I play—and unlike many of the other NHL legacies I've played with, I don't mind it.

My dad has always been my hero.

Which is why I know he's asked me to work with the First Line Foundation today—a charity my father started after retiring from the NHL—purely as a way to check up on me. Where we used to talk hockey for hours, we barely share surface-level conversations now and I *know* he knows I've started avoiding him altogether.

The foundation funds scholarship programs for kids who want to play hockey but don't have the means to do so. I've worked with the program before, I've even enjoyed it before, but now . . .

It feels daunting, like I know even now that the smiles of children won't drive away the constant dread filling up the void of my body.

"Rhys," he calls again, his voice still too loud. I huff a breath, sliding my shoes on and grabbing my bag before heading into the warm June air. "Just . . . try it today. And then, if you feel like it, take the keys tomorrow morning to run a few drills before the rink opens."

I nod, tossing the bag into the backseat of my BMW. I'd been cleared to drive for a month or so but have barely left the house in all that time.

"I will," I finally say, tightening my hands on the steering wheel in the silence that follows. The swishing sound through my father's crackling speaker tells me he's driving with the windows down in his ancient truck that my mom refers to as "that *thing.*"

"And if you're not ready this year, there's no reason to push yourself. An extra year might be good, to make a better impression on the scouts before the next draft—"

The next draft . . . My shoulders hike defensively, but I can't help the slight appeal of it, waiting until I don't *feel* this way about hockey anymore, until I love it again, just like I always have.

This is ridiculous. I'm not a soldier. I play NCAA hockey . . . I should be over this by now.

I cut him off before this entire conversation sends me spiraling and right back into my room with the blackout curtains shut tight.

"I want to play. I feel ready to play again," I lie. It's one I've been practicing, so it rolls off my tongue easier than breathing. "I'm good."

A deep sigh over the line before we exchange quick goodbyes and I finally start the car.

• • •

The rink is crowded, especially for a Thursday evening at dinner time. Kids ranging in age from five to thirteen skirt and swerve around the rink with a few volunteers that I recognize from previous functions—some retired players, some parents with relevant experience. I even spot Lukas Bezek—one of the new star players for the Bruins—with the social media team working with a few of the older kids on slap shots.

Just as I step onto the ice, a little blur slams into my legs with a belatedly screamed, "Watch out!"

I catch the small kid before he can bounce off my thighs and fall flat onto the ice.

He giggles as I hold him up by the little pads and jersey he's wearing and wait until he gets his feet under him again. He looks up at me the entire time. He has a dusting of freckles and a gap-toothed grin that makes him look just like a mini hockey player. He slides a bit again, not quite the best skater out there, but he doesn't frown or seem agitated in the slightest.

"Sorry," he offers, a little whistle coming from the hole where he's missing a front tooth. "I'm still working on my stops."

The old Rhys would have laughed and said something gentle or funny, like *"That's all right, bud. I am too."* But even the idea of laughing seems impossible, so I offer as much of a grin as my face can manage.

"Good thing we're gonna work on those stops today," a chipper voice announces as a tall, pretty girl glides up and stops short next to us, a gaggle of little ones behind her. "And good job, Liam, on finding our special guest coach for today!"

Liam, the boy still clinging to me with a little gloved hand on my leg, laughs again and leans back.

"He's so tall!"

The group of kids now surrounding us all giggle and smile at me, waiting on something. Sweat slicks the back of my neck at the sight of all their hopeful faces looking up at me, relying on me.

Maybe this was a mistake.

"This is Rhys." The girl takes over. "He's a center for the Waterfell Wolves, so he plays hockey in college, just outside Boston! He's been playing since he was your age. And he's gonna help you guys with skating today."

"Will we play today?" a little girl asks with her helmet in her hands, cheeks blushing immediately at the attention of her fellow classmates.

"Probably not today. We're gonna mainly work on skating, all right?" The girl smiles lightly at the group as they all cheer. "We'll do a bit of stick handling with our hockey captain here." She nods to me. "And then finish with some fun games. How does that sound?"

A consensus of excited shouting commences before she dismisses them to some warm-up laps.

"Hope you don't mind me taking over," she says, reaching her hand out to shake mine. "I'm Chelsea. One of the leads told me you'd be helping out today with the little ones."

"Yeah," I reply. I skate gently beside her, following her lead to the other side of the rink where a stack of cones sits by the boards, and try to pull it together. "Thanks for that. Was a little out of it this morning."

"I understand." She chuckles. "We all have some of *those* nights."

I should laugh, or nod and agree—as if my lack of emotion is just due to a bad hangover from a rough night out—but I can barely muster a half-grin as we set up for drills.

"Anyway, for the littles, it's mainly just a skating lesson. The ten-and-up group is with the Bruins for media today." She nods toward the stumbling crew headed back in our direction. "And the little one who tried to knock you over is Liam—he needs some extra care if you want to focus on him today. Make it easier."

So I do.

Liam is easy, an eager—albeit clumsy—learner who never loses his smile. He clings to me easily, watching the other kids every now and then with a little determined scowl.

Chelsea closes the session with a quick round-up huddle. Only half of the kids are able to kneel, the rest sprawling on the ice with happy smiles.

I keep waiting for that little reminder of myself at this age, holding my dad's stick and letting him glide me almost too fast across the ice. Watching his games on the TV, decked out in his jersey and shouting just like my mom. The first time I got a goal on my own, even if it was nearly accidental. I wait . . . and still, nothing.

"My brother's real good too," Liam says a little breathlessly as he holds on to the pocket of my joggers once again. The kid's a terrible skater, but he's happy.

"Is he?"

The kid looks over his shoulder at the older group finishing up across the ice.

"Yep. Oliver. I think he'll be jealous you skated with me today."

"Jealous?" I quirk a brow at the little guy.

He nods and another giggle escapes. "Oh yeah. You play Wolves hockey, and Oliver wants to play for them *bad*."

I glance over, now wondering why exactly Liam hasn't been called over by the gaggle of parents surrounding the kids gorging on the goodies at the snack table. The older kids scatter, all heading for the gate, except one—a taller boy with hair long enough that it hangs just out of his helmet, who is skating right for us.

Chelsea is nowhere to be seen; in fact, the ice has cleared. Parents and children cover the bleachers and huddle around the table of snacks, their laughter and chatter echoing and bouncing off the walls of the open rink. I wait for someone to step up to the glass and notice the two boys still on the ice, but no one bats an eye.

"Is she not here?" the older boy, Oliver, asks, pulling his helmet off to hang in his hands. His hair is darker, but the gray eyes are identical to his brother's so it's easy to spot their connection.

Liam shakes his head, silent for the first time all afternoon.

Oliver makes a frustrated sound. After a quick wary glance up at me, he looks down at Liam with his hands on his hips. "I told you, if she's not here, you wait for me by the snacks with Miss Chelsea."

Liam pouts, his hand releasing me so he can skate, or trip, to his brother.

"But it's a Wolf!" he explains in a semi-hushed voice, letting out a quick little howl. "Like, he plays hockey for Waterfell."

The kid waits for his brother to react, but Oliver looks embarrassed, almost angry. Liam howls again, then turns his head toward me and says, "Right, Rhys?"

I let out a smile and nod. "Right, Liam."

"He's gonna teach me so much hockey stuff, I'm gonna be even better than you."

Oliver smiles, albeit reluctantly, at his brother's antics, as Liam skates little circles around him. He probably feels like he's flying, but he's tripping along on one foot.

It's easy to see the camaraderie between the brothers, and it makes me think of being six and chasing Bennett around like a lunatic. He was always bigger, but I was faster. He's my brother, even if not by blood, and an ache emanates from my chest at the thought of him, of the one hundred missed calls and texts on my phone that I've yet to listen to or answer.

I haven't seen him since the hospital, despite knowing he's made multiple visits to my house, only to be turned away by my parents over and over.

My phone vibrates in my pocket, and I grab it.

BENNETT REINER: 152 Unread Messages
I know you're alive dumbass. Answer your . . .

Not bothering to read more than the preview, I slip the phone back into my pocket and ignore the niggle of guilt that threatens. I refocus my attention on the boys who are staring blankly up at me.

Chelsea suddenly joins us. She's smiling brightly at the boys, and offers me a little shrug before leaning over to whisper in my ear.

"They're always the last ones here." As she speaks, I look over and see that the snack table has cleared out and we are the only four left in the whole rink. "Someone has to stay with them until—"

A door slams and a girl sprints down the ramp toward the gate.

She's slight, covered in tight black leggings and an oversized blue sweatshirt that she's practically swimming in, her ponytail loose and fluffed up by the hood hanging around her shoulders. The undone, barely-there look on her face makes me wonder when she last slept.

I watch Liam's face light up, his little knees bending like he might jump up and down from excitement if he wasn't afraid to fall. Next to me, Chelsea huffs and rolls her eyes, giving me a look that says this is far from the first time this girl has been late.

"I'm here," the new arrival shouts, her bag bouncing hard against her back where it's slung on her shoulders. She sprints onto the ice in slip-on sneakers, sliding aimlessly for a moment before she regains her balance and takes quick steps toward us.

"You're late," Chelsea sneers. "Again." Her hands fall to Oliver's shoulders in a protective gesture, and red spreads further across the new girl's already flushed skin.

"I know," she says, kneeling onto the ice to get at eye level with Liam, who is still excited, with no sign of frustration toward his . . . mother? She seems too young, especially with Oliver looking to be around eleven.

The girl looks around briefly, and it's only then that a flash of recognition hits me. I've seen her before, but I can't place where.

She doesn't bother speaking to Chelsea, only giving a big smile to Liam, who is looking at her like she's his entire world, before shifting to speak directly to Oliver, whose face is red and slanted down, disappointment emanating from him.

"I'm sorry, bud." She bites her lip hard, her wide gray eyes pleading. "I tried so hard."

"I got even faster today," Liam offers, completely and blissfully ignorant of his brother's obvious frustration.

She gives him a wink and rubs his head lightly, mussing his hair as she stands back up. "I'll bet you'll be even faster than Crosby one day."

I almost snort, partially because I'm now imagining a Sidney Crosby poster in her childhood bedroom. Despite the fact my lips don't even begin to rise—no hint of a laugh threatening—I am taken aback by how quickly she got any kind of reaction out of my empty body.

"Crosby's not the fastest. And you swore you'd be here to see," Oliver accuses, scowl still in place, cheeks heated.

"Oliver, killer, I'm sorry. I promise I'll be here—"

"You say that every time, and you only don't show because of *him*." He spits the word like poison and her expression shutters.

It's clear whoever this *him* is, he's a constant issue for them. A boyfriend, maybe? I cross my arms, finding myself somewhat in agreement with Chelsea.

"How about you show me now?" the girl offers in a hopeful tone, attempting to turn the conversation around. "Give me a minute to put on my skates and I'll even race you—"

"Actually," Chelsea cuts her off, "we need to be off the ice now. They've got to clear it before the beer league game tonight. Come on, Oliver, let's get you one of the cookies from the snack table. I saved some for you."

Oliver follows Chelsea as she skates off toward the exit, and I realize only now that the girl is staring at me, eyebrows furrowed.

Self-conscious in a way I would never have been before the accident, I fix my stance, straightening my spine. My arms hang loose at my sides for a moment, but somehow that seems worse. I cross them before feeling more ridiculous and letting them drop again, one hand finding my pocket.

"Who's the big guy?" she asks Liam, quirking an eyebrow at him before he smiles.

"Oh, yeah, I know—stranger danger—but that's Rhys."

"I don't know who Rhys is, bug."

"He's gonna help us get *real* good at hockey," Liam says, just as his skate slides out from underneath him and he slips onto the ice, stomach first.

I reach for him immediately, easily picking him up and holding his arms until he gets steady again. Easy enough, especially after repeating this process about twenty times in the last hour.

"You good?" I ask, bending down to his level and sending another quick, albeit restrained smile to the girl looking down at us. I wait a beat for something—a smile, a hum of approval, a *"How sweet"* or *"You have such a way with kids."* All normal responses to my easy charm before. But she gives me nothing but a wide, blank stare.

I hate it, feeling like her cat-like gray eyes can see everything. Like there's something physically wrong with me that signals the absolute shit show stowed beneath my skin.

"I'm good," Liam replies, skating ahead on shaking legs. "Rhys is, like, the best hockey player."

"Ahh." She nods, eyes still infuriatingly locked on me. "All right, welp, say goodbye to the hockey hotshot, bug. Time to go home."

"Bye, Rhys! Next week I'll bring my helmet. It's got stickers on it," Liam practically shrieks, picking himself up quickly from another fall before trying another howl with me. I know I should join him, make him feel like I'm his friend, but there's a pressure on my chest that keeps me from breathing, let alone howling with him.

He falls twice more on his way to the boards and bleacher seats where his brother is unlacing his skates. Oliver carefully watches the girl, like he's worried about her despite his anger.

She blows a raspberry; her bangs and the multitude of loose tendrils of silky brown hair whip and whirl around her face. I wait a moment, poised to introduce myself when I spot the hang tag on her bag.

"You go to Waterfell?"

Not just Waterfell—that's a skate embroidered into the end of the logo: a figure skate.

She spins back toward me so fast, her entire balance gets knocked off. I grab her, not shocked that she feels light as air from how small she is, and place her back on her feet before she can blink.

Her name is lost to me, if I ever knew it, but I remember her. I've seen her in and out of the complex before, always in a rush of some sort, always barely put together.

But the memory that's hitting me hardest is seeing her burst into our practice one day when we ran late, shouting her head off at our even-keeled coach before a tall, stern-faced man picked her up by the waist and carted her off.

I stayed after my practice let out, lingering in the tunnels for a moment as she started blasting loud, vibrant music and blazed onto the cut-up ice, keeping the Zamboni from clearing while she skated like she wanted to kill someone.

Pure passion.

She's beautiful this close, even with her haphazard look—her hair is shiny and dark, skin flushed but pale with a unique little patch of freckles under her right eye.

"Glad I caught you." I try to smile, my old charm covering me like a thick coat, a shield. She blinks once, twice, then sharpens her brow in deep frustration and shoves away from me.

"I'm sure you catch all kinds of things."

Smiling still, in spite of the cold response and the emptiness hollowing my gut, I offer, "I play hockey for Waterfell."

"All right, kiddos," she calls, ignoring my words and presence completely as she marches off the ice with an upturned nose. Something inside me twists, whether at her dismissal of the thing that once made me so valuable, or the lack of any recognition. "Let's go."

The two boys grab their gear bags and strut behind her, Liam just as animated as before and Oliver just as dejected. Looking at his beaten-down expression feels like a punch in the chest, and I rush off the ice to follow them.

"Hey," I call, waiting as all three turn around. "Can I talk to you for a minute—uh, sorry, you didn't say your name."

Liam giggles and points up at the slip of a girl guarding him.

"That's Sadie."

"Thanks, nugget." She rolls her eyes, hip-checking him in the shoulder as she looks up at me. "What for?"

"It's about . . . the boys. Just—" I cut myself off as she struts down to me. The closer she gets, the faster my heart races at the idea of arguing with her.

"What?" Her tone is just as aggressive as her stance, arms crossed and glaring up at me, as if *she* is the 6′3″ center with three extra inches of skates.

"I know I'm new to the scholarship program, but Liam and Oliver are great—even as young as they are."

"I know."

I manage to keep the smile plastered to my face, mainly because something warm is thrumming in my gut. "And, well, I think parental support is important to kids, especially about their interests—"

"Get to the point, hotshot."

All right, fine. No more charm. I harden my stare and cross

my arms. "You should make an effort to be here. Not a forgotten promise."

Her eyes turn molten before me, fire beneath the slate gray, and for a moment I think she might tackle me, attempt to check me into the boards.

Maybe it'll help, force me to feel something besides the empty chasm of nothingness yawning inside. Maybe, if she turns out to be stronger than she looks, she'll knock me flat on my ass.

Honestly, I hope she does.

"Noted. Anything else you'd like to spout off from that high horse of yours?" Sadie doesn't wait even a second before continuing. "Great!" Her hands clap sharply together. "Glad we had that talk."

"Wait." I try again, my frustration mounting as I reach to grab her wrist and stop her retreat.

She flares, igniting at the contact and pulling herself from my touch like I've tried to set her on fire. I release her immediately, only to see her little hand now wrapped, as much as it can be, around my wrist. She's bending it like a bully on the playground in some attempted self-defense move that sends a zing up my spine.

"Don't ever grab me like that again." She bends my wrist a little more, and I want to ask her to keep it there in her warm grip because this is the first *anything*, other than pain, I've felt in months.

But I can't, because by the time I work a swallow down my throat and unstick my tongue from the roof of my mouth, all three of them are gone.

CHAPTER TWO

Sadie

For me, Tuesdays are the worst day of the week.

"Sade, please."

Tuesdays are paydays, which means my father is more inclined to outright ask me for money rather than dropping hints or stealing from our food budget.

"I can't."

I try not to look, focusing instead on lacing up my sneakers and double-checking that my bag has everything I'll need for practice, as well as clothes for the café. After stuffing an extra pair of socks into the side zipper pocket, I'm forced to look at him as I descend the rickety stairs.

"Just an extra few. I just need something to get me through the week."

I try to remember that there was a time when it wasn't like this. When my father was someone who loved us dearly—who put me, and even baby Oliver, first.

"I said I can't," I say again, crossing my arms and wanting so badly to shove past him. His head is hanging lightly, hair shaggier now than it has been, but his eyes are still mine despite how red-rimmed and dark they are. "Oliver needs new skates; his foot was bleeding yesterday from how tight his old ones are."

My brother tried to hide it, but I caught him last night in the kitchen putting Band-Aids on his ankles.

My dad's mouth tightens, and I can almost hear the argument in his head, the line he walks so carefully. He's never hit us, never physically hurt one of us. But his mere presence is enough to feel like someone is pressing down on my shoulders. He wants to argue that this is his house, it's his money, but it isn't really. Not anymore—not since I got a job at fourteen and saved every penny until I had enough to keep skating. Not since earning the scholarship that ensured I didn't have to take a single one of his handouts—if they could even qualify as one.

My mother had money from a trust her wealthy family bestowed on her too early, before her habits got harder to break. She pays child support to my father—checks I work tirelessly to find in the mail before he can blow them on top-shelf whiskey.

Once upon a time, I believed they were a cute romantic story: the rich girl falling head over heels for the boy from nothing. But now I know better.

My mother doesn't love anyone except herself.

And my father might love us, deep down, but he'll always love his vices more.

Maybe that's why I can't stop myself from reaching for the fifty in my jeans pocket from tips the day before and slipping it into his hand.

"That's all you can have from me for the week," I warn, a swirl of anxiety threatening my stomach as his eyes light up. "I'm serious. I have to pay for Oliver's skates."

"It's fine," a raspy voice huffs, my brother sliding underneath my arm and into the kitchen. "I can stay in my old ones for another month."

"You can't, killer. Besides, you have a tournament coming up."

Before I can get to it, Oliver fills up the filter and starts a pot of coffee for me. He keeps his back turned to our father, the actual adult, still stationed by the doorway like he might bolt at any moment.

"When's your tournament?" Our father's voice is shaky, eyes still a little bloodshot as he walks farther into the kitchen, apprehension in his every move toward Oliver. When he's drunk, he's fearless, but sober he's almost scared of us. "Maybe I could come—"

"Don't bother," Oliver mutters beneath his breath, cutting him off. I hip check him lightly as I grab creamer from the fridge and happily take the to-go cup my eleven-year-old brother is already holding out to me.

"It's next weekend if you wanna come to mine," a sleepy Liam says from the kitchen door before dragging his Star Wars blanket across the floor with him and planting himself in a seat at the table. "Are you making pancakes again, Sissy?"

I grab my bag from the table and sling it over my shoulder before ruffling Liam's curls from behind his chair. "Not today, bug. There are some toaster waffles in the freezer for both of you, and your lunches are packed on the second shelf."

Liam slumps dramatically in his seat. "No pancakes means a bad day, Sissy."

Oliver grumbles, harshly shoving the plate of already-prepared cinnamon-toast waffles toward his brother. "Eat and shut it about the pancakes."

I pull his ear as I pass him. "Be nice," I reprimand, before softening my voice and giving him a pat. "And thank you."

"Whatever."

A pang in my heart weighs my shoulders down, twisting in my chest until a scream is almost pushing through my lips. It feels like my body is on fire from the inside, every bit of anger and resentment and fear bubbling like an active volcano, and I know I'll explode on *him* if I don't get out of this room right now.

"Can't you see what you're doing to them?" I want to shout. *"I know what happens next because it's already happened to me. And I can't do anything else to stop it—wake up!"*

"Do you have to go before the bus comes?" Liam asks, his voice still overly loud for the early hour, but I can almost feel the discomfort in it.

Do you have to leave us with him? That's the real question. Oliver might remember Dad before all this, but Liam doesn't. Liam only knows this father—the one who doesn't show up, who continues to grow weaker and nearer to death every day.

Oliver might be bursting with anger, but Liam is wrestling with fear.

I hate to leave them; I hate sending them to summer camps and endless distractions that don't break our budget. But without skating, my tuition isn't paid, and both jobs I currently hold are barely enough to supplement the checks from our mom.

This is for them. One day, maybe, they'll understand it.

"Love you, nugget," I whisper, kissing Liam hard on the cheek. He dives in for a hug and latches onto me until I tickle his sides to get him to release me. Oliver is leaning against the kitchen counter, his ever-growing lanky body rigid with his arms crossed tightly over the hand-me-down USA Nationals shirt. I give him a nod, knowing how much he doesn't like to be touched, before passing my father's figure, leaning in the doorway.

He opens his mouth like he wants to say something, and I wait, because some part of me is clinging to the possibility that he'll come back.

But he stays silent.

And I want to scream.

• • •

Blaring Deftones's "Cherry Waves" does little to clear the fog of anger, but the sight I'm greeted with upon my arrival at the ice plex easily empties every thought out of my mind.

There's an expensive car in the otherwise empty lot, and the lights inside the complex are on.

I should be the only one here. I use Coach Kelley's key before my shifts at the concession stand for extra ice time. Public skate doesn't start until eight a.m., so no one should be here before—I double-check my phone again—six in the morning.

And yet, with a quick glance through the large panes of glass surrounding the ice, I can see a blue figure—a goddamned *hockey* player—*sitting* on the ice in the corner.

I drop my bag, push my sneakers off by the heels, and slip on my skates, lacing them fast. My headphones are still blasting, only amping me up; I'm ready to pick a fight.

Bursting through the doors, I shout a quick, "Hey! You can't be here!" and march myself into the already lit-up rink, ready to give whatever moron is hogging *my* ice time the screaming match of the century.

Only something is wrong.

The man on the ice isn't sitting—he's collapsed, like he's hurt.

He's panting heavily, his skin gleaming where it's exposed. His hockey sweater is half pulled up over one of his shoulders, like he was in the middle of trying to get it off and couldn't finish.

Sweat clings to every part of him, sticking his long dark hair to his forehead and against the back of his neck. His abs are flexing over and over, like he might be hyperventilating. The golden skin is taut and distracting—so much so that I shake my head to clear my derailing train of thought.

I yank out my headphones, and the sound of his gasping breath immediately fills the silence of the rink. Sliding the guards off my skates, I hop onto the ice to skate over to him and come to a harsh, scraping stop.

"Hey," I call, my voice shakier than I want it to be. "Are you all right?"

Stupid question considering the circumstances.

My hands, still bare because I didn't put my gloves on, grab at his arms and try to stop his constant shivering. His eyes are dilated, taking me in slowly, almost like he's not sure if I'm real.

This close, I recognize him—the hockey hotshot *Rhys* from the other day. Dark brown hair, pretty brown eyes, and a sharp jawline like hard steel, with a dimple in his right cheek that makes me wonder if there's a matching one on the left when he smiles.

He slumps back again, but his teeth start chattering harder and he swiftly pulls his knees tight against his chest, skate blades slicing against the ice.

"I c-c-can't breathe," he manages to gasp out.

He can, he's breathing right now, but I'm no stranger to a panic attack. My mind settles, the chance to focus on someone else always a welcome distraction against the endless screaming in my own head.

"Hey," I call, a little harsher, even while I plaster on a pretty smile, trying my best to look sweet and calm in hopes that it will bring him down from whatever dangerous precipice of panic he's hanging from. "Look at me."

He does, brow furrowing lightly, brown eyes glistening beneath.

"You can breathe."

Something wrestles in his eyes before he shudders and grasps his half-on practice sweater in a death grip, like he's going to pull it off. My hand closes over his, releasing his grasp and stopping him from nearly choking himself on the collar in his desperation.

"I'm s-s-sorry."

I need to get him off the ice, but I know I won't be able to lift him alone, and it'll be at least an hour before anyone else shows up.

"C'mon, hotshot." I try for something between gentle exasperation and flirtation in spite of my own racing heart, hoping to relax him. "You're okay," I say, like telling a baby they're fine to calm them when they fall. "We're gonna have to get you off the ice. Can you stand?"

"Y-yeah," he says, his breaths labored and too fast at the same time. "I'm sorry."

"Don't apologize, just help me, okay?" I reach around his middle, grabbing on to the padding of his hockey pants on his lower back and using it to hold him steady as he slowly finds his footing.

"I don't know if I can skate," he mutters between shuddering breaths, his eyes squeezing tightly closed. "I—"

"You're fine. I'll use it as an excuse to get my hands on you," I say, my nerves fried and mouth stumbling over anything to distract him. "Just stay upright on your skates. I've got you."

He looks at me again, brown eyes still dilated as he locks onto my gaze. A little nod lets me know he's as stable as he's going to get, and I dig my skate into the ice to press off slowly with his added weight.

God, he's heavy and tall—albeit lankier than most hockey players his height.

It takes almost a full minute to make it to the gate while skating carefully and carrying double my weight. He doesn't peel his eyes off my profile the entire time; I can feel them almost searing the side of my face. I manage to slowly set him on the bottom step of the short bleachers nearby.

His hands reach down for his laces, fingers shaking so hard they keep missing the loops until he's sawing out a curse beneath his breath with a bitter expression of hopelessness. But I've been a caretaker my entire life, and no amount of annoyance can keep me from kneeling before him and taking his hands in mine.

"Focus on slowing your breathing," I offer before he can open his mouth for another pitiful apology. My fingers are numb but make quick work of his laces and pull on the tongues so he can easily slip out of his skates.

I draw the line at pulling the no doubt foul-smelling hockey boots from this stranger's feet.

"You got it from here?" I ask, rocking back on my skates and looking up to see his eyes still locked heavily on my face.

"You're Liam's mom."

I snort. *Closest thing to it.*

"Sister, but yeah. We met. Sadie." I smile brightly at him, praying that he doesn't really remember meeting me.

"Rhys." He puffs a few breaths, almost like he might laugh if he could catch his breath. "You wanted to knock me on my ass," he says with a smile, and I see the peek of a dimple on his other cheek. *Knew it.*

"Yeah, well . . . you did that all on your own today."

Another one of those light, huffing laughs leaves his open mouth. His hands and arms are still trembling. It's silent again, only the buzzing hum of the lights and systems as the background to my second perusal of him. I want to speak, to fill the space with comforting words, but I find myself empty of them.

"You're the figure skater that looks like fire."

My brow furrows. "What?"

He huffs and smiles lazily, looking more like a sleepy drunk. "Never mind."

Why is he here? What happened to him on the ice? The questions are piling up, pushing against my lips to fly out. But one look at his lax, vulnerable body position and I clam right back up.

Not my circus. Not my monkeys.

Cutting my eyes away from the depth of his, I check my watch.

Damn it.

Six thirty a.m.

After scooping my hair up into a high bun, I slide my lounge pants off and plop them into a heap a few feet away from Rhys's resting body, leaving me in tight undershorts. Part of me feels terrible just leaving him here, but the other part of me—the part that knows how easily I could lose *everything* I've worked for if I don't focus—

strengthens my resolve. With any luck, Mr. Hotshot here will get it together and get out of here.

I pause at the gate, biting my lip and glancing back over at him.

"Can you get out okay? Are you good now?"

He nods slowly, barely opening his eyes and giving me a quick thumbs up. He grabs his skates in one hand and braces the other on the railing, leaning on it heavily before he slips his hand to the wall to walk up the ramp to the exit doors.

With the sound of the door slamming shut, I re-center my focus and hook my phone up to the handheld speaker my coach gave me so I can work on my short program choreography before my shift starts.

At least, I try.

But no matter how loudly I play the music, or how many times I fall while trying—and failing at—a triple axel, nothing can pull my focus from the hockey boy with the sad eyes.

• • •

As I push through the door, a blast of warm air from the interior of the ice plex hits my pinkened skin before I stall at the sight of the hockey player I'd assumed would be long gone.

It's as if he barely made it out of the rink's doors. He's sitting against the half-wall beneath the window with his eyes closed and head tilted back. The long column of his throat works with a heavy swallow before he opens his eyes to look up at me.

I should ask if he's all right, but the only thing that comes from my lips is a bitter, "Were you watching me skate?"

It isn't a question so much as an accusation.

His brown eyes are less glassy now, but his skin still looks pale, like the panic is taking a long time to truly drain from his system. He shakes his head, and a minuscule grin ticks his lips crooked.

"No, but I might like to," he snickers, looking a little dazed and unkempt. "I'm imagining you skating like Liam, since that's all I have to go off."

There's no stopping the grin that stretches across my mouth; as much as Liam loves to "play hockey," he can barely keep his little legs underneath him.

"Well, considering I used my warm-up time helping some hockey player, I don't think your imagination is too far off."

I'd meant it as a joke, but hearing it out loud it sounds like a reprimand—even worse is catching Rhys's near-wince as he absorbs what I just said.

God, has it really gotten this bad? Having things under control has never really been my specialty, nor has self-preservation. Feeling too much all at once until the dam bursts is much more my speed.

I sit down to unlace my skates and pull my bag closer.

"I don't know what's wrong with me," he says, and laughs.

"I think you're crashing," I offer. "From what looked like a major panic attack. Has this happened before?"

"I'm good," he says, shrugging off my question.

My spine stiffens. I'm ready again to fight with him if needed. "If it *has*, then it was really stupid for you to be out there without anyone around."

I wait a moment, but he doesn't say anything.

Finally, I ask, "What are you still doing here?"

"I was trying to work up the nerve to drive home." He laughs, but winces at the same time. "If you can get my keys." He wobbles to his feet, his footing unsteady until he slumps back against the glass door.

"Yeah, you're definitely not driving, hotshot."

"What are you even doing here?" he asks, but there's no bite to his tone, just mild curiosity. "My—I was told no one would be here this early."

Technically, no one is allowed to be.

"I don't know what you're talking about because I wasn't here this morning. Just like *you*, hotshot, didn't have a panic attack and nearly pass out alone on the ice."

He grimaces but nods, walking carefully with his bag slung on his left side and his right hand braced almost painfully on my shoulder.

"*No one* was here this early," I concede with a pleasant little smile on my lips. "Which is the only reason I'm going to help your big ass to my car and get you wherever it is you need to go."

"I can drive, honestly. I just need to sit in my car for a few."

I don't want him to drive, but I know at any moment now Coach Kelley and the rest of the summer staff will start arriving, and I can't—*God*, if I get any more demerits this year . . .

Stop.

Shaking my head, I straighten. Going down that path will only lead me to my own cryfest in the car and to speed-skating through my ice time while throwing sloppy jumps.

This year won't be like last year. This year is going to be better.

"All right, if you swear."

Rhys nods again and seems to try a charming sort of boyish smile.

We push through the doors of the ice plex, stepping into the cool morning. My beat-up Jeep Cherokee looks almost ridiculous next to his sleek black BMW, but I manage to keep the snide comment on my tongue from tumbling out.

Releasing him once he has a hold on the driver's side door, I clasp my hands together and rock back and forth on my heels.

"Thanks," he begins, looking at me with that same searing, annoying intensity. He looks less vulnerable now, almost tired but forcing some sort of charismatic mask. "I genuinely app—"

"Save it." I hold my palms up to stop him before he can irk me anymore. "I wasn't here and neither were you. Don't worry, hotshot."

His brow furrows, the same sadness from before crawling back into his eyes, and for a moment, I hate it. Every word to him out of my mouth is infected with taunting, and I can hear it but I can't stop it.

I wait for him to chew me out or push back, but he just looks tired.

"Right. Well . . . I'm sure I'll see you around."

The vulnerability slips slightly back onto his face as he sighs, unlocking his BMW to slide in. The longer I stare at his open expression the more my stomach churns, almost like I'm going to be sick, so I turn on my heel to break the haze of my mind and march toward the doors.

And no matter how deeply I want to check on him once more before I head back in, I keep my head screwed on straight. The urge to tease and kiss away his despair is too great, and it will only end poorly for me.

"Not if I see you first," I mutter beneath my breath. A little vow to myself to steer clear of the boy with the sad eyes before I try to take his healing into my own hands.

CHAPTER THREE

Rhys

Since the accident, waking up drenched in sweat has become my new normal, so it isn't a surprise when I turn over to ice cold, soaked sheets. What *is* a surprise is the soft voice of my mother pulling me from yet another night terror instead of my alarm.

"Shit," I mumble, blinking through the bleary smear of moisture over my eyes.

My mother is leaning over me, her hand brushing the side of my face where I've turned toward her voice.

"You're sleeping on your stomach again," she begins, keeping her voice soft like she has for the past months. It makes my chest clench tight because that isn't like my mom—she is loud and invasive, and this summer of my demons has turned her into . . . this. "You really scared me this morning."

Shit.

I close my eyes a little tighter, afraid of the look that I know is plastered across her face. While my father is more like me, my mother is all heart with zero hard exterior.

Growing up, she'd been the soft place for me to fall; hell, even Bennett had let her tend to every scrape and mend every loss with a proud smile and kiss on the head while our numbers were painted on her cheeks. Now, and especially in the last three months, she's been almost overwhelming in her care for me.

Nearly to the point I could swear my dad was about to re-enter the NHL and get checked into the boards to gain back her doting attention.

"Did I wake you?"

She's smiling gently, dressed in long sweatpants that pool on the hardwood and one of my father's old threadbare Winnipeg team shirts. I push up onto my elbow and flip completely over, taking the proffered cup of water from her hand.

"No, your father's getting a cold so he's snoring like the dead." I half-grin and see her real, genuine smile break through. "Are you all right, Rhys?"

If it were my father asking, I wouldn't hesitate to lie, but my mom has something that pulls the truth out of me no matter how deeply I try to bury it.

"I'm trying to be."

She nods, sitting on the edge of my bed. "School is back in session soon. Are you going to stay here this semester?"

"No," I answer, thankful that she's allowing me the space to distract myself. "I'm going back to the house next month." And I'm dreading that conversation with Bennett more than I am my first practice back. "I need to get back into my routine."

While it isn't a lie, it might as well be. Getting into my routine won't help; nothing will.

Except for a pair of gray eyes and a flirty smile.

The thought is like a shot to the gut, and I have to clench my hands in the bedspread to control the quick reaction.

God, Bennett is going to have to tie me to my damn bed to keep me from seeking out that particular vice. I can feel the thrum of my blood at just the thought of her, the immediate warmth that her voice and scent and face provide.

Whatever control I had before that game three months ago is

gone—maybe it's a piece of the part of me that died that night. Nothing that's left seems worth anything anymore, and I'm still walking the razor's edge of giving up.

Guilt threatens at the racing, hate-filled, darkened thoughts plaguing me while my mother sits there, desperately trying to push the sunshine that glows from her toward me. I can't bring myself to tell her that I feel nothing.

You felt something with Sadie.

A sneaky grin stretches across my mom's face and she rubs her hands together. "Wanna make biscuits and chocolate gravy?"

"What time is it?"

"Four, but who cares?"

"You know you'll wake dad the second he hears a pot clang," I warn, but I'm already shoving the sheets off my body and heading for clean, non-sweat-soaked clothes to change into.

"Serves him right, the little *mudak.*"

My eyebrows shoot up, and I wait for the humor to force the laughter from my chest the way my mother has always been able to do. Yet nothing comes up.

I try to shove off the self-hatred. Shrugging and turning away to head into the bathroom, I offer a quick, "Your Russian is getting better, but I doubt that's what he expected you to use it for."

"Cursing me out?" My dad's booming voice is scratchy with sleep as he steps into my room, shirtless, wearing only his sleep pants. "Nah, that's exactly why I wanted her to learn, my little *rybochka.*"

Tensing until I'm sure my shoulders are at my ears, I clench my fists and take a deep, heaving breath.

I wonder what kind of treatment that expensive sports psychologist would recommend if I told her even my dad's voice is becoming a trigger for me.

"What are you two doing up?" He comes to stand behind my mom's seated form, hands dropping to her shoulders to squeeze before he pulls lightly on her loose ponytail of strawberry blond hair. "Are you bothering my son?"

My son.

I try to breathe again, intentional and slow, relaxing my fists.

Because she's big talk and no action when it comes to her husband, my mom only smirks up at him and nods. "Yep. Craving some biscuits and chocolate gravy."

She doesn't utter a word about what we both know. That my dad doesn't snore. That she's become a light sleeper since she found me nearly suffocating through a panic attack in my sleep months ago. That tonight she woke up to the sounds of muffled cries and probably almost gave herself a heart attack when she realized I was on my goddamn stomach again.

My dad wrinkles his nose, because as much as he loves anything my mother does and would gladly eat raw meat if she served it to him, he *hates* chocolate gravy with a passion.

"Well, then what are we still doing here? Preheating the oven alone takes an hour."

They both stand and start for the door but pause and wait for me. My mother is all masked concern, now smiling and lovesick, drooping lazily in my father's arms.

But my dad's eyes are relentless as they take stock of my every muscle, seeing too much and yet nothing all at once. Does he see a stranger where he once saw a twin?

"I need a shower, and I'll be down," I say, shutting my eyes and then the door before I can hear anything else, desperate for a break to just be empty without the pressure of pretending I'm not.

• • •

Seeking any feeling, even pain, has clearly become some sort of hobby of mine, because I find myself at the rink by five a.m. two days later. Even earlier than my last little visit.

I follow my dad's directions again, flipping on the overheads and saying a quick good morning to the night-shift manager, grateful that Max Koteskiy's celebrity status provides access to slick, fresh ice and an empty rink.

I get through my warm-ups off ice easily, stretching slowly to release all the tension from my horrid night of sleep.

But once I'm sitting in the vacant locker room, it only takes a wave of dizziness to completely derail my focus. My vision goes blurry, my hands clenching around nothing as I release the laces that were nearly wrapped around my fingers. I try to stop the mounting panic, leaning over to hang my head between my knees, forearms pressed to my thighs to keep me somewhat upright. A shiver works down my spine as I fight against the squeezing in my chest, the fear growing as my eyes blink fuzzy again.

I close them.

"This is pathetic. Stop it."

But speaking the words out loud does little to drown out the sound of my own screaming, *"I can't see,"* like a broken fucking record in my head. My hands reach up and cradle my head as the pounding of my temples rises to a sickening level, and my eyes won't open because I'm too damn afraid that *they won't work*.

"Get it together, goddamn it." I clench my hands in my hair, resisting the urge to slap myself in the face.

"We have to stop meeting like this, hotshot."

Fuck.

Even the rasp of her voice is enough to pull me back.

I gently raise my head, trying to pull myself together enough to sling a smile onto my ashen face.

Without thinking, I open my eyes, blinking rapidly to clear away the fog. Still, I see her clearly. Her face is calm, forehead relaxed and mouth set in a sweet little smile—the perfect image of unbothered ease. Except for that tiny divot between her eyebrows and the concern in her gray eyes so deep I could swim in it.

"I'm sorry," I rasp.

My breathing has already started to calm now that I'm distracted by the way Sadie struts around the locker room and makes herself at home, dropping her bag in a corner by one of the long benches.

"Need me to give you mouth-to-mouth?"

The flirty taunt is so sudden it works like a cold-water shock to my nervous system. Everything settles, my focus turning away from my half-on skate and wholly onto her.

Her muscular legs are wrapped in smooth black fabric, a school-issued athletic long-sleeve shirt tight on her upper body. Her hair is down today, thick and straight with fringe dripping from behind her ear that has my fist closing to prevent myself from reaching out and tucking it back.

Instead, I try to focus on the cluster of freckles beneath her eye.

"A-are you flirting with me?" The words slip out fast, my voice sounding nowhere near normal, still breathy and weak. I almost want to take it back because I'm a hollow shell of nothingness and she's so goddamn *full*.

"Me? Flirting with the hot hockey player who keeps showing up in my space?" Sadie smirks down at me, pulling one of the earbuds out of her ear, the cord dangling in her hand. "I'd be stupid not to."

She's so up-front, be it with anger or teasing, so brutally honest in the face of my weakness that it settles something in me.

Or completely sends every brain cell I have left into an absolute frenzy, which might explain why I suddenly blurt out, "Do you want to do something about that then?"

It's a taunt more than it is a flirt, and the old me would *never* say something so bold. The old version of my controlled, captain-on-and-off-the-ice persona followed a strict three-date rule before any hookups, which were already a rarity. I didn't want distractions—I just wanted hockey.

Until hockey decided it didn't want me.

Maybe I want a distraction from how much I hate what hockey has become in my head.

Sadie hums, a sound that's both snarky and sweet all at once, her body gliding over to me.

"Put this in."

I take the earbud from her outstretched fingers, brushing the skin lightly with my knuckles as I do, letting the sensation of her nearness coat my stretched, tense muscles. The headphones are old, the cord connecting them dangling between us as she sits on the bench next to me.

Desperate, I spread my legs until my sweatpants are pressed lightly against her legging-covered flesh. She doesn't move away, only watches me patiently as I put the earbud in my left ear.

There's a quiet stillness to the music—soothing and just repetitive enough to drown out the mass of older panic taking over my brain. Like the sound coming from the bud in my left ear is enough to overpower everything else.

Except for the warmth of her beside me. Somehow, that's more.

CHAPTER FOUR

Sadie

Seeing him this way hurts.

I've experienced panic attacks before, but the worst weren't mine—they were Oliver's. I could barely help him function before we got him medication. Now, the attacks are fewer and far between, but the sight of Rhys curled in on himself, huffing for breaths like he can't quite catch them, brings back memories of laying a bag of frozen peas on my brother's chest so he could settle his nervous system.

Only I don't have frozen peas right now.

"Is this helping?" I ask as José González's gentle strums echo in our ears.

Rhys nods, his eyes flickering over me in a little pattern—eyes, mouth, the grasp of my hand in his.

Eyes. Mouth. Hands.

"You're helping," he blurts, cheeks red from embarrassment or exertion.

I nod. "Okay."

"Okay."

We sit back, like every movement is just as in sync, connected by the headphone cord between us.

Music plays while he slows his breath and I slow my heart. I lose track of how long we've been here.

"Music helps me," I say. And Oliver, though I don't add that even as I remember slamming headphones over my brother's ears as his principal and I verbally sparred over his "unbecoming" behavior at school and "lack of parenting" outside of it.

There's a tickle on my skin and I look down to see Rhys's hand absentmindedly playing with my fingers in a too-familiar way.

I stand, stepping back.

"Did you skate?" I ask, suddenly desperate to fill the charged silence between us.

He smiles in that sad, sleepy way as he continues to climb down from the high. "Didn't even make it on the ice."

"Do you want to skate with me?"

This time it's a cocky grin. "That's a line. Now I *know* you're flirting with me."

"Am not."

"Whatever you say, Sadie," he snorts out.

"I'm offering to . . ." *What am I offering?* His smiles and taunts are making me lightheaded. "To split the ice."

"Okay." He nods, standing over me in his now-laced skates, turning from a ball of anxiety into a tower of a man. "And your music."

"What?"

"I want your music." He shrugs. "It feels good. Helps me focus, I guess."

Something about his words makes me want to hug him, a light burn behind my eyes.

"Okay," I agree.

· · ·

Seeing Rhys heading toward me, I realize maybe I wasn't as sly as I thought in attempting to sneak off the ice while his back was turned.

For a moment, I contemplate slamming the metal door down over the concessions window so I can scream, "We're closed!" when he approaches.

Unfortunately, that would mean crushing the fingers of the un-suspecting mother who looks close to falling asleep atop my counter space as I slide her coffee to her.

"Thanks," she offers. She picks up a second cup of hot chocolate and sheepdogs two hyperactive hockey kids away.

"Didn't know you worked here too." Rhys smiles, pushing a hand through hair that's a little wet, like he might've dunked his head under the sink after finishing his morning skate. A few tendrils keep falling into his face, too short for him to shove around the curves of his ears.

I clench my hands, because some stupid part of my brain wants to push those hairs back myself.

"That's how I have a key." I shrug.

It's not how I have a key at all—I don't think working a concession-stand job usually reserved for high schoolers warrants an entrance key to the ice plex. I only have it because that's part of my summer compromise with Coach Kelley. He won't hover and drag me across the country when I have my brothers out of school if I continue to practice here at the community rink and send him updated footage of my routines weekly.

"Can I get a coffee?"

I smile, but heat crawls up my spine. "All out."

"Out of coffee at seven thirty in the morning?"

"Unfortunately," I say, stirring creamer into the cup in front of me.

"Not even a little bit left for your favorite customer?"

He smiles and it makes me pause. Two matching dimple imprints form in his otherwise chiseled cheeks, a little bit of light bleeding into his usually saddened brown eyes. I want to stand in that smile like a flower preening in the sun.

"Rhys, you're not even in my top ten. Besides, I highly doubt your prep-schooled ass has ever purchased anything from a public ice complex concession stand."

His hand thumps on his chest like what I said was deeply hurt-ful. "Consider me a card-carrying member of the concession-stand loyalty club now."

"Well, in that case." I grab a half-full Styrofoam cup before slid-ing it toward him.

"What do I owe you?" His eyes glimmer at me.

"A break from your continual presence at my place of work."

"That's a high price."

"I'm expensive."

He takes a sip of the coffee black and curses.

"Maxwell House," I say, taking another gulp of my own.

Rhys shakes his head. "That's shitty coffee."

"Very," I agree.

"I think I was just hustled."

I can't help but smile. "Hustle my favorite customer? I would never."

His laugh bursts out, beautiful and tinged with the boyish vul-nerability of a kid talking to his school crush. It makes me want to bat my eyelashes and preen—which only makes me sick when I re-alize his presence is turning me to mush.

"Favorite, huh?"

I shrug, "You tip the best."

He laughs again and takes out a high bill, sliding it my way before leaning toward me on his elbows. "I guess I do."

It would be so easy to kiss him. The boy is a hazard to my per-sonal boundaries and health.

"Like I said, I'm expensive."

Rhys's mouth opens for a second before snapping shut as he shoots upright and shoves away from the counter.

"Sorry—I'll uh, see you."

He's gone so fast it gives me whiplash.

I look around for a moment, cheeks heating at how closely I'd leaned into him. My eyes flicker over a tall, handsome, middle-aged man and a group of players decked out in Waterfell hockey T-shirts and hats, and my face flushes with the clear implication.

Good enough for a quick morning flirt, but embarrassing in the face of his friends.

Forget him.

• • •

"Rhys Waterfell hockey" sits in the search bar of my browser; the cursor blinks, waiting for me to make a decision. I glance around the empty interior of Brew Haven, before hovering over his name.

"What's that?" Ro pops up beside me.

"Jesus Christ, Ro," I seethe, hand on my chest to stop my now-racing heart. "We need to get you a bell."

She giggles, pulling a cherry lollipop—my favorite—from her waist apron and handing it to me. "I wouldn't need one if you weren't so distracted by"—she draws out the *Y* and leans across me with her long-limbed form, slamming the ENTER button on the search bar—"Rhys Maximillian Koteskiy. Sheesh, that's a mouthful."

I can only nod, my tongue suddenly stuck to the roof of my mouth at the image of him displayed across my screen.

Rhys Maximillian Koteskiy: 6'3". 210 lbs. C. Shoots Right.

"You have that look on your face like you're thinking about how much you wanna eat him."

"I'm only thinking about how obnoxious it is to spell *'Reece'* like that. God, could he be more cliché?" My finger taps at the screen beneath his stats, at the prep school background I'd been joking about. "Berkshire School? That's a private hockey academy, Ro. And look, his dad is an NHL Hall of Famer. He's been raised like a perfect little prodigy."

The words feel heavy, but I spit them anyway, ignoring the memory of Rhys panting and terror-struck, lying on the ice. The mental image of him flushed, panicked that he couldn't breathe, sits in such deep contrast to the headshot across my screen.

He looks younger, decked in a navy hockey sweater with the Waterfell University wolf howling across his chest, seeming larger than life with a smile meant to be in front of the world. Dimples. Shorter, well-kept hair and clear eyes.

"Sadie?"

I shake my head, exiting the screen as fast as I can before looking back up at Ro.

The girl is gorgeous, and it isn't just her lean, athletic figure and mess of ringlet curls that somehow always seem perfectly styled in a thousand new, different ways; it's something deeper, like sun is shining from within her bright, tawny skin, stretching out and over everything she sees.

"Yeah?"

"Gonna tell me why you're looking him up?"

"Because I didn't know who he was, and he's been . . . bothering me lately."

"We'll get to the second part, but let's start here: How in the *world* do you go to Waterfell and *not* recognize that guy? Even I know who he is, and I've never been to a game."

I try not to roll my eyes, because while that's true, Ro is more aware than I am. The little wallflower knows so much because she listens, she watches everything.

"You're in that arena all the time, where I'm sure life-size cutouts of him are lining the tunnels and hallways, if the massive posters of his face on campus are anything to go by."

God, had I been that far gone last semester?

Yes. I can hear Coach Kelley's voice invading my thoughts, telling me exactly how absent I'd been, how much of a letdown both my programs had been at the finals.

"I hadn't noticed, I guess," I reply half-heartedly, because I won't talk about it. I'll be better this year, for my team, for Oliver and Liam—but I won't talk about last year anymore.

Ro has that look on her face now, arched perfect eyebrows over her sparkling green eyes, pursed lips. She wears her every emotion on her face, and *this* is her concern.

"All right, well, you said he's been bothering you," she reminds me, letting whatever she was going to say die before reaching for the multicolored mugs soaking in the sink. I take the waffled washcloth from her outstretched hand and help her dry. "Gonna tell me about that?"

"I've just run into him a few times lately at my early practices. He has a tendency to beat me to my pre-skate." I shrug again, feeling ridiculous as I turn toward her.

Ro's squeal is immediate, and I have the urge to cover her mouth despite the closed, empty café around us. Whatever sharp look I give her seems to be enough as she settles.

"That's adorable," she offers, nodding excessively as she starts again on a homemade sunflower shaped mug that's started to lose its color. "I mean, hockey boy and figure—"

"Nope," I snap, cutting her off and reaching in to drain the water from the big sink. "Stop it, you cannot go around romanticizing everything—how many times do we have to have this talk?"

She looks at me like I've kicked a puppy, but Ro is a hopeless romantic, and she's been my friend for three years now—my only friend, really. But it doesn't matter how many guys she watches me take into a bathroom or sneak out of our dorm in the morning, she's convinced that my love story is out there.

"Understood?" I ask while washing my hands. She nods almost aggressively, moving to the side to take off her apron and allowing me room.

Ro waits only a minute for me to put my apron in the little cubby next to hers and grab my backpack before the dam bursts.

"So . . . can we go to a hockey game?"

This time, I can't help the smile and slight roll of my eyes. But the flutter of laughter that escapes me and the feel of her arm looping over my shoulder as we exit together, giggling over some inside joke, makes me feel normal and good. Like a regular twenty-one-year-old college student, if only for a moment.

CHAPTER FIVE

Rhys

"No."

"Rhys," my father calls, the sound of his voice making me grip the marble counter until my fist goes white. "Please. I'll come with you. We haven't skated together since . . ." He trails off, combing a hand through his salt-and-pepper hair.

"Well aware," I snap, immediately regretting it as the words slip out. "I know you want to check on me and see how I'm skating, but I need to do this on my own, okay?"

There's a vulnerability in my father for a moment before he nods and turns back to the expensive espresso machine, working quietly, almost sullenly.

"Another coffee already?" I ask, trying to relieve the tension that keeps my feet stuck to the kitchen floor.

"For your mother." He smiles, slowly making her overly complicated latte, complete with some sort of foam art that he barely finishes by the time my mother pads lightly into the room. She's bundled in a fuzzy robe with little fruits and vegetables dotting the material and has thick glasses sitting atop her head, tangled into her hair.

"Morning," I call, getting a happy smile from her as she settles herself on the barstool next to where I'm standing.

"How'd you sleep?" she asks, yawning, attempting to seem casual despite the clear, hidden check-in her question poses.

"Good."

It isn't a lie. I got a full night's rest, a rare occurrence that I'm trying to convince myself has nothing to do with distracting thoughts of a certain figure skater.

"Good." Mom smiles. My father steps up behind her. He sets the steaming cup in front of her and kisses the top of her head, then massages her shoulders.

"What is it today?" I ask, leaning over to study the latte's foam art.

"I think . . . a flower?"

My father frowns. "It was supposed to be a heart."

"It looks like a big mushroom blob," my mom says, her tone affectionate.

I laugh, a real one that makes both of my parents look up at me in surprise. Guilt chases away the good almost immediately. Have I been so empty, even with them?

"I'm late," I say, jumping up and grabbing my bag from beside the door.

"For an empty rink?" My mom smirks.

"I—uh, yeah." Not bothering to explain, I grab my keys and head out to the garage.

. . .

I half expect the rink to be empty when I enter—that Sadie really is just a figment of my imagination, invented so I don't feel so goddamn alone in my anxiety and nothingness.

What I see on the ice only seems to prove that claim.

She skates with that same energy I remember from before, all passion, like watching a living flame on ice. None of her movements look that fluid—she's all punchy between delicate dance moves, like some hybrid powerful gymnast-elegant ballerina—but it works.

Music is playing from a small Bluetooth speaker in the corner, the beat heavy and loud, not what I've imagined from her. Her phone is upturned on the bench, so I touch the side, lighting it up so I can see the song title, "Run Boy Run," scroll across the top. I try not to read below the music, but when I spot a text from "DO NOT ANSWER," I can't stop myself.

Please Sadie I need your . . .

The rest of the message isn't visible. Something stirs in my stomach, making me nauseous at the endless implications. Looking back at her, gliding on the ice, I can't get over the overwhelming urge to lock us both in this quiet open rink forever, never having to face anything outside of it.

I'm psychotic. I guess nearly dying on the ice didn't take away my control-freak mentality.

Sadie's going fast, turning to face backward and leaning like she's prepping for a jump. She takes off from the ice and does three turns in the air before slamming down hard enough to slide on her ass toward the curve of the corner boards.

I'm over the boards before I realize, skating to her and stopping short like some strange reverse of that first day she saved me—only I'm still the one panicking.

"Sadie?"

My voice feels hollow, my hands numb.

She blinks up at me, pushing up slightly. "Hey, hotshot."

Relief blares through me so quickly, I nearly join her in lying on the ice.

"You went down pretty hard. You okay?"

"That was easily the fall that hurt the *least* this morning." She smirks, a gentle curve of her lips that makes my stomach drop and the back of my neck heat.

And I can't *not* touch her; I grab her biceps and lift her gently until her skates are steady beneath her body.

There's concern mixed with the light humor still on her face, like even now she's more worried about *me*. That little divot between her eyebrows appears, contrasting with her beautiful smirk.

"Were you watching me?"

"Maybe."

"You keep catching my worst moments," she grumbles, skating slowly. I follow her, trying not to pant like a fucking dog behind her.

"Only fair," I add. "Considering today might be the only day you're not hauling my big ass off the ice."

"I've seen bigger."

Everything in me perks up at the verbal spar, the offer of flirting. Every part of my usual numbness starts to fade away at the promise of *her*.

"Have you? An ass girl?"

She stops and smiles. "Not particularly. But I've heard lots about hockey players having *giant*—"

I clap my hand over her mouth, pushing into her and sending us both lightly into the boards. She's a small thing; even the height of her blades doesn't give her an advantage since I've got mine on as well. Small, but not delicate, and shapely in a way I can easily see through all the tight black material covering her muscular body.

She giggles into my hand, gray eyes crinkling with humor at the effect of her taunt.

"Got it out of your system?"

She nods, but I hold on a moment longer, desperate for the feeling of her pressed to me. I want to grab her, caress and touch every inch of her.

I shouldn't—Sadie's my *friend*, if even that. But I'm in her orbit now, and she's becoming my goddamn center of gravity. Whether she realizes it or not.

"What about you?" she asks.

"What about me?"

"You ever gonna tell me why I keep pulling your big, handsome ass off the ice?"

I smirk. "So you *have* been checking out my ass."

She's silent, a half-smile still on her face, but she's also clearly studying me. She's worried about me *again*, and a knot starts to form in my throat.

Sadie suddenly pushes me, switching our positions and pressing me into the boards and plexiglass in a much softer, more sensual way than I'm used to. The top of her head just reaches my shoulders.

"All right, hotshot, let's make a deal."

No deal needed—if she keeps looking at me like this, I'll do anything she says.

"I don't ask about your shit, you don't ask about mine. We share the ice—"

"And music," I butt in.

"And music." She laughs and my chest feels lighter. "But that's all. Nothing else, just . . . partners."

She pulls away from me and does a little spin, keeping her eyes on mine.

"Don't look me up," I add desperately as she starts to skate to her usual side of the ice.

Sadie's brow wrinkles and her mouth opens like she might tease or ask a follow-up question, but she doesn't. Something she sees on my face must be enough.

"Okay."

• • •

"I think I got it!" Liam shouts, slamming down again as his stick spins away with the puck.

I smile, skating over to scoop him up and hold his arms while he tries to steady his blades underneath his little body.

Volunteering again had originally been my mom's idea, after hearing my dad pester me each morning about skating together—and after having to distract him each morning so he didn't follow me.

I adamantly requested no details of said distraction. My parents have always been affectionate enough to make me sick on a normal basis.

So now I tensely skate with Liam, desperately trying to ignore my father's stare from the other side of the rink. He's helping the older kids, which means he's with Oliver, so I can't help but check on them both.

Oliver is slightly tall for his age, and from what I've seen in the last hour of distracted teaching, he's gifted. Good enough to be watched by the line of coaches chatting on the side of the rink.

My father, tall and strong, is still very much the NHL star player he was before retirement, except for the gray now scattered through his dark hair and the wrinkles at the corners of his eyes. Just like any time he's been on the ice with me, he's smiling as he works with the players on pivot drills around two bright orange cones.

I maneuver Liam so he's holding the low side pocket of my joggers before removing my glove and offering my hand.

A loud laugh bursts from the circle of kids waiting on the drill space, alerting me to the group of preteen boys surrounding Oliver.

"Oh no," Liam mutters, sighing like a mother exhausted over her disobedient child.

"What? Oliver?"

Liam nods, looking up at me and releasing my hand. "Yeah. He fights with those boys sometimes—the ones in the red jerseys."

"He doesn't like them?"

"They don't always come here. Only when they're with their dad, I think. Oliver doesn't like anyone, but he really *really* doesn't like them."

The kid is observant, I realize. I have to stop myself from asking him to tell me everything he can remember about his older sister.

"Do you know why?"

"Not really." Liam sighs again, mimicking my pose with his arms crossed. "But one time when we were all playing sharks and minnows, I heard them talking about Sadie."

My stomach sours as I watch Oliver toss his gloves off and tackle one of the kids. I want to start cheering and whistling like I'm watching his first NHL fight, but I manage to keep myself in check.

Instead, I tell Liam to hold on to the boards while I skate over and insert myself between the grappling kids.

"Back it up," I snap, easily yanking them apart. "Calm down."

My dad tries to hold Oliver's shoulder, but he jerks away like he's been burned.

"Don't touch me, asshole."

I blow out a breath. *Jesus, this kid.*

"Calm down, Oliver," I try, my voice a little softer as I keep ahold of the red-shirt kid's collar.

Oliver's heated stare shoots to mine like a caged animal ready to scratch. He looks like Sadie, defensive and ready to fight.

"They started it," he spits out, anger rolling off him in waves. I can see the vulnerability in his gaze begging me to believe him.

"I know," I say calmly, releasing the other kid with a shove toward my dad. "Let Coach Max deal with them. Let's go cool off."

Something flickers in Oliver's eyes before he sighs and drops his head. "Okay," he says and follows me toward where Liam is now lying flat on the ice.

The session is nearly over, but I claim a corner of the rink for the three of us, dragging Liam around as I correct Oliver's edges.

It isn't until my father joins us that I realize the rink has cleared out. "Where's Chelsea?"

"I sent her home; told her we would wait on their parents."

I nod, keeping my gaze on Liam chasing Oliver around the circle he's creating with his edges. If I look at my dad, I'll see the question that I know is there about these kids and my connection to them.

But he doesn't pester. Instead, my dad steps forward with his stick, pulling Oliver from his current pattern and shifting his focus to catching a fast shot on his backhand. It takes a few minutes, but Oliver warms up to us easily, following every correction given to him. I can see the spark ignite in my dad when he recognizes the level of talent the kid has, his bright potential.

I spot Sadie instinctually, as if she's a homing beacon forever drawing me back to her piercing gray stare. She stops mid-step, her bag dropping off her shoulders as she watches Oliver with apprehension in her eyes and her guard *way* up.

Liam is shouting for her as I pick him up and skate us both over. Oliver pauses, but my dad has him run his current drill again.

Sadie watches him, eyes bright—like this isn't something she gets to see that often.

"He's gifted," I say, letting Liam climb down from me.

The younger kid shouts, "Watch me!" And tries to join his brother across the rink. Even with his resilience and quick recoveries, he'll never make it.

I can tell Oliver is showing off a bit and Sadie is glued to his every move. It stirs something in me, like I should apologize for what I cornered her about that first day. Perhaps I read this situation wrong.

But then I think about that text to her phone.

"Your parents aren't coming?" I ask. It feels like testing a field for land mines.

"We have a deal, hotshot," she answers, refusing to look at me. "They're busy. I can take care of the boys. Any other questions?"

Thousands. Like *Why are you so angry? Why do you skate like you're on fire? Who is so bad that you listed them as DO NOT ANSWER in your phone? Are you safe? Are you okay?*

Still, I shake my head.

Crumbs.

I'll eat every last one.

CHAPTER SIX

Rhys

It's been three weeks of this routine, getting my feet under me again sans panic attacks while tying my skates. Two weeks of waking to the promise of seeing Sadie settling my stomach, skating to her eclectic music taste that swings from Steely Dan to Ethel Cain to Harry Styles in the same hour.

By now, I feel as though I can read her mood by the song she first selects. I can tell she's in need of settling when she plays Phoebe Bridgers, or that she's desperate for a fast dancing skate when she blares Two Door Cinema Club and MGMT back-to-back, usually smiling from endorphins as she freestyles across her side of the ice.

But sometimes, she starts Tracy Chapman's "Fast Car." Those days, she usually doesn't speak to me—only stares at me on our way in with eyes that look half full of tears.

I try to listen most on those days, as if the lyrics she hears might be another language for her. I want to pick up on the smallest of hints, desperate for as much of her as I can consume.

Today, however, she's late.

Most days that Sadie comes in late, she's having an angry day, so I prepare to shoot and race the rink to something loud. But today doesn't seem to be one of those days.

The anxiety at being on the ice without her settles as I hear her entrance echoing from the tunnel into the silent rink.

It takes all my strength not to turn and stare as she comes in, to wait until I hear her skates slice the ice before looking.

Sadie's wearing her usual outfit: a threadbare gray Waterfell University shirt and leggings with a flare over her white skates, hair pulled up and mostly off her face.

She skates over to me in her usual style: a little angry, graceful, but with a touch of vengeance.

"I made you something," she says, and there's that divot between her eyebrows, like she is frustrated or questioning everything nearly constantly. Her hands hold nothing, but she sticks them out to me like I'm the one with a gift.

"What?"

"Your phone."

I open it and hand it to her, watching over her shoulder as she settles right next to me. She pulls up the music app, selects her profile, and clicks the first playlist.

There's a picture of a very sad-looking beagle spread flat on the floor with a party hat on his head. Across it in sparkly letters, the name of the playlist is bright.

"Sadie's Songs for Reece's Sad Demon Brain," I read aloud, before adding, "You spelled Rhys wrong."

"Your parents spelled your name wrong on the birth certificate. Your way looks like *Rise*. So if anything, I fixed it." She rolls her eyes, but her teeth clamp on to her lip a little self-consciously. "I made it last night. I . . . well, graphic design isn't my major."

My heart pinches like a lingering stab wound at the thought of her in her bedroom, up all night curating songs and making art for the cover so it looked like this. For me.

"I thought maybe you could listen to it while you skate and . . . I don't know. It's stupid—"

"It's not," I cut her off vehemently. "You made me a playlist."

"Yeah." She nods, rocking in a wide circle on her skates back and forth, pushing off my chest each time. I grab her when she returns this time, my hands on her wrists to keep her touching me. I transfer her wrists into one of my hands, selfish with her touch as much as her time. Digging a second set of AirPods from my pocket—a gift I'd been working up the nerve to give to her for nearly a week, I slip them into her ears and gently let her go.

"Do you want to pick first?"

"I think you should just shuffle it. That's what I do, then you focus on that instead of panicking."

I hover my finger over the button as she starts to skate off to the other end, before I see her pause and swizzle backward.

"It might not work, and I don't really know what's bothering you, but music helps me."

She stops there, but the unspoken words are just as loud. The look in her eyes says *I wanted to help, and this is all I have* and *I see you.*

"Thank you," I offer, but it feels too insufficient.

I press shuffle and chuckle a little when "No Sleep Till Brooklyn" starts blaring in my ears.

Sadie skates around quickly, zigzagging along and warming up, focused like always. But when she passes me again, her eyes meet mine and she mouths along with the words playing through our headphones.

A laugh rumbles in my chest. I want to stay just like this with her forever.

. . .

"Your father mentioned something interesting—*damn it!*"

I look up from my perch at the countertop, checking over my mom as she rushes her finger under the tap while boiling sauce bubbles over the pot behind her.

"You okay?" I smile, watching as she wipes her hands on her overalls and turns back to the stove.

My dad might have been an incredible hockey player, but my mother was well-known in her own right. "Architecture's Darling," according to many news articles and magazines. Anna Koteskiy is known for designing grand gazebos and extravagant gardens. Now, she mostly spends her time running a few charities for sustainable housing projects.

Anna Koteskiy is notable for many things, but her cooking skill isn't one of them.

Still, my mother loves to cook—no matter how hazardous it is for her and everyone in the vicinity.

Somehow, my father's entrance scares her enough to hit the pan with her forearm, shouting a little curse and still managing to keep ahold of it. My father and I both race toward her. While I take an oven mitt from the counter to grab the pan, Dad dotes on her like she's suffered a life-threatening injury.

As he mutters to her in a mix of Russian and English, my mom and I share an eye roll.

"Maybe I'll take over dinner," Dad says. He sighs, letting her go with another kiss to the burned skin. "It's nice outside; take our son out to the patio and set the table."

Mom grabs the stack of dark green pottery plates with silverware, napkins, and other table necessities piled on top. I grab the pitcher of ice water and stacked glasses. We both leave the large kitchen through the attached glass conservatory and step out onto the back patio. The string lights are already on, their warm golden light casting an added glow to the amber of the six o'clock sun.

The custom oak wood table needs a slight dust off, which is usual for this time of year with the obscene number of flowers and blossoming trees near the outer perimeter of the sunken patio.

"So who's the girl?"

I choke on the gulp of water in my mouth, coughing repeatedly as my mother—the traitor—laughs and waits for me to regain my composure.

"What are you talking about?"

"Clearly there's a girl."

My fingers dance through the condensation on my glass. "Did Dad say something?"

Her eyes twinkle like I've confessed my love for whoever she's imagining. "Should he have?"

"No."

"Rhys, if your father knows about a girl before me, I will never forgive you." She glares at me for a minute before relaxing with a knowing smile. "Besides, I thought you were still keeping him in the doghouse when it comes to your dating life after the prom incident."

A full-body cringe rolls through me at even the mention of prom, and I shove the memories back behind the brick wall in my brain.

"Don't remind me." I shake my head again. "What makes you think there is someone, anyway?"

I wait for her light teasing, but her voice drops into the soft whisper she used for every failure and scrape and bruise when I was a child.

"Because you are my son, a piece of my heart, love, and you have been *drowning*. Maybe you still are."

I feel sick. Of course my mother would know, saving me from nightmares as often as she has.

"Probably." I sigh, my knee kicking up, bouncing anxiously.

"But lately, you've seemed different."

She's waiting for me to fill in the blanks, but I'm not sure what to say. That there *is* a girl, at least on my end, even if she'll hold me at arm's length forever? That's fine; I'll stay an arm's distance away as long as it means she's still near me, chasing out the shadows crowding my empty body.

I know it isn't healthy. I just don't care.

"Sadie is just a friend."

"Sadie? Pretty name."

Pretty girl. I bite down on my tongue, smoothing a hand over my knee to try to slow the shaking.

"We've been sharing our ice time in the mornings. She's a figure skater, for Waterfell actually."

"Yeah?"

"I don't think she really likes me," I snort, unable to stop talking about her now that I've started. "But she's funny. And she plays good music."

"Sounds like a cool girl."

"I like skating with her." The words pour out like vomit.

"The angry one?" my dad asks, slipping beside me to plate the eggplant parm in the center of the table, letting me help with the large serving dish of sides balanced on his hand and up his forearm. "Her brothers are adorable."

"She has brothers?" Mom asks, giving Dad a quick kiss on the cheek before settling as we pass around roasted veggies, Caesar salad, and pasta.

"Oliver and Liam," I offer. "Oliver is pretty good."

"More than good. That kid's a star. And little Liam is the cutest kid I've ever seen, *rybochka*, all his freckles and missing teeth."

Mom waits to finish her bite before asking, "They're in the program, then? That's good."

"Didn't know you were skating with someone at the rink those early mornings." There isn't an accusation in my dad's words, not really, but my back is up anyway.

The lie slips out quickly. "I invited her. We, uh, had a class together last year."

"World's Worst Liar Award still belongs to you, Rhys." Mom sighs, reaching for the wine bottle across the table. My dad beats her to it, refilling her glass for her.

It feels good to talk about Sadie, at least a little, but it's another reminder that, no matter how often I think of her—of the way her gray eyes settle on me, of her music in my headphones after another nightmare, of the fantasy of her hips in my hands—Sadie is not really anything to me. I doubt she'd even call us friends.

Meanwhile, I find myself desperate to be near her.

CHAPTER SEVEN

Sadie

It's a good night. Really, really good.

The warm, late July air sails through the rolled-down windows while "Waterloo" plays through the staticky speakers. Liam sings every word at the top of his lungs from his car seat, and although I don't know where his ABBA obsession came from, I've definitely encouraged it. Even Oliver smiles and hums along from his seat.

I pull into the drive-thru of Oliver's favorite fast-food place, which he swears makes the "perfect milkshake-dipper fries." His face lights up with another bright smile that I pocket away; they're so rare nowadays.

But tonight, he's made of them.

He played the game of his nearly-twelve-year-old life tonight, scoring two of the team's three points for the win. Even playing on this mixed exhibition team, Oliver shines; I know, come fall, he'll shine even more on his school team.

Oliver like this—wet hair drying in the summer heat, mouth smudged with chocolate shake remnants, smiling through too-large bites of waffle fry—that's the brother I remember. The one buried beneath the hurt.

He plays the alphabet game with Liam without complaint, both of their giggles giving me more sustenance than the spicy grilled chicken sandwich I'm scarfing down.

I leave the car in park for a while after we're all finished, watching the sunset over the slight hilltop that rolls down to a small park and a popular lake that we have skated on many times when frozen. It's moments like this when I can imagine another life for us all, when I'm torn by the urge to drive off into the sunset, chasing the light until we're somewhere new. I'd never skate again if it meant an endless supply of nights like this for my brothers.

My phone rings, cutting the low playing music in the background. Mitchel Hanburgh.

The lawyer.

I excuse myself, stepping out of the car and under the cover of a tree far enough away that their little ears can't hear, but close enough to keep watch over them.

"Hi, this is Sadie."

"Sadie." Mitchel sighs. I can almost picture him the way I saw him on the video call before. "Listen, I still need Oliver's birth certificate—"

"I found it," I cut him off. "I can send it over tomorrow if I go by the school."

"Great," he agrees, but there's enough hesitancy that I know what's coming next. "And your father? Did you speak with him?"

"I-I haven't had time."

"Ms. Brown, I have to have his signature on the consent documents. And I haven't even broached the topic of Liam's—"

"I got it," I snap, then run a hand through my hair. It snags on the tangles before I yank it free. "Sorry, I just—I'll see what I can do."

"All right," he sighs, resigned. "I'll let you go. Send me what you have and I'll see what I can do on my end with the custody papers."

"Thank you," I reply before ending the call.

It's like my perfect frozen snow globe moment has been shattered. The smile I give my brothers isn't as bright as before.

I hate that Oliver notices, even more that he doesn't ask. Watching his smile sink and dim until it fades entirely—the tightness in his body as I start to drive toward home—makes tears prick behind my eyes.

The emotion is overwhelming. I know I won't be able to sleep without something—something to push everything bubbling within me *out*.

My hands are shaking as I type out a quick *Busy tn?* text to a usual hookup. I don't wait for a response before jumping out, seeing Oliver already unfastening Liam's seatbelt.

The house seems quiet, but that isn't a good or bad sign—something my elder little brother and I know well.

I hate that the front door is unlocked, because it means Liam, still chattering and singing under his breath, is the first over the threshold. It doesn't matter that I shout at him to stop and wait; he takes off, Oliver and me chasing behind him until we all crash into one another like dominoes.

"Is he asleep—"

Liam's question is cut off by Oliver's hand over his mouth.

Our father isn't asleep—if anything, he's passed out on one of the kitchen chairs, arms cradling his head on the top of the table. There's a torn-up box of beer, empty on the floor of the living room, an empty broken bottle of whiskey in the corner of the kitchen just before the stairs.

No, I realize with my heart leaping into my throat. *He's crying.*

"Take Liam to my room."

That's all it takes before Oliver is ushering a now-quiet Liam up the creaking stairs.

"Dad?" I start, inching slowly toward him, unable to decipher his mood. "I—"

"Oh God," he cries, lifting his head up from the cradle of his arms. His eyes are red and sunken, cheeks rosy with intoxication and wet with tears. "Sadie, I'm so sorry. I just . . ."

"I know." I don't, but I want to stop him now before the pieces of me still held together crack entirely. "I thought you were out of money. How did you get all this?"

"Please. I'm sorry," he blubbers, ignoring or not hearing my question, his hand tightly gripping my wrist.

"Don't touch my sister," Oliver sneers, storming into the kitchen and grabbing Dad's hand off my arm.

"I'm your father," Dad snaps, turning from pathetically sad to furiously angry in the blink of an eye.

"Barely," Oliver spits back, but he's pulling me away from the kitchen. He's all brave talk when facing off with Dad, but the fear is in his eyes—he's still scared. We all are.

"Is Liam okay?" I ask, rounding the corner to the stairs.

Oliver shakes his head. "There's some fucking woman up there saying she's Liam's mom, and now he's hiding."

My stomach drops.

Liam doesn't know; Oliver probably barely remembers. Five years ago, I woke up early for a before-school practice, hoping to bring Oliver with me to avoid anything with our dad. But when I walked down the stairs, Dad was passed out across the couch hugging a bottle, and a baby was on the floor, just looking at me with wide gray eyes.

I was terrified, a sixteen-year-old high school student who already had too much responsibility with Oliver, and suddenly, there was a bouncing little baby boy to add to the absolute shit show of my life.

My coach stepped up. He knew I needed to keep it all a secret until I was eighteen at least, or we'd all be taken away and separated. So he helped me find sitters, and helped me deal with my father so that I could skate and keep winning.

I owe him everything.

The pit in my stomach churns to anger, fueling my loud steps toward my brother's room. Oliver is on my heels; as much as he is my baby brother, he's a protector through and through beneath all that anger.

The woman is clearly drunk, swaying on her hands and knees as she tries to draw Liam out from hiding beneath his bed.

I grab her by the collar of her shirt, dragging her back. I'm sure if she were standing, I'd be at a height disadvantage. But I'm strong and she's strung out.

"Get the hell out, psycho!" Oliver shouts.

I manage to drag her out of the room, demanding that Oliver check on Liam, before shoving her to the top of the stairs like I might fling her off.

"Are you really his mom?" I ask, hating the word. "Did you give birth to him?"

"Yes, I—"

"Prove it."

"I-I-I think I have the birth certificate. I can't—"

"I don't care. You have two options. Either you sit here while I call the police and my lawyer to make sure you pay the years of missing child support. Or you go the fuck home and send me that document. And you sign my fucking custody papers."

It takes barely a minute before she says, "Okay. Just let me go."

As soon as I hear the door close behind her, I burst into action. My hands won't stop shaking as I pack Liam's clothes into a bag. Oliver sees what I'm doing and takes off to his room, leaving Liam perched on the bed.

"Spend-the-night party?"

"Yeah," I breathe out, pushing his hair back off his little freckled face. "Are you okay, bug?"

"Yeah . . . Is that weird lady gone?"

"Yeah. She's not coming back."

"She said she was my mom."

"She's not," I say fervently.

"Oh." He nods, thinking hard. "Do you think, maybe, one day I'll have a mommy?"

My heart hurts.

"Maybe one day, bug."

His words haunt me the entire drive. It must be written across my face when we pull up to the dorms, judging by Ro's reaction, where she stands outside, waiting. We tuck the boys in and Ro tells me to shower in her room while she starts a movie for them. She's already playing Tracy Chapman through the soft speakers by her bed.

I cry until I can't breathe.

For a moment, while lying on Ro's bed waiting on her, I think about trying to contact Rhys. Like something about him would make this better—which is ridiculous, considering who he is and what he's dealing with himself. But I can't shake the thought.

Ro scratches my back and holds me until I fall asleep.

CHAPTER EIGHT

Rhys

Somehow, Sadie got to the rink before me, which makes me rush to get on the ice like an overeager kid for his first real game.

I don't even bother to try to wipe away the cheesy smile that hangs off my face almost constantly around her. She turns every hesitancy into excitement, every anxiety back into near bliss in the way it used to be for me on this ice.

I wonder if I could convince her to *She's the Man* herself onto the men's hockey team so I never have to be on the ice without her.

God, I've got to get it together if I'm going to be "Captain Rhys" again by next month.

Trying not to disturb Sadie mid-routine—because I can tell it's full-out from the intensity of her movements, the artistry so beautifully woven into it that it makes my chest ache. I clench my fists to trap the anxious monster in my head that's so desperate for more of her, worried if I even stare too long at her, I won't be able to stop myself from doing something insane—like pinning her to the boards again. Or seeing how light she is in my hands. Could I hold her up with one hand while the other presses—

A loud crunch and hard bang rip me from replaying my inappropriate dreams, shooting the heat in my body away with an ice-cold plunge of terror as I watch Sadie slide on her stomach into the boards, hard.

She doesn't move.

She's on her goddamn stomach on the ice and she isn't moving.

Fuck.

I think I'm going to be sick.

I shout for her in a blind panic, jumping the boards in my sneakers and racing to her sprawled figure. I briefly wonder how in the world she stayed calm that day she found me lying on the ice, because I'm losing my mind at the image of her here now.

When I make it to her side, she's shaking.

"Sadie?" My voice is quiet as I kneel down to pull her up. She's like water in my hands, boneless and slipping away as I try to at least prop her back against the boards.

My hands hover in the air over her body. I'm desperate to check that she's unharmed, but too scared that I'll frighten her or expand her anxiety.

She's crying, nearly sobbing, like she can't take a breath. Panic is still racing through my veins, but I try to concentrate on her.

"Hey, breathe—remember?" My hand presses back the tangled pieces of her hair that have escaped her ponytail. "I know it feels like you can't, like you're dying, but focus on my hands."

I reach down and press her hands into mine. For how flushed her cheeks and neck are, her hands feel like the ice we're sitting on.

"Try the threes rule," I say, whisper-quiet in the vastness of the rink. "My therapist tells me to think of three things you can hear, three things you can see, and three things you can feel."

"Okay," she huffs, her voice catching in a sob.

"Start with what you can hear."

"My music." She pauses and closes her eyes tightly. "Your breathing. The air-conditioning."

"Three things you can see."

Her red-tinged eyes open again, but only a few tears escape. "You."

I can't help the smile that slips out. "Try to be specific."

"Your dimples when you smile. The pink cap on my skate laces. An old Bruins logo flag."

"Good, last one. What can you feel?"

"The ice under my legs, the boards behind me." She keeps her eyes locked on mine. "You holding my hand."

"Good girl." I squeeze her hands in mine. "Okay, Gray?"

The question makes her smile as she calms further and she nods, tears only slightly leaking down her cheeks. I hate the sight of it; I'm unable to stop myself from bunching my sleeve and wiping beneath her eyes.

"Gray?" she asks.

"It's your eyes." I smile.

She giggles, but it turns into a sob. "Sorry," she says.

"Nope. Not doing that apology thing." I wince as my mouth opens again. "I know we said no questions—"

"Rhys—"

"—but I have to ask, because this is new."

Sadie starts to stand, climbing me like my body is purely there to support her—a thought that intrigues me more than it should. I help her, towering over her even without my skates on, while she steadies on her blades.

Finally releasing her lip from between her teeth, Sadie huffs a breath and lets the words fall from her mouth like a waterfall.

"They're cutting the concession area hours for the rest of the summer, which means I'm losing that job. And I can't do coaching on the schedule they offered so I won't have that to replace it. Not to mention, I wouldn't be like this if I could just get laid, but apparently that's not happening for me right now. So I'm trying to just work all the time. But my job near campus only has so many hours until the semester starts. And Oliver needs new skates—"

Her chest starts to heave. I firmly press a hand down on her sternum, trying to bring her back.

"Stop for a second." She nods at me appreciatively. "Let's go somewhere else today."

She's already shaking her head.

"I need to practice. You need the ice time—"

"One day won't kill us."

If Bennett or any of the team could hear me now, they'd think they'd entered an alternate universe.

Instead of waiting for Sadie to acquiesce, I slip my arm under her legs and pick her up in a bridal carry. She squeals lightly but doesn't complain as I walk slowly back to the gate and all the way into the locker room.

"Do what you need to do and then come out to my car. I'll go wait there."

And without thinking, I drop a kiss to her forehead and pick up my gear bag, turning to leave the room before I can consider how ridiculous that move might have been.

• • •

"Extra cream cheese?" I ask, faking a gag. I'm quickly rewarded with an angry little push.

"No cream cheese?" Sadie fakes a gag, eyeing my savory breakfast sandwich. "Sweet over savory every time."

We're in my car, parked by a lake near town that Sadie had—reluctantly—suggested. It's gorgeous and busy, but even with the golden morning light shining like a halo over the painting-esque view, I'm distracted by her.

She's so beautiful; dark lips and thick lashes over her darting, intense eyes. That little patch of freckles that I want to touch almost constantly. Brown hair that I imagine would feel just like silk if I ran my fingers through it.

"I'm glad you seem better."

"Thanks for the food. I think I was just hungry."

I don't think it's that simple at all. But I can't help the warm feeling that feeding her has given me.

"Sure." I nod. "But I mean, I'm great at listening. If you want to talk about anything."

Especially the part about getting laid.

I bite my tongue.

"I need another job, I guess, is the main point."

I nod. That's something I can help with.

"I need another instructor for the Learn to Skate classes, for the First Line stuff. I was going to ask one of the guys, but it would be great to have a figure skater there. We always get kids who want to figure skate one day."

Her eyes go wide, fixated on me. "Really? And . . . and it pays?"

"Yeah." I shrug. "Though, not much, but . . . probably close to what you made concession wise . . ."

"I'll take it," she blurts, cutting me off. Sadie blushes, but it quickly disappears as she turns away from me. "Sorry, about earlier. I'm not usually, I'm not so . . . sensitive. I have a better handle on things when I'm not so . . . amped up."

"Amped up?"

She rolls her eyes, gulping down another sip of her iced coffee.

"I just need to work out my stuff . . . get laid, you know. Athletes do it all the time."

"I don't," I blurt out, immediately wishing I could take it back. I bite down a little harder on my tongue to keep from asking her if she wants *me* to help with that.

If she wanted you, she would've asked. Fucking look at her—she's not afraid of anything.

But the image of her vulnerable on the ice, looking up at me, flashes through my mind. I don't want anyone else to see her that way.

"Serial dater?" she snorts.

"More like serially monogamous. But not anymore. I don't—" I shrug, trailing off because I'm not sure what to say.

"Maybe you need to get laid too."

My face burns and my hand fumbles to turn my side of the A/C colder before scratching at the back of my neck.

"I— What—"

"I wasn't offering, hotshot." She smiles but turns away just as quickly. "Trust me. That's just . . . not a good idea."

"Right." I try to laugh. But I can't help the singe of embarrassment staining my cheeks.

Of course not. Look at her and look at you.

Pathetic.

"For the record," I say, looking out along the lake, across all the life around us. "I am offering."

She's silent. Smiling and shaking her head, she avoids every ounce of the eye contact I'm directing toward her.

But I can't bring myself to regret it.

CHAPTER NINE

Sadie

"Gorgeous spiral," Coach Moreau says, her accent thick in the airy quality of her voice.

Celine Moreau, Canadian bronze medalist and one half of a very famous brother-sister pairs team, is the university's current pairs-team coach. Only two pairs currently train as part of the Water-fell team, along with the eight singles. Today, she's the only coach present for first season practice; really, it's more of a warm-up skate mixed with team bonding.

My coach is strangely absent, but I try not to think about that. Try not to let that anxiety even take root.

Instead, I find myself, unfortunately, thinking about Rhys.

His massive hands, his stupid pretty doe eyes and dimpled smile. Everything. I'm distracted—sloppy—and I know Coach Kelley wouldn't be pleased, that I'd get reprimanded and told to do it again until perfect. I'd prefer that, it's what I need, so I let Moreau's compliments roll off my shoulders, passing my ears as background noise.

Eventually, practice ends and the entire team circles up for a quick meeting. I've got blinders on, and thanks to Rhys's extravagant gift that I begged him to take back last skate, music still plays through the fancy headphones in my ears—which is the only reason I don't hear Luc approach.

He plucks a headphone from my ear.

"This is sex music," Luc whispers. I elbow him discreetly, pretending to listen to the encouragement from his coach.

Luc Laroux is a handsome—and unfortunately, skilled—pairs skater. If he would stop dating and dumping his partners, he might be on his Olympic tour right now. Instead he's here, with a set of skills that the other pairs team obviously envy and a heartbreaker reputation.

Currently, he's found himself partnerless again.

"I saw Rose on a magazine cover the other day," I say. "Still too proud to grovel?"

His jaw clenches tight, all mirth melting from his face at the mention of his longtime partner, the now popular Olympic prospect currently plastered everywhere in the skating world alongside her new endearing partner.

The ice king himself almost looks jealous.

"Aw," I say mockingly. "Do you miss her?"

There's a flash in his eyes before he covers it with a wicked smirk that I know has gotten him under many women's skirts.

"Why? Are you offering to be my new partner?"

I fake a gag. "Over my dead body."

Luc's snicker is hidden under the loud double clap from Moreau signaling the end of practice.

"You sure? I need to practice my lifts. Was looking for a partner."

I roll my eyes as we slug slowly behind the rest of the team. The innuendo is one I'm unfortunately familiar with. Usually, I'm quite repetitive in my motto of not mixing business with pleasure, but in this case I already have mixed. Which makes it easier to say yes.

And yet, I'm hesitating.

And a stupid pair of brown eyes are taking over my entire brain.

So I shake my head and shove Luc's shoulder. "I've got to get home."

• • •

It's a pancake breakfast morning, which, by Liam's standards, assures it will be a good day.

Ms. B, our neighbor who often helps us, offered to watch the boys today. I don't usually need her on the weekends before noon, but Coach Kelley called a last-minute practice at the community rink in a midnight email.

Which means I need to be there a few hours early to make sure my current jump combo and my spiral are as clean as possible. I'm desperate for this year to be different; starting with not disappointing Coach Kelley.

But then, I see Rhys's car.

Emotions soar through me too quickly to home in on just one—anger, frustration, fear, worry . . . excitement and anticipation.

I want to see him, I realize, as much as I want to scream at him to get out of my rink and out of my head.

You can't touch him. Stop it.

I mentally chant it as I march into the rink and down to the locker rooms, ready to be firm. To tell him we can't skate together anymore, for my sanity.

Fuck.

Rhys is sitting on the bench, back resting against one set of lockers, bent and sweating, skates on, legs splayed out as he heaves breaths like he's been drowning.

My bag falls off my shoulder. My anger falls away into nothing.

The sound alerts him, brown eyes shooting toward me in panic—then going half-lidded as he realizes it's just me.

"We have to stop meeting like this," he mutters, his plump mouth arching into what I assume is meant to be some sort of smile, even if it's barely there from exhaustion. My stomach hurts. Finding him like this again . . . a week before he has to be back at practices . . .

My heart feels like it's lodged in my throat.

"Rhys," I barely get out, my hand reaching for his face. It's only as he circles my wrist that I realize I'm shaking.

"Worried about me, Gray?"

"Terrified," I admit. "I thought it was better."

"S-so did I." He groans, his head slumping into my palm, as if it's the only thing keeping his neck upright. "Today is just a bad day."

"I should've brought you pancakes," I say, not realizing how insane that sounds on its own.

He laughs, breathless but happy. "Please explain that one."

"Liam thinks when I make pancakes, it'll be a good day."

He smiles at me, doe eyes glittering, dimples deep. "I'll try that one next time. I bet you make the best pancakes, though."

"I'll make you some sometime," I whisper, sitting next to him as he wipes off his forehead and leans back. "You okay?"

Rhys nods. After sitting up, he takes a few gulps of his water. "Yeah. But just a fair warning, I will take you up on that. I love breakfast food."

"I thought you liked savory over sweet."

"I like anything when it comes to you," he confesses, and my heart clenches.

His hand dips into his pocket, handing me a headphone. I realize only then that he's got my old pair in his ears, that he's listening to music.

"I couldn't find mine fast enough," he sighs.

I take the proffered earbud, letting the cord link us as he hands me his phone to select the music.

CHAPTER TEN

Sadie

Rhys might as well have a sign plastered across his forehead saying KISS ME. And I should be wearing one that says THIS IS A HORRIBLE IDEA.

None of this has gone according to my plan.

Seeing him like this makes my chest ache, hunched over in just his sweatpants and an athletic tee stretched across the broadness of him. With his head in his hands, fingers scraping through the thick, unruly brown locks, and breath shuddering from the tight line of his lips.

"Make This Go On Forever" is playing in my right ear, the music of Snow Patrol kicking up in intensity every few moments, feeding the energy between us.

My previous hookup experiences have been quick, handsy, in-the-dark moments, usually over before they really began. They're a personal favorite distraction when I feel so much it seeps from my home life into everything else.

But the way Rhys is looking at me isn't just lust—it's that desperation I know so well in the darker parts of my mind that close me off from everything.

The need to feel something, just to ground myself.

I have to remind myself of what this is before I dare to touch him. To let myself be this for him. He's a popular hockey player with

a mask that must be as good as gold. I've seen him vulnerable, repeatedly now, and I *know* he won't ask outright, even as he leans in
a little closer.

So I match him, breath-for-breath, move-for-move, until his
tensed forehead is pressed to my own, the sweat on his brow now
cold in the chill of the room.

His breath is minty and cool as it puffs against my lips, and I *know*
how terrible this is, how much I truly should pull away, take back my
headphones and dial in my focus, skate off my bubbling emotions
like I usually do—but something is keeping me here, drawn to his
deep well of hopelessness like a moth to a flame.

I can't save him, even if I wanted to. If anyone needs saving, it's
Oliver and Liam, and it's definitely not my place to try to hold up the
drowning hockey boy in front of me now.

He needs me.

Yeah. Sure. For this, maybe.

It isn't slow, just a hitch of my breath before I shove myself into
him, lips meeting his with no hesitation, only need.

A low moan rasps from his throat that sounds like absolute relief, and then he's responding, giving me back the passion I'm feeding him until it feels like we're part of a continuous loop. His hands
reach for my waist, pulling almost harshly; I seat myself across his
hips, legs straddling him on the low bench. His back hits the lockers
behind him as the skates half-tied on his feet dig into the rubber mat
flooring.

Pulling back to look down at him, I take in every detail: the thick
brush of his dark hair falling over his forehead, the pink flush of his
cheeks, and the darkness of his swollen lips that are lightly open,
huffing quickened breaths. His hands are still bracketing my hips,
making me feel so delicate with the way they span the entirety of my
waist as they move upward.

"Is this what you want?" he breathes out, voice raspy, as he gazes up at me with half-lidded eyes. I reach out for him, but he catches my wrist and holds it. "Tell me."

My voice is gone, my mouth so dry it feels like I've gone months without a drop of water. I can only nod.

A breathtaking smile I've never seen before breaks through Rhys's lips, two dimples showing in his cheeks as he laughs and closes his eyes before pressing his mouth to the skin of my wrist and muttering against my pulse, "Good. Me too."

I can't decide what I want to do with him first.

I slide my hands up his shoulders and neck, and into his hair. I grip it lightly and dive for the strong column of his throat this time, licking and kissing it rapidly. He moans again, long and loud with lips right at my ear, sending goose bumps across my skin. The movements of our bodies are harsh enough to dislodge both headphones; his phone clatters to the floor, leaving us in echoing silence.

Rhys's hands trace a pattern across my lower back, and for a moment they wander south. I wait for him to do *something*, anything—I just need more. But after a brief hesitation, his palms soothe up my covered spine and into the hair at the base of my neck, moving to cradle my face in his hands as he kisses me again.

I grab his massive palms in my own hands, hard and insistent, and slide them down, down, down to cup my ass.

Rhys groans, squeezing me, and I smirk and dive in to swallow the sound.

It's intoxicating, the feeling of being on top of him and in total control. We're only kissing, but it feels like more than any of my previous hookups.

Minutes or hours—there's no real concept of time while I'm here across his thighs. The only thing keeping me sane is the space I maintain between us, my knees planted on either side of him so I hover over the prominent distraction below me. I won't even allow myself to look.

Which is possibly the only reason I hear the loud, echoing *bang* of the back rolling door slamming, signaling someone's arrival.

I scamper from Rhys's lap, tossing myself onto the floor.

"Jesus," he mutters, but I can't look at him as my phone lights up.

It's barely even six, so there shouldn't be anyone strutting the back hallways at this hour. Still, it's a reminder that these aren't our summer mornings together anymore; this is real life.

Which means a very specific someone will be here before I can remove the blush from my cheeks.

Standing, I fix my hair into a messy bun and spin back toward the hockey boy who will, unfortunately, be starring in my fantasies from now on.

I sit on the bench across from him as if nothing has happened, ignoring the searing feeling of his gaze on me yet again.

"Sadie—"

The spell is broken. Everything warm in my stomach is rotting the longer I look at him, guilt taking over.

You can't help anyone. You'll just mess them up forever.

"I need to practice." I slip on my skates and quickly lace them with shaking hands, like I've absorbed every bit of his anxious energy into my body. He opens his mouth, but I raise my hand to stop him. "Seriously, Rhys, don't mention it. It was good."

"Then why are you leaving?" I hate the vulnerability in his voice almost as much as I hate myself.

Because this changes everything we've built in our quiet mornings. I can't be your savior if I'm pulling you down with me.

I need to focus. Oliver, Liam, Ro, skating, work, school. That's what matters.

Don't disappoint Coach Kelley. Don't let this year be like last year. Don't get distracted.

Oliver, Liam, Ro. Skating, work, school.

I want to say something kind, apologize even, but the only thing that manages to leave my swollen lips is another brittle, "I need to practice." Standing on my covered skates, I finally look at Rhys once more. "And I need to *focus*. This can't happen again."

His brow dips, and he watches me while I toss my hoodie into my bag and nearly sprint through the tunnel to the ice.

I skate for only thirty minutes before I decide to head back, hoping he's where I left him. I practice my apology in my head once or twice, because apologies aren't exactly a regular event for me. But before I can round the tunnel into the locker room, I hear two voices.

One is a now-familiar male voice.

The other one I also, unfortunately, recognize.

Turning the corner, I see Rhys standing, sans skates, stretched to his full height, towering over Victoria's lithe spandex-clad body. She's gorgeous, her lean muscles easy to see with her tan tights and ruffled skirt, complete with baby blue leg warmers bunched prettily on her bright white skates. She looks like the posters of girls I had in my room as a child; the Olympians cut out from magazines that I pasted to the insides of my school folders. She looks exactly like I thought I would now.

Graceful and strong, yet beautiful.

Not this tired, overly emotional—even hateful—skater that I've become.

Victoria looks good with Rhys, I realize. Both of them are long-limbed. She has her buttery blond bun secured tightly, has plump lips and skin still tanned from her summer on the Italian coast that I watched play out with envy on social media while underneath the comforter in my bedroom, eating far too many chocolate-covered cherries.

And Rhys, with his mask of perfection, every trace of fear and vulnerability now gone. In their place is the handsome college hockey star I imagine that he usually is: messy hair like he just came off a hard skate, flushed skin, and a smile that looks like stars—bright and glimmering. It even flashes in his irises, the little flecks of hazel brighter as his eyes crinkle and dimples pop.

He's exactly the campus golden boy I imagined. A slightly more rugged version of his team photo that my illicit internet search yielded.

Something about it makes my stomach hurt.

Victoria lays a delicate hand on his arm as she speaks again.

An irrational flare of jealousy has my spine straightening before I sit far away from the both of them on the bench, slamming my bag down with more force than necessary.

"Oh!" Victoria perks up at the sight of me, turning slightly so she can face us both, her hands holding lightly to the strap of her bag where she clasps and unclasps a pink claw clip. The sound is grating in my ears, but not more grating than her chipper giggle.

"Good morning, Sadie. I didn't see you. Have you met Rhys?" She gestures to him, angling her shoulder into his bicep like they are familiar.

While I can still taste him.

I lick my lips.

My eyes slide to meet his curious gaze, fixated on my face in the same way it continually has been.

"I haven't. Didn't know it was 'bring-your-boy-toy-to-work' day, or I wouldn't have shown up empty-handed." While the words are voiced toward Victoria, it's Rhys who I want to hear them. The quick set of his jaw and flare of his nostrils are the only proof that I've succeeded.

My phone is buzzing again, and I finally grab for it, answering without even looking.

"What?"

"Sadie." The tearful voice of my youngest brother comes through the line and my heart slams into my stomach. "You-you have to come back."

There's not even a moment of hesitation before I whisper into the receiver, "I'm on my way, bug," and hang up.

With my back still turned away from them, huddling in the corner like I might disappear into it, I hear Victoria's heavy sigh.

"I'm sorry," she says, her voice a soft little whisper intended only for Rhys in this echoing room. "Sadie is . . . kind of a loner. She doesn't really play well with others."

I've played just fine with him for a month.

The way she speaks about me like some sort of problem child only ratchets up my rising anger at her well-rested face and bright-eyed beauty, until it's bubbling out of my mouth.

"Well, there's only room for one person on the first-place podium, Vicky," I snap with a hateful smirk across my sullen, pale face. "But maybe you'll get there one day."

"Sadie."

The bottom drops out of my stomach, making sweat bead on my brow.

Coach Kelley is standing tall in the doorway with a glowering stare and furrowed brows. His disappointment has always been a great weakness of mine as the single male figure I've looked up to most of my life.

He took me on when I was eleven after watching me throw a tantrum over ending my first-place streak, with no parental figure to stop me from pulling the plastic crown out of the other girl's slicked-back hair. His coaching career was only five years young at the time, starting immediately after tearing an ACL and being unable to recover his quad lutz status from his previous Olympic run.

He followed me from juniors to college once I missed the Olympic qualifier. But his disappointment in knowing his prized pupil would never skate for Team USA haunted me. It was part of what caused me to spiral.

And part of the reason I am now on probation, not able to compete until I pull my attendance up to at least seventy percent.

"Coach." I grimace, nearly unable to swallow under the panic.

God, why is everyone here so fucking early today?

I reach to untie my skates to avoid every single eye now directed toward me.

"We gonna have a problem again this year?"

I keep my head held high, but my cheeks are warm with embarrassment at the obvious reprimand—even worse, in front of Victoria and Rhys.

"We talked about—" he starts, before realizing that I'm *unlacing* my skates. His eyebrows climb his forehead. "What are you doing?"

I shake my head, frustration, anger, fear swirling to the point that my eyes are stinging.

This is your *fault. You kissed Rhys. You got distracted.*

You left Oliver and Liam alone.

"I can't." Shaking my head, I grind my teeth together until I'm sure my jaw will break. "I have to go."

"Sadie," Coach Kelley snaps, gripping my arm as I try to maneuver past him. "You know the rules. You're still on probation. You can't miss—"

"I know." I shrug out of his grip, not bothering to look behind me as I sprint outside and to my car.

"Sadie," a voice calls just as my hand grips the handle to my driver's side door. "Wait—where are you going?"

Eyes closed tightly, I snap out a quick, "Leave me alone, Rhys."

"We should talk—"

"We don't need to talk." I toss my bag into the passenger seat. "I need to go, and you need to relax. You're coming off as clingy, hotshot."

I hate this version of myself—the desperate, fear-driven, and

hateful girl who wants everyone and everything away from her because it's too much. But Rhys needs to see this so he realizes what a
mistake that moment in the locker room was.

I hear Liam's little voice looping like a record in my head.

Slamming my door and locking it, I try to start the car, only to
hear the grating scream of my engine refusing to turn over.

"No," I huff, tears stinging my eyes. "No, no, no!"

I try to start it again and again.

Nothing.

There's a *tap tap tap* on my window before the hockey golden boy
with the sad eyes is plastered to the side of my car, gesturing for me
to roll down the window. I want to ignore him, but heart-pounding
fear has my hand reaching for the handle to manually roll it down.

"What?"

Rhys sighs, running a hand through his long, beautiful hair in a
way that's irritatingly distracting. "I know you said we're not friends."

I'm being ridiculous, but I can't stop myself from spitting,
"Well-established point there."

A strange laugh bubbles from him, and it almost sounds like it's
causing him pain.

"Right, well, you're the one who stuck your tongue down my throat,
kitten, so your brand of not-friendship is one I can handle, I think."

"Kitten?" I spit out before I can let the embarrassment of his
crass comment overtake me completely. "Watch it. 'Gray' was bad
enough."

"It's the eyes." He smirks, and for a moment I can see him from
before. Maybe our paths have crossed before, because right now he
looks every bit the campus hero, hockey golden boy, and exactly the
type of one-night stand I'd be rolling around with.

"No." I glare at him.

He holds his hands up like a quick surrender. "I'll pick another
nickname for you, then."

"No nicknames," I barter. Nicknames seem too familiar.

He snorts. "Says the girl who keeps mocking me as the hockey hotshot. Trying to give me a complex?"

"Hard to give you something you already have."

In truth, I *don't* know him. In fact, everything I've seen from him so far should only prove that he isn't the hockey *hotshot* I'm so fond of calling him. In the month I've skated with him, he's either been heartbreakingly sweet or devastatingly panicked and sad.

No part he's shared with me has been the hockey captain, Rhys Koteskiy—until today.

"Right," he says. But his face looks a little forlorn, and I wish I could take it back. I hate this. I bite down hard on my lip, hoping to keep anything else horrible from spewing out of my mouth.

My phone rings again, Oliver's and Liam's grinning faces brightening the screen and sending another heated wave of anxiety through me. I answer quickly, waiting with my eyes shut tight for Liam's small sobs, but it's Oliver this time.

"Sadie?"

"Hey, killer," I barely force out. "Are you okay? I'm on my way now."

"We missed the bus for the early program. And Liam peed his pants again. Are we gonna get in trouble since it's the first day of school?"

A breath of relief puffs through my lips and I shake my head, even though he can't see it. "All right, that's okay. And no, you're not going to be in trouble. Don't worry. I'll be home soon and we'll figure it out."

After hanging up, I jerk my entire body toward my rolled-down window and grip the ledge with both hands.

"Were you going to offer me a ride? 'Cause I'll take it."

"Yeah." Rhys's expression is a mix of relief and confusion, most likely from my extreme hot-and-cold attitude.

"Great!" I nearly barrel him over when I unexpectedly push the door open. He only falters a moment before grabbing the handle and holding it for me.

He takes my bag from my shoulder, hauling it toward his sleek, shiny car—that I've already admired once this morning—and dropping it in the backseat.

When I climb in, the leather is cool on my skin. I lean back as if I've been here in this car with him a million times before.

The bubble that forms around me in his private presence starts to encase me as he settles next to me and takes my address. His eyes are keen on his backup camera and then on the road, as if he's just earned his license.

"I hate driving," he huffs after a few quiet minutes, cheeks glowing and eyes wide as if he hadn't entirely meant to say that aloud.

"Why did you agree?"

His brow furrows again, hands squeezing tight on the steering wheel before he blows a hefty breath that ruffles the thick hair hanging over his forehead. And then he smiles that same dimpled shining-star smile, and I realize . . . it isn't fake; he's just that goddamn beautiful.

"You needed my help."

I don't trust myself to say anything.

It's quiet in the car, but my ears are keen on the music he plays, as they always are. It's just the local pop station, rolling through top hits. Rhys doesn't sing along, doesn't even tap his fingers; it's like he's too focused on driving to notice anything else. Meanwhile every muscle in my body is tight with the restraint of not belting out every song or dancing in my seat. Music, like sex, is a form of release for me. When everything feels like too much, it's a safe place for me to channel it all—much safer than my tendency to indulge in late-night party bathroom hookups or not-even-one-full-night stands.

Music, any style, makes me feel good.

I'm so tight with the swirling tension in the cabin of the car that I try to burst out of the door like a spring toy the second he gets slightly close to my cul-de-sac turnoff, pushing the door hard to open it.

"Jesus Christ!" he shouts, slamming the brakes so hard the open door swings, nearly hitting me despite my grip on the handle. "God, Sadie—please don't ever do that again."

I want to spout off something sarcastic, but there's genuine fear in his eyes. His face looks stricken, like he's just seen a ghost.

It's the same look he had on his face when I fell into the boards.

So I bite down on my lip and mutter an apology, tacking on a thank you as I point over my shoulder at the shoddy redbrick duplex behind me, the grass too high and filled with weeds. I'm not ashamed—I've had enough of that to last me a lifetime—but Rhys in a shiny black BMW screams silver spoons and daddy's money, even if he has a deep well of secrets and emotional trauma beneath the pretty hair and handsome smile. Showing him my home, where all *my* secrets live, doesn't really rank highly on the list of things I'd like to do with the hockey boy.

"I need to go. Seriously, thank you, Rhys."

He reaches across the console, his massive wingspan stretching until he's able to keep me from closing the door. It's surprisingly attractive and my cheeks blush with heat.

"Are you sure you're okay?" he asks, the concern on his face steadying me. He leaves the rest unsaid, but I can see it in his eyes. I've helped him when he couldn't stand; he's offering to do the same.

But I know inviting him into my prison as my backup will only endanger the ones relying on me, and reveal everything I've been able to contain for years. Not to mention, I can still *feel* him—and I know that continuing to allow myself to be around him will only make it worse. Even now, all I want to do is let his hands grab my hips and haul me across the console into his lap with the strength I know he has, and press me into the steering wheel—

No. Not with him. Stop it.

"I have to go. Thank you," I repeat, closing the door.

The next morning, before I can even consider what I'll do to get back my own car, I step outside to see my Jeep is in the driveway, freshly detailed. It starts without any complaint.

CHAPTER ELEVEN

Rhys

"Remember what the doctor said about the noise and about drinking, Rhys," my mother rambles on, her voice crystal clear over the sound system in my car. My head stays pressed lightly against the overly plush material of my seat, trying to keep my breathing even in the cool interior despite the sun beating down through my window. "In fact, why don't I just send this all to dear Ben. He'd be glad to help—"

"Mom." I make my fifth attempt to end this anxiety-fueled conversation since I parked in front of the redbrick house. "I'll be fine. No need to give Ben anything, all right?"

"Rhys," she half-sobs into the phone and my entire chest constricts. "If you want to come back, you can, and we can work something out—"

"*Uspokoit'sya*, my love."

I shut my eyes tightly, my hands gripping the wheel as my father's voice echoes in the soft space of the car, suddenly making everything feel smaller. Making *me* feel smaller. "Let my son go now, yes? You've talked to him since he left half an hour ago. He needs time."

"I'm all right, Mom," I say, swallowing hard at the lump in my throat. "Promise. I'll call you tomorrow."

With that promise, she finally agrees to hang up, the sound of my father's quiet Russian words echoing as he presses the *end call* button for her.

A loud thump draws my attention to the window, where I see the openmouthed, exaggerated shock across Freddy's face. He pulls the aviators off and opens my door.

Matthew Fredderic, left winger and resident pain in my ass. With helmets on, gliding on a sheet of ice, we could be twins—we have the same height and build, which works wonders for our first line forward play as winger and center. But off the ice, we are night and day. Freddy is blond, with innocent green eyes and an overly flirty smile to match the "love-'em-and-leave-'em" personality that continues to leave a trail of broken hearts in his wake. He's got a reputation already, has had one since freshman year—and according to rumor, he was just as wildly promiscuous in high school.

He's the kind of guy you're worried about introducing to your *mother*, let alone your sister.

"I knew I was dying." Freddy sighs dramatically, resting his body weight against the open door as I step out. "Those fish tacos from that truck have finally done me in, Reiner. I'm having hallucinations."

I just manage a smile before my eyes lock onto the looming figure behind him, arms crossed, still standing next to his truck.

Bennett Reiner has been my best friend since we were five years old. Our fathers played together in juniors, and in the NHL for only one year before Ben's father tore an ACL and ended his career in his rookie season. Our first Learn to Skate lesson shoved us together before hockey, before school. We were inseparable, to the point that we were sold like a package deal to high-end coaches from prestigious hockey academies in the area. While my skills and speed developed into offensive positions, eventually landing me at center, Ben just kept getting taller and bigger without any of the aggressive play, before coaches settled him in the goal.

He's the best goalie I've ever played with, someone I can rely on to stay calm and even-keeled no matter the score. Always meticulous, especially with his routine, Bennett is a solid presence.

One I haven't allowed myself to lean on, expecting I'd pull him down with me.

"Hey," I say, nodding my head and letting Freddy close the car door behind me. There's a lot I could say, words muddling together inside my head.

I'm sorry, Ben. I could barely manage to open my goddamn eyes, let alone look my father in the face.

Talking to you, being honest with you, felt like climbing Everest because the idea of never being on the ice again was suddenly just as terrifying as being on the ice again.

I hated myself almost as much as hockey hates me, and I didn't want to feel anything even remotely comfortable, and you're a savior, a protector—you couldn't protect me from this.

You're my best friend, and I never wanted to hurt you, but everything inside me turned black, decayed, and it's still nothing good. I am nothing anymore, and it's selfish, but I didn't want you to see that.

Instead, I run a hand through my hair again before shoving my hands into my short's pockets, nodding. "How've you been?"

He's silent, staring at me without moving, a stillness only I've seen in him.

"I'm gonna put the beers in the fridge," Freddy offers, his smile faltering. He slaps my shoulder. "Good to have you back, Rhysie."

Freddy stops by Bennett on his way to the truck, squeezing his shoulder tightly and ignoring the way the larger guy throws his shoulder back slightly to disengage his touch. Freddy grabs the groceries out of the still-open door of Bennett's truck, then heads past us into the house with arms stacked with paper bags.

The silence stretches between us, just like the immaculate green yard that I know Bennett probably mowed himself this morning. Routines, sameness, they're what keep Bennett alive.

"Bennett, look—"

His massive hand lifts, stopping whatever word vomit was near to spewing from my mouth.

"It's not that hard to pick up a phone, Rhys. Even for just a text." He sounds stoic, but his blue eyes are deep pools of hurt and betrayal. "I thought you were going to die."

He might as well have punched me in the gut.

"Ben—"

"No." He shakes his head, pressing his lips together and running a hand through his hair. He takes his sunglasses out of his shirt and slides them on, like blocking the redness of his eyes will keep me from hearing the hurt in his voice. "The last time I saw you, you were in a fucking hospital bed. Do you realize that? You left me in the dark, begging your mom for any information. Going to summer intensive without you, keeping up the team momentum, telling them you were at some fucking intense recovery camp? I felt like a goddamn idiot, shut out by my best friend."

Every word from his mouth feels like the lash of a whip, but I'll gladly take them all. If anything, it only feeds the festering thing inside me.

You did this to him. And you can't even feel bad about it, because you're empty. Nothing left, even for your best friend. Selfish.

So, instead of anything else, I nod. Bennett doesn't like to be touched, otherwise I'd have pulled him into a hug already. His emotions are written across his face, easy to see even with his well-maintained beard and dark Ray-Bans.

"I won't apologize now because it'll sound like I don't mean it." I shrug, before nodding resolutely. "But I'm back. Moving back in today, going out tonight or something, and practicing on Monday. I'm not leaving."

I'm not leaving you again goes unsaid, but I can see that he takes my peace offering as he readjusts his sunglasses and closes the door to his glossy, black truck. I reach for my bags in my backseat and turn back toward him, ready to let him have another go. He comes by my side, but I stay a few feet back, following him as we head toward the house.

"Welcome back, Captain," he quietly offers as he maneuvers ahead of me to pull open the front door. "I'm still mad at you."

Bennett's service dog, sitting just inside the doorway, huffs at me, like he's as grumpy as his owner. It sends a bursting feeling of home through my body.

"Glad to be back, Reiner."

And even if it's just for a moment, fleeting and small, that warmth in my chest is enough.

It has to be, for now.

• • •

We don't end up at a party that night, but in a booth at our favorite local burger joint. Bennett sits across from me, Freddy on my right as we pick at the leftovers of our overly large order. Three plates of wings, potato wedges, and veggies are scattered across the table, the centerpiece a nearly demolished giant pretzel, the last piece barely hanging on to the hook it was delivered on.

Bennett is smiling now—a genuine one that shows all his teeth—as Freddy retells the story of hitting on the Bruins' player development coordinator during summer intensive and getting nearly leveled by her NHL-player boyfriend on the ice right after.

"No *way* that guy 'gets back to you' on helping you with that fancy little deke shot," Bennett says as he gulps down another swig of his nearly orange local IPA. He's a beer snob, refusing to split the half-empty pitcher between Freddy and me.

"It's called *the Michigan*."

Bennett's smile only widens. "Should be called the mission impossible. No way you'll get it good enough to use in a game."

Their chirping pushes a smile to my lips almost too easily; last year Bennett was ready to put his blocker through the kid, fed up with his arrogance and obsession with fancy deke-style trick shots. They weren't moves he could really do during the heat of a game, but Freddy *loved* to piss off our usually calm goalie by treating warm-ups and practices like a damn shootout.

"Heard from Tampa?"

The question comes from Bennett, and I have to swallow hard before I shake my head.

Before I even came to Waterfell, I was drafted by the Tampa Bay Lightning. I knew that after my degree was secured, I'd have my spot with them. But right after the injury, they rescinded their offer and I haven't heard from them since, which has left me desperate to prove to other professional teams that I am still just as good—if not better.

I can feel my best friend watching me closely, keeping track of my drink in a way that makes me question whether he received a text from my mother, but I try to ignore it. Still, sweat starts to gather on my brow and the rush of heat on my neck makes me pull at my collar.

If anyone is going to sense something wrong with me, it will be Bennett Reiner.

"You have to be kidding me," Freddy grumbles through a mouthful of pretzel before groaning and slumping against the booth, slapping his phone down on the sticky table.

"What?"

"Fucking puck bunnies ruining my life," he moans, ripping off the rest of the pretzel like a caveman, shoving it into his already full mouth. "Paloma's story is making me regret listening to you two idiots."

Bennett's nostrils flare, jaw locking as he bites back a retort. Usually, this would be the minute I change the subject to keep the peace, but I'm distracted by the video playing on a loop on Freddy's phone.

I don't care about the blonde in front of the camera, spinning in a little circle so the entire frat house party is displayed. But there's a familiar brunette in the light of the flash as the camera quickly moves over her.

She's only visible for a second before the image moves on to several snapshots of shot glasses and toasts, and before I can think better of it, I snatch Freddy's phone off the table and click to go back, pausing the video with my thumb pressed down hard.

It's her.

Sadie, sitting on the arm of a questionable-looking red sofa, her posture terrible and slumped so her chin rests on her palm. Her nails tap against her cheek as she stares emptily at the guy sitting on the actual cushions next to her with his hands drifting up and down her calves.

She looks terribly bored and so beautiful, with the frown I'm now so used to playing across her painted lips. She is close enough behind Paloma that I can see her entire face, her smoky colored eyes, her hair slicked back into a pretty braided ponytail with a gray slinky dress that looks like it's for a sophisticated night out instead of a frat party just off campus.

My chest aches, a strange bleed of panic working its way down my spine.

"Don't mention it. It was good."

That's what she said. Not good enough, though, because she didn't seek me out again. Didn't show up at our morning skate or the second night of Learn to Skate.

I don't blame her. I know I've been a husk when it comes to desire or passion—too afraid to try anything with *myself*, let alone another person.

I've thought about it, but the emptiness and depression gnawing in my gut always overcome any want. Even when I tried once or twice in the shower, the pain rushing in my head and lack of anything to think of that felt even remotely *good* just made me feel more broken.

Pathetic.

But I *did* feel something with her—something real and warm that chased every scrap of darkened shadows away from me while I focused on her. Just her.

"Jesus Christ, Rhys," Freddy barks, shaking my shoulder and grabbing his phone from my too-tight grip. "You good?"

My breath comes out a little too loudly for my preference, kicking up at the concern splayed across both of my friends' faces. Bennett's brow is somehow furrowed deeper, a bit of frustration and anger blending with the distress.

"Are you with her again?" he asks, his voice low and quiet.

It takes me a moment to realize he isn't talking about Sadie, because of course he isn't. He doesn't know her, let alone anything that happened between us.

No, Bennett is asking about Paloma, puck bunny extraordinaire and a previous situationship of mine. It was only for a few weeks, and I can count the times we actually slept together on one hand, but everyone talked about it for months, as if Paloma Blake had officially achieved her ultimate trophy in bagging the captain.

"No." I shake my head, gripping my thighs under the table to quell the tremors now rocketing through them. "No, I'm not."

"You know her? Sadie?"

My head whips to Freddy, giving me an instant headache at the too-sudden motion. His eyes twinkle as he screenshots the frozen screen and pulls up the photo, tossing his phone to a curious but quiet Bennett.

"How do you know her?" The words spill out before I can stop them, muscles too tight as I wait for Freddy's answer.

"I barely know her. I've just seen her at a few parties, is all." He waves me off before smirking too widely. "Now, how do you know her?"

She pulled my body off the ice after I had a goddamned panic attack just trying to skate, which I can't really do anymore without losing my shit, then flirted and smiled at me until I could breathe right.

She kissed me to the point that I almost felt like I wasn't broken anymore.

"Yeah," Bennett adds, sliding the phone back across the crowded table after finishing his perusal of Sadie. "Considering you've been locked away all summer."

I wince, but let it roll off my shoulders just like every shot Bennett takes. I deserve it. "She's a figure skater—"

Freddy snaps his fingers and points at me. "I fucking knew I recognized her from somewhere."

"You just said you saw her at a party."

"I mean, like, somewhere *else*. Anyway, continue."

"I've been getting some private ice time over at the community rink, and apparently she had the same idea."

"Are you guys . . . ?"

"Absolutely not."

Freddy raises his hands in quiet surrender. "Just wondering. I mean, you're the one staring at my phone like it's the fucking Stanley Cup."

I don't deny it, but instead opt for the slightest bit of honesty. "She seems cool. I barely know her, but . . . yeah."

"So should we head over to the party then?"

A fantasy fills my head of showing up at the house, walking in and stealing her attention and time, putting my own hands on her bare skin—so much more of it than I've seen at the rink. Seeing if her lipstick will stain my skin so I'll wake up from nightmares with a tangible memory of something good.

"Don't mention it."

Her rejection would work like a shot to the head, but one I'm not ready for, so I stop the *yes* from spilling out of my mouth and shake my head.

"I need to get some sleep before our preseason meeting tomorrow."

"C'mon, Rhys," Freddy begs. "We'll only stop by—we won't even drink. Promise."

Promises from Freddy are as reliable as ones from a politician, but a thrilling rush raises the hairs on the back of my neck at even the thought of seeing the girl plaguing my psyche.

CHAPTER TWELVE

Sadie

Getting Ro to a party is like pulling teeth—but somehow, getting her to leave one is even worse. Especially tonight, because despite my efforts to keep her sober, she is bubbly drunk.

I bang on the bathroom door again, brow furrowed in concern.

"Ro?" I call again. "You okay?"

There's a long silence, and for a moment I think about trying to bust down the door. Instead, I press my ear against the door again and play with a lock of my hair from my now-unbraided ponytail, twirling it round and round, looping through my fingers in a pattern.

Finally, there's a loud clatter, and then, "I'm okay!" shouted a bit too loudly from inside. I hear the sink running and settle myself against the wall, closing my eyes and tipping my head back.

The party had originally been my idea, but Ro had agreed after I took a Sharpie to her College Bucket List and added attending this specific party with me. It's partially for me, but also for her to feel something good again instead of getting lost in her head. Her "I have a boyfriend now" complaints were heard and blatantly ignored by me because no way in *hell* will I be tolerating the way I've seen him treat her in the very few times we met over the summer.

Tyler is still at an intensive program for biomedical engineering.

Ro wouldn't tell me what happened, but I saw the texts over her shoulder while doing her hair in our dorm bathroom. She let him know about going with me to the party; he requested photos of her and then ghosted her in the middle of their conversation after a flippant text that said "*ok.*"

She isn't as overtly sad now, burying her feelings beneath the shots of tequila we took before dancing until all she could think of was pulling at the high hem of her patterned lilac shorts. All *I* can think about is putting my skate blade through Tyler's neck the next time I see him.

"That bad of a party?"

The familiar voice feels like cool silk against my heated, flushed skin.

I open my eyes and I'm greeted with the sight of Rhys, looking completely put together and very un-vulnerable—a first for our interactions.

Having not seen him in a week, the urge to ask him if he's okay, if he's had another panic attack or if he's ready for his first real practice back—still marked in blue Sharpie on my own calendar—is overwhelming.

My eyes eat him up. His long, lean body is fitted into dark jeans and a crisp black tee that molds lightly to his biceps as he rests against the wall across from me. I notice the clear quality of his eyes and a light flush to his cheeks; he isn't drunk, but he's had something to drink. Which is somehow more confusing because I hadn't noticed him anywhere in this house.

"Why do you say that?" I ask, pressing my hands down the skirt of my dress, pulling at the hem slightly. I hate the wave of self-consciousness that buzzes through me as he takes me in, his eyes quick in their scan of my very short gray silk dress and white platform Converse that have double insoles for my aching feet.

I might be slightly overdressed in a sea of denim and leather, but

I look a thousand times hotter than I actually feel. Not to mention that the dress makes it much easier to get in and out of this party with what I came for—a quick distraction.

Which my traitorous mind is now thinking should be the hotshot who has appeared at my side like a wish granted.

"Because it's almost one in the morning and you don't even look buzzed."

"How do I look then, hotshot?" I ask, smirking despite my earlier self-promises to forget about the boy with the blues.

"Like you're in pain," he snaps out, more fire in him now than he's had in our previous interactions. The snippiness of his statements and the gleam in his eyes make me warmer, my pale skin flushing red.

Like you're in pain.

Jesus Christ.

Is that how it goes then? All the depth of truth I've seen from his eyes and his obvious panic are reflected back at me—where I saw through him so easily, he can now see through me, like some twisted, broken mirror.

"Way to ruin a party mood," I manage to grit out beneath a sudden suffocating wave of nausea before turning to knock on the door again, praying for an escape from the torment of his warm chocolate eyes.

"You weren't in a party mood."

"No?" I snap, eyes squinting toward him over my shoulder. My ponytail tosses with the swiftness of my movement. "Why do you think—"

The door bursts open and a tipsy Ro stumbles out, giggling and hiccupping like a drunken little fairy. She spots us both, her eyes going wide as she finishes fixing the strapless striped top to her matching shorts, before pulling at her tall pale cream boots that give her an extra few inches over me she doesn't truly need.

Grabbing me around the shoulders, she leans in and offers her hand to Rhys, who takes it gently.

"I'm Ro." She smirks, continuing to side-eye me and wiggle her eyebrows.

"Rhys," he offers. His smile toward her is dazzling, and I see tipsy, overly romantic Ro looking a little starstruck.

"Ro." I smile, but it comes out more like a grimace. "Can you give us a minute? I'll come down and meet you, and we can go."

"I thought you and Sean—"

My hand slaps over her freshly re-glossed lips before I pull it swiftly away and wipe the sticky residue on my bare leg. Ro frowns dramatically at me, her cheeks burning as she takes in my face while I dutifully ignore the heat of Rhys's gaze on my skin.

"Tell Sean I changed my mind. Since your English class buddy is hanging around, maybe you can talk to him."

Ro's face only flushes further as she giggles and backs up to hold onto the wall—but it isn't a wall she's grabbed, it's a boy. One I also recognize.

The tall, lean, and muscular body comes to a halt, letting Ro completely mold to him as she stumbles and holds on to him. He settles his hands on her hips to catch her stumbling, his boyish face glinting with stars in his eyes like a perfect prize just fell into his lap—and, in all fairness, it kind of did.

"Sorry," Ro breathes out, her face tilting up toward him. Her curls cascade down her back, the flower clips I spent an hour meticulously putting in sliding down the strands, barely keeping them half-up now.

The man holding her bursts into a wide smile, his famous one that every girl at this party—hell, nearly every girl on campus—has probably succumbed to before. It's not hard to guess why—tall, muscular hockey god Matt Fredderic looks like pure gold. He has a handsome face, somehow angular and soft at the same time, with carved smile lines like a supermodel version of a young Heath Ledger.

It definitely doesn't help that he's dressed like he walked out of some Greek vacation ad, the white linen short-sleeve button-up unbuttoned at the top to offset his golden skin, a chain and medallion of gold glinting in the dim hall light.

"You're good, princess," Freddy tells Ro. His mouth curves, hands touching the ends of her curls, which fall all the way down her back. "Need some help?"

"Nope," I snap out, grabbing Ro's hand and yanking her away from Trouble with a capital T. I know for a fact that if she were sober, her entire body would've jerked away from this man the second she accidentally brushed him. "No funny business, *RoRo*—now go. I'll come find you."

Ro grumbles at the nickname but releases the wrist of the playboy behind her and slinks down the stairs, albeit unsteadily. Freddy watches her with that same little glimmer in his eyes.

"Absolutely not," both Rhys and I say at the same time.

"I didn't do anything!" he barks, hands raising high in surrender. "I was only up here looking for your dumb ass." He points an accusatory finger at Rhys. "Text Reiner back. He doesn't believe me that I don't have you completely wasted."

"I'll tell him we'll be home soon."

"Why?" I ask, regretting the word vomit immediately as Rhys looks up, a little shell-shocked and a little confused, but with the corners of his mouth lifting slightly. Freddy is smirking, walking backward and making himself scarce. "I mean—"

"Want me to stay?" Rhys asks; the smile aching to burst forward is barely held back. He stays where he is, like I might scare off if he gets too close.

"I'd like to see your stamina when you're not fresh off an adrenaline-high crash."

He lets out a quick laugh that he looks nearly shocked by, before shaking his head and closing his eyes, stalking toward me.

Before he gets to me, a different body cuts him off, pressing me into the wall and grinding down—ignorant of present company and oblivious to my disinterest.

Sean—last name redacted since I can't seem to remember it—seemed like a good idea when he joined me on the dance floor earlier in the evening. He'd been a regular hookup of mine during the absolute downfall of my life last semester. He'd seemed like an even better idea when he'd started massaging my calves while chatting away about nothing I cared to hear. His hands are strong, rough enough that they might leave a mark, or so I'd subtly hinted at him earlier.

It seems after seeing only Ro come back downstairs, he took that as an invite.

"Are you trying to eat me?" I snap, shoving him off, flooded with the embarrassment of this happening while Rhys can see.

I hate that prick of self-consciousness as much as I hate the immediate, obvious flush to my cheeks. It's not the hooking up I'm embarrassed about—I've always been unashamed of my sexuality, my choices to do what I want with who I want. Hookups only, that's my MO, and I refuse to apologize for it; if men don't have to, why should I?

I enjoy myself and get what I need—most of the time.

So why does Rhys being here make my stomach hurt?

"That's the plan, babe." Sean smirks, crowding into me again. "Ready now?"

My face only flushes further as I shove him off *again*. "Not interested, actually. Get. Off."

"That's what I'm trying to do." He laughs, backing off barely an inch, but it's enough to notice someone lurking behind him. Spinning on his feet, he braces back against the wall, angling into my shoulder like he might slip around me at any moment. He nods his head toward Rhys with a quick smile. "Oh, shit. Koteskiy, hey."

The drawn out *hey* does nothing to erase the tightness around

Rhys's eyes. Still, he plasters a smile across his mouth and drops his chin in a quick, cool acknowledgment, before he glances back at me. It's hard to wrestle with the want in my chest; my heart thrums with the effort not to sprint toward him and use him like a personal shield from the ghost of my lowest moments.

"Gonna make it to Frozen Four this year?"

"That's the plan," Rhys replies, hands shoved into pockets, quirking an eyebrow at my tense stance. "Okay, Gray?"

His question to me isn't any softer, but something about it is different . . . familiar. Genuine, but quiet, like the soft sadness etched permanently into his eyes that no one besides me seems able to see.

"*Gray?*" Sean mocks, laughing, his arm dropping onto my shoulder like a heavy weight. I wonder if I stopped trying to stay upright, would I sink into the floor? "Oh, am I interrupting something?"

"Yes," Koteskiy says, at the same time I blurt, "No."

Rhys's gaze turns darker, a feat I didn't think possible, before I shrug Sean off and slink away from them both.

Sean guffaws loudly, the sound grating to my ears. "Koteskiy, huh? Upping the competition this year, Sadie?" He bumps me with his hip, green eyes on fire as he takes me in again.

It's my fault that Sean feels this way. Last semester, I spent an exorbitant amount of time playing with his drunk frat buddies just to get some kind of fire beneath him, so he would pull me upstairs and wreck me instead of trying to romance me. If Sean sees Rhys Koteskiy as some sort of game between us, it's only because I put that thought there.

I should be nicer about it, but I find myself somehow angrier— at myself, at Sean. Even at Rhys for whatever painful dance we are doing with each other.

"That's not what this is," I finally concede, hating that a part of me still wants to grab Sean by the hand and lead him into the now-vacant bathroom, let him slip into my body while I close my eyes and think only of Rhys . . . his deep brown eyes gazing up at me perched on his lap and the sound of his heavy breaths against my skin . . .

It would be so much easier to leave after that, to pull down my dress and get the hell out of this suffocating house.

But I *can't*.

"Listen—"

Whatever Sean is going to say is cut off sharply as Rhys grabs ahold of his shoulder and stops his attempt to crowd me again.

"Having trouble hearing?" he says, shoving Sean back hard enough that he trips, even though Rhys has barely moved. "She's told you no repeatedly." His voice is calm even as the storms gather in his eyes.

"You don't know Sadie. It's all fucking games to her, man."

Every bit of confidence I walked in here with tonight is gone, shredded. I wait for Rhys to pull away, but he only looks at me. Like he wants me to refute the claims, instead of standing here, avoiding his gaze, completely shrunken in on myself.

Normally, I would. I'd love to bite Sean's head off. But I feel so full of everything, I *need* a release . . .

"Fine," Rhys offers, stepping closer to me. His stance is all power, towering over Sean's too-relaxed form and semi-shielding mine. His hand settles on my waist, slipping around to press against my lower back. "Then she can play them with me. Get the fuck out of here."

The warmth building in my chest spreads throughout my body, head to toe, my pulse racing. The weighted heat of his palm is searing through the thin silk of my dress.

I want to kiss him, like some schoolgirl who's had her virtue protected, like he's some knight in shining armor.

"It's my house."

Warm brown eyes go nearly black, fists clenching, and from Sean's unintentional step backward, I realize maybe this erratic behavior isn't normal for the hockey star. I reach for Rhys's hand quickly, wrapping a hand around his wrist.

"We're leaving," I say with more confidence than I feel, snapping my entire body forward hard enough that it jolts Rhys into me. His hands mold to my middle, keeping me upright and making me hyperaware of how large his palms are compared to my waist.

I stop short as Sean shoves past both of us and stomps down the stairs, his angry mumbles barely audible above music so loud the walls shake.

Rhys's breath flutters against my hair in the opening of the stairwell where I've abruptly stopped. "Some kind of warning would be nice next time, *babe*. Unless you want to sideline me for my last season."

His use of that little sneered name works like a drug, relaxing every tense muscle through my neck, back, and arms. It's almost ridiculous how much I can tell he's trying to calm me, when I barely acknowledge my anxiety in the first place.

I snort without meaning to, tilting my head up at him while I snip, "A fall down the stairs would end your entire season? I thought you hockey boys are indestructible."

It takes only a moment to realize I've said something wrong, crossed some unspoken boundary with my words. His face tightens, eyes filling again with that deep well of pain I've seen in them more often than not, before he adjusts his mask and grants me a small, quick smile.

"I need to find my friend." It's the only thing I can think of to say.

He nods toward the stairs leading to the thumping party. "Me too."

But neither of us moves.

Something is making me hesitate, keeping my body pressed to his as "The Hills" by The Weeknd starts to blare from downstairs. I should go and find Ro. Go back home and finish myself off. I should . . .

Spinning, I grab Rhys's wrist and pull him again, straight into the still-vacant bathroom. I slam the door shut and lock it behind us. There isn't much light, just a dusty red glow from the painted bulbs someone has installed for the party. The walls shake with the bass from below, the song bleeding through the cracks around the door as I grab onto the black fabric of his shirt.

"Sadie, I—"

"Yes or no, hotshot." It's more of a statement than a question, but my entire brain feels like it's hanging by a thread, barely sane through the overwhelming thoughts that could've been drowned out by someone else's touch by now.

Rhys looks nearly in pain, his brown eyes dilated, red light flickering over his chiseled, handsome face while his sharp jaw stays tight. I watch the thick column of his throat work, only getting hotter with the image of him as he makes his decision.

"I'm only doing this if we talk after."

"What if I don't want to?"

"Sadie." He grasps my hair in his hand and holds me still while angling his mouth to my ear. "I don't do this . . . party bathroom hookups? That's not . . ."

The rejection stings, and I jerk out of his hold, ignoring the slight pain in my scalp as I wrench my head from his grasp. "But locker rooms are perfectly fine? As long as it's to soothe your shit, not mine, yeah?"

It doesn't register what I've said, what I've revealed, until I'm reaching for the doorknob, desperate to escape.

CHAPTER THIRTEEN

Rhys

For once, I'm not thinking. Not as I blindly followed her upstairs. Not as I let her lead me into an empty bathroom. Not now, as I grab at her shoulder to stop her from leaving and spin her, easily pinning her small body against the door.

"This is what you want?" I ask, making sure that this time, she can feel me entirely. Every bit of my body is pressed completely to hers, connecting like a perfect puzzle piece.

She's so much smaller than me. In our previous interactions I've mostly been on the ground looking up at her like some deity coming to save me, so it's something I only really notice now that I'm towering over her with my hand broad against her trim waist.

"I just . . ." she starts, but fades off again. Her pupils are blown, and the red light somehow only highlights the freckles beneath her eye, the angular shape of her face.

"Tell me," I nearly beg. Maybe it's the too-loud music giving me a massive headache, or the red light that makes this almost like a foggy dream, but I can't make myself shut up. "Because I'll tell you. I can't stop thinking about the locker room, and I—"

She shuts me up by slamming her lips onto mine. I'm all too eager to reciprocate, tilting down to wrap my arms around her little waist and lift her closer to me, pressing her back into the panels of the door. Her muscular legs twine around my waist in return, holding herself up with ease while grinding lightly down my stomach, chasing friction like a fix.

Sadie's like a goddamn drug, the effect just as immediate, my mind relaxing and something *good* chasing the dark out of my veins until I feel like *Old Rhys* again; even my headache dulls to an ignorable level. I gulp down her presence like air after breaking the surface from drowning. I soak it all up, knowing from my experiences with her before that the switch will flip.

This won't be enough for her, and I understand it. There's barely enough of me left to make a complete human. Why would I be able to hold her together when she's becoming the one keeping me intact?

My lips take their time, slowing from her frantic beginning. I sweep my tongue across her mouth. My teeth lightly graze her lip, pulling the plump bottom one to suck between my own, before releasing it and heading south. Two kisses to the corner of her mouth, a drag of my tongue down the underneath of her chin, before I press harder, slowly sucking kisses into the skin of her neck.

The moan Sadie releases is soft and light, so opposed to the intense scratch of her nails on my arms and the back of my neck beneath the light shag of my slightly-too-long hair.

My stomach is swirling, nausea from my headache mixing with intense lust and my anxiety about doing this here, with her, in this damn bathroom.

I pull away to talk to her, to ask her to follow me home, to beg *her* to talk to *me*; but she latches on to my neck, sucking and licking against the skin so fast my vision blurs and I stumble into the wall, hands gliding underneath her dress to grip her upper thighs to maintain some kind of hold on her.

She's so strong, I feel like I could let go entirely and she'd hold tight, keeping herself up easily.

There's a knock at the door, to which Sadie quickly offers, "Fuck off!"

I smile into her neck, feeling almost high off her.

But the person on the other side is insistent, shouting through the crack in a high melodic voice. "Sadie Brown! You can get off with Sean later."

A wave of frustration rolls through me, as if I have some automatic claim on her, like a fucking third grader. *I licked her so she's mine.*

"What do you want, Victoria?" Sadie calls.

"Ro is jumping off the high dive like a psycho!"

That makes her pause. She drops from my arms entirely, pulling her dress down just as a flash of black peeks at me. Not giving a second thought to her reddened neck, swollen lips, or loosened ponytail, she rips the door wide open and takes off at a near sprint.

I'm frozen for a moment, watching her escape me like she's on fire. My eyes flick to the mirror, the light of the room half glowing from the overhead bulbs in the hallway, half red, cutting me nearly down the middle. My collar's looser now, shirt askew, with marks from Sadie's mouth across my neck.

I can't help the warmth that radiates up my spine and turns my cheeks slightly dark.

I think I like what the aftermath of Sadie Gray looks like on me.

Victoria stares from the doorway, eyes wide, with a pretty smile across her face.

We've crossed paths before—both captains of our sports in our junior years, both communications majors with a few classes together. I've never dated or slept with her, but she was my type before. Perfectly put together at all times. Intelligent, kind, elegant, blond.

"Rhys," she finally manages to speak. "I didn't know you were here . . . with Sadie?" She says it like a question, and if it were anyone else, I might refute the claim. But that interaction in the locker room comes to mind too quickly, the hurt defensiveness from Sadie that makes me want to protect her—even if I know she wouldn't let me if she were here.

"Yeah, I'm just here to pick her up." *Literally and figuratively, I guess, since her ass was just in my hands.* "I should go see if she needs help."

Victoria smiles at me, even if her eyes look a little less sparkly, and I edge around her and head downstairs.

. . .

Thankfully, the music is quieter on the large back porch, only two speakers blasting "Wasted" at max volume. I spot Sadie easily, crouched over the lip of the pool on her knees with only two inches between the hem of her dress and her bare ass.

It's that sliver of pale skin that has me launching down the small set of wooden stairs to stand behind her, blocking her from the small audience forming at our backs. Only then do I realize that Sadie's friend Ro isn't the only one in the pool; Freddy is right behind her, a few feet away but close enough for me to know, whatever this situation is, my winger was involved.

I eye him quickly, shaking my head and pressing my thumb backward over my shoulder, desperately trying to remove him from the situation.

He only shakes his head, crossing his arms like a pouting child and casting a quick, hesitant glance toward a very wet Ro, her curls now pulled high atop her head in some crazy knot that looks like it's tied with—a shoelace?

I try to pay attention to the whispered argument between the two girls, but I'm far too distracted by my stupid friend getting closer and closer to the duo.

Sadie falls back from her whispered conversation, her ass tapping against my shins. It doesn't seem to startle her—far from it, so it seems, as she grabs on to my jeans and starts to heft herself back up.

Instead, I grasp her biceps easily and set her on her feet.

"Can you find a towel?" she asks.

"Yeah," I agree without hesitation, despite knowing I have no idea where I could get one.

As I spin away, my foot taps against the two sets of shoes sitting perfectly by the pool: one set of flopped-over cream boots, the other a pristine set of white-and-navy Air Force 1s with a missing shoelace.

"Don't touch my shoes," Freddy barks, close behind me, and I'm seconds away from shoving him back into the water for getting snippy with me right now. He walks right past me after barking out the order, heading for a wicker dining set beneath the overhang of the porch where two bath towels lie.

"Planned this one, did you?"

Freddy smiles that same stupid smirk that's etched nearly permanently on to his face, and grabs a towel to sling over his shoulder, taking the other one back to the girls heading toward us.

A quick, "Sure," is all I get from him before he's handing the towel to Ro. She fumbles with it for a moment until a concerned Sadie grabs it and circles it around her shoulders like a blanket.

"Thanks for watching out for her," Sadie says, albeit reluctantly, as she guides Ro toward the wooden staircase. Freddy nods, swiping his towel over his hair and letting it rest around his shoulders as well.

"Not a hardship to get a beautiful woman soaking wet," he quips before I can elbow him in the gut, or tape his mouth shut, or find a way to rewind time and never let him become my friend.

Sadie and I both jump in simultaneously, barking over each other.

"Jesus, Freddy."

"Back off it, Freddy."

But a loud hiccupping laugh bursts from the nearly-drowned girl, cutting off every reprimand sitting on my tongue.

"That was a good one, Freddy," Ro agrees, dropping the towel and stumbling as she attempts to pull on her boots. "At least, *I* thought so." She nearly falls again, but Freddy wraps a hand around her arm to steady her while she gets her shoes over her wet calves.

My gaze finds Sadie immediately. With her arms crossed and lips pursed, she looks altogether much smaller than she did mere minutes ago, straddling me against a dingy bathroom wall.

"Okay, Gray?" I ask again.

The question seems to jolt her, her eyes snapping to mine with such sharpness that a shiver rolls down my spine. She bites down on her lip, and my hands tighten inside the confines of my pockets, keeping myself from reaching to pull it loose.

"Yeah. We just need to call an Uber."

I'm shaking my head before she can finish. "Don't. We'll take you back to . . . ?"

"The dorms," she finishes. "Not far. Honestly, we could walk—"

Freddy shushes her, making that little divot form between her brow again as he passes by her and taps on her head like a child.

"Rhys is an overprotective crazy person, and Ro here is walking like a baby giraffe, so let us drop you, yeah?"

It's clear she's battling her agreement, but there's no way in hell they're walking home alone. If she won't take our offer, I'll just have Freddy drive slowly alongside them until they get back to the dorms.

"Okay," Sadie nods, while her friend jumps up and down in place, using Freddy's arm as a stabilizer and shouting a chorus of yays.

Freddy easily joins in too, a glint of mischief in his squinted eyes that I'm sure is now permanently stuck there.

We leave quickly, piling into Freddy's ancient SUV that shouldn't be road-legal. It takes a few minutes to maneuver out of the piled-up street parking, which Freddy does one-handed while opening his phone and tossing it to Ro, who has to lean on the console to use it while it stays connected to the cord hooking it to the outdated system.

"I don't have connection, but there's lots in my downloads. Play whatever, princess." He smirks, winking over his shoulder at the already-flushed girl. I elbow him hard in the side, but he only smiles wider. "Just make it good."

Ro purses her lips and looks quickly at Sadie, who sighs deeply, like a parent—but it's more out of amusement than annoyance—and leans forward to set her chin on Ro's shoulder.

Both girls smile brighter as Ro clicks on something and sets the phone back on the console.

"Oh, hell yeah," Freddy shouts as the song starts, cranking the volume to an absurd level and rolling down all four windows so the heated summer-night air breezes through. They all sing at the top of their lungs to the blaring Taylor Swift song, so loud I can't really make out their voices in the mixed chorus.

My eyes flicker between both the rearview and side mirrors, where I can just see Sadie, dancing side to side, hands in the air, ponytail wild behind her, eyes closed. Her eyes open and her body stretches across the backseat as she and Ro hold hands and yell the chorus into each other's faces, giggling.

As many times as I've seen her, Sadie's only really smiled at me twice. But this smile—this is different. It's so big, her pillowy, faded-red lips stretching, the apples of her sharp cheeks softening and creasing the collection of freckles beneath her eyes that I'm just as desperate to touch as I am to get close enough to count them.

Too distracted by the indecent path of my thoughts, my entire body jolts as Sadie suddenly grabs ahold of my shoulders, leaning into the front seat as far as her seatbelt will let her. Her hands settle and squeeze, and it's embarrassing how difficult it becomes to hold back a moan.

Her lips are nearly at my ear as she shouts over the music, "Why aren't you singing?"

Sadie is infectious, so much so that a smile to match hers dances quickly across my face.

"I don't know the song."

"You don't know 'Getaway Car'?" Ro joins in, smooshing in next to Sadie. It presses Sadie's cheek to mine for a second, the corner of her lips hitting my skin like a goddamn fire poker.

Freddy graciously turns the volume down. "He's not really a Taylor Swift guy; unless they're playing it in the arena, I doubt he knows it. And even then"—he shakes his head—"Rhys is too focused to hear anything besides 'Get. Puck. In. Net.'"

Sadie rolls her eyes at the robotic impression, sharing a look with me like she understands how deep that implication goes for us.

If you play it, I'll listen.

She gestures toward him with her chin. "And you're not focused?"

"I'm a good multitasker," he says. In usual Freddy fashion, it's embedded with a perverse double meaning, making Sadie and me groan while still-drunk Ro laughs again.

I grab the dial and turn the music back up to save us all from Matt Fredderic's relentlessness, letting the music blare as we cross South College and head to the edge of campus.

"We're in Millay," Sadie offers before either of us can ask, pointing to the redbrick buildings facing each other at an angle, the fountain and benches between them barely lit by the orange sidewalk lights, disrupted only by the blaring neon-blue of an emergency box.

Freddy pulls right up to the curb, and I nearly spring from the car, terrified that if I don't try something now, Sadie's going to slip through my fingers once again.

Sadie looks a little shell-shocked at the sight of me standing, but she keeps her arm around Ro's waist and doesn't say anything as I walk them both up to their dorm entrance. Sadie swipes her Waterfell ID and lets Ro through with a strict command to wait, before spinning back to me.

"Thanks for the ride," she says. "And for my car. I didn't mention it before, but that was . . . You didn't have to do that, so thank you."

My head is shaking before she finishes her sentence. "Of course."

From her position a few steps higher than me, she's slightly taller, so I have to look up at her. I've been looking up at her from every panic-induced dream I've had since that day on the ice, like she's meant to be there.

A fucking guardian angel, I guess. Which is something I'll never say out loud because I'd never live that down. Especially considering how much I crave that from her.

Like she would *want* to save me.

Pathetic.

Self-hatred swirls again, and now I want to tape my mouth closed before I say something stupid.

"You could repay me by getting coffee. With me, I mean."

Something stupid like that.

My laugh is self-deprecating, and I want to tell her that I used to be *good* at this—that I was charming and not whatever this shaking, pitiful thing is that's replaced that part of me.

Sadie doesn't laugh, but she does start shaking her head.

"I'm not really the go-and-get-coffee girl . . . honestly, not really the get-anything-together kind of girl. And definitely not the girl to date someone like you."

I smile, completely forced and fake, somehow accepting the absolute kick to the gut her response is. My mouth starts to open, to beg her not to say anything else, but she keeps going.

"Tonight was—"

I groan, my hands covering my face as I beg, "Please don't say good, I don't think I can handle that again."

Sadie laughs lightly, stepping down to my level.

"All right, duly noted," she says, reaching her hand into my pocket and grabbing my phone. She doesn't ask, or say anything, but turns it to my face to unlock it. She texts herself the most recently used emoji, which is, unfortunately, a hockey stick. Her eyes dart to mine with a quick eye roll as if to say *typical*.

"What's that for?" I ask, taking my phone back from her outstretched hand. We've spent over a month together, but never crossed the line to communicating outside the rink.

I don't want to get my hopes up.

She takes two steps up the short staircase before turning to look at me and shrugging.

"I don't know yet. Have a good night, hotshot."

I can't help the small smile that appears. Despite everything else, I now have something of hers.

"Good night, *kotyonok*."

CHAPTER FOURTEEN

Sadie

Taking on the early shift at the café is always a gamble, especially a week before school starts. With everyone returning to campus, it's hit-or-miss how busy five-to-nine mornings will be.

Thankfully—for the sake of my slight headache and the pinch of anxiety at the top of my spine—this morning is a slow one. I serve a few regulars—the summer crowd of town locals that will make themselves scarce again once the semester fills the warm brown paneled walls with drowsy students.

At half past ten, I start another roast of the new but popular Ethiopian blend, dumping a bag into the grinder while I have an empty moment at the register.

"Here," Luis, our main—and really only—chef, calls from the slot of the kitchen window. He sets down a plate of crunchy avocado toast with two poached eggs and extra chili flakes, with a drizzle of honey in the shape of a heart that I *know* will be spicy when it hits my tongue. As if on cue, my stomach growls, and I offer him a big smile.

"Thank you," I say as emphatically as I can, because I'm starving to the point I'm almost dizzy. My hair is a mess of semi-straight tangles and I've lost my trusty wrist elastic, so I can only tuck both sides behind my ears and hike my shoulders up to keep the strands from interrupting my meal.

Luis smirks and leans through the window on his forearms while I sit on the countertop to easily balance my plate in my lap and eat, while still having a view of the entire café.

George, a local writer, sips coffee that I know has gone cold by now, while a trio—parents and a freshman girl—enjoys a full spread because the mom was too excited about moving her daughter into her alma mater not to order everything on the menu to sample. Only one table has emptied in the last few minutes, the tabletop scattered with a blueberry-dotted ceramic mug and a few empty sugar packets.

"I was planning on trying my çilbir recipe on Ro."

I smile, swallowing down another too-big bite of messy toast. "She'll love that; especially knowing she doesn't have to fly all the way to her mom to get good Turkish food."

Luis nods, wiping down the steel top of the window again. I'm quite sure he has a slight crush on Ro, but he's gentle about it. If Ro knew, even for a moment, that he felt that way for her, she'd probably never show up for work again; not because of him, or even really the fact that he's a lovestruck high schooler, but because for all her sunshine personality, she is suddenly a clam when it comes to real-life romance.

The girl can read chapter-long filthy sex scenes without a flinch, but tell her a boy thinks she's pretty and she turns into a tomato.

The chime of the door sounds just as I stuff the last bite of my toast into my mouth and slide the plate into Luis's outstretched, callused hand. My gaze flicks over to the two patrons approaching the cash register while my churning stomach takes a free dive off a cliff somewhere.

Of *course* it's him.

Of course it's Rhys, looking like a goddamn wet dream in gray sweatpants and a navy Dri-FIT long-sleeve shirt that hugs every single inch of his tight upper body. His smile is soft and a little sleepy as he continues to speak to his very large friend waiting patiently at the counter. His hair looks damp, like he popped out of the shower just before this—which is a dangerous thought because now I'm picturing him beneath the spray of some high-end rain shower, washing his abs and thick thighs.

My eyes trail down his body again before someone clears their throat and I start choking on the bite I didn't even chew, too struck by the absolute karmic punch of seeing him.

Rhys is looking at me now, his eyes like burning fires that scald my skin as I gulp down water and hop down from the counter.

"Morning," I offer, smoothing a hand over the black half-apron tied around my black jeans.

I feel that little pinch of anxiety growing as Rhys peruses me just as I did him, his eyes clocking my tight gray short-sleeve shirt that's most likely littered with coffee stains and, yep, crumbs of sourdough. I tuck my hair behind my ears again, wiping the back of my hand over my mouth and finding a stain of yellow from the corner of my lips on my hand.

Jesus.

"Not the get-coffee-together kind of girl, huh?" Rhys teases, no hint of his hesitation or unease from last night present in his expression now.

"Just the serve-it-with-a-smile kind," I quip.

He smiles more genuinely, the indent of one dimple showing. "For some reason, I doubt the 'smile' part. I don't remember that from the last time you served me coffee."

My mouth splits wide into an over-exaggerated, all-teeth grin as I offer to take their order.

Bantering with him brings my anxiety down, calming me in an almost unsettling way, where I crave the next little interaction between us. Maybe it's the quickness of it, the permanent deep well of sadness in his eyes, or the fact that he's distractingly gorgeous like some old Grecian marble statue of *male beauty*.

"Have a seat and I'll bring it out to you," I say, spinning the iPad toward them with the total. Rhys tries to grab for his wallet, but the large, surly-looking man beside him is quicker, tapping his heavy metal card against the system before leaving the counter without another word.

Rhys leans in over the counter and I mimic his movement, watching a light flush paint his cheeks.

"I, uh . . . I had my first practice back this morning."

"Yeah?" I have the urge to grab his hand and hold it. "And? All good?"

The idea of him panicked and alone makes my stomach hurt. I can't explain it, but I feel an intense protectiveness over his pain.

"All good. I listened to that song. The one from the locker room, with the weird band name?"

My throat feels clogged. "Rainbow Kitten Surprise."

"Yeah." He smiles; dimples.

I freeze, because if I move, I will kiss him. Grab his usually shaking hands. Tuck my fists against his neck until the heat of his skin releases them from their tight hold. Splay him across the counter and mold my entire body to his. See if the golden boy captain can release his tight control for me.

"Anyway, I'll wait over there. Thanks, Sadie, for everything." Rhys lingers for a moment, locking me in his gaze again before ducking away and following his friend to a clean table close by.

I study them while making their orders: an iced black coffee with three tablespoons of almond milk for the grumpy one—Bennett Reiner, going by the name on the order—and a cold brew special, which means maple syrup, toffee nut, and a splash of condensed milk, for Rhys. I nearly swallowed my tongue as I listened to him order my go-to drink.

They're both speaking quietly, both on their phones as much as they are off them, and despite the constant discussion flowing easily between them, they both have a tightness in their shoulders, while Rhys bounces his leg beneath the table.

I've never seen Bennett Reiner before, but I'll never miss him after this—his height alone is like a calling card. He's got to be pushing 6′6″, which is daunting to me, sitting as a solid 5′2″. Rhys is tall, but Bennett is like a mountain with his broad shoulders and tree-trunk thighs. He doesn't look like a college student, really—not only from his size, but from his hyper-masculine features that make him look like he might be leading stuffy board meetings and climbing mountain faces in his spare time. His light brown hair is a mop of messy waves and curls, and he has a well-maintained scruff of a beard, thin enough to see the masculine squareness of his jaw. His eyes are slanted beneath thick brows like a permanent furrow, even with a smile on his face as he speaks quietly with Rhys.

"Here," I try to announce myself as I step up to their table, holding their drinks out carefully.

Bennett swipes his immediately, sliding a coaster under the plastic and a foam holder over the sweating cup. Rhys takes his from my hand directly, smiling up at me. It's gentler this time, less fake than I've seen from him, with that lightly bleeding sadness like invisible tears on his cheeks.

"Thanks." He takes a quick sip. "By the way, this is Bennett. Ben, this is Sadie."

"The figure skater." Ben nods to me, not quite meeting my eyes.

"And coffee maker, apparently," Rhys supplies.

"A good coffee maker, you mean." I smirk. "The best cup of coffee you'll ever have."

"Should I stand and announce it for everyone? Best coffee in Waterfell?"

The door chimes and I barely have a moment to straighten from where I've leaned forward, a hand on the back of Rhys's wooden chair, before a little body rocks into my legs with a delighted giggle-scream.

"You almost knocked me over, nugget," I scold, but a happy grin solidifies on my face as I lean down and ruffle Liam's hair. He's got half of a Darth Vader mask painted on his face, which I know is thanks to Ro's artistic abilities. Said artist is speaking lightly to Oliver as they walk into the café at a more normal pace. The black paint has smudged a bit now, some of it across his arm where he must've been rubbing at it earlier, but the kid adores Star Wars. I firmly believe it started because Oliver loved the movies first, and Liam was desperate to be just like his big brother. Now, I see the same thing happening with hockey.

"Sorry, Sissy." Liam doesn't rest for a moment before launching into the entire story of their very normal morning as if he's telling a daring adventure story. He ends the quick tale with a rushed, "Are you making pancakes?"

Before I can answer, he suddenly freezes, before breaking into a howl so loud I have to slip my hand over his mouth. He's babbling through my hand, pointing frantically at Rhys.

Oliver reaches my side. He nods lightly, hefting his bag farther up on his shoulder.

"Hey, killer." I nod to Oliver and let go of Liam's mouth but keep a firm grip on his shoulder. "Was he good today?"

Liam is still nearly shouting, ecstatic to see Rhys again. It's a little unnerving.

Oliver runs a hand through his hair. "Everything was fine. My practice ran over, but Ro kept him occupied."

I nod to what Oliver is saying, though he seems hesitant for a reason I plan to flush out later. Right now, I'm more focused on the worry that if I let go of Liam, he will jump into Rhys's lap.

"Sorry," I offer quickly. "Liam, remember what we've talked about."

"Rhys isn't a stranger, right?"

Rhys laughs. "Right."

"You're not?" Bennett asks with a little tick of his mouth. "Since when?"

Though the question is posed to his friend, my little brother decides to intervene again with a screeching, "Since he's teaching me hockey. Rhys is the best hockey player, probably in the world."

Bennett smiles lightly. "Humble, too."

Rhys shakes his head, eyes flickering to Bennett, then to me, before settling back on Liam. There's a new tenseness to him though, I notice. His shoulders are pinched, his smile tight, fake; he's wearing his mask once more. It makes me bristle as I realize that Liam's infatuation with Rhys might make him uncomfortable.

Grabbing Liam's hand, I nod toward a large open table next to the counter. "Wanna chill for a minute while I close out?"

"Sure." Oliver shrugs. He takes Liam's arm and pulls him along behind him. "Come on, Anakin, leave them alone."

Liam's lip furls, his head whipping back and forth between his brother and the table of hockey gods like he can't decide exactly what to fight for. What ends up spilling from his lips is, "I'm not in my Jedi robes, Oliver. I'm Darth Vader."

I turn to Ro and give her arm a thankful squeeze. "It'll only take a minute for me to close out and change over everything. Do you mind? I'll be fast."

"They can sit with us if you need," Rhys says, standing before I can disagree and dragging Liam's chair—with him still in it—back toward their too-small table. Liam squeals a laugh, eyes shining as he looks at Rhys's upside-down profile.

Rhys smiles up at me. "We're friends, yeah?"

I want to stop them, to argue with Rhys, but Ro stops me when she smiles and gives him a quick thanks, pulling us both away to change over.

"I don't—"

"Relax." She sighs, dragging the word out into four extra syllables. Her hands squeeze my shoulders as she forces me around the counter corner, smacking my ass to send me to the break room.

"I'll close your stuff out," she says, pulling an apron off the little hook beneath the POS station and tying it before tying up her curls into a springy ponytail on top of her head. "You stop trying to control everything and let the nice hockey boys play with your brothers while you take a moment to *not* be their mom."

She pats her fist down in a gentle rhythm on the top of the counter—not that she needed to, since Luis is already gazing at her.

"Luis, can you cover the front for a few?"

"Sure," he replies a little too quickly as he shrugs off his gloves and hair net. It's wild that he accepts it, considering his family owns the entire café and the restaurants on both sides of us, but his dreamy-eyed look is all the explanation I need.

We push into the small break room that doubles as a manager's office and connects to the back rooms of the restaurant to the right of us. Sitting down on one of the chairs, I blow out a breath and look up at where Ro perches on the desktop.

"So," she starts. "How did your meeting go?"

"Okay." I breathe, nodding as if that will make me more confident. "I think. I mean, it was short? So I don't know. I'll meet him next week to speak more and bring the documents I have. He said that'll be all we need for Liam."

"That's good, Sade. Honestly."

"Right? I think it's a good sign—it has to be."

It *has* to be. I'm running out of other options, and dragging myself between campus dorms and my home, shelling out money from the already tight budget for babysitters when our neighbor Ms. B is busy—it's piling up, and school hasn't even started.

Ro helped untangle me last year, but I refuse to put myself in that position again. And this is the only way left.

"Yes." She smiles, all reassuring and supportive. "And if he won't take you on, we have tons still left on the list, okay?"

Ro is my best friend, no matter my best efforts at keeping her at arm's length. She shoved her way in freshman year, not deterred by my attitude or attempts to rid myself of her. Instead, she stuck like glue, until she was so attached I couldn't exist without her. Then she watched me suffer from a paralyzing panic attack and held me through the entire thing, rocking us both on the little twin bed in our freshman dorm.

After that, I showed her everything. It was like I couldn't stop.

She took it all in stride with a pursed mouth and determined brow, babysitting and helping me get the little ones to and from school while I balanced figure skating, and everything else. She tutored me when I was put on probation for my classes, scooped me off the bathroom floor when my hookups didn't succeed in chasing away the pressure in my chest.

I'll do anything for her, protect her endlessly, forever.

Oliver, Liam, Ro. My family.

"Okay."

Ro stands, hugging me tightly and letting me breathe for a few moments. Her hands run gently through my hair, combing out little knots and snags, then braiding it loosely down my back.

"Good?" she asks. I nod into her stomach before pulling away and tucking the loose tendrils behind my ears.

"Good."

"Okay, then go get the boys and just enjoy some time with them. Why don't you bring them to the dorm for a sleepover? We can make a pillow-fort and check them into school late tomorrow."

"Sounds perfect."

CHAPTER FIFTEEN

Rhys

With our first preseason team practice and meeting under my belt, I feel somewhat light as I stroll into our second practice.

The first day I'd woken up late on purpose so Bennett wouldn't try to drive us all together, even if I only waited until he turned off our street to head out. I needed the time in the quiet space of my own car to calm myself. I wore an all-black ensemble, hoping it might hide the anxious sweat nearly dripping from me—at least until dressing out.

I nearly called Dad, letting my finger hover over his contact for a solid three minutes before tossing my phone to the floorboards of the passenger side and driving in silence.

Somehow, nothing cracked—not my phone or my mind—even through the semi-easy first skate together. I spent time getting to know the new freshmen, apologizing for being the absentee captain over summer intensive camps, and thanking Holden, a defenseman who'd taken up as my alternate after the injury.

Coach had asked Bennett to be captain more times than I could count, but he refused each time.

I'm not sweating as much now, at least not from anxiety—more from the hard pace as I round the rink, working the puck on my stick on the sharp turns before hitting a quick stop as Freddy takes off, our relay team quicker, smoother than the others. Practice is officially over, but that only means it's my time for team-building drills before the conditioning stretches.

Leaning against the boards, I lift my chin toward Bennett where he sits with his cage off, spraying water into his mouth.

"They look good."

Bennett nods. "Better than this summer. That Sinclair kid's quick as fuck."

"Yeah?" I smirk at his clearly displeased face. "Got a wicked backhand too."

Bennett shakes his head again, left shoulder twitching up to his ear, even if it only shifts his pads a hair. "You caught that, yeah? Had to get used to the zigzag he runs for it, but he's only gotten a few past me. He's killing Mercy."

That makes me smile a little, flicking a glance at Bennett's tandem, Connor Mercer. He looks exhausted and soaked, having already emptied his water bottle over his head.

"Mercy needed a little knocking down."

"Coach wants to start him more this season, and trade off more games."

That does make me pause, but instead of offering a reaction—because I know Ben—I only flick up an eyebrow.

He shrugs. "Doesn't bother me."

"Scouts?"

"They'll see me. They saw me last year too." He takes another swig of his water. "Besides, we're supposed to be a tandem and I played twenty-six out of thirty-four games last year in regular season."

"Because you're near perfect."

He shrugs.

Freddy skates up, heaving breaths through a smirk as he pulls his own cage off. "What are we talking about, ladies?"

"Bennett's not talking to you after that stupid shit you were pulling in the shootout drills."

My tone is filled with unreleased laughter, but Ben looks like he might be ready to snap Freddy's stick, if not his spine.

"C'mon, Reiner, you can't be mad at me for keeping you on your toes."

"I was in butterfly for so long I thought I pulled something, you blockhead."

Freddy raises his hands in surrender. "Not my fault the freshies want to be just like me."

"You had your entire team of fucking wingers dangling all over my zone."

"You did?" I ask, smiling despite Bennett's seething tone. "They all just did what you said?"

"Just call me Daddy." Freddy's smirk grows teeth and gleams like the sheet of ice we're standing on. Holden gags, only catching that last golden nugget of our conversation.

As the rest of the team finishes up the race, offense beating defense by a smidge, I call a quick huddle and plan a team cookout at our house for Wednesday. First day of school, but not the first weekend, so that the freshmen don't get the wrong idea of what this event is—bonding, not boozing.

The locker room is buzzing lightly after practice, and I feel the desire to participate and joke around, but each time someone tries to engage with me, there's only exhaustion. A bone-deep numbness.

It's something I recognize easily now, from all the expensive therapy my parents have paid for: *masking*. Dr. Bard calls it a *negative coping mechanism* and says it's a symptom of PTSD, which I definitely don't have and she will not convince me otherwise.

I took a hit playing a sport—I wasn't in a goddamn war.

It's easier this way: to pretend to be who I was before that game, to be the same team player and leader who earned the *C* on my jersey sophomore year. It's who I am, who I should be—just lost beneath the dark cloud insistent on following me everywhere.

After stepping into the warm sun outside the athletics complex, I pause to wait for Bennett—who is most likely stacking his pads in the exact order he prefers them.

My phone lights up again, a text from my dad.

Lunch?

Above it sits a trail of long paragraphs and ridiculous uplifting quotes that read like the inside of a self-help journal, along with quick one-word responses from my end.

I hesitate in my reply, waiting for an excuse.

It's not that I don't want to spend time with him. My dad is my hero, always will be. It's just confusing and complicated now. And I can't get the echo of his voice out of my head.

My son.

Bennett steps through the door, hair perfect, decked in slacks and a dark green polo that looks a little out of place considering we should be headed home to gorge on food and rest. His phone is pressed to his ear, and he uses his free hand to slide his Ray-Bans over his eyes against the sunlight.

"I said I was going to be late," he mutters, jaw tight in a way that quickly tells me exactly who it is he's talking to. "I told you last time that *this* week was the first week of practices, so I needed to push lunch back."

He's close enough now that I can make out the gruff, identical tone of the other caller.

"It's fine, Bennett, I can wait."

Adam Reiner: former NHL prospect, current cutthroat corporate lawyer.

Bennett comes from more money than he'd ever know what to

do with—the kind that ensures generations could choose not to work and be fine with it. His father was a silver-spoon baby with a trust fund larger than a full roster of NFL contracts, which makes it somewhat surprising that he became best friends with the Russian transplant who'd been living in a dingy apartment after turning eighteen in a boys' home and learning to speak English from an elderly college professor who lived above him.

The rich-kid center whose future wasn't dependent on anything, and the poor, scrappy defenseman whose future was entirely dependent on that rookie year—and yet, they'd never stopped that friendship.

I have no problems with Bennett's father, never have—but after the divorce, Bennett could barely stand to be in the same room with him.

So his father missed more games than he attended, stopping altogether during our time at Berkshire. Now, I know that once a month Bennett meets his father at Bar Mezzana in South End.

Besides the extravagant gifts that often bless our home or garage—most recently the undriven new Bronco sitting with a tarp still tucked over it—Bennett and his father do not have a relationship.

"Don't bother," he snaps back. "Go back to work. I'm not driving into the city for twenty minutes of staring at each other over stupidly expensive food."

He hangs up without a second thought.

"Missing another lunch?" I ask, realizing after that I wouldn't know either way.

Bennett shakes his head, rearranging his hair and glasses again with trembling hands.

"I went to the last one, but it was the first time I'd seen him all summer."

"Still bad?"

"I'm just . . . My mom's happy, finally. Her and Paul are gone for the next two weeks to Europe. I don't want the reminder."

"I get it."

I don't, actually. Bennett's parents' divorce has always been a strange topic for me.

My parents are sick in love, and always have been. To the world, there's nothing Maximillian Koteskiy loves more than hockey. But anyone who truly knows him knows he'd give up every Stanley Cup win and his entire career if it meant he'd hold on to my mother.

"Headed back to the house?" Bennett asks, holding the button on the side of his phone to turn it completely off.

"I think so—"

"Pool party at Zeta," Holden announces, walking out shoulder to shoulder with Freddy. Both are haphazardly put together in a way that almost makes them look like twins, but where Freddy is all play-boy smirk, Holden is boyish innocence.

"I'm good," I say. I have other plans in mind, namely attempting to sneak another hour of a certain punky figure skater's time.

"I'll come," Bennett says surprisingly. At my look, he shrugs. "Need something to do."

"Fair enough. I'll see you guys back at the house later."

With a final few chin lifts and waves on my way to the car, I tuck in and shoot a quick, *Can't today* text to my father.

I grasp the handle before I curse, realizing I've left my keys in my locker.

Thankfully, everything is empty now, making it easier to run in, grab my keys out of the cubby, and get out without the need to stop and talk with anyone.

Coach's office is the only room with lights still on, the door half open. I pay no mind to it at first, but the conversation inside is loud enough it makes me pause against the wall before crossing the doorway.

"You swore that it wasn't on the schedule," a deep voice growls. "You said it was a home game."

"It was." Coach sighs. "Look, if you really aren't going to play—"

"What's the consequence of not playing?"

My brows dip. A player then, but I don't recognize the voice. It isn't that surprising though, considering how absent I've been.

A slam like a hand to the desk, and then, "I won't be in that damn arena with even the possibility that she—"

"Listen—"

"You asked me what my deal was. *This* is my fucking deal." The other voice is nearly a growl, intense and low. Angry. "I don't play in an arena she might be in. I *can't* see her. Otherwise, I'm going to *fucking* kil—"

"Okay, Tor. Okay."

I don't recognize the name beyond an inkling of familiarity that I can't really follow. He sounds insane, but I trust Coach enough not to have someone like that messing with our team mojo.

I retrieve my keys and leave, quiet and quick, before driving to my new favorite coffee shop, hoping for even the slightest chance at spotting Sadie.

• • •

It's Ro I find inside the cozy, well-named Brew Haven, standing at the counter chatting with a well-dressed guy.

I stand behind him for only a moment before Ro catches my eye and the reserved expression—which seems strange for the enthusiastic girl I only recently met—melts from her face. Maybe she is more reserved when not drunk off her ass and screaming Taylor Swift into the night air.

"Rhys Koteskiy." She smiles, but her eyes track to the guy still leaning against the counter next to us. "Here for a coffee or for a girl?"

"You two know each other?" the guy asks, eyebrow ticking up as he directs his question at me instead of her.

"Rhys," I offer, reaching my hand out to him with my captain's smile. He takes it, giving a hard quick shake before letting me go.

"Tyler. Ro's boyfriend."

Got it. I keep the smile plastered across my face as I look back to Ro, her nervous expression making me feel a little nauseous. I lean in and pointedly ask, "Is Sadie not working today?"

Tyler laughs, nodding at me with a renewed twinkle in his eye. "Sadie really does have a type, huh? Surprised she isn't the one thirsting after—"

"Tyler, stop. Please," Ro quietly begs before looking up at me. "She's not, but she is at the dorms—at least, I think." She clicks the side of her phone where it rests on the counter. "Yeah, she's still there, but she'll go home for the weekend so . . ."

She trails off with a little shrug.

"So I should text her instead of showing up unannounced and sending her into a spiral?"

Ro smiles again, somehow broader, like the thought of me understanding some of the complexities of her dear friend makes her ecstatic. "Exactly."

"Gotcha." I nod, sticking a five in the overly decorated yellow tip jar with multicolored flowers drawn all over it. "I'll see you around, I'm sure."

"I hope so. She deserves something good."

It warms something in me that this enigmatic girl, Sadie's best— and I honestly think only—friend, approves of me. Even if Sadie herself doesn't.

I do text Sadie later that night after gorging myself on the pre-made meal marked with my name that Bennett labored over at the beginning of the week. Lying back on my sloppily made bed, staring at the ceiling with a movie playing off my PS4 on the mounted TV,

I can't get her out of my head. I've listened to Sadie's Songs playlist until I can pull it up in my head like a file, mentally playing my favorites and trying to imagine what she was thinking when she added them. But it isn't long before my own feelings and thoughts invade each one.

"Barely Breathing"—the way she unlaced my skates for me when my hands were shaking.

"Don't Look Back in Anger"—the raging look in her eyes when she does her long program.

"Sleep Alone"—her smile, her laugh.

My current favorite, Beck and Bat for Lashes' "Let's Get Lost," plays over my speaker as my fingers pull up her contact information and shoot off the text before I can think twice about it.

> **RHYS**
> *Hey.*

> **SADIE**
> *Is this the equivalent of a Koteskiy "You up?" text?*

> **RHYS**
> *Do you want it to be?*

Panicking, I send another text right after.

> **RHYS**
> *I'm just lying in bed and listening to music.*

Instead of a text back, I get a picture of her that has me shooting upright in bed, dropping my phone through suddenly slippery hands before pulling it up to my face as if I'll miss the image if I close my eyes for even a second.

She's lying down, her hair in a mess of waves playing around tangled blue sheets and a white comforter. She's not smiling, really, but her lips tick up lightly in one corner of their slightly pursed position. Her eyes are sharp, the dark gray piercing even through a screen. Her skin is slightly flushed, and the worn wire of her old headphones—which she must've stolen back from me—dangles across her sharp collarbones.

My eyes trail over her bare shoulders; one of the straps of her tank top is slinking half off, revealing a multitude of freckles scattered like stars across her skin.

I wonder how long would be too long not to respond—if I have time for a shower while imagining my fingers touching every single freckle I can find in a very thorough search.

Shaking my head, I spot the text beneath the photo—after I save it to my phone so I can stare at it for an embarrassing length of time.

SADIE
Funny, I'm doing the same thing.

I feel ridiculous for a moment while retyping my texts four times, knowing full well she can see the little dots appearing and disappearing repeatedly.

RHYS
Too bad I don't look as good as you doing that.

SADIE
Yeah, then Freddy might try to sleep with you.

A laugh threatens to burst out of me, pulling at my lips—even just this, just her written words, are enough to chase away a little of the anxiety from sitting in this too-empty room.

SADIE
I'm as exhausted as I look tho, so I'm probably gonna crash
*   soon and ghost you.*

It takes me another too-long moment to decide what to say, finally settling on:

RHYS
You don't look exhausted.

I wait, uselessly bringing my phone up to my face and then dropping it face down on the bed, as if it will prevent me from checking again and again. But her lack of response must mean she's sleeping now.

Standing, I leave the phone in my bedroom and head into the large, dark bathroom that's been spotlessly cleaned this summer by Bennett to the point it looks as if no one has ever lived here. I strip and close the door behind me before turning the shower all the way hot.

For a moment, I look in the mirror as I run my hand along the light scar over my eyebrow, the smaller one beneath my eye that's nearly unnoticeable unless touched—both from visor injuries during the hit, both of which I don't remember receiving.

My body is healed fully, every bit of it pressed back together. My mind is the thing that's permanently broken.

There is a video out there of the game and the injury. I tried to watch it once, but got sick and didn't make it past the first intermission. I couldn't remember when the hit happened; the constant anticipation made me so nauseous, I gave up.

I wonder if Sadie's seen it, but I'm too afraid to ask her. One Google search is all it would take.

Shaking my head, I step into the steamy, warm shower, letting the hot water roll over my tightly coiled muscles, dipping my head under the spray and pushing my hair off my forehead.

The change of temperature makes me dizzy for a moment, and I try to ground myself, placing both hands against the still-cold tile wall.

Sadie.

Sadie with freckles over bare shoulders, with her messy waves, bare-faced and looking up at me with her gray cat-like eyes.

Just the thought of her settles me immediately, the image burned into my mind of her hovering over me in the locker room like a queen atop a throne. Does she know I'd kneel for her forever if it meant she'd look at me like that?

My cock hangs heavy between my thighs, pulsing as my thoughts take me through every moment I've touched her soft, supple skin. She's burned into my every thought, like some sweet scent that brings back every *good* memory I've locked away.

I picture her here in my shower beneath the hot spray, because I want her in my space. To feel like she's wholly mine, even for a minute. She's so fucking small, but larger than life to me.

Rhys, she breathes.

In my head, I press her against the tile and drop to my knees; I picture her above me as my hand glides up and down my shaft, slow. Steady.

With her, it'll never be slow and steady.

No. I imagine her bucking wildly as I fight to hold her still, until I sling her legs over my shoulders. Her skin probably feels like silk here, too, even with the hard muscle beneath.

God, I know she tastes good, and just the thought of it has me gripping harder, faster. I imagine her climbing with me, her sighs and moans growing louder until the entire house can hear that she's mine. That *I* make her feel like this, like a fucking man pleasing his woman until she can't help but scream.

I chase the high with the Sadie in my head, just wanting to feel the euphoria that I *know* I can make her feel. I'm desperate to please and worship her like this, but to control it—to have the wildcat figure skater at *my* mercy for once.

Her gray, taunting eyes are forever locked onto mine as I close my eyes and my legs shudder under the effect of the fantasy of her. I brace a hand on the tile, my head fuzzy, but not with pain.

In my head, she says my name again, that same light whispered moan, and it sends me soaring over the edge. I come with her name spilling out of my lips like a desperate plea.

My forehead presses into the tile as I nearly collapse under the relief. *Fucking hell.*

Maybe I should feel ashamed for thinking of Sadie like that, but it's hard not to when she's everything good. For the first time since March, I feel . . . alive. Which is somehow more dangerous, because now, I don't think I *can* let her go.

I want to cling to her, to prove that whatever is left of me is worth something.

I send one more text to Sadie before plugging my phone into the charger.

RHYS
You look beautiful.

CHAPTER SIXTEEN

Sadie

My skate slides again, the edge not catching in the slightest, and I tumble onto my back and across the ice.

I close my eyes and it's there again.

A flash of a dimple, eyes like chocolate, massive hands gripping my waist so hard I swear I can feel it even now. Rhys, using my body, tossing me around like I'm light as air, his voice a smooth tease in my ear. Calling me his "new favorite distraction" before he flips me over and takes me again from behind.

The same fucking fantasy that's been haunting me for days.

The same fantasy I regrettably indulged in last night, alone in my bed, fingers fast between my thighs.

The same fantasy that had me coming harder than I had in months.

I try to catch my breath and shove the image of Rhys—the invented one that I would swear he'd never truly be like in bed—out of my mind.

Rhys is too golden to fuck me hard enough that I feel nothing.

That's why he scares you.

Shutting my eyes tightly, I try to focus on the music still playing before it cuts off.

Fuck.

Coach Kelley is standing over me now, arms crossed and eyes narrowed even as I refuse to look at him, like a child avoiding a reprimand.

"You've gotten sloppier," he says, reaching down and roughly jostling my shoulder to pull me to sit up. I shrug him off and stand on my own, skating to the bench for water.

"I'm just tired."

He follows behind me, and only when he's nearly in my ear does he add, "Weigh-in. Tomorrow."

I hate the ease with which that threatens me, the sick feeling that roils in my gut at the obvious implication. I fell because I wasn't paying attention to my edge, treating the axel like it's second nature to me when it's my worst jump. I fell because I was distracted.

I did not fall because I've gained some minuscule amount of weight.

"Do it one more time, Sadie. Make it fucking perfect," he whispers in my ear before jolting back.

He cues the music and grabs the water bottle from my hands, tossing it over the bench.

It's always like this with him. My practice is always last so that he can push us over my time, messing with my carefully created personal schedule.

Which is why I find myself grateful for Victoria's late arrival, meaning we've overlapped and she has the last fifteen.

I finish my routine—almost perfect by my own standards and a barely-there improvement by Coach Kelley's. Still, he *has* to focus on Victoria now, so I rest gently on the bench, scraping the ice from my blades with my plastic guards.

"I thought your attitude was just for me on the ice, but it seems like you're just as prickly here."

My heart races, my entire body lighting up like a Christmas tree at the sound of his voice.

He's still *my* Rhys, but he's more now—Rhys Koteskiy, captain

the Waterfell University hockey team. His hair is combed, still shagging a bit, his eyes bright and without their usual deep pit of sadness. He almost looks refreshed.

He brings a hand to his chest as he looks down at me affectionately. "I'm hurt, Gray."

I can't help but match his smile with one of my own.

"I think you'll survive, hotshot." I pat the bench. He sits right beside me, pressing his thigh to mine. "Besides, I save my really, *really* bad attitudes for you. No need to get jealous."

Victoria's music cuts off, followed by some loud yelling that carries easily across the cavernous rink. As much as the girl annoys me, she takes Coach Kelley's brutal corrections in stride with a quick nod and a frozen smile, hands clasped.

"Is he always like this?" Rhys's mouth is nearly touching my ear, his breath cool. I shudder.

"L-like what?"

"So . . . intense?"

"No," I say, a fake little smile gracing my lips. The part I don't say is that he's usually worse, especially with me.

But I need that. Coach Kelley's unflinching, severe support only shows his dedication to my success. He's like that because he believes in me. He's the only one who does.

"Here early then?" I ask as Rhys settles his body against mine.

"Actually," he says with a smirk, "you're the one on my ice time."

As if planned, the stern-faced hockey coach I've seen around a few times comes from the tunnel with a frustrated sigh. His hand taps lightly on Rhys's shoulder as he steps past us to talk with Coach Kelley, who is blatantly attempting to ignore him.

"Give me five and we'll be off," my coach finally snaps, thundering over the surprisingly soft voice of Rhys's coach. He doesn't argue with him, only comes back to us.

"Koteskiy." The coach nods, scratching at his beard. "And?"

"Sadie," I offer.

I take a sip of my water and nearly spew it back out when his coach asks, "Girlfriend?"

Rhys blushes and I find myself suddenly aching to say *yes* and tackle him to kiss his heated skin. My fingers twitch because just the thought is so intensely overwhelming—to see Victoria's face of shock and Coach Kelley's fuming at my disgusting, unprofessional behavior.

To feel Rhys again . . .

Suddenly my cheeks are the ones heating.

"A friend," Rhys corrects. "Her brothers play. They, uh, practice with the foundation."

My stomach churns; the implication that my brothers are charity cases flashes like a neon sign announcing every shame I carry every day. I hate it.

The girl who kisses his sadness away and needs help with her little brothers.

Pathetic.

"Actually, I have to go." I jump up from the bench with my guards on my blades. "See you around, hotshot."

I don't need him or his help.

Or his stupid dimples.

I'm barely through the tunnel, heading toward the girls' locker room—which is a ridiculous distance away from the ice, because the hockey team gets most of the arena space—when he catches up to me, grabbing my arm.

"Listen, Rhys—"

"How humiliating," a different voice sneers into my ear, fingers curling into my bicep. "My office, now."

He jostles me hard, and I duck my head as I follow behind the lean body of my coach. Victoria passes us, flicking her gaze over me sympathetically.

When Coach Kelley turns in to his office, I pause, but only because Victoria is reaching for me.

"Your practice slot is over." She clears her throat, looking at me a little hesitantly. I don't blame her; not only are we not friends, but I don't think I've ever been nice to the girl.

She looks around again before dropping her voice. "You don't have to follow him in there. He's our coach, not our parent."

He's been more of a parent to me than my own father, I think but don't say.

Instead, I shrug off her concern with an eye roll.

"I can handle Kelley. Worry about yourself."

I straighten my stance, like preparing to march into battle, before entering his office and closing the door behind me.

"I'm sorry I was distracted—"

"Who's the boy?" He cuts me off harshly. I turn and watch as he strips his skates off and shoves his feet into overly expensive sneakers, tossing the black skates into his bag.

"What?" I blanch.

He sneers at me. "Who is the hockey boy you're wasting time making passes at in my practice?"

"I don't . . . I'm not—"

"Do it again, you're back on probation," he says, snapping his fingers at me. As if this conversation is done.

"You're not being fair."

I'm not arguing about Rhys—one day of being a little off-center isn't going to destroy years of skating ability, of complete dedication.

"Not fair?" Coach Kelley slams his fist down on the metal desk between us, standing and hovering over me. "Victoria lands her axel better than you every single time. Want to talk about fair?" His voice rises with every word, and anxiety rushes down my spine. "I've put *years* of money and time and effort into *you* and you're so ungrateful I can't keep your attention for an hour."

drafted—he wasn't. Now, Holden is without his usual line match. I'd assumed an underclassman would replace him.

Coach Harris clears his throat before setting his face firmly in a way that only further pricks the hairs on the back of my neck.

"So we picked up a transfer from Michigan. Toren Kane."

A wave of nausea hits; the massive lump in my throat is the only thing keeping my breakfast from spewing.

Toren Kane.

Massive defenseman for Mt. Hart University, our rival school's hockey team. Top NHL prospect for three years running, but consistent fuckups have prevented him from making it onto a roster. The player who'd nearly killed me last spring.

And Coach Harris wants me to play with him—not just on my team, but on my goddamn line?

"Are you fucking serious?"

It isn't me that speaks, but my father, his voice a menacing whisper while his hands white-knuckle the arms of the chair.

"I know—"

"Are you out of your damn mind?" His voice is louder this time, rising over my coach's. "You *know* what he did to my son, Harris. He's a goddamn nightmare."

Harris looks as if this is the last argument he wants to have, and I know the coming words before he says them.

"It was a legal hit, Max. He's a talented de—"

"He's a liability, is what he is. His entire team agreed with us, wanted him suspended."

"Max—"

"There's a reason he didn't go to the draft, remember? Multiple times. That scandal was *everywhere*!" My father's voice rises again, the light edge of his accent sharper as he mixes Russian curses into his shouting.

"Max—"

"Thousands of kids will come after this one, better than him—but you *need* him? At what cost? We're talking about my *son*, this team's captain!"

Coach doesn't raise his voice or attempt to calm my father down, only nods and flicks his gaze from me to my father, and back again.

I stand abruptly, accidentally knocking my chair back. They both pause for a moment, but the room keeps shrinking until I'm convinced I'll suffocate if I stay in here for one moment longer.

I stalk out, ignoring their calls to me in both English and Russian, taking the corner by the door too quickly and clipping my shoulder. The halls are empty, but I keep my head down as the pounding starts to overtake it. I try to concentrate—to do the grounding techniques I've learned, to stop the real panic attack before it starts.

My body slams into someone and I barely mutter an apology before heading off, my vision hazy and tunneling as I stumble forward.

A hand grabs my wrist hard, little fingernails pressing into my skin, and I almost moan; I'd know the feel of Sadie's skin even if I were blind.

I spin easily, letting her back me into the cool blue-painted brick behind me. She looks so powerful like this, never mind the fact that I physically tower over her—she just seems so in control, like she can calm me with a quick press of her skin to mine.

I realize, as my gaze tracks across her face, that she's speaking to me.

"Sorry," I say, just as pathetic and shaky as always. Apparently this is to be my new normal. I've never been the aggressive one, always controlled on or off the ice, but now I want to put my fist into something.

I can't help the self-deprecating chuckle that slips free.

God, no wonder she doesn't want me. *Pathetic.*

"Rhys, what's wrong?" Sadie asks, in a way that makes me sure she's asked it already and I'm freaking her out by acting like a psych patient in some catatonic state. "You're shaking."

"I—"

I'm not scared—not of Toren Kane. I'm pissed. I feel betrayed by someone who's had my back since freshman year, who has never once treated me like I was just some mini clone of my father, who stuck by me through my injury. It doesn't matter that I know my team will have my back; why would he bring him here?

My team screamed dirty hit, and so did Kane's team, but the officials said it was clean. So he's cleared—it doesn't matter that he might cost me my career if I can't get this shit under control, or that he stole everything from me; and he's got the nerve to show up on my team, at my school?

Everything in my head is swirling around like water through a drain, leaving me with that eerie numbness leaking into my fingertips.

I reach for Sadie, picking her up easily while shucking her duffel bag off her shoulder. A second of worry slams into me that she could very well reject me again—and who would blame her—but she doesn't. Her legs slip over my hips, tightening to hold herself up as I press my lips to hers. Once, twice, then I bite down on her plush bottom lip and soothe the nip with my tongue.

"Rhys," she half whispers, half moans. "Not here."

It makes me pause, because she's right—we're in the middle of a hallway in the ice complex during the day. My dad drove here with me, otherwise I'd be halfway home with Sadie in the passenger seat, creating some reason to keep her in my room, in my bed—anywhere, as long as it's in my space.

"I think that you're mad at me for something, but I—"

"I was." She sighs quickly. "I'm over it."

She doesn't really look over it, but I feel a little too waterlogged and dizzy to investigate.

"I want you," bursts from my lips, because she's all I need. I don't care about being in the open, getting caught. But if she does, then it matters to me.

Sadie leaps down from my arms and wraps a hand around my wrist, fingers pressing against my pulse as she drags me down the hall and into the showers.

The room is empty, but she shoves me into the farthest stall, yanking the curtain to close us in with speed and lust bursting in her eyes, only feeding the monster in my veins.

I've never done anything like this. I've never been like Freddy or Holden with their puck bunny hookups. I've always been boyfriend material. The good-guy all-star athlete, straight-A student that girls want to take home to their parents. A serial monogamist.

Not anymore.

Another laugh escapes me while her soft little hands explore up my stomach and chest.

I broke more than my body during that game; my mind is fucking splintered.

Sadie shoves into me, her hands climbing quickly beneath my shirt, fingers slipping into my belt loops . . . I reel back.

Nope. I don't need her in control—I need the control, something to grasp ahold of while I'm spinning out.

I flip our positions, letting her shoulders hit the tile as I slip a hand to the soft skin of her inner thigh, tracing a finger along the line of her spandex shorts. I press hard, demanding kisses to her mouth, her neck, the spot behind her ear.

"I know you like to have control," I whisper, crushing my lips against her cheek. "But I'm not some boy you're using to try to feel nothing. You're going to feel everything with me." My teeth clamp down on her earlobe, just a nip, before I cut off her moan with another hard press of my mouth to hers.

She follows my lead, but continues battling me for dominance even still.

I sink to my knees in front of her, laying kisses on her stomach. She's wearing that same fucking threadbare Waterfell shirt that only feeds my fantasies of her in a shirt that looks almost identical, except with my name on the back.

Before I can move further, Sadie's hand grasps my chin and tilts my head back.

"I'm exhausted," she confesses, relaxing back against the tiles and looking down at me as our breathing still stutters, hands roving each other's bodies. "Rhys, I've been at practice for hours. I should shower—"

"Great. I've got enough energy for the both of us." I turn my head into her palm and plant an open-mouthed kiss there. "Just relax and let me take care of you."

I put my hands underneath the length of her shirt, fingertips dancing along the top of her shorts.

"Tell me, Gray. What do you want?"

Her eyes flash as she realizes that I will do whatever she tells me. "I want you to eat me out."

A groan leaves my throat before I can stop it.

"Thank God," I whisper, tugging on her shorts until they pool around her ankles. "Do you trust me?"

Her brow furrows, teeth letting go of their tight hold of her bottom lip. "To eat me out? I think so." Her tone is still sassy, but filled with a distinct breathiness as a lusty haze takes over her face.

A part of me—distinctly old Rhys—wants to stop at that answer, to force myself off her until she can say yes. Trust and sex are one and the same, especially for me.

"Please."

I am gone for this girl.

"Okay, Sadie Gray," I whisper, before reaching my hands to her knees and pulling them apart.

CHAPTER EIGHTEEN

Sadie

Rhys's hands feel like fire along my cold, bare skin, every bit of my icy exterior melting as he sweeps his fingers over all the shattered pieces of me.

I don't let the guys I hook up with eat me out. Mostly because for what I want, it's a waste of time. And it usually doesn't feel good—not enough to make the intimacy worth it. Not that many even offer.

My heart is racing.

Rhys's fingers reach the thin strip of my seamless thong. He curls them around the fabric and pulls it tight so a burst of pressure ignites against my clit. It surprises me so much I cry out before he yanks them down over my hips, pulling them slower as he reaches my ankles.

His eyes are searing, staring directly into mine as he prompts my feet out from each leg hole, his grasp warm on each ankle. Every ounce of confidence that I usually feel in this situation has simmered into nothing but vulnerability.

He might be the one on his knees, but he is the one in control.

I want to touch him, but I'm not sure where I want to start.

Rhys lifts his hands. One grabs ahold of my hip with a solid pressure. The other drifts softly, almost reverently against the skin of my inner thigh as he finally breaks my gaze and stares down at my bare pussy.

"Fuck, Gray," he whispers, and I can feel his breath against the overly sensitive skin. "This for me?" He smirks, all cocky arrogance—a flash of that hotshot hockey captain I know he can be when he wants.

I huff, "Easier to keep it bare for my costumes." I try to use the words to build a wall because everything with this boy feels danger- ous already, like I'm suspended on a tightrope, the threat of falling for him permanently imminent.

He shuts me up by pressing a warm thumb into his own mouth before lightly playing along my slit.

"That's not what I meant," he rasps. He pulls his hand away to show me.

I'm near to dripping, embarrassingly wet considering he hasn't done a single thing besides kiss me. But he's gorgeous, a disarray of the perfect picture he's been before.

The panic is gone from him, his hands steady and eyes bright, but it makes him more beautiful. His brown eyes seem warmer in the yellow light of the showers. He looks just as large as always, his thick thighs straining against gray sweatpants and a bulge distracting me enough that I turn my head. And those goddamn dimples are on full display. He's a blend of boyish excitement and manly self-confidence as he slides my thigh easily over one broad shoulder.

I'm fully exposed, my skin turning pink beneath the sudden sti- fling heat of the room and his attention.

"So beautiful," he whispers. Before I can try any response, he licks a wet strip along my slit, flicking his tongue lightly against my clit and then pulling back to blow across it softly.

"Oh, fuck," I cry, then bite down on my lip because my control is slipping.

He peeks up at me, eyes half-lidded but burning like warm choc- olate. "That's all it takes?" he taunts, but there's a question in his eyes.

It comes out before I can stop it.

"I don't usually do this."

"What? Hook up in a bathroom?" He smirks at me again, eyes twinkling. "Funny—every time I've had my mouth on you has been in a bathroom."

It's now, when he's so relaxed, that I can see the bright shooting star that is Rhys Koteskiy.

This is going to burn. He is going to burn me.

Except I don't care. I'll let him burn me if he keeps touching me like this.

I shake my head, leaning back as he presses his nose into the pale flesh of my pussy, just above where I need him most.

"Please," I beg, hating myself for it, even as my legs tremble beneath his hands.

He licks another long swipe before circling my clit.

Good God, I'm going to melt into the floor. My entire body is alight, and I'm embarrassingly close already. I avoid looking at him, my head tilting back against the brick.

"This is exactly how I pictured it." He breathes in, almost like he didn't mean to say it.

My head tilts down toward him with a smirk on my lips—like I might regain control.

"What? A dingy locker-room shower stall?"

Rhys huffs out a laugh, his eyes twinkling with mischief as he presses his entire mouth to my clit, sucking hard.

"Fuck," I gasp.

I slip just slightly, enough that my hands reach for him, sinking into his soft brown hair. My nails scrape his scalp a little as he circles me in some witchcraft-like pattern that has me gasping as if I've been underwater and I'm just breaking the surface.

He groans and jolts my thigh higher, just over the ball of his shoulder. His big hands are holding me nearly completely off the ground. My toes are scrambling, and my shoes squeaking as I writhe.

With his left hand still melded to my ass, squeezing every few moments, Rhys takes his right hand and gently parts me, sliding one finger into me. I cry out, far too loudly, but he lets a pleased noise rumble from his plush mouth against my clit. I jerk, but he steadies me, sliding another finger in and speeding his lips and tongue to contrast with the firm, slow stroke of his fingers.

He curls them, just slightly, and I make the mistake of looking down at him.

His brown eyes are glowing, locked intently on my face, watching my every move. And then he smirks, letting me see just one goddamn dimple.

I go off like a rocket.

"Already?" he teases as I pulse around his fingers, gripping them. My shoe squeaks again against the tile beneath me as he lowers my leg. He gently kisses the inside of my other thigh as he pulls it from his shoulder and then sets me back on both feet. "Fucking perfect. So beautiful."

A lump catches in my throat.

Rhys is still on his knees, his hands gentle on the curves of my calves. He reaches for my discarded underwear, and pulls them up my legs after helping me step into them.

My heart stutters as he presses another kiss to the fabric, this one more reverent than sensual; I hate the way it makes me ache. The way, *"Do you want to come home with me?"* almost spills from my lips. I feel vulnerable, undone, and somehow more full of feeling than before—not the usual emptiness and restraint I bask in after a hookup.

Dangerous, my brain repeats, but my body is ready to tackle him to the floor.

After he helps me with my spandex, taking his time sliding it over my legs and smoothing his palms over covered and uncovered skin, I grip Rhys's wrists and pull him to stand. Ready to take control back. Ready to—

He lifts his hand, his wrist still enclosed in my grip, and presses his fingers into his mouth.

The noise that comes from my lips, some sort of whine in the back of my throat, turns my cheeks maroon. Still, I can't look away as he pulls his long fingers from his swollen lips.

He's everything.

The way I think about him scares me. I need distance before this really hurts. And yet—

"We should do this more."

His smile is like spun gold. "Yeah?"

"Yeah," I repeat, feeling a bit like I'm floating. "Yeah, actually, I think this would be good for us both. You need a distraction and I need a . . . release."

Something dims in his eyes, his dimples disappearing. A little pain throbs in my chest, but I ignore it.

"What do you mean, exactly?"

I shrug and play at the hem of my shirt. "Like . . . hook up? Unless you don't—"

His hand rises to stop me.

"Friends with benefits. That's what you're suggesting."

I nod.

"I don't really . . ." He trails off, seeming to be engaged in some sort of mental battle. "Never mind—I'm not missing my chance. Yes."

"Really?" I smile brightly.

He mimics it. "If that's what you want, Gray, then yes."

He kisses my forehead on his way out, with a quiet, "Call me," pressed against my skin.

CHAPTER NINETEEN

Rhys

"You good, Cap?"

It's a hard question to answer, but Freddy looks worried—hell, the entire locker room looks apprehensive. I want to say no, but the tension is thick already and I know as captain, I should be defusing it, not adding to it.

Today is our last practice before our first exhibition game, away against a small school in Vermont whose coach is close with ours—which I assume is part of the reason the game is so early in our pre-season.

It is also our first practice with our new defenseman.

News spread quickly, thanks mostly to Freddy and Holden's big mouths, which made it that much easier for me to play ignorant and drown myself in Sadie.

Nothing has happened yet beyond quick make-outs in my car, hands pressing to cloth or skin, both of us desperate for relief. Some days, we just skate. Some days we never make it to the locker room, intense and gasping into each other's skin in the wide trunk of her Jeep over the blanket she told me was for "drive-in movie emergencies."

When I told her that I'd never heard of such a thing, and had never been to a drive-in movie, she looked so deeply hurt that I laughed louder than I had in months, a smile stretching my skin until my cheeks hurt.

Then, after class that night, she'd met me outside her dorm and demanded we take *her* car. She drove, which she usually asks to do—I wonder if it's because she remembered how I blurted out my new anxiety over driving that one day.

We rolled into a drive-in theater, to my surprise, backing in and opening up her trunk to lie there. I bought two hamburgers and a plethora of most likely expired candies from a teenager at the single concession booth, then we laughed and talked and barely looked at the distorted flickering screen of the double feature, with me soaking every part of Sadie up like water to grass after a drought.

She told me at the end that it wasn't a date.

But I didn't care; it *felt* like one. And we hadn't even kissed once.

It's easy to pretend, when it's just us, that maybe she is completely mine. My girlfriend. That I could convince her into my arms again and again, somehow smuggle my jersey on to her body, bribe her to cheer for me and stand in the cold bleachers because she wants to show everyone I am hers.

And I want to be hers, almost more than I want her to be mine.

"You sure you don't want to say something before?" Freddy asks, probing after my lack of an answer.

Bennett shrugs, shucking his leg pad on. "Why? Everyone knows he's coming. Everyone here has Rhys's back."

"Damn straight." Holden nods.

I shake my head. "He'll be your partner, Doherty. No reason for us not to take every advantage we can this year."

We are going to the Frozen Four. We are winning it—one player isn't going to change that.

The door opens, then slams closed behind the hulking figure of Toren Kane.

He doesn't glance at anyone, keeps his eyes down as he struts to his assigned cubby beside Holden, tosses his gear bag on the floor, and begins to change.

Besides last spring through my helmet cage, I've only seen him in photos on Elite Prospects, and the same high school composite plastered across the internet during the height of his scandal years before.

Hockey players, in general, tend to be on the taller side—most are at least six feet. Height and size are just as much of an advantage as speed and skill can be.

Still, Toren Kane is tall even for a hockey player. He's not quite as hulking or as broad-framed as Bennett, but close; probably pushing close to 6′6″. As a captain, his size and obviously honed physique should make me happy to have him on first line defense, standing in front of Bennett.

But the only thing I feel is hatred—a foreign, unwelcome well of it.

The silence of the dressing room is deafening, everyone pretending not to watch us both, their eyes flicking back and forth between us.

"Kane," I call, gaining some grip on the tsunami within. "We should talk."

He glances at me quickly before shrugging off his shirt and reaching for a Dri-FIT undershirt from his bag.

"We can't pretend nothing happened," I continue. "If you want to be part of this team, we have to talk."

I hate this. I hate that I have to be the bigger man here, when he's the one who ruined my life. But I'm trying. I sink into the numbness, hoping that the thing I hate most will keep me from bashing his teeth in.

Kane glares, pulling the shirt down over his abdomen and shaking out his damp black hair.

"Nothing to talk about, Koteskiy. Get over it already."

My fists clench, body jerking toward him. *So much for numbness.*

"Are you fucking insane?"

Freddy snorts, coming to stand by me. "Certifiable, from what I've heard."

There's a slight rise in the tension of Kane's shoulder as chuckles echo in the room. I remember the news outlets covering the hit had called him a psychopath, said that he'd shown no remorse, kept repeating the same sentiment over and over.

"It was a clean hit," he says.

"Bullshit."

"He's fucking crazy."

"Clean hit, my ass!"

A chorus of support and disbelief rings from behind me.

The weight of the words I want to say—but can't—feels suffocating, and for a moment I'm Atlas, ready to drop the entire weight of the world from my shoulders if it means only a minute of relief.

Still, I refuse to drag any of them down. Refuse to see pity in their eyes or, God forbid, hear their laughs at the expense of my pain; their disbelief in my ability to lead them, even if I've lost that belief myself. How would any of them look up to a captain, and trust me to lead them, if they knew that every second on the ice, I'm fighting an internal war?

"Clean hit?" Freddy jumps in, crossing his arms as he steps forward. "Your own team, hell, your *own coach*, wanted you out for that."

"Refs said it was clean. I didn't do anything. Grow the fuck up."

Bennett grumbles at that, his voice still quiet, but thundering in the locker room because it's rare for him to speak out. "Take some responsibility for yourself."

Kane's tan face flushes red with anger, his eyes narrowing as he takes us all in, realizing he's cornered.

"I'm not here to fight." He smirks. "Off the ice, that is. I'm just here to play fucking hockey." He shrugs again, continuing to unpack and make himself comfortable.

Something about the casualness of it, as if he didn't end my season early last year—as if he couldn't have easily ended my life—ignites me.

I shoot forward, slamming my hands into his chest and tipping him back into his cubby. His head knocks back against the top shelf.

"This is my fucking team. Show some respect."

"Fuck off," he sneers, smirking again like he's daring me to really hit him.

I slam my fist in his face like a knee-jerk reaction. No one will stop me or pull me back. If anything, they'll join in. This is my team.

You took everything from me.

"Enough."

The only voice that can stop this confrontation isn't booming; it's soft and firm in the way only Coach Harris can be.

It takes a moment for me to realize I'm still locked on Toren Kane, hands gripping his shirt while he only smiles with a trickle of blood sliding over his white teeth, lips, and chin.

"Let him go," Bennett says. "It's pointless to fight like this."

I follow Ben's instruction—a reversal of how it was between us for so long—and let him lead me away.

Coach Harris stands in the center of the dressing room, holding our attention easily, as he always does. Even, I notice, Toren Kane's.

"I know that there are a lot of emotions in here right now, but get it together. Let it out on the ice; not on each other." He looks toward me and sighs. "Toren is a part of this team now, and I expect you all to act right and treat him like he's any other member of this team. Whatever you need to do to get to that point, I don't care. Just don't do this shit on my ice or in my dressing room. Hell, nowhere in my goddamn complex. Am I understood?"

"Yes, sir," we all agree.

"It's gonna be a long practice. Get the hell out there."

CHAPTER TWENTY

Sadie

Falling into Rhys feels like what I imagine falling into addiction might be like.

Everything with him feels easier. This isn't the first time I've had a sort of friends-with-benefits agreement with someone, but it's the first time it's felt like *this*. Before, it was all just to get rid of the boiling inside me, a form of exercise and relief. With Rhys, waiting longer than a *day* to see him again, to touch him, feels like torture.

I'm torn between loving the way it feels to be with him, and hating how much I love the way it feels to be with him.

Not to mention, the man eats my pussy like it's his fucking *job*.

Even right now, stuffed into a storage closet before all the parents of the Learn to Skate classes have vacated the building—when it would make more logistical sense for me to be on my knees for him—he's got me half-hoisted in the air, his face pressed between my thighs as my bare ankles dig into the muscles of his back.

I'm on the cusp of a climax, can *feel* my legs starting to shake, when he pulls back. I nearly slap him as my hands grab for his silky hair to push him back where I need him most.

"What the hell, hotshot?" I gasp, voice whining as much as I try to make it harsh. "I'm so fucking close."

"My birthday's next week," he says, as if now is a perfect time to have this discussion.

"Happy birthday," I growl. I grip his scalp a little harder, which only makes him smirk.

"Thanks." He sighs, pressing a kiss into my inner thigh that has me grappling for the wall again—I'm so close that he could *breathe* a little harder on my clit and I'd combust. "But I figured you could tell me that the day of."

My stomach sours a little as I realize what he's asking. And yet, my traitorous body is still reacting like this man isn't holding my orgasm over my head like a carrot.

"Rhys," I say breathlessly.

He licks a solid, hard swipe against my pussy and I bite out another curse.

"If you want to come," he threatens, his voice dropping as the darkness he's always trying to hold back bleeds into the edges of his golden boy persona, "then you'll agree right now to be there. As my birthday present, if that makes it less serious for you."

I can barely register his words because he's fucking *breathing* them into my pussy, dark brown eyes glazed and half-lidded as they stare up at me. That one stubborn dimple pulls his smile up lopsidedly.

"Please, Rhys."

"Need an answer, Gray. Then you can have whatever you want."

I close my eyes tightly, trying uselessly to erase the image of him on his knees that's forever burned into my brain. I shouldn't. I *really, really* fucking shouldn't. But—

"Okay," I whine. "Okay, okay, okay. Just *please.*"

He chuckles and presses one hard kiss right on my clit before leaning back.

"That's my girl." He grins, before his hand that's been resting on my thigh suddenly presses two fingers straight into my dripping center.

I moan, loudly and desperately—too loud for where we are hiding, but I don't care. It barely takes a minute of his full attention to pull the orgasm from me, my lip bruising as I bite down hard enough to break the skin while my entire body combusts.

I come down from the high slumped against the wall as he cares for me so gently it makes a lump form in my throat. We do this dance every time. Him, too sweet and caring and gentle. And me, shoving his embrace off with some half-hearted excuse for leaving while I try to pretend I don't see the sadness re-entering his eyes.

This time, I don't say a word, kissing him hard and nipping lightly at his lips as I carry my discarded skates outside.

He shoves his skates off at record-breaking speed and follows behind me. After tossing his bag over his shoulder, he gets close enough to tap me.

I can't outright ignore him. Our cars are parked right next to each other.

"So you'll come?" he asks, and I'd feel a bit like I'm throwing a puppy in the trash if I reject him now.

"Yeah." I nod as we reach our cars in the empty lot. "Yeah, I'll um . . . I'll try."

Rhys smiles and nods, bouncing on his toes. Despite my slightly noncommittal response, he's still as excited as if I promised to show up with a banner and balloons.

"Seeing you will be the best part of my birthday." He smiles a little sheepishly, like he didn't mean to say it. Then rubs the back of his neck and bids me a quick goodbye before hopping into his car.

And, just like every time before, he waits until my car starts and drives to follow me out of the lot.

. . .

I almost don't show at all.

But about two hours after the time of the party that he texted me

earlier in the week, I show up at the Hockey House, feeling a little ridiculous about getting *this* dressed up—my go-to gray silk slip dress
with an oversized leather jacket thrown on—to show up *this* late.

I checked my lipstick twice before I even got out of the car, but
I do it once more now on the screen of my phone. I'm wearing a
heavier layer of makeup than usual, but it's a special occasion.

Is it? So Rhys is special?

Shaking off the conflicting thoughts about the sad hockey captain that constantly plague my brain, I walk through the half-open
door and into the clustered throng of people. Some I recognize,
some I don't.

But I definitely don't see Rhys Koteskiy.

Making my way back to the kitchen after a full sweep of the
downstairs, I spot at least two familiar faces: Freddy and Bennett,
both glaring at me unhappily as I saunter in.

"Freddy." I nod. "Hey, have you guys seen Rhys?"

"Look who finally decided to show." Freddy downs the rest of
whatever is in his red plastic cup. "A little late for him, actually."

I frown, playing with the hem of my dress a little self-consciously
and feeling small even with the three inches of heels provided by my
black boots.

Bennett doesn't speak, but looks uncomfortable as he avoids my
eyes from his perch on the barstool, massive shoulders curved in-
ward as he slowly peels the label off the bottle of beer he's drinking
from.

"I know I'm late. But I need to talk with him."

Freddy sneers, cheeks flushed enough that I can tell he's a little
looser with his reactions. "Not happening. Get out."

"Freddy," Bennett snaps. His eyes flutter to me briefly before angling back to his teammate. "Back off it."

"No." Freddy crushes the cup in his hands, tossing it over his
shoulder with a perfect arch into the trash can, which garners an

ill-timed cheer from the guys gathered there. The campus playboy looks furious—an expression I'm not used to seeing on his model-esque face. He flattens his hands on the counter and glares at Bennett. "You saw him, Reiner. He stared at the fucking door all night waiting for her." Freddy jerks his attention back to me, eyes dark as he sizes me up again. "You've already hurt him once tonight. Considering your track record, I think it'd be better if I stop you now. You don't give a shit about him."

I don't know him well enough for that to hurt as badly as it does; maybe it's his connection with Rhys that makes the words land like a slap.

I do wonder how much Matt Fredderic has divulged to Rhys about our paths crossing last semester. How often he saw me take one of his athlete friends into a bathroom at a house party, or grind into the lap of some overgrown football star just to feel nothing. I barely remember last semester; I was spiraling out of control and desperate not to feel so much all at once.

This year is different. Rhys is different.

"If I didn't give a shit about him, Freddy, I think you'd know. But this isn't like last semester." I push the words through clenched teeth, hating the vulnerability of it all. My eyes flick to Bennett for a moment, but he's just as stoic. "And Rhys is . . . different."

"Please." Freddy snorts, rolling his eyes.

Fury ratchets up my spine. "I love sex just as much as you do, *Freddy*, and that's not a fucking crime just because I'm a girl. But I *guarantee* I care more about Rhys than you have *ever* cared about a girl you put your dick in."

Now it's Freddy who looks like he's been slapped.

"He's in his room," Bennett cuts in, jerking his shoulder a little.

I'm gone before either of them can change their minds and try to stop me.

I've never been in the Hockey House, that I remember—and

definitely not while Rhys Koteskiy was one of its inhabitants. Still, I find his room on the first guess, with a *51* poster taped to the door signed by all his teammates. I look a little closer and see all the signatures are marked with "Get well soon" or "Thinking about you" or "You're stronger than this."

"O Captain, My Captain" is written the largest and signed by Matt Fredderic in a script that looks ridiculous next to the size of everyone else's.

I raise my hand and knock a little beat against the wood.

"For the last time, Freddy . . ." Rhys huffs from inside, throwing his voice like he's far from the door. "I knew she might not come, okay? You're right. It was stupid of me to ask."

My brow furrows and I knock again even as he's still speaking.

"She's not my—" He throws the door open in the middle of his sentence, angry as he looks for the culprit of the knocking and only finds me. ". . . girlfriend."

CHAPTER TWENTY-ONE

Rhys

She's so goddamn beautiful. I feel every ounce of anger at her fade the longer I look at her.

Sadie Gray is in my house, in the doorway of my room, looking like every fantasy I've ever had, wrapped in a silk bow.

"Hey," I choke out, throat hoarse, as my eyes scan the expanse of her pale legs from knee to the high cut of her very short silk dress. I've touched that same silk before, I realize, and there's some dark possessive part of me that warms at the sight of it.

"I'm sorry I'm late," she says, and I realize I'm smiling like an idiot.

I swallow back the immediate insistence I want to make, that this is *fine. No worries, I'm just glad you're here.*

She could've showed up in a shirt that said STOP TRYING, HOT-SHOT. I'M NOT YOUR GIRLFRIEND, and I'd still be as happy to see her.

Because I crave Sadie like an addiction.

"You're here now," is the best I can do, because I don't want to waste any of the time I have with her on anything but comfort. She makes me feel warm and solid, whole again.

I step to the side and stretch my arm behind my head, cheeks going pink at the slight disarray of my room. It's not messy, but it's well lived-in, as I've barely left my room this week.

The anxiety has been worse. Enough that I skipped two days of classes, fully unable to get myself out of bed. I rolled through multiple nightmares, showering off sweat and washing my sheets every day because they were soaked through.

But now, everything seems still. And seeing Sadie standing in the middle of the room, sliding off her leather jacket and hanging it off my desk chair, there's an innate rightness to it. Like she's finally where she's meant to be.

Here. With me.

"Happy birthday, hotshot," she says, but there's an apologetic tinge to her usually fiery taunt. It chips away at the lingering resentment until I want to toss her on the bed and shove that silk up to her stomach.

I wonder if she notices it's *her* music playing soft and low through my surround sound, The Neighbourhood crooning "A Little Death" in the background of this fantasy come to life.

"Thanks." I smile, genuine and small, as I pass her to sit on the bed. She's just a smidge taller than me like this, the heels of her boots—black leather I'll be unable to get out of my fucking head from now on—giving her the added height. She steps between my legs, one hand held behind her back with a little pouch that I saw her pull from the pocket of her jacket.

"I got you something."

Her other hand grabs mine from my thigh before dropping the pouch into it. I pull on the ribbon to open the plastic, then dump the contents into my palm.

A black hockey puck and a stretchy bracelet. I squeeze the hockey puck in my palm, watching it give and release.

"It's, um . . . a stress ball. Like, you squeeze it and it helps distract your thoughts or center them? My brother has one, and it helps his anxiety," Sadie says, shrugging and tucking her hair back again.

"That's . . . that's really nice," I say, feeling lame as the words leave my lips. It's more than that. It's *everything*. It's a piece of me that only she holds the key to. It's the acceptance of me as I am, by the only person that matters right now. "And the bracelet?"

She giggles as I pull the blue-and-gray beaded bracelet up to inspect the little block-letter beads that spell out *hotshot*.

A laugh bursts from me and I slide it on immediately.

"It's a joke."

Not to me, I want to say. I'll never take it off.

Instead, I wrap her in my arms and tug her down into my lap with a groan.

"Time for me to show my thanks, yeah?" I ask, breathing lightly into her ear and pressing kisses just beneath it. "Lay back."

Sadie shoves off me too fast. I grapple for her, but she escapes my hands.

"Take off your pants," she says.

I'm standing before I can even think about it, looking at her as she lazily leans back on her elbows on the bed. Sadie, just like this, with the thin little strap drooping off her freckled shoulder, pulling the gray fabric enough that I'm close to getting a glimpse of her pert, pink nipple.

My mouth waters as she reaches up and pulls all her hair high on her head, cooling her neck, before letting the dark strands spill across her skin.

I shove my jeans to my ankles, stepping out of them without tripping as I refuse to take my eyes off her for one second. Her hands only hesitate once—her fingers curl into the top of my boxer briefs and she looks up at me for assurance.

I nod like a fucking bobblehead, groaning as she pulls them down to stretch over my thighs and free my dick.

"Oh," she says, her face so close I can feel her breath. My hips flex involuntarily, and her hand pauses before grasping me at the base.

"You're . . . very big." She blushes, and it's the first time I've seen her look at all intimidated.

I'm not small, but she is—which makes me look huge in her little hand. Too delirious to speak, I just nod.

"I've never . . . I mean . . . the guys I've been with—"

My hand grips her chin hard, jealousy boiling in my gut at the suggestion.

"Finish that sentence, I dare you. I guarantee it'll be you on your knees this time, not me."

The mild threat and my hard grip seem to wake her from her shyness.

Sadie bites her lip and sinks to her knees in front of me with a sultry smile.

"You're acting like that wasn't the plan all along."

Without warning, she takes me deep, and my breath stutters out in a moaned curse. My hands grip her hair because I feel like my knees are going to give out.

When I regain my balance, I look down to see her wicked attitude still shining through the watery, cat-like gray eyes locked on my face.

I'm going to come too fast.

That, or tell her I love her or something worse.

So I pull her back off me, trying not to focus on the way spit drips from her mouth, her lips still perfectly colored. Seeing the print of her lipstick on my fucking dick makes me squeeze myself at the base to calm down.

I shove Sadie back onto the bed, covering her body entirely with mine. I pull that silk between my fingers, pushing it up her stomach so I can cup her pussy.

"It's my birthday, so I get to choose my prize, don't you think?"

Her eyes are glazed, all the fight gone from my spitfire skater. Her body always relaxes under my touch, and it fills me so fully with satisfaction and possession that I have to smother the urge to bang on my chest.

I pull down the straps from her shoulders, baring her chest to me. She's braless, with skin flushed all the way to her fucking nipples. My mouth seeks them first, licking and sucking softly, almost teasing in a way that drives her wild.

For such a fierce girl, she thrives under a softer touch.

Her body shivers and I grip her bare waist a little harder in my hands.

"Mmm." I hum against her skin. "Do you like that, Gray?"

She nods and I grab for her chin again, pulling back to look down at her.

"Say it," I beg.

Instead, she brings her hand to her mouth, then licks her palm and reaches down to grasp my cock.

I buck instinctually into her fist, whimpering into her neck as she works me.

Fuck. Fuck. Fuck.

Sadie hums a little louder and my eyes blink open to look at her, so small beneath me and yet in total control again.

"Do you like that, hotshot?" she taunts, and I groan.

This. The push and pull for control—*God*, I want her forever.

"You're killing me, Gray," I growl out, jerking her up. I'm so fucking close already and seeing her skin flush as she pleasures me only makes it worse. Her eyes are glittering, a little smile quirking the corner of her red mouth.

I kiss her hard and insistent as we both moan into each other's mouths at the contact. Her tongue wastes no time in tangling with mine until she rubs her hand over the head of my cock and I pull back with a gasp.

Her lips press their way down my chin, and I hope she leaves a mark on me.

Like she's granting my birthday wish, Sadie's teeth sink into the skin at the base of my neck with a little bite and I come hard, stars flashing behind my eyes.

It takes me longer than normal to come down from the high, but I do, slumping back onto the mattress as Sadie pushes my weight down and climbs over me. I hear her heels on the floor, the sound of the sink turning on and off, and then look toward my bathroom to see her leaning on the doorframe.

She's still dressed, silk straps pushed back up onto her shoulders, leather boots still on, while I'm splayed naked across the bed.

My dick twitches at the sight of her.

I prop my head up, flexing my abs lightly as she saunters toward me.

"It's *my* birthday, remember," I say, eyes sparkling. "And I still want dessert."

She leans over me and we kiss again, slow and steady.

"Whatever you want, hotshot."

I should tell her to climb on top of me and sit on my face in the way I've been thinking about for weeks.

Instead I say, "Stay the night with me?"

She freezes for a second, her body still where she's straddling my abdomen. I can feel the heat of her against my skin and for a moment I want to say *never mind* and drag her up to devour her.

But I wait, and Sadie finally huffs a breath.

"Okay," she whispers. "I'll stay tonight."

I make her come three more times—like a reward for her answer, or proof of why I'm worthy of her time—before we fall asleep naked under the sheets of my bed.

But when my alarm goes off the next morning, she's gone, and the sheets are ice cold.

CHAPTER TWENTY-TWO

Rhys

Nothing is helping the tremors in my hands as I sit on the bus for the last hour of our trip.

I faked sleep for the majority of the drive to Vermont, avoiding conversation with Freddy to my left.

Growing up, Bennett had always been my seat partner, which was perfect for my focus.

That didn't change at Waterfell, despite the slight discomfort of our oversized bodies shoved into the chairs. I don't think Bennett could change a ritual if he had to.

Freddy cranks the volume on the Bluetooth speaker in his hand after Coach gives him the nod, which means we are close enough to the arena for it.

Gym Class Heroes starts blaring, "Cupid's Chokehold" reverberating throughout the bus and gaining smiles from the upperclassmen and confused interest from the freshmen. No one really knows where the tradition started, but music blasts on the bus for away games and in every locker room—before a game and after a win. A few of my teammates yell and sing along as Holden and Freddy start rapping back and forth, dancing around the bus.

When I was a freshman, it was fun bonding, a quick hype-up. Now, with Freddy and Dougherty, it plays out like a full-fledged production.

"He's getting weirdly good at this," I mumble to Bennett at my right, running my fingers along the bracelet on my wrist.

He messes with his baseball cap and shrugs. "Not that weird. Freddy loves this."

"What?"

"Attention."

I laugh, even though I know Bennett isn't trying to be funny. It feels good for a minute, like I'm me again.

It isn't until I'm in full gear and stuffing myself into an equipment closet to hide the signs of an approaching episode that I'm reminded this is my first game back.

Fuck.

The phone in my hand is trembling as shakes wrack my body.

I dial before I can think twice about it.

"Hey, hotshot," Sadie answers quickly, a smile in her voice that drips through the receiver like syrup. "Miss me already?"

The tightness in my chest starts to ease immediately.

"Hey," I say, breathing out.

It's silent for a long moment before her quiet giggle sears my skin and shoots goose bumps down my arms.

"Just calling to breathe in my ear?"

"Working on my Darth Vader impression." I flirt with an ease that reminds me of before. "How am I doing?"

She sighs deeply, something rustling like she's settling against fabric. I picture her in bed, on gray sheets that mimic the shade of her eyes.

"I don't know; you haven't said anything about being my daddy—I mean father."

A laugh bursts from my chest, full and surprising and warming me entirely.

"I'm working up to that one. Too iconic."

"True. Best to just focus on the breathing."

There's a quiet surety underneath the joke. It almost feels like she's pressing her hand to my chest like she has before, calming me down while I hide in a musty storage closet in full gear.

I must be silent for too long again; she sighs into the phone, not patronizing, but quietly gentle. Like blowing breath on my over-heated skin.

"Are you sure you're okay, Rhys?"

I want to ask her to say my name again, but I manage to hold it together by gnawing on my lips until I'm sure they're bloody.

"Yeah." I shake my head, a chuckle escaping and reverberating in the room. "Yeah. Actually, I have a game today."

"Your exhibition game against Vermont."

"Yeah." I breathe. I love that she knows. "It's right now."

"You'll be okay, hotshot. Besides Oliver, you're the best player I know."

I laugh, the conversational, relaxed tone of her voice soothing me. "That's good company to be in."

"I need you to go play your game and win so you can get back to the hotel room for me. Otherwise I can't give you your surprise."

"Surprise?" I ask, feeling a bit like a kid at how my heart kicks at the idea. Like she's promised me ice cream for being a good boy.

And I'll do anything she says.

"Yeah, but only if you hang up with me now. Okay?"

"Okay," I say, but wait for her to end the call herself.

She pauses and we're both just breathing again. "Kick their asses, hotshot." Finally, she hangs up.

I walk back into the locker room with a beaming smile on my face. The same smile stays on my face throughout warm-ups. The caress of her voice plays on a loop in my head as I start my first game since the accident.

. . .

I don't play much, just a bit with my first line.

Coach spends the majority of the time letting the new kids get used to their lines. Holden and Kane play the most, clocking high ice times during every period. The first couple of shifts, they're a hot fucking mess, to the point that the assistant coach, Johnson, is close to ripping his hair out.

Every time they come back to the bench, Johnson leans over Toren's hunched body and berates him. Holden picks up a few corrections, but it's easy to see that Kane shoulders the blame for their terrible coordination.

It makes me smile.

Until Coach Harris jerks Johnson back by his collar and takes over the defensemen coaching for the third period.

I hate how much it changes everything—the obvious improvement once Holden and Kane learn more of each other's patterns. The difference in Toren now that Coach offers him slight praise and useful corrections.

And then I hate how good he is, how seamless he fits with his line.

Fighting in an NCAA game is a severe penalty—one Kane's received quite often. He sounds like a team's worst nightmare in the news, but he's a dream on the ice.

If he wasn't my personal nightmare, maybe I'd be able to—

No. I stop myself before that ridiculous notion can take hold. *Not my problem*. Toren Kane is a nuisance, a liability to my team. Nothing more. Not a friend or a teammate; he's a parasite, one I intend to get rid of if I can. And if not, I'll at least protect myself as much as I can from his venom.

The game ends in an easy win. The small private school in Vermont has a new team that's still learning to mesh and move as one, which is why Coach scheduled the exhibition with them.

We'll stay overnight, because we'll play one more exhibition with them in the morning.

Hotel rules are strict, and as usual, I'm with Bennett. They'd tried to separate us once in freshman year, saying we needed to make other friends on the team, but it ruined the surly goalie's routine enough that we lost the game and Coach Harris nearly fired the development coordinator who'd made the decision.

The team gorges on catered food in one of the hotel conference rooms, the table loaded with meat, veggies, and above all else: pasta.

All our plates are piled high, matching our hunger and energy levels. For a moment, it feels good to be back.

Bennett hefts two perfectly plated dishes high as he steps around the jostling of our teammates. He sits to my left while Freddy takes the seat across. He's on a roll now, telling us all the chirps he enjoyed using, and some new ones he picked up from a talkative defender on the other team.

Kane looms like a dark cloud in the background, a loaded plate in his hand as he examines the two long tables before backing out of the room and leaving.

Doherty is the only other person who notices, watching a little warily as his partner exits.

After dinner, we all part ways to our rooms, and I bolt for the shower before Bennett can even open his mouth.

I throw on athletic shorts, my hair dripping onto my shoulders as I fluff the pillows, lean back, and stare at my phone.

Bennett eyes me again with his bag over his shoulder as he heads to the shower, brows slanting.

"You'd tell me if something was wrong?"

My heart slams into my stomach.

"Yeah," I lie, hating how easy it comes. "Of course."

CHAPTER TWENTY-THREE

Sadie

The incessant flutter in my stomach is to blame for how quickly I put Liam to bed.

I checked the score for the last time on the couch with Oliver and Liam earlier, which Oliver promptly watched over my shoulder. He tried to play it cool, but I could see the sneaky smile he tamped down after seeing the Waterfell victory.

The point division shows Matt Fredderic as a top scorer, along with two other names I don't recognize. As I mindlessly scroll through the play-by-play, Rhys's name pops up on my screen with an incoming video call.

I check myself in the mirror of my bathroom while spitting mouthwash into the sink.

The phone continues to buzz, only further igniting the swarm of bees attacking my belly. I slap off the bathroom light and slide on the wooden floors of the hall in my fuzzy socks, practically vaulting into my bedroom. I answer the phone as soon as the door closes.

"Hey." I check myself in the top corner of the screen, making sure he can even see me in the low lamplight of the room.

"Hey, Sadie Gray." He smiles.

He's breathtaking even through the screen of my phone, with

damp bedhead hair resting on a pile of bright white hotel pillows. His skin is shining with a light flush, his dimple gleaming from an excited smile I now recognize.

"Where are you?" he asks, and I remember just how often he's been in my dorm room between and after classes. Enough that he would recognize my decorated walls or checkered blue bedding.

"Home." I move a little and find a comfy spot on my bed, sinking into the old twin mattress. "Congrats on the win, hotshot."

His mouth opens to speak, but a deep voice rolling from the background cuts him off.

"Don't congratulate him. He tweaked his ankle in the first shift and rested most of the game."

My eyebrow crinkles, the words Bennett has said rolling around in my head as I try to make sense of them. The sheepish look on Rhys's face doesn't help the inkling of disbelief.

But then he smiles, his eyes glazing.

"I love that," he says.

"What?"

"When you get that little wrinkle in your eyebrows. Like you're thinking really hard about something."

"About you." I roll my eyes. I drop my phone to point at the ceiling, hiding the blush, and kick my feet.

I've never been this way with anyone. Watching my dad mourn my very-much-alive mother—drowning tears with alcohol, drugs, and women since I was twelve—left a bad taste in my mouth about relationships. Hell, people in general.

But with Rhys, it's different.

Real.

"You didn't play?" I ask.

Bennett walks close enough I can just see him out of frame.

"Want me to bring you anything back?" he asks, slapping a base-ball cap on his head as he leaves the frame again.

"I'm good," Rhys replies. The door slams and he visibly relaxes when it's just us.

Like he always does.

"So." He sighs, a mischievous glint to his eyes. "My surprise."

I giggle—not a sound I make often, but there's a thrill to this.

I'm not nervous, I'm excited . . . and a little worried that I'll regret this later, when he's moved on to a real girlfriend and his big career.

Still, I take this moment to be selfish.

"I don't remember anything about that," I say teasingly, slipping the stretched neckhole of my oversized T-shirt off my shoulder with a strategic shrug.

His eyes track the movement, shoulders slumping as he relaxes further into the bed.

I open my mouth, but he cuts me off.

"You're so beautiful."

Something warm and unwelcome wriggles in my chest. So, instead of responding, I strip my shirt from my body in one fell swoop. This isn't romantic. We aren't a couple—this is sexual only.

"Oh, fuck," he curses, eyes wide as he takes in the baby-blue lingerie set Ro gifted me for my birthday last year.

"You like it?"

He nods like a bobblehead.

"Good. I like that you like that." I smirk when he almost reflexively flexes his abs. "Do you want to touch yourself?"

"I want to touch *you*," he responds immediately. The warmth in my stomach tries to grab hold again.

I shove it away, finding a spot to prop up my phone before sliding my hands across the translucent material against my stomach.

Rhys tracks my every movement, now clearly holding the camera one-handed.

I watch with fire in my eyes as his arm moves up and down.

I've felt and seen exactly what he's packing down there, but even so I bite my lip to stop myself from asking to watch.

Slowly, I slide the straps of the bustier down my shoulders, shimmying closer to the camera to give him a better view. This way feels safer, cutting off my head from his sightline so he can't see my eyes. I've already let my guard down too much—this is me taking back my control. I desperately need it, before I drown completely in everything *him*.

He lets out a low moan as I bare my breasts to him. The movement of his arm quickens, jostling the camera.

"Fuck, Gray," he grinds out, before the door clicks and the phone goes flying with a non-pleasurable shout from Rhys.

I knock my own phone down and pull my duvet up and over my head to cloak myself, leaving only my face visible.

Bennett appears on my screen as he picks Rhys's phone up. I see a flash of his blushing, bright red cheeks, before there's rapid movement and Rhys is in the camera again.

He walks somewhere, a bathroom it looks like, before sighing and apologizing over and over.

"It's okay," I mumble from my cocoon.

He smirks at my new ensemble even more than he did at the lingerie. And I try desperately to smash out the growing warmth when he says, "You look so adorable."

But that warmth is taking up permanent space in my chest. And so is he.

CHAPTER TWENTY-FOUR

Rhys

There is just the slightest nip in the air now, enough for the non-northerners to don light jackets for the trek across campus. We're having two-a-days quite often now that we're a week out from our first home game.

I feel better than I have, partially from how well the team seems to be meshing even with the parasitic Kane looming over me every practice, but mostly because of a snarky figure skater who has her little fist clenched into my chest.

Bennett pretends the night in the hotel room never happened. Just like he and Freddy pretend not to notice how often I leave after dark for a quick "midnight run," which is only a mile to the dorms—and back with a little guest in tow. I sneak her in, but I know they know.

I find myself at Sadie's door in between classes more often than I'll admit. I go down on her often, my favorite position being her on her back on the bed, her legs over my shoulders while I kneel and jack myself off. It's impossible not to with the sounds she makes, her taste, her blunt little nails on my scalp.

Her touch soothes me as much as it ignites me. I was floating before, feeling nothing but numbness. Sadie makes me feel alive for the first time since that game. Like I'm a whole man again.

We haven't slept together, not yet. Partially because, by the time I get my fill of her, she's come at least three times and I can't keep myself from following her over the edge with a slight touch.

The other reason—the one I can barely admit to myself—is that I'm scared.

Sadie is ingrained in my body and mind; going even a day without her makes me anxious to be near her. I want more than just her hands on my skin in dim light. I want her everywhere—her hair all over my room, her voice in the noise at my games, her toothbrush in my bathroom—and I worry she'll get her fill of me and move on. So I hold back the one card I have to play in our friends-with-benefits agreement.

Like the mythical cheerleader waiting to give it up to the quarterback, I'm waiting for her.

I walk beside Bennett from the calculus class that I've put off until this year. I'm not even sure why Bennett is taking the class because I'm fairly certain he took it freshman year. Not to mention he's a genius in his own right.

Freddy and Holden meet us on the green with some freshmen teammates in tow, and we all head toward the wellness café for lunch.

"Do we have a two-a-day Friday?" Holden asks, sliding his backpack strap over his shoulder again after it slips.

"No, just an early day."

He nods. "Great, then party?"

"Which house?" Freddy asks, his eyes flicking to Bennett like he really wants to beg. Bennett's face is a little harsh, but he blows out a breath and shrugs.

"We can use ours or theirs—I don't care."

Freddy and Holden slap hands like twins and start to discuss which of the two off-campus hockey houses we want to use to host our annual back-to-school party.

We live in the "Hockey House." It's been passed down to team-

mates for longer than I really know. Bennett and I got first dibs when
the former seniors moved out of the two-story colonial, painted pale
blue with the Waterfell Wolves' flag flying off the wide front porch.

It's close to campus, an easy walking distance to the main hub
of shops on South College and only a little farther from the dorms
and campus. The other team house, affectionately called the "hockey
dorms," is a seven-bedroom with split bathrooms that wasn't so ap-
pealing to Bennett, who likes full control of his spaces. Still, Holden
and Freddy lived there happily their first year. Freddy moved in with
us last year after he joined the first line, like a bonding experiment.
The fourth bedroom, that's been vacant since Davidson left, will
probably be filled by one of the underclassmen.

"The dorms are bigger . . ." I offer before trailing off.

Because she's here.

I spot Sadie just as she spots me. She's across the green, walking
in the direction of the arena and dressed like she might be headed
to practice.

There's a guy with her. Tall, muscular, dressed in a similar tight,
all-black ensemble. Sadie's bag—complete with that same fucking
hang tag—is slung on his shoulder. The sight shoots a pang through
my already-tight chest.

She says something to him quickly before running toward me
with a wave. I preen under her open attention, the way her eyes
never leave mine as she jogs over.

Sadie bounces on her toes for a minute, smiling as she blurts, "I
found a song—oh."

She steps back, cheeks glowing as she takes in the group around
me. Freddy smirks at her, Bennett quietly raises an eyebrow, and
Holden and the freshmen stop their conversation to look at us.

"Sorry." She steps back again. "You're busy."

"I'm not." I laugh, but there's a kick in my chest like maybe this
isn't what she wants. *Is this a secret too?*

Afraid to think about what that means, I nod goodbye to the guys and cart Sadie off with my hands on her wrists, pulling her a few feet away.

"You found a song?"

She smiles again and it feeds my soul. "It reminds me of you. I added it to the end of the playlist last night."

"I'll listen to it on the way to my class."

That sentence makes her smile somehow grow until her eyes nearly disappear, crinkling at the edges.

It makes me want to do more of whatever will get her to look at me like that, so I add, "I'll text you what I think."

"I won't see you tomorrow?"

My stomach drops. Fuck. *Oliver's game.*

The one I promised him I'd attend after he mentioned it offhand, which made Liam immediately invite me. Oliver hadn't asked, but I'd seen the slight question in his eyes, whether I might show up.

"Shit," I mutter. "Gray—I'm so sorry. I have . . . fuck, I have two-a-days all week. I forgot I have practice."

Her face shutters, offering only a glimpse of real, raw disappointment before she builds a wall of resentment. I've seen it before, the movements of her face almost identical to Oliver's. It's another sign on a list of things that make me worried about that family—something has happened to them, made them like this.

"I'm sorry—"

"Don't apologize to me. Oliver's the one you promised."

I try to reach for her as she shuffles back, hating how quickly this conversation has changed. "Sadie—"

"It's fine, Rhys. We aren't dating, you don't owe me anything. My family is fine without you."

It feels like I've been punched in the stomach, and again when she stalks back to the handsome, arrogant fucker still holding her bag for her and they take off together.

The boys are gone from the green, Bennett strict enough about his schedule not to bother hanging back, but Freddy has waited for some reason that I don't care to know. He settles in step next to me, backpack half-slung over his shoulder. A girl sends him a happy, coy greeting when she passes, which he enthusiastically returns while slapping an arm over my shoulders and pulling me away, blocking my view of Sadie.

"Still *just* sharing ice time?" Freddy asks, his tone serious despite the easygoing smile he has. "'Cause with the death glare you're giving Luc, I'm thinking it's a bit more than that."

"If it was more, I think I just fucked it up."

"One step forward, two steps back. You'll be fine."

I shake my head. "Who's Luc? The guy she's with?"

"Oh God, you don't know that guy?" I shake my head and Freddy laughs, patting my chest. He pushes open the doors to the university's wellness center and kitchen, blasting us with a burst of cold air. "Good for you. I can't fucking stand him."

That doesn't help, considering Freddy likes everyone. "Who the hell is he?"

We grab trays for the wellness kitchen food line—it's the major hub for athletes here at Waterfell for any meal. They offer grilled chicken, full-fledged salad bars with every topping imaginable, greens, potatoes—anything we can and will eat, especially during the season.

"Luc's a figure skater, part of a pair . . . or he was. He has trouble staying with his partners and not sleeping with them."

There's nothing I can do to stop the slight surge of adrenaline that pumps through me. My fingers grip the tray tightly as I grab nearly every piece of grilled lime chicken that Freddy leaves behind. I take a calming breath.

It's not like he said Sadie's sleeping with him.

"He was Olympic-bound before he ended up here, I think. Thinks he's God's gift to women, or some shit."

I snort. "Takes one to know one, eh, Freddy?"

He laughs, nodding. "Sure, sure." He's already got a little potato popped into his mouth as he chews and talks, walking us toward the hockey table.

A couple of people nod their heads as we settle, myself at Bennett's right, Freddy directly across from me. Where we all have heavy smorgasbords of food within our set diets, Bennett has a sectioned bento box meal he made at home.

"I know you said you're not together or anything," Freddy continues, his voice quiet even amid the roar of the crowd. He rubs a hand along the back of his neck. "But I swear I think he and Sadie used to be a thing."

Damn it.

Bennett looks up at me for a second. "Sadie likes Rhys. She's at our place all the time. I don't think she'd have time for anyone else."

I sigh and nod toward him in a silent thanks. "She's got plenty of time for it now."

"Yep—and if that's the case, Captain, you've got plenty of time for other girls. What about P?"

As if she's been wished into existence by the hint of her name, Paloma sinks between Bennett and me, her arms brushing both our shoulders while she angles a wink at Freddy.

"Bragging about me again?" She smirks, stealing a potato wedge from my plate and dancing it around her painted lips.

Paloma Blake is gorgeous and she knows it. Blond hair; lightly tanned skin; thick, pouty lips; and a body nearly every player at the table—hell, maybe the entire student population—has salivated over at one point. Everything about her looks like a sexed-up runway model, with an overconfident attitude to match. She might be all flirty winks and blown kisses, but I've always suspected the girl has hidden claws.

"Rhys pretends you guys never dated." Holden laughs, flicking his head toward her with a wink. "If you want someone to brag, just give me a night, P. I'll never shut up about it."

Paloma smiles again, all sultry, and every piece of her demeanor is so fake I want to jerk my entire body away.

Bennett does, pulling away entirely, and she melts into his seat as he leaves the cafeteria.

"What's his problem?" she sneers, body spinning to watch Bennett leave and leaning entirely into my side. I lightly jostle her off me.

"Maybe he didn't want you all over him," I whisper. I'm not mean, I just don't care anymore. Old Rhys would've let her lie there, let her flirt a bit before refocusing on practice. "You know how he is."

"I don't, actually," she argues, her tone defensive. "But what's your fucking problem?"

"No problem."

"Clearly." She rolls her eyes. "What crawled up his ass and died?"

Holden snorts, stuffing the last of his grilled chicken in his mouth in one overly large bite. Freddy looks up and laughs, nodding his head toward me as he answers Paloma.

"He likes a girl that isn't falling all over him for once."

Paloma raises one perfectly plucked eyebrow as she peels back the lid of a brightly colored kid's yogurt that seems like it appeared from nowhere.

"Who?"

I don't want to say, because if Sadie's reaction is anything to go by, she might be keeping us a secret. But I know that if anyone on this campus knows everything about everyone, it's Paloma.

"Sadie Brown."

There's barely a twitch in her face; her flawless features stay perfectly in place, no reaction to my words.

"The figure skater?"

I pause and look at her. "Yeah—you know her?"

She smiles and it makes my stomach hurt. "Oh, I know her—she's fun."

Something about the way she says it makes me uneasy.

"Fun?"

Paloma shrugs, but that gleam in her eye doesn't disappear. "She's wild. She pops into parties for quick, not-so-quiet hookups and bounces, so it's given her a reputation. I don't think she's slept with anyone on the hockey team, but other sports? Yeah. She has a type—athletic, rough. I haven't seen her around in a while, but last semester she was *wild*."

I want to ask more, but I force my mouth closed. If I learned anything from the time I spent dating her, Paloma isn't who this information should come from.

I force myself to eat despite the sour feeling in my stomach. We've got practice in a few hours, which might give me enough time to talk to Sadie and make it up to her if she wasn't already at her own practice.

But I know her schedule like I know my own, because I *want* to know it. I want to see her every second I can, and for two busy student athletes, that's a scheduling nightmare. It's surprisingly easier for me to find the time for her than she can for me. More often than not, she is taking care of her brothers. I get the sinking feeling in my gut, the more I am around her, that she is the *only* one taking care of them.

I excuse myself quickly, shoving back from the table and tossing my scraps in the bin on my way out. Then I dive into my phone and pull up Sadie's text thread, debating over exactly how to fix it.

But first I open her playlist for me, queuing up the new song: "Yippie Ki Yay" by Hippo Campus. I can't help the smile that spreads from knowing *exactly* why she chose it.

CHAPTER TWENTY-FIVE

Sadie

It's Friday night and I have a shift at the café that I'm already late for.

Practice was awful. I angrily ran through the jumps for my long program, sloppy the first handful of times because all I could think about was Rhys.

He texted after our mishap on the quad, but I'd ignored it at first, focused solely on the weekend's schedule: work, practice, and Oliver's game.

I planned to message him back after Oliver's game, to apologize for getting so upset—because the truth was that Oliver didn't care, not enough for this to bother him. I was the one who was hurt and I should have been honest with Rhys about it.

But then, Friday night came, and we never made it to Oliver's game.

Instead, I spent the night hunting down my father, who'd stolen my car while we were packing Oliver's gear bag and getting Liam dressed after his bath. Oliver missed his game, Liam became more aware of exactly how terrifying his father could be, and I called every bar within fifteen miles until I found him.

I had to hitch a ride in a too-expensive taxi, fight off grabby hands from drunk older men in a seedy dive bar, and grapple with my own father for my car keys.

So Rhys's text sat unanswered, and the self-hatred swallowed me whole until I made a decision: bringing Rhys Koteskiy into the mess of my life was something I wasn't willing to do.

I texted a quick, *I don't think we should do this anymore.* I couldn't bring myself to block him, but left the rest of his messages unread and unopened.

It has been a week of absolute hell since then, avoiding Rhys at every turn and focusing solely on school, work, skating, and my family.

Tonight, my coach kept me late after practice, running me ragged with new additions to level up my short program.

Then, because of my academic probation, he had me do my homework in front of him, sitting in his cramped office until well past my clock-in time for work. I knew Ro would cover me, but it made me sick with anxiety. Being at the rink late meant I hadn't had time to see my brothers before work, and I had to trust that Ms. B, our elderly neighbor, would hold down the fort until I clocked out.

I know that Coach Kelley is very aware of that fact, of my other responsibilities, but I can't hate him for pushing me to be my best.

He's only like this because he believes in me. He's the only one who does.

Even though I hate how *much* I have to work, I love weekends at Brew Haven. Especially Friday and Saturday nights, when the shop stays open late for open mic nights.

Some people sing or play the guitar, some do poetry or excerpt readings—we've even had a stand-up comic before, which, while cringy, was definitely a fun distraction while washing dishes.

Tonight is the first open mic night of the school year, so we're expecting a semi-small crowd. Partially because it's the first one we've hosted this year. But mostly because there are about a hundred parties on and off campus we will have to compete with until close. Including one at the "hockey dorms" that both Ro and I received invitations to via text.

I was surprised to receive one, from Freddy of all people, to celebrate their first home game win. But I know I can't go—I can't risk running into Rhys because I know I'll give in.

Ro is sitting on the countertop, staring intently at her phone while I make a decaf latte. I imagine she's poring over Matt Fredderic's text again. "Are you going to go?" I ask her. "You should."

"I can't," she answers, but her eyes don't leave the screen and she's nearly drawing blood where she's gnawing on her bottom lip.

There's only one thing I know of holding her back.

"Where is he?"

"Who?"

"Satan—I mean, your boyfriend." I giggle, but cut myself off at the sight of her slightly stricken expression.

"He . . . he blocked me again. I think we're broken up." There's a little quiver in her voice as she says it, even as her shoulders attempt a casual shrug.

It isn't the first time Tyler has done something like this. I try to limit my time around him as much as possible because I have neither the patience nor self-restraint to keep from causing a problem, and the little I've seen of him, I despise.

It's a vicious cycle too; if Ro breaks up with him, he pesters her at our apartment and place of work for weeks until they get back together. But when he decides he's changed his mind, or that Ro has messed up in some way, he blocks all contact from her with no notice.

Once, I had to pick her up off the side of the road ten miles from campus because they'd fought at dinner and he'd left her there.

I hand the latte I've finished to Ellis, one of the new freshman employees, before putting my hands on either side of the counter where Ro's perched, trying to stop her legs' anxious swinging.

"You okay, Ro?"

She smiles, but it doesn't reach her eyes. "Yeah. Actually, I think I'll go home after shift and have a self-care night."

I smile back. "I'll see if Betty can keep the boys at her place tonight. You and I can do face masks and watch *Because I Said So.*"

Ro's smile grows as she spoons a heap of homemade whipped cream into her mouth and nods. She lets the spoon dangle from her lips as she pushes off the countertop. "Perfect."

The door chime goes off and I look over my shoulder to see Paloma Blake flounce through the door.

As usual, she's dressed in a way that makes me want to simultaneously tear her hair out and steal the clothes off her body for myself. Sometimes, when our paths unfortunately cross, I imagine she's walking in slow motion to a personalized soundtrack of "Maneater" or "Bubblegum Bitch," the click of her heeled knee-high boots on beat.

Paloma Blake and I have woven in and out of each other's lives since sophomore year, attending most of the same parties and often, we realized, hooking up with the same guys. For that reason, it almost felt like a competition between us.

She comes to stand in front of Ellis, but her eyes are only on mine as she leans lightly on the counter like a feline stretching in the sun.

"Paloma." I nod, crossing my arms subconsciously as I can't help staring at her cleavage sitting on display, almost spilling from her lavender corset top.

"Sadie Brown," she coos, plump lips spreading wide over white teeth. "Just the person I was hoping to see. Mind if we chat?"

Yes.

But I slink around the countertop, promising Ellis that I'll be right back, and slip out the front door. Paloma and I walk together to the little alleyway between Brew Haven and the off-campus bookstore.

"What do you need?"

"I hear you and Rhys are talking." She leans back against the brick.

The sound of his name hurts, and I hate it.

"Fascinating," I say, deadpan. "Nothing better to do with your time than play town crier?"

She rolls her eyes. "I came to ask if it's true."

"Paloma." I scrub my face with my hands. "You are constantly dating someone, particularly in the sports arena. Why don't you just ask him?"

"I dated Rhys," she spouts.

I hate the possessive clench in my gut. I know he's dated before—*look* at him—but hearing it makes me a little nauseous.

"And?"

"And so I know him. And, unfortunately for my psyche, I know you." She drops her fake smile and stands up straight. "He doesn't need you around him. It's their final year to win the Frozen Four and get attention for the draft."

I clench my jaw, hating that, as much as I want to fight her in this alley, I can understand her worries.

Not only that, but I agree with them.

"You think he gives a shit about taking time away from your dreams? From your brothers?" Coach Kelley's heated whisper reverberates in my head. *"He'll never understand."*

"Last year, we—"

"This isn't like last year," I snap, cutting her off.

For a moment last year, Paloma and I had almost been friends. A little truce as we self-destructed together. I'd seen her spiraling the same way I was, so the implied accusation cuts deeper. As if she's suddenly all better, with her refreshed highlights and summer tan.

If she gets a fresh start, why not me?

Paloma starts to speak again, but I raise my palm.

"Save it," I whisper. "I was talking to him, I guess. But you're right. Don't worry, I've already told him it's over. I'm leaving him alone."

I wondered briefly if he's doing the same thing, but I muted his messages, trying to quell my need to look.

"If you want him, fine. Just leave me out of it."

Oliver. Liam. Ro. The custody hearings. Work. School. Skating. Surviving. That's what is important.

"It's not a question of if I want him." Paloma rolls her eyes, adjusting her top just so. "It's just—you know what? Never mind."

I walk away before she can.

I expect to feel lighter somehow, as if I'm truly shedding Rhys and his haunting, sad eyes.

But I don't. If anything, I feel worse.

CHAPTER TWENTY-SIX

Sadie

"You swear you haven't had sex with him yet?"

We're sitting on a pallet of pillows and blankets, almost all of them Ro's; half are homemade gifts from her grandmother, in a whole assortment of colors that looks like a muted rainbow threw up. Both of us lie flat on our backs, nearly cheek to cheek with legs outstretched to either side of our small living area. Ro's lengthy curls fan around me, tangling with the straight silk of my own hair.

My cheeks heat under the slight embarrassment at Ro's question. If anyone else asked, I might rip their head off, but I know Ro means well.

"I swear," I say.

And it's the truth. Rhys and I have done nearly everything else, but every time we start to go in that direction—with me leading the charge—he redirects me with his mouth on me so quickly I can't complain before he's wrenching endless orgasms from me.

The boy has a magic tongue.

"Why not?"

There's a lot of ways I could answer, but I don't want to say what I really think—that he doesn't want me in that way. Maybe he heard about last year after all.

"I think he was taking things slow," I say, the sting of past tense hot on my tongue as it falls from my lips. *Was.* "But it doesn't matter. And besides," I say, sitting up on my elbows and leaning over Ro so my hair forms a little curtain around us, "I thought *you* said no talking about boys. If that's back on the table, you need to tell me about the Student."

The Student.

Ro is a tutor for mathematics, English, and multiple sciences. She's an overachiever in all aspects and has been since freshman year. She has always stayed professional.

Until recently, where she started talking about one of the people she tutors. He's labeled in her phone as *Student*, which is odd already because she uses email to contact her tutees, not her personal number.

I haven't seen the messages, but I know she likes him—just from her perpetual smile while she schedules their sessions.

If that's even what she's doing.

"Oh, suddenly someone is silent," I say with a laugh.

We both push up and rest our backs against the small sage sofa we found on the side of the road and spent weeks cleaning, only to spill an entire glass of red wine on it while celebrating the following weekend.

Ro shrugs, but still refuses to say a word about the Student.

"Right." I sigh. "Well, how is tutoring Matt Fredderic going then?"

She takes a big gulp of her Big Gulp. "It's fine. Easy."

"I'm surprised he needs a tutor. Isn't he sleeping with all his professors for good grades? Or does he just not have any female teachers to seduce this year?"

Ro rolls her eyes. "Very funny."

I start to say more when my phone starts ringing.

It's an unknown number, but the area code is local. Normally I wouldn't answer, but I've had too many scares when it comes to Oliver and Liam, so I hold up a finger for Ro and quickly apologize before answering.

"Hello?"

There's loud music for a moment before a door slams and it's slightly quieter.

"Is this Sadie Gray?"

"Sadie Brown," I correct, my stomach sinking; there's only one person who calls me that.

"The figure skater?" the guy asks, sounding puzzled by my correction.

"Yeah," I say breathlessly. "Who is this?"

"Bennett Reiner. I'm Rhys's friend. We met once at the coffee shop."

I nod, even though he can't see it. "I remember. Bennett . . . what's, I mean . . . Why are you calling me?"

He takes a deep breath, seeming to struggle to get his words out. "I didn't want to call you unless I had to, but I think something's wrong with Rhys."

My stomach drops, heat flaring over the back of my neck. *What's wrong? Is he okay? Is he hurt? Did he have another panic attack?*

"Why are you calling me?" I ask again, anxiety mixing with anger—not at Bennett, but at *everything*.

Rhys is not mine. We aren't dating.

"I thought . . . look, I don't know what's going on between you two—"

"Nothing is—"

"—but I know that Rhys isn't okay. I don't think he's been okay for a while, and for some reason, I think you know that. So, if he's told you or confided in you, it's not *nothing*." He spits the last bit out, like he's angry with me for calling it that.

"Bennett, I can't—"

"You don't have to date him or whatever you're doing, but please, can you just come help him? I can't get him to leave, and he's locked himself in a bathroom and said only Sadie can come in. If he doesn't want people to see him like this, he needs to get the hell out of here, and none of us can drive."

Oh my God.

Ro cocks her head at me, and I know the call is loud enough that she can hear at least some of it. She shrugs, letting me know it's my choice.

"Send me the address. I'll come take him home."

• • •

After I park the Jeep, we both hop out and walk the short distance from the street to the bumping, loud, aptly named "hockey dorms." Ro crosses her arms, hands gripping her shoulders self-consciously. It doesn't help to cover her, especially with her hair piled into a pretty ribbon-bound ponytail; she's all bare, tawny skin.

We look terribly out of place: Ro in her blue-and-white-striped silk pajama set—because the girl doesn't own a simple T-shirt—and me swimming in an old ratty band tee that comes down to mid-thigh, covering my shorts entirely.

Still, we brave the murmurs when we climb the stone steps to the porch and front door, where a few stragglers are talking and laughing. Walking through the open door, I look around for the mountain that is Bennett Reiner.

I see far too many familiar faces. A few ignore my angry, bare-faced stare to tell me they're happy to see me or glad I'm back on my "usual shit." Shoving past them all, I'm a second away from calling Bennett when a shoulder slams me hard enough to toss my body into the wall.

"Nice outfit, Ro," a snarky voice taunts.

I'm spinning around, ready to knock him on his ass before he can blink, but Ro stops me, stepping in front of me to block my path to Tyler. He's flushed, clearly more than a little drunk, and something about it makes me nervous.

"I can deal with this," Ro tells me calmly, but her eyes are dilated and there's gooseflesh across her bare skin. "Go find Rhys."

"I won't leave you here—"

"It's fine." She smiles. "Tyler and I are done, but I can handle him. Besides, we're in the crowded front room at a party. What could happen?"

A lot. I want to argue, but I catch a familiar set of bodies approaching from the back of the room near the kitchen: one hulking and decked in a long-sleeve shirt and jeans, backward baseball cap, and a scowl; the other, slightly shorter, but still outmeasuring most of the guys in the room, dressed in his usual Matt Fredderic fashion of a semi-unbuttoned shirt and a chain around his neck.

I start for them, pushing through the throng of people.

Bennett spots me first, both of us now heading toward each other, cutting the distance in half. Freddy comes too, but his eyes are focused beyond me.

"Your friend okay?" he asks when I'm close enough to hear.

"You mean your tutor?" I joke, but my mouth can barely form the hint of a smile. "No, she's not. I-I need to . . . Can you just, like, go hover around her and make sure she's okay?"

He nods and taps me on the shoulder, scooting by.

Bennett looks unflinchingly calm, but there's a flush to his cheeks like he might have had a few drinks. He messes with his baseball cap and looks at my shoes, a hand-me-down pair of slip-on clogs, then nods over his shoulder.

I follow him through the kitchen to a narrow back stairwell that is, thankfully, empty.

Bennett takes the steps two at a time, and I follow close behind until we reach a closed bathroom door. He takes off his baseball cap, rakes a hand through a mass of messy amber brown curls, and readjusts the hat back on his head, gesturing toward the door with his other hand.

"Right," I whisper, hating my clammy hands and seasick stomach. I knock on the door.

"Busy!" a female voice yells. Her tone is angry, but that doesn't stop me from grasping the wall like I might pass out, or vomit—or both.

Bennett huffs a little derisive sound and slams his fist so hard on the door it rattles.

"Open the fuck up." He doesn't yell, but it has the same effect.

"Go away," Rhys slurs through the door, and I'm sure my face is ashen now. "I'm fine, Ben."

"Rhys?" I ask, pressing my entire face nearly into the wood. "It's Sadie. Can you open the door for me?"

It's barely a second before he does.

Or she, because the girl is the first to slip out of the room, adjusting her high ponytail and jeans as she does. She gives a sneer of disgust toward the bathroom and her eyes flick to me before snapping to a fuming Bennett.

"Freddy told you not to mess with him," Bennett practically growls.

She rolls her eyes. "Whatever—he's a mess. Threw up for the last ten minutes while I just stood there. I'm assuming you're—"

"Gray," a voice croaks.

We all whip our heads toward Rhys.

His body is slumped into the doorframe, his gray shirt slightly darker around the collar in a way that tells me he was either sweating or tossing water from the faucet onto his face. His skin is flushed, his hair a tangled mess that he tries to curl behind his ear as some of it plasters to his damp face.

He looks . . . terrible. Yet . . . he's smiling at me, dimples deep and eyes foggy.

"You're so beautiful." He slurs so much that his words all come out as one.

I feel another wave of heat as a light pulsing starts up in my head.

"Was he this drunk when you went in there with him?" I ask, vision hazing as I glare at the girl trying to leave our little alcove.

Rhys stumbles, catching his weight on the doorframe again as he looks between us. "She pulled me in there," he hurries to say, as if it's him I'm accusing. "But I didn't want to—"

He hiccups and I see Bennett step toward him, like he's planning to be a shield in case he throws up again or passes out.

"Are you fucking kidding me?" I ask, whipping back to the girl. She's tall, even more so with her heels; I wish I was wearing shoes like hers so I could take one off and stab her in the eye with it. "He's blackout wasted and you took him in there? For what? To hook up with the hockey star while he's literally so drunk he can't see straight?"

The girl's cheeks go red and her eyes widen a little, as if she's just realizing what she did. She might've had a drink or two, but she's not drunk.

"I didn't know he had a girlfriend."

Flames shoot out from the sides of my head.

I launch myself toward her before I really think it through. We tumble into the wall, my arms around her waist. Then I use my foot, now missing a clog from my jump, to take her down to the hardwood flooring.

"We didn't do anything!" she screams. "He threw up all over the place before—"

I hit her—which unfortunately isn't a first for me.

The very few people in the hallway around us are starting to chant or yell. I only get in two good hits—one to her face, the other to her arm—before she finally blocks me. She's screaming at me, but I can't hear her beyond the red haze.

She touched Rhys. She took advantage of him.

Then, I'm pulled away.

Bennett easily walks me backward, even as I squirm in his arms.

He's huge, and I'm sure it looks like a Newfoundland taking a Chihuahua by the scruff. My ears are still ringing as I try to come down from the burst of adrenaline, so I can't hear as he barks something at her over my shoulder.

Rhys is sitting in front of the bathroom, looking up at me in Bennett's arms with watery brown eyes.

I hate how vulnerable he looks, but it brings me back under control. *Focus on Rhys.*

Easy.

I stop fighting against Bennett and he drops me after I nod. He switches me for Rhys, tucking an arm around his waist to lift him as Rhys leans heavily on him.

"I didn't want her here, Sadie," Rhys coos, his voice slurring even as his eyes shine. He reaches for me, but I sidestep him. "I promise."

"It's fine, Rhys. I know." I sigh. "*You* didn't do anything wrong."

"I think I'm in love with her." I hear Rhys tell Bennett, but his voice doesn't lower even a notch. "And she won't let me *in*."

My heart clenches and I can't help glancing over my shoulder, maneuvering quickly down the stairs.

Bennett winces, helping Rhys along as we walk out the back door. "Calm down, bud."

"Sade doesn't think I'm a golden boy, Ben." Rhys smiles, but it's all wrong. "I don't have to pretend now that she's here. She *knows* I'm broken." He lets out a huffed laugh.

"Rhys . . . you're not broken." Bennett sounds as distraught as I feel behind the hard mental wall of steel I have raised in a last-ditch effort to protect myself.

"I am, Ben. And she's the only one who sees it."

Bennett gives me an unsettled look, but continues on.

"Let's get you out of here, man," he says, his tone softer.

Bennett leads, staying close to the side of the house and avoiding the other half of the party enjoying the cool autumn air.

As we make it to the front lawn, I step forward to navigate us to my car.

"Where are you going?" a voice shouts—Paloma, I realize as I turn around.

She's standing by the front steps, having leapt up from the lap of a very large, very terrifying-looking man I've never seen before the second she saw us approach. Her eyes keep flicking between the three of us, like she isn't sure who she addressed with her question.

Maybe it's the already-high adrenaline echoing in my veins, or the vulnerable, heart-wrenching words spilling from Rhys's drunken lips, but I can't seem to stop myself from heading toward her.

I must look slightly unhinged, because a little bit of fear widens her eyes as she steps back.

"If you want him, Paloma," I snap, "take better fucking care of him. Or leave him alone."

She flushes, crossing her arms. "I didn't say that—"

"Whatever. Be with him or don't, I don't fucking care," I lie, my teeth aching as I push out the words. "Just—" A humorless laugh bursts out of me before I can stop it. "You know what? Never mind. You can't have him, okay? I don't get him and neither do you. Leave him the fuck alone and we don't have a problem."

Paloma nods, but she isn't looking at me. No, she's looking past me, toward Rhys. Bennett scoffs and calls for me to leave.

"Stay out of my way," I whisper. I look over her shoulder at the small crowd gathered. The black-haired guy is watching it all with a sinful smirk across his lips, leaning back on the steps as if this is his favorite reality show. But above him, sitting on the highest step and being tended to by some football player, is the girl from earlier.

I gesture to her, making her face turn ashen as I call louder, "And tell your little friend up there to watch her fucking back. I don't need unbruised knuckles to skate."

It's easy, now, to leave, something in my gut is satisfied by the red skin on her cheek, the thoroughly reprimanded look on Paloma Blake's otherwise perfect face; all of it pushes me forward, leading Rhys and Bennett to my car down just two rows of cars from the lawn.

Bennett sets Rhys in the Jeep's backseat, gentle as the giant can be. Rhys tucks against the seat and I turn to see a running Ro headed my way. Her sandals smack on the pavement and the silk of her pajamas ripples in the cool wind.

She grabs on to Bennett, who flinches under her touch and draws back.

"Someone's gotta stop him."

"Who?"

"Freddy."

Bennett curses and takes off back toward the party with Ro, leaving me with Rhys.

It's quiet, the wind whipping through the trees and the muted party noise gentle in the background. I can't stand the silence, so I play boygenius's "Revolution 0" on loop in my head.

Rhys is just breathing, but I glance at him quickly to make sure he's still awake and alive. Despite his drunken stupor, he sees my concern.

"I'm good," he says. He sighs deeply again, pressing a hand to his chest before letting it fall. "Just those Darth Vader impressions again."

The words are still slurred, but it's the droopy smile that has me looking away fast.

"I can't believe you're here," Rhys whispers, his voice fitting seamlessly with the sounds around me and in me.

It's almost painful not to look at him.

"Where've you been?"

"Rhys . . ." I beg.

He reaches out, almost falling out of the car, to grab my hand. It forces me to look at him, to see the glittering pain like drops of a deep blue in his dark brown eyes.

"I called you over and over. I just . . . Sadie, please."

"Don't do this right now. You're drunk and I'm tired."

He bites his lip and nods, but the movement is slow and lethargic. I want to kiss him again, but it's selfish because it's *my* need.

It's overwhelming, the way I feel around him. The need to touch him, to hold him—and not in the way that my own emotions usually overwhelm me. This is . . . it's soothing, like it melts away all the bad thoughts in my head.

"Close your eyes," I murmur, letting my thumb rub circles over his warm hand. Letting myself bask in the comfort of *him*. "You should sleep it off, hotshot."

His lips tilt at the nickname. He keeps his eyes closed and his hand folded in mine.

"You'll still be here when I wake up?"

"Yeah," I murmur, stealing a moment to caress his overheated forehead and run my fingers through his hair. "I've got you."

Even like this, perched in my backseat with a boyish sleepy smile across his face, Rhys looks larger than life. He's destined to be something *great*.

We wait patiently, before Freddy—who's sporting bruised knuckles and a red cheek, and Ro come back, both barely speaking to each other, other than to tell me that Bennett isn't coming with us.

I drop them off at the Hockey House, the four of us silent as Freddy helps Rhys walk into their home.

I hate leaving him there, even with Freddy. It feels wrong, leaving him.

Because I've begun to think of him as mine, I realize as I pull away from their nice little house.

He deserves so much more. He's temporarily broken—there's no fixing me.

That thought stays with me like a mantra, far into the night and through the next day.

CHAPTER TWENTY-SEVEN

Rhys

My hands are shaking.

Considering there is nothing on the table, apart from a misshapen mug from my mother's limited foray into pottery, I clench my fists as I wait.

This is ridiculous. A bad idea.

Except I know this is the right choice.

After waking to a pounding headache and an exhausted Bennett slumped against my bedroom wall where he'd kept watch over me all night, I was tormented by a replay of the previous evening.

"I think I'm in love with her."

Good *God*. But fuck if it wasn't true, at least somewhat.

Give me two more weeks of her snappy attitude and smoky giggle and I would be.

Immediately after Bennett finished telling me what I did—and said—I reached for my phone and sent an apology, arguably too quickly and desperately. And, like all my messages since Sadie's last one, it went unanswered. If she's still receiving my texts, I'm sure I look insane. Maybe she thinks I am, considering we were only hooking up in her eyes and I told the girl I was falling in *love* with her.

Bennett hadn't been willing to let it go, so I told him. Everything. About the initial pain, the self-inflicted sleep deprivation, the panic attacks, Sadie . . . *everything*. He looked angry the entire time, but that's a usual expression for the controlled goalie.

But then, he hugged me. Tight. Loving.

His eyes were wet with tears as he looked at me and said, "If you'd told us, told me, we could've helped. Things would've been different."

I knew that was true as he said it, but I told him not to tell anyone else on the team. Bennett could know—he should have known from the start—but this isn't for everyone. This pain is my own, as is the choice of who I share it with.

But . . . there is one more person who deserves to know.

"*Chto eto?*" The Russian words sound gruff but chipper as my father pads down the last step into the kitchen. "What's this?" he repeats in English, finishing off the top button of his shirt.

He's dressed for work, which for him means an interview, a press event, or something for my mother.

"Do you have a minute?"

I watch as he measures the expression on my face, perhaps even my body language. He's always been good at that; it was one of his strengths in the league. His face turns stern and he nods.

"Do we need your mother here?"

"No." I shake my head. Mostly because no matter how I try to hide, she knows everything. "Just you."

He sits at the table without prompting. I'm at the head, while he takes the side closest to me.

"Do you want a coffee?" I ask, suddenly desperate to stall.

He shakes his head, waiting patiently.

My parents and I have always been close. I think if I'd chosen to go anywhere else in the world for school, they would've found themselves moving there. And . . . I've never minded it. It was a saving grace when I was hurt, even if it was hard to see that through the pain.

"My son," he whispers, his hand patting mine before he mimics my posture almost exactly—not intentionally, but because we are made of the same materials. I'm like a replica of his youth. Is that what he sees?

My son. My son. My son.

It plays again, like a permanent scratch on a skipping record, a glitch in my memory that brings an immediate headache. I try to play Sadie's playlist in my head, looping the Oasis song again and again.

Still, I can't get the goddamn words out.

"I'm not okay," I shove through my lips.

"*Vchistuyu,*" he whispers, a sad smile stretching across his face. It's a word I don't recognize from my partial, limited Russian.

"I don't know that." I shake my head, my throat catching.

"Finally." He smiles but it's watery. Between him and my mother, the intensity of emotions in this house has always been welcoming. After the hit, it was stifling. Now . . . now it is starting to feel like *home* again. "It means *finally*, Rhys. You're going to tell me what's going on now. What is hurting you?"

My brow furrows as I look up at him. "How did you—"

"I know I am not your mother." He raises his hand to silence my protests. "But along with her, you are the most important thing in my life. I would bleed myself dry if it meant I could take your pain for you. Now, tell me."

So I do. Working all out of order, because I know what is going to be hardest to say.

I tell him of the panic attacks at night, the night terrors that Mom has had to shake me awake from multiple times. I tell him about starting the sleeping pills prescribed to me, how they made me lose memory, or how one minute I'd be in the kitchen making lunch, and then suddenly I'd be driving nearly to the harbor—that it scared me enough to stop taking them and just deal with the nightmares.

I'm honest when he asks if I still have them. I do.

I tell him about the panic attacks on the ice when I first started back, and his face looks distraught with the details. I know it's because I didn't ask for his help, that he knows I was hurting and scared and alone—only I wasn't alone. So I tell him that too, about Sadie and her music and everything else about her that brings me some kind of peace.

Dad smiles at that, his eyes wet as he stays silent and lets me get it all out.

And then, I tell him why this is the first time he's heard it.

"In the hospital," I begin, looking at my hands splayed on the oak. "I couldn't really see anything or remember much that I could. But I could hear you, over everyone that was there. I kept hearing you."

I can still smell that harsh antiseptic mixed with metal, can remember my hands trying to pat down and rub at my unseeing eyes, until a nurse had to hold them down. My mother was crying, but I could just faintly tell because the loudest noise was my father's sobbing yells.

"My son! My son—help him. Please."

And then, *"I can't live without him. Not my son—he can't do this to me."*

It wasn't some grand hurtful thing, and it would take more than a few sessions of therapy to understand it, but his screams haunted me. I'd never seen my dad upset or afraid before. And when I was at the peak of my fear, the calm, steady presence of my father wasn't there—just panic.

So I chose to keep everything to myself. Because I love my dad, and I never wanted to hear him like that again.

I tell him all this before I work up the courage to look at him.

His eyes, so like my own, are shining as tears drop down his face.

And then he's moving, his arms closing around me before I can blink, trapping me to my seat in a fierce hug.

"My son," he whispers into my hair, and this time no bolt of fear or panic rushes down my spine. Just warmth. "I'm so sorry, Rhys. *Prosti menya, pozhaluysta.*" *Forgive me, please.*

"You didn't do anything—"

"I did," he says, holding me somehow tighter before letting go and settling back into his seat. The lump in my throat is hard enough to swallow through, so I don't reach for the coffee that I desperately want. "I should have been there, should have stepped back and asked what it was you needed. But seeing you like that, the blood on the ice, the way your body gave out—"

I stop him with a hand and he nods.

"It's still too hard to think about it. Makes my head swim," I say.

"Because you can't remember it?"

I nod.

"Thank you, Rhys. For telling me everything, for letting me in." My dad clears his throat and wipes the tears from his cheeks before meeting my gaze. "Listen to me closely. I don't care if you toss your skates in the trash tomorrow. I don't care what you choose to do for the rest of your life as long as you're happy." He chuckles and relaxes back into the chair.

"If you'd picked up a basketball all those years ago, I'd be courtside for the rest of my life with one of those big foam fingers. If you take up a paintbrush, I'll buy every piece that we have wall space for. If you use that big brain of yours for engineering or law, I'll do whatever I can to show I support you until my last breath."

"I want to play hockey. I do," I insist, because I know I still want this—it's just buried beneath panic and pain.

"Still. This"—he gestures widely—"this life we have, it's *nothing* without you safe and happy. That is all I want. I love you, son."

Tears form at the corners of my eyes, and I try to hold them back. "I love you."

There is a long stretch of silence, as something new settles into my bones. The numbness is still there, but it isn't overwhelming. It's . . . it's just *there*.

"Let's go to the rink today," Dad offers just as my mother descends the staircase, dressed in slacks and a nice shirt. He goes to her instantly, like it's muscle memory, and I wonder if he felt this all-consuming craze for my mother like I do with Sadie.

I shake my head. "You've got things to do today—and I do too. But this week?"

He smiles and nods. I do the same.

It feels a bit more like I'm really home.

CHAPTER TWENTY-EIGHT

Rhys

It's been nearly a week without Sadie now, sober or otherwise, and it's started to affect my game. After playing our first home games last weekend, we are scheduled for two away games this coming weekend. So far, we're sitting about where we were last year—close to the top, with Boston College, Michigan, and Harvard as our top competitors.

My focus is good, but not great, disrupted a bit as I find myself arriving earlier and lingering later every day at the rink, hoping to catch even a glimpse of her.

I miss the way she makes me calm, sure.

I just miss her.

Sadie was my friend before anything else, even if her stubborn mouth wouldn't let her call me that out loud. Those two months of morning skates are now some of my favorite memories on and off the ice. I want more of them.

And yet, she is out of reach.

For the time being, I am waiting on her and making myself worthy of her.

A week back in therapy isn't enough, but it's a start. Sadie can't be my crutch if I want her to be *mine*. I won't put that on her ever again.

The library is slightly cool, matching the temperature outside.

Like most of the old on-campus buildings, it's usually either freezing cold or boiling.

I've kept up with my studies—it's required for the team, but also for my captain duties, which include hosting team study days so we can all exchange professor information, helpful hints, or common test questions. It's still hard being around my teammates and faking smiles, but there is a wound in me that hasn't healed. It won't happen overnight.

I have to remind myself of that a lot.

The good thing is that Toren Kane usually makes himself scarce for anything team related, which means the ever-present reminder of our ice time doesn't follow me off it.

Before I can make it to the table at the back of the library's first floor that's slightly rowdier than the rest, something catches my eye.

It's the little figure skater who I've been looking for, dressed in tight jeans and another large T-shirt, half-huddled beneath the brawny figure skater, Luc. The one who makes my spine prick with uncomfortable jealousy—something I'm not exactly used to.

"Wait, Sadie," I call out, getting a stern glare from the librarian at the desk nearby. I shrug at her, considering we aren't on the silent floor.

Sadie and Luc are both ignoring me, I realize with rising frustration. They don't stop their hurried movement through the front doors, but I follow anyway.

Slamming out of the library, I start shouting a little louder as we empty into the small parking lot.

Sadie spins, her ear to her phone and a panicked look in her wide gray eyes as she takes me in—and for some reason, my presence seems to make her more upset. It feels like a kick to the gut. She spins away, marching in a figure eight as she continues to dial and redial someone.

Luc sighs, and nods toward me like we're friends.

Which is fine, unless he's sleeping with Sadie, and then I think I'd like to knock him on his ass.

He walks to stand next to me. He's about my height and build—an athlete through and through—which somehow makes me more infuriated with him, despite having never spoken to the man before.

Shoving a hand through his jet-black hair, he cocks his head toward me, while I refuse to take my eyes off the angrily pacing figure skater in front of us, wishing I could do *something*.

"Rhys, yeah?"

I nod, clenching my jaw a little while Freddy's voice rings in my ears. *"He has trouble staying with his partners and not sleeping with them. . . . I think he and Sadie used to be a thing."*

"Luc." He looks over at Sadie again. Another possessive urge to rip his eyes out rolls through me, but I manage to hold on to my sanity. "This is ridiculous. She shouldn't be this scared to miss practice."

"What's happening?"

He starts to speak, but stops.

Sadie shoves her phone into her back pocket and spins with a little shriek, kicking at the ground hard enough that both Luc and I jump forward like we can stop her.

"What's wrong?" I ask, suddenly feeling like I'm intruding and hating every second. It's hard to swallow; harder not to reach for her.

"Rhys, please, I can't do this with you right now," she says dismissively, her hand waving as she curses and redials on her phone again. "Where is she?"

"Relax, Sadie—just miss the fucking practice," Luc says as he steps closer to her. I feel a little sick. "He can't—"

"He *can*. And it doesn't matter—if I miss, then by the school standards I could lose my scholarship."

Swallowing down the doubt clogging my throat, I step forward again, tightening my hand on the strap of my backpack. "Can I help?"

"Rhys." Sadie sighs, looking like a volcano about to erupt. "Please, I—"

"I know," I cut her off, stepping closer until my shoulder pushes Luc out of our little bubble. She starts to soften under my gaze, enough that I dare to touch her; I reach out and grab her hand, rub circles into the skin of her palm. "Just tell me how I can help you, Gray. Fuck—I hate seeing you look like you're about to panic."

Growing bolder with her, I release her hand and grasp her chin gently, tilting her eyes to mine, heart aching at the hopeless, frightened look in her eyes.

"Tell me."

She melts into my hand and part of me—the very ridiculously male part of my brain—wants to look at Luc now and smirk at him, display her in my arms as if to say *See? She's only soft for me. I'm the one she comes to—not you.* But I manage to keep my attention on Sadie.

"My brothers are home from school, and my neighbor who usually watches them can't." I nod as she whispers to me, never letting go of my gentle grip on her chin. "And Ro should be home, but she's not answering her phone, and I can't miss my practice—"

"You need me to get your brothers?" I nod. "And take them where?"

"It's fine." She jerks back, immediately defensive about the help being offered. "No, I just—"

"Sadie," I say more firmly. "I know where your house is, I remember it. Where do I need to take them?"

Her eyes fill with tears, but she doesn't let any of them free as she finally caves. "Okay, yeah. Just . . . Can you bring them to the dorms? Ro's probably napping between her classes. Just—yeah. I'll give you her number and she can pick them up outside the dorms."

I nod, and let her take my phone to input Ro's number. "Now, just go—"

She hesitates, even as Luc picks up her bag from the ground and waits for her. "Rhys—"

"I know . . ." I swallow down every word I want to say and offer her one of my mask smiles. "It changes nothing. Doesn't mean we can't be friends. Okay, Gray?"

She bites down on her lip hard, nodding her head even as her eyes refuse to stop scanning over my form. "Okay, Rhys."

I can't explain why it hurts so much that she doesn't call me *hot-shot.*

She grabs her bag from Luc's outstretched hand and spins on her heel, not bothering to wait for him. When she's out of earshot, Luc turns to me and slaps a hand on my shoulder.

"I don't know if you've met Coach Kelley."

I shake my head. "Only briefly."

"Well." He huffs another breath, closing his eyes and shaking his head as if this is the last thing he wants to do. "If you have feelings for her, real feelings—and I think it's clear you do—then you need to watch out for her."

I fight the urge to shove him and growl, *I do watch out for her,* paying attention to the tone of his voice, the defeated look in his eyes.

"She might listen to you about that overly intense coach of hers."

My brow furrows and I adjust my backpack on my right shoulder, slipping the other strap on. "She said that's normal—that he's just like that with everyone."

Luc shakes his head with a sigh. "Kelley's not normal. And if you don't know what's going on in that fucking *rink*—"

"Laroux!" Sadie shouts, stamping her foot. "If you make me late, I'll cut your fucking balls off and hang them on my dash."

A smile pulls at my mouth just watching her, and Luc takes off, not bothering to finish his statement before he's jogging after her.

● ● ●

On the front steps of a house that's identical to Sadie's, if slightly brighter, Liam and Oliver sit with their backpacks on, alone.

And on their own lawn next door, there's a man lying flat, face down.

The sight of the body so close to the boys scares me enough that I barely get the car in park before sprinting toward them. Liam howls when he sees me, a confused smile taking over his face as he stands and slaps Oliver's shoulders.

"Hey, buds," I call, slowing my gait and donning a smile as if that could distract them from the situation screaming *danger* over the stranger mere yards from them. "You okay?"

"Are you here for us?" Liam asks instead of answering my question, and a pit starts to form in my stomach. "Ms. B isn't home, so we don't know what we're supposed to do." He shrugs his little shoulders.

I look over toward their house again. The man is surrounded by a few cans and bottles, as well as a puddle of vomit, but he's breathing. I step back and survey the rest of the cul-de-sac.

"Yeah, I am."

Liam howls again, jumping up and down in place like he can't hold in any of his enthusiasm.

Looking at Oliver, I ask, "Do you two know that man?"

Oliver doesn't respond, but Liam chews on his lip and nods, albeit hesitantly. "That's my dad."

Fuck. I think I'm going to be sick.

"Sadie's gonna be mad," Oliver says, standing beside his brother, his backpack sliding off one shoulder. The look he gives me is wary at best. "She hates when people know about him."

Liam looks worried at that. "But she *likes* Rhys."

"Exactly." His brother chuckles before staring back at me with that same skeptical gaze. "Sadie sent you here?"

It's clear Liam doesn't understand, but I do. Oliver's twelve, but he knows Sadie didn't tell me, that she hid this from me.

I try to focus through the racing thoughts in my head.

"Yeah. I'm just your chauffeur."

"I don't know what that is," Liam says with a sigh.

"It means I'm driving you guys to Ro."

"Yes!" Liam shouts, fist punching into the air. He darts to my car without a second glance at his father passed out in a twisted mosaic of beer bottles across the lawn.

As if this is a regular occurrence.

Oliver waits with a strange mix of fear and want across his face, hidden just slightly behind his mask of anger.

"I'll stop by The Chick if you want," I offer. "We've got time."

A hint of a smile pulls at Oliver's face and Liam squeals, "That's Ollie's favorite!" while continuing to pull at the door handle on the car.

I know it's his favorite. I asked Sadie weeks before, after a grinding make-out session in the passenger side of her car, with her straddling my thighs. I saw yet another bag of to-go trash from a trip to The Chick and teased her about her addiction, which she clarified was Oliver's addiction. She made it sound like a convenience at the time.

Now, I know better.

"Let's go." I nod over my shoulder. "We'll get some food and I'll let you control the music."

And just like his sister, Oliver brightens. My heart is twisting in my chest, but I keep it together and let them sing ABBA songs the entire way to the drive-thru, trying to latch on to their happiness as if it'll erase the anxiety of Luc's words mixing with the image of their house.

CHAPTER TWENTY-NINE

Rhys

After the boys have eaten their fill of chicken sandwiches, fries, and milkshakes while parked at a nearby park that Sadie took me to months before, I open my phone and pull up Ro's contact, stepping out of the car and slightly to the side before dialing her.

It rings twice before a gruff voice snarls, "What the fuck do you want, asshole?"

I pause, nearly choking on my own spit at the furious male growl that definitely isn't Ro. Something uncomfortable slithers down my spine.

"Is this not Ro's number?" I ask, my voice steady, slightly calm, but still firm: my "Captain Rhys" voice, some on my team might call it.

There's a long pause, then a much lighter sounding, "Rhys?"

My eyes bug out and I cough. "Freddy?"

I've never heard Freddy sound like that in my life.

I hear some fussing in background, before Matt fucking Fredderic is back. "We're, um, studying right now." His voice drops, like he's farther away from the phone, and I can just make out a quiet, "It's Rhys, princess—I can handle it."

Suddenly, he's back at full volume. "Sorry—um, wait—why the fuck are you calling Ro?"

His voice is almost gruff, like he's a little annoyed with me.

"Why am I—" I cut myself off from the tirade I'd like to spring on my forward that definitely ends with *Find a new fucking tutor and leave that girl alone*. Instead, I run a hand over my face and sigh. "Sadie wants me to bring her brothers to Ro at the dorms."

Another bout of rustling, and I can hear Freddy complaining in the background as Ro takes over.

"Hey," she starts, voice light and airy. "Sorry, I've been having a problem with spam calls. Um, I can—I won't be back for a few hours. Shoot."

"It's fine, Ro." I smile and look back at my car, seeing the boys dipping the last of their fries into the shakes, chocolate smeared all over Liam's mouth. They look calm—even Oliver has relaxed just a bit. "I can keep them with me until later if you want. Just let me know when you're ready for them, okay? Take as long as you need."

She sighs into the phone with an audible smile. "Thanks, Rhys."

"No problem."

. . .

As I pull up to my parents' house, I hear Oliver almost choke on his milkshake—that is somehow not empty—while Liam audibly squeals.

"You live in a castle?" Liam asks, blinking wide at the colonial that's been completely refurbished.

The front retains its original style, but the back has been added on to and stretches farther than it did when it was first built. The house is painted gray, but it's bursting with life from multiple trellises and trees; one of the gardens, where brightly colored flowers dot the canvas of summer green, is visible even from here.

It's a pain during the winter months, but my mother's green thumb shows brightly in the spring and summer, and even now in the beginnings of fall.

I smile. "No, but my parents do."

"His dad played hockey, Liam, what did you expect?" Oliver mumbles beneath his breath, even as he stares out the windows with wide eyes.

"Our dad played hockey," Liam snips back, but the withering look from his brother shuts him up before I can ask more about it.

Speaking of, I see my dad come out of the garden, hearing my car approach. His face is all happy surprise as he steps down from the raised terrace, dressed in slacks and a button-down that are speckled with dirt, indicating he *was* somewhere for an interview or meeting, but didn't bother to change before joining my mother in her gardening.

My windows are too tinted and I want to give him a warning, so I idle the car and tell the boys I'll be right back before slipping out.

He sets his hand on my shoulder, eyebrows dipping as I whisper, "I need your help."

"What's wrong, Rhys?"

My voice is shaking as I tilt my head toward the car. "Sadie's brothers are here with me. She needed help—"

"Rhys, calm down," he cuts me off, squeezing my shoulder lightly.

Why am I so upset?

Because Sadie has been taking care of them alone and you made her take care of you too. Selfish.

I close my eyes tightly. "Yeah. Yeah, okay." I swallow again, brushing a hand through my tangled hair. "I, uh, I took them for food. Sadie—she wanted me to drop them off with a friend, but—I don't know. It's complicated. And they're kids, so I didn't want to take them to the Hockey House in case some of the players were there, or what if they don't like strangers? But . . . she asked me for help, and that's—"

"Rhys, it's fine." He nods to the car and smiles, waving to the boys inside. "Just get them out of your car and we'll bring them inside, okay?"

"Okay."

He stands back as I return to the car and open their doors. They both hesitate. Liam looks at my dad with wide awestruck eyes, straining over the seat to see him out of the window.

"Is that Coach Max? He's your dad?"

I smile as I unbuckle him. He should probably be in a car seat, but that's not something I currently have on hand. I barely stop myself from pulling out my phone to blindly order one off Amazon. "Yes, that's him. He's my dad."

"That's so cool. He plays hockey with you."

Oliver rolls his eyes, but keeps looking a little nervously at his sometimes coach.

"Yeah?" I ask, pulling him out and into my arms.

"Yeah," he mumbles, his little hands reaching up to play with the ends of my hair as they loop around my neck. "I wish my dad wanted to play with me."

At that, Oliver lets himself out and slams the door, standing on the side of the car and waiting for us.

"Oliver," I hear my dad greet him. "Good to see you, champ. How's your season going?"

The question seems to relax the older of the Brown brothers, as he starts to reluctantly brag about his stellar season.

Liam interjects a few times, wild compliments about his brother being "*the best hockey player in the world*," but it only serves to make Oliver blush. He doesn't show it often, but I'm starting to see that to Oliver, Liam's and Sadie's opinions hold more weight than even the praise of an NHL Hall of Famer.

The garden gate opens again, a loud creak that makes both kids jump a little, before my mother appears, tucking her hair back as she slowly steps out in dirty overalls and equally dirty green gardening boots.

"Who is that?" Liam asks, holding on a little tighter to me, his mouth nearly in my ear and voice a little too loud.

"That's my mom."

"Oh." He nods and looks again at her, like he can't peel his eyes away from her.

While Liam is almost plastered to me, like he wants to be invisible, Oliver is suddenly standing like an army sergeant, glancing warily at her as if he's worried she'll get too close.

I'm starting to think that there's something deeper here, anxiety spooling out through my body, tightening like a noose at my neck.

"Is she nice?" Liam asks, his voice a little softer as my dad turns and waves to my mom, who stays there.

"Yeah," I say gently, fighting over the lump in my throat at the question. "She's very nice. She would love to meet you."

Liam nods, but his eyes never leave her.

"That's nice," Liam mumbles quietly.

"What is, bud?"

He tucks his head into my neck. "That you have a mommy. And a nice one."

I have to close my eyes for a second. *Fuck fuck fuck.*

"Yeah, bud, I'm very thankful." I am now, and always will be, because this kid is hurting my soul.

My mind wanders back to Sadie again, the distraught look on her face at the very thought of asking for help—anger mixed with fear roils in my gut at the thought that keeps circling and I can't let it go now.

Sadie is more alone than I thought.

Previously, I might've seen her as stubborn, but the words from her brothers, the image of her house . . . it's plaguing my brain like a waking nightmare.

I decide to carry Liam inside, since I suddenly don't want to set him down. His arms are wrapped around my neck anyway, head ducked—the first time I've seen the brave little one shy about anything.

Oliver walks just a step behind us as we approach the door where my still-smiling mother stands.

"Hi there," she offers, her attention solely on Oliver first. "I'm Anna, Rhys's mom. What's your name?"

"Oliver. I'm Sadie's brother."

My mom smiles brightly. "I've heard a lot about you. My husband says you're a really, *really* good hockey player."

"A star," my dad says, standing at Oliver's back.

Oliver blushes under her attention, rubbing a hand over the back of his neck and nodding. My mom doesn't reach for him, but I see her hesitate with her hand raised like she wants to. Maybe she can see what I see, what my dad clearly sees—that he's a bit like Bennett, tense and desperate for space, at least physically.

"And who are you, love?" She gentles her voice further, stepping up to look at Liam, who's ducked his head back into my neck while his little fingers play with the collar of my shirt.

He doesn't speak, just continues to glance at her, like he doesn't want to look away.

"Jesus," Oliver sighs, rolling his eyes while his cheeks blush like he's slightly embarrassed by his brother's hesitancy. "You can tell her your name."

"Liam," he finally murmurs, slinking from beneath my chin just barely. But I know, if I look at him, I'll see the same stars in his eyes from before, like she's a magic fairy who's come to grant his every wish.

"Liam," she savors his name and I watch him raise his head from my shoulder in response. "It's nice to meet you. Let's go inside now and have some dessert, yeah? You can help if you want."

"Really?" His eyes go wide. "I can help?" He wriggles until I finally let him down from my arms.

Liam pauses, staring at her outstretched hand and raising his, but checking back over his shoulder to his older brother. There's a hint of fear there, like he's just trying to make sure that this is safe, that it's okay.

Oliver nods, and Liam grasps onto my mom's hand as they trip forward into the kitchen as she explains how *delicious* biscuits with chocolate gravy are, despite sounding not-so-appetizing.

Oliver hangs back, just behind me as Mom and Liam step forward, Dad following close behind after I nod at him to go first. I wait for the kid, settling into a slow pace as we all take the long way through the garden and into the house.

My phone vibrates in my pocket, and I check it to see a text from Ro—several crazy, but happy-looking emojis followed by an all-caps text that she would make sure Sadie got rest.

You should make an effort to be here, I'd chided Sadie the first day we spoke. The memory of my words makes me trip in my steps. Oliver looks at me for a moment and the guilt hits harder.

Selfish, entitled asshole.

I can feel it again now, that voice that leaves me alone whenever Sadie's entire presence mutes it. The dark thing that has lived under my skin ever since the day I hit the ice and woke up to gauze all over my face and my body, struggling to breathe.

The anger only faded, until it was just emptiness, and I missed the anger.

Now, it's only self-hatred left.

But I'm learning the tools for it. I'm also learning that I might need better tools when it comes to handling Sadie Gray.

"Oliver . . . is your dad normally like that?" I ask.

He tenses for a moment and avoids my eyes as he nods.

"Your mom?"

It's hard to talk around the knot in my throat, but I try to clear it, try to keep my wits through this land mine of a conversation.

"Sadie and I had a mom, but she—" He shrugs. "She didn't want us. So my dad kept us when she left." There's a begrudging defensiveness to his tone.

We walk a few more steps up to the door. He stays just outside of the open door, the smell of dough and melting chocolate slowly beginning to permeate the air, and his expression is one of anxiety mixed with fear.

But I'm patient. I'll be patient with him just like I will be with Sadie.

"Are we staying here long?"

"As long as you want" slips from my mouth before I can think twice.

Oliver nods, though, accepting it. "You should tell Ro. Maybe she can make Sissy get some sleep—she never gets any."

"Because of your dad?"

I've stepped on one of the land mines—his stance turns defensive, eyes sharp.

"She takes good care of us," he cuts back over his shoulder, like he can't quite look fully at me as he says it. He's defensive, sure, but he's scared. "Sadie—she takes care of me and Liam; and I help. We don't need anything."

He steps into the house without pausing, and I know that's all I'll get from him for now. He doesn't trust me yet, not really. But I'm keying into his words—*Sadie and I had a mom*. Does that mean that Liam's mom is someone else? Is she in their lives?

Or is Sadie alone?

Oliver hangs back in the kitchen, unsure of what to do, while Liam spends every second looking at my mom, watching her every move and following each command.

I finally get Oliver to sit at one of the barstools. He nervously taps his fingers on the marble, quiet, almost pensive in his guardianship over his younger brother.

Where Liam chats constantly, answering any questions my mom or dad throw at him, Oliver is cautious, observing my family's routine quietly. My dad grabs a bag of chips from the pantry and a few containers from the fridge, sitting at the counter and placing all the goods between the three of us.

Oliver looks at the food, then to me, before quietly informing my dad that I already gave them food and thanking me again.

"You're a growing boy, Oliver. Rhys used to clean out the entire pantry in one sitting at your age."

His hesitancy grows, but there's a little smile from my father's words working its way onto his face.

"Are you sure?"

My dad smiles a little sadly and drops his shoulders so his words are quiet enough that I can just make them out.

"I know how hard it can be to accept things when you've spent your life working very hard for very little. Saving up and still ending up hungry."

My chest clenches, and I see Oliver trying to understand how the famous man, someone he's probably idolized in his own head, was once a hungry child too.

"Yeah." Oliver swallows lightly, but he continues listening intently.

"But it's okay. I want you to eat it all. In fact"—he opens the container of buffalo chicken dip—"I want you to try it first, and if you hate it, we have tons more you can try."

Oliver softens slightly, enough to melt into it when my dad pats his back.

"Okay."

Hours later, after the sun starts to set and Ro sends me a text for where to drop them off, I load up the car with the boys and a few things I need at the Hockey House and buckle Liam in tight, still a little worried that he isn't in a car seat. I drive ten miles under the speed limit just to be safe.

We're only halfway there when I hear Liam call my name.

"Do you think I was a good helper today?"

I smile and flick my eyes to the rearview mirror. "You were a great helper, bud."

Liam turns to his brother and lowers his voice just slightly. "I hope I was the best helper today. Then maybe she'll wanna keep us, Ollie."

Oliver flips his head, his tone biting as he chews out, "Stop it, Liam. They're strangers."

I frown a little at his quick dismissal, but I know he's defensive and probably uneasy with the turn of events today. A prick of worry needles me at the two different ways the recap of today will be told to their older sister—Liam in his fairy-tale way, while Oliver might make it sound like we held them hostage.

Liam yawns audibly, slumping back and mumbling, "I think I wish Anna was my mom. I think she'd love me a lot."

Oliver looks toward me as I pull to a stop at a red light, his cheeks pink from embarrassment or anger, I'm not sure.

"Sadie takes care of us," he chides his brother. "I told you to stop saying stuff like that."

There's a warning in his tone, like this isn't the first time they've talked about whatever this is. It makes my stomach churn, worse when I see a few tears well in Liam's eyes.

"I don't want anyone to take us from Sadie." Liam looks at me, eyes still red and teary. "You're not gonna make us leave Sadie, right, Rhys?"

It's the first time the youngest sibling has looked at me like that, wary and suddenly unsure.

It's a sharp reminder of exactly how shaky their trust is, even Liam's.

"No." I check the light again, before turning in my seat to look them both in the eyes. "Never. You and Oliver will *always* be with Sadie. I'll make sure of it."

I'll just make sure she's not *alone* in this ever again.

CHAPTER THIRTY

Sadie

I'm exhausted.

I'm sure there are tears leaking from my eyes, but my skin is so clammy I don't think I can tell the difference.

"Again."

Coach Kelley's voice isn't booming; it's calm. I wonder exactly how much pressure it would take to cut him with my blade if I spun a little too close.

"I have to—"

"I didn't ask."

My lips part like I might scream, and whatever he reads on my face makes him gleam, looking practically giddy as he claps his hands.

He starts my music, the heavy beat of the instrumental piece wild against my chest, in my throat. Kelley doesn't even give me a second to find my position; he doesn't care about that. All he wants out of me is power.

And it works, like it always does. I hit every jump better than I have all night. Every pose is powerful, even thrilling. I'm electric, so much so that there's a bright smile on my face when the program ends and I head toward him.

"Feels good, doesn't it?"

I smile and nod, because it does feel good—it feels amazing. Kelley's praise is just the cherry on top. I go to grab my water, but he stops me with a hand on my arm. He clasps my chin so he can lift my head and meet my eyes.

"Beautiful, okay? You are so strong." If possible, my smile grows wider. But then he adds, "See how capable you are when you're not so distracted? Leave the stupid boy in the past, yes?"

I jerk my head out of his grasp. Just the mention of Rhys is enough for a bolt of longing to strike through my chest.

"Yes," I mutter, pulling my guards from the board they're resting on.

"Have you given any more thought to what I offered for your brothers?"

Yes, and the answer is and will always be no.

"I'm thinking about it," I lie. I haven't told Coach Kelley about the meetings with the custody lawyer, or about accidentally stumbling across Liam's birth mother and basically blackmailing her into signing away her parental rights. Not that it took much convincing. "I haven't made a decision."

He says he knows a lawyer who would help me make sure the boys go to a family who can properly care for them.

It doesn't matter. I'll give Coach Kelley every part of myself to succeed. But I won't give up my brothers.

"You know I am only thinking of you, my terror." He's called me that since I was twelve, probably because I was terrorizing every other girl in my age bracket at the time. "I have your best interests at heart." He touches my shoulder as he walks by, leaving me alone in the arena.

I sit on the bench for a long moment, trying not to feel overwhelmed by the sudden racing thoughts he's left me with. But when I realize I've left my phone in the locker room—which means I've had no contact with my brothers, or Ms. B, or Ro—I shoot up, sliding my left guard on as I step.

There's a figure quietly sitting in the stands just above the tunnel. I squint up at him in the muted light of the arena.

"You can't be in here—it's a closed practice," I grumble, loud enough to be heard.

A smoky chuckle reverberates in the empty room.

"I can see why," he says with the kind of voice that makes my subconscious scream *DANGER*.

"Who the hell are you?" I bite, feeling myself bristle like a feral animal.

He jumps over the lowest railing, which still sits fairly high, and lands with the grace of a jungle cat. When he straightens, he towers over me in black track pants and a black Dri-FIT shirt, looking so much like what meeting the devil might look like.

Especially his eyes—bright gold, almost ethereal even in the dark. His mouth is tilted half up, in a crooked grin that makes him appear like an insane *GQ* model who just finished a killing spree.

"Kane," he supplies. "And you're the little figure skater that knows all Captain's secrets."

He's unfortunately attractive, with golden tan skin and black hair that's slightly shorter on the sides and a rasping mess of waves on the top that look repeatedly combed through. His face is all sharp angles, highlighted by a scar down one side of his cheek and jaw, another nick on the side of his neck, a small one pulling at the Cupid's bow of his pouty lips.

"Are we on a fucking pirate ship? You're pulling a real evil villain thing right now."

He shrugs and rolls his eyes, still grinning, then crosses his arms casually.

"Aren't I always?" He's speaking more to himself as he rolls a stick between his sharp, gleaming teeth—a lollipop, I realize with a jolt.

Satan is sucking on a lollipop.

I almost want to laugh, but I'm anxious enough in this rink alone with him that I manage to snuff it out before it bubbles over.

"Look, I don't know who you are or what your deal is, but I've got all the annoying assholes I can deal with right now, okay? Move."

"Does your perfect little boyfriend know that your coach over-trains you?"

I growl, which in this face-off probably looks like a feral toy poodle barking at a German Shepard.

"One, he's not my boyfriend—"

"Does he know that?" he asks, removing the lollipop. It's purple, so I assume it's grape flavored. He swirls it on his tongue before biting lightly on the stick as he smiles.

"And two, my coach doesn't overtrain me. I'm just the best one on the team." I grin brightly at him, eyebrows fluttering with my taunt. "Jealous? What? Is your coach too busy with his star center to mess with whatever the hell you are?"

He smirks, eyes like fire. "Considering I'm on this team *at all*, I don't think Coach gives that big of a shit about Koteskiy."

I wait for a moment, trying not to let my confusion show. I'm not very good at it.

His eyes light up. "Oh my God." He laughs, and I get that same flash of a sinister comic book villain trapping the hero. "You don't know?"

"Know what?"

"Who I am?"

"I don't really give a shit—"

He holds a hand up, smile widening until I can see a slip of sharp canines that adds to his villainous look. "You will. Google him—or better yet, google me. Toren Kane—I've got better articles. Just see what you can find."

He pushes past me, reaching beneath the end of the home-team bench farthest from me and grabbing a bag. I realize he's putting on skates.

Dumbstruck and a little shaken by the conversation, I take off to definitely *not* google him.

. . .

I have First Aid Kit blaring, windows rolled down so that by the time I stop in my assigned parking for the dorms, my cheeks are pink and flushed from the wind.

I'm rushing, and very nearly forget to put my car in park before lurching out and toward the dorms, catching the door from someone on their way out.

I live on the third floor, but I take the stairs instead of the elevator to avoid any waiting time.

I have exactly *zero* texts from Ro or Rhys, which gives me just as much anxiety as if I'd missed an emergency text. But I'm already extremely late for my meeting with the lawyer. I spent most of my definitely-speeding drive here planning exactly how to beg Ro to bring my brothers food and spend the night with them at our house—something I would *never* ask her to do otherwise—so that I can still possibly try to make the meeting.

When I burst through our door, Ro is in the kitchen. The smell that wafts over is mouthwatering.

She gives me a bright, beaming smile that I definitely don't deserve, considering how many of her texts and calls I've let go unanswered as of late.

"Hey," I drag out, slumping against our wrapping-paper-decorated door.

I wait for the onslaught of noise from the boys that is normal for nights they spend here.

Ro's got a wooden spoon in her mouth, like she's just finished tasting whatever's in the pot on our sketchy stove. A bright orange scrunchie is keeping her hair up high on her head.

"What's wrong?" she asks, mumbling around the spoon as she

drops everything she's doing and comes toward me. "Everything is okay."

"No." I shake my head. "Where . . . The boys. They aren't here? What the hell?" I rake my hands through my hair, pulling out my bun and redoing it again. "I need to call Rhys, and then after I'm done losing my shit with him, I *have* to meet with the lawyer—"

"Hey. It's okay—my, uh, seminar went over and Rhys offered to grab food with them." Ro smiles, but there's a hesitancy in her eyes. "Actually, I'm going to go pick up the boys in, like . . ." She glances at her watch. "An hour. Trust me, he's probably showing Oliver some cool hockey moves while Liam laughs like it's the funniest thing ever."

I take a deep breath, trying to calm my racing thoughts. Because she's *right*; as much as I'm furious with the hockey boy haunting my every thought, I do trust him. Especially with the boys.

Even if this feels like a trial by fire.

"And I made *you* dinner. So eat," Ro says, shuffling me over to sit at our little table. "And then sleep. I'll call the lawyer and reschedule. Trust me."

There's a sinking feeling in my gut, a slight unease. But if there is anyone in this entire world I trust, it's Ro.

"Okay."

"Good." She smiles. "I'll take care of everything, okay? Now eat."

I smile as she sets a heaping plate of chicken pesto pasta in front of me. "Smells amazing."

She bats her hands at the compliment. "Yeah, yeah—you know cooking isn't my thing. But I need to keep my little skating rock star fed."

She sits to eat with me and we chat, light and absentmindedly, avoiding anything too deep. It feels good, and I find myself relaxing and getting more tired as I polish off the entire bowl. Soon after, Ro leaves to get the boys and I set up their cots in my room, laid out like a big pallet on my floor.

It used to make me happy to look at it, because I knew they'd be here with me: safe. Now, it fills me with dread. Can I do this? If I get custody of them, can I even stay here?

I pad to the shower as I think about it.

I know the answer already, which is why I overloaded my courses this semester to try to graduate in the fall. But I'm just avoiding academic probation, barely clearing my check-ins with my counselor and Coach Kelley. Which is ridiculous for a simple communications major.

By the time the shower goes cold, I'm standing dead on my feet. So I laze to bed, only waking briefly when I hear the pitter-patter of Liam's feet.

Oliver crashes to the floor almost instantly, quietly begging Liam not to wake me. But Liam ignores his plea and walks right over to my bed. I shut my eyes tight, feigning sleep, and he presses a gentle kiss to my forehead before whispering, "Sweet dreams, Sissy."

I don't know how I'll manage it. But I know I *will*, somehow.

Because those two boys deserve so much more than this.

CHAPTER THIRTY-ONE

Rhys

It's Thursday night, which usually means my friends and I are out at a team dinner or floating through a few parties. Nothing too crazy, because we often have to travel on Fridays, but something to get everyone excited in a controlled environment.

Tonight, however, Freddy, Bennett, and I are hosting most of the team at our house for dinner, drinks, and bonding.

Holden even invited Kane.

He ran it by me first, in a stumbling phone call that made me feel strangely guilty. He wasn't trying to take sides; he was actually doing his job—getting to know his defensive partner.

Kane didn't show, and I see the slight disappointment on Holden's face when he looks at the empty seat next to him that he insisted people save for our missing teammate.

Now, dinner is over, but we sit with dirty plates and full bellies, laughing and talking. And even though I don't participate as much as I did before, it feels . . . normal.

A loud, swift knock interrupts the laughing, and Holden looks up at me before pushing back his chair and offering to get it. I know he's anticipating the black sheep to have finally made an appearance. But after only a few moments, he comes rushing back to me.

"Who is it?"

"Um." He rubs the back of his neck. "It's Sadie, the figure skater? She asked to talk to you."

I feel a brief flare of irritation that everyone seems to know her—the irrational part of me wants to take her and her brothers and keep them for myself. Still, I nod and stand, trying to stop my shaking hands. I breeze too quickly toward the door—so quickly I jam my hip into the entryway table where all our keys and wallets lie.

Cursing lightly, I pull open the door, a little miffed that Holden closed her outside instead of inviting her in.

And she's there.

Beautiful—like always—in a way that catches in my throat.

Her hair is down, damp, and I want to touch it because I know how silky it is after she's showered. Her skin looks a little pink, sensitive in the wind, and there's that stupid divot between her brows that makes me nearly sigh. I start to wonder if cartoon hearts are popping up over my head.

Everything in my system calms.

It's never like this with anyone else. Absolute peace. It leaves me full, unprotected, unaware of anything except the softness of her skin and the hard pillars of stone that guard her heart. And how much I want to sink into her body or nip at her neck—leave some kind of evidence that I've affected her as much as she has me.

"Hey," she starts, her voice gruff. I can't tell if she's going to cry or yell at me, but she doesn't sound happy.

"Hey?" I say, but it comes out like a question. "Do you want to come in?"

A loud laugh rumbles like thunder from the kitchen and she winces.

"I didn't realize you'd be busy—I mean, God, that sounds so conceited—"

It doesn't. It sounds *good*. Like she thinks she could show up out of the blue and I'd drop everything for time with her, and she's right. It's just how our arrangement was before—and still is for me.

I don't give a shit what's happening in this house, she's the first priority I have.

I don't care if she never wants to touch me again. I won't leave her alone when it comes to her brothers and whatever is going on with her dad.

So, I reach for her wrist and gently tug her inside, closing the door behind her before I back up to give her space. I know her enough to *know* she needs it.

"Okay, Gray?"

It slips from my mouth before I even think about it.

Her face crumples, tears weaving down her cheeks as she breaks into slightly shuddering sobs—like she's holding back a complete meltdown.

"Why did you take my brothers to your house?"

My eyes widen. This isn't what I expected her to be upset about, but if I've crossed a line—

"I just got them some food," I whisper, crossing and uncrossing my arms. "Ro was busy, and I didn't have anywhere else to take them." It doesn't matter how soft and understanding I make my words; I still watch them hit her like a slap.

"You could've just called me. I mean, why didn't you? You didn't have to be the fucking knight in shining armor—"

Sadie stops, and I can see the anger slip over her skin like a veil. But she looks exhausted, so the fury is almost too weak to hide the pain in her eyes when she stares back up at me.

"I was just trying to do the right thing," I say, trying to get her to understand.

I prepare myself, knowing what's about to happen.

"Is that an accusation? Am I not doing the *right thing*?"

"Sadie—"

"You have no *right* to judge me."

I'll take all the anger she needs to release; I'll be her punching bag if I need to. If it helps. I don't care, as long as it wipes that despairing, empty look from her eyes.

"I am not some charity case for you and your rich little family to rescue. We don't need your help. I can take care of them by myself—I've been doing it for years." The last word is a ragged sob.

The match is lit; fury, dark and coiled, releases through my veins as the implication of her words takes root.

For years. It echoes in my head like a pounding war drum.

"You shouldn't have to. Not alone," I snap, but my voice doesn't rise even a notch. "You're not their parent, Sadie."

"I am!" she shouts back, and I realize that there is only silence behind me. "For now—I am. I'll be whatever they need."

I lower my voice, hoping she'll follow suit.

"I just wanted your brothers to be safe. And Oliver wanted you to get some rest. They are worried for you—Oliver probably more than he worries for himself."

"Stop."

I step forward, crowding her just slightly toward the door. "Be mad. Yell at me if you want, but it's not going to stop me from caring, and it's not going to stop me from trying to help you, no matter how many times you push me away."

"I—" She lets out another shuddering breath, and I wonder if she's ever felt as helpless with my demons as I do facing hers now, worried that any moment is going to devolve into panic.

"I didn't come here t-to yell at you." She swipes at her eyes, her chin tilting down. But I catch a glimpse of her resigned features.

Shame.

That's an emotion I'm all too familiar with.

"Sadie," I whisper, raising my hand just slightly. Her pretty gray eyes flick up to me, a softness appearing in them as she takes me in. It makes my chest tight. "Why did you come here, Gray?"

Her throat works. The slim column of it is distracting enough that I cup her jaw, letting my fingertips dip to the skin along her neck.

"I don't know how to say it," she grumbles with a little half-whine, half-sob. It brings a strange smile to my face, and she mimics it slightly.

"Just try."

It takes a long moment, but she does.

"Besides Ro," she starts, "no one has ever done anything like that for them. For me. No one cares, and I . . . I'm sorry. That text—"

My brow furrows, but I can't bring myself to care much about it when I'm touching her now. Who cares what she thought weeks before? She isn't pushing me away now.

"I think I was trying to keep you away from all that."

"All what?"

"My life." Sadie shrugs, and then her hands grasp my wrists. "And you still just . . ." Again she finds no words, but she shakes her head and looks up at me in a way I'm not sure I've seen from her before.

She looks . . . wonderstruck. Like she's seeing something for the first time. There is still that softness that's new to her features and I desperately want to put this moment in a snow globe so I can see this, us in this semi-embrace, forever.

Too soon though, she pulls back.

"So I just . . ." She shakes her head, looking a little dazed. "Sorry. I didn't come for this. I-I came to apologize, and to say *thank you.* So thank you."

She turns to the door. I can feel her slipping away, and I don't want her to. I don't want to do this dance with her anymore. Even if I never see her again, I won't be able to stop wanting her.

"Sadie?"

She spins back to me, the divot forming between her brows. "Yes?"

"I don't want you to keep me away, okay? I want to be part of your life."

"No," she chokes out. "You don't, Rhys. It's messy and way too complicated."

"I don't care."

"Rhys."

"Sadie, if you told me you were joining the Witness Protection Program, I'd ask, 'Where are we going?' and 'Can I pull off a beard?'"

It makes her laugh, and the sound turns my skin to gooseflesh.

"Gray?"

"Yes?"

"I want to kiss you."

If she rejects me again, I think I can take it. In fact, I worry more that, if she lets me, the dark thing that lives in me will just want to take and take and take from her. I worry I will be too much, and yet still not enough.

Sadie doesn't speak anymore, just takes deep breaths with her mouth parted as we stare at each other.

And then she jumps for me.

CHAPTER THIRTY-TWO

Rhys

I catch Sadie easily, like I've been doing it my entire life. Her legs wrap around my waist, tight enough that I wonder if my belt will leave an imprint beneath the leggings on her pale skin that I can trace later with my mouth.

Her mouth slams into mine with no hesitation, no battle for control. Just pure want, affection, and admiration pouring from her lips and sinking so deep into my skin that I know I'll never get her out.

I don't want to.

I cup her ass, squeezing because it's impossible not to, keeping her on me even as I pull away from her mouth to eye the stairs. I climb them, hoping I don't send us both careening back down in my clumsy hurry.

She never stops kissing me, her mouth achingly sweet in little presses and licks against my neck, my chin, and my collarbone. Her hand tugs lightly at my button-down and I'm worried she'll rip the buttons off in her haste. I think I'd like her to.

I slam into the side of my doorjamb, knocking us both into the door and wall like a pinball in an old arcade game.

"Shit," I curse, pulling Sadie off my neck to make sure she isn't hurt.

She's smiling, teeth bright against lips that are now flushed and swollen. I want to make every part of her flush to match the slight pink running down her cheeks, neck, and toward her chest that I can just see beneath the white long-sleeve shirt she's wearing.

"Sorry. You okay?"

Sadie laughs and leans in to kiss me again, tightening her legs around my waist. The groan that pulls from my mouth doesn't sound human, but I can't help it.

Her laugh. Her smile—that damn mouth of hers.

I kick the door closed behind us and toss her lightly onto my bed.

"Where are your brothers?" I feel like kicking myself for asking in the middle of this moment, but I'll be damned if I take any more time from them.

"With Ro at the dorms."

She's stripping before I can say anything else, her shirt disappearing somewhere off the end of my bed, leaving just a thin blue bra in its place. It looks soft, and I find myself frozen, waiting to see what happens next.

I've dreamed about this moment for months; dreamed about Sadie for months. It feels surreal to really have her *here*.

"Take off your shirt," she demands. My hands slip as they work furiously at the buttons, and I'm sure the lack of coordination isn't a turn-on. I slow down as I slip my shirt off and lay it across the desk chair in the corner.

I reach for my belt as I settle just in front of Sadie's perch on my bed. But her hands knock mine out of the way, reaching for the buckle and slipping it loose. My belt hits the ground with a *thud* that I barely hear over my racing heartbeat.

My jeans come off, leaving me in only black boxer briefs. Sadie pauses before her hand tentatively reaches for the bulge beneath the fabric.

She's touched me many times, always with her hand, usually while my fingers played between her thighs; but this feels different.

She grips along my length, caressing me slowly.

Then, Sadie peers up at me. Gray cat-like eyes and a patch of freckles I know better than the back of my hand. Her mouth parts, my name whispered like a caress before she reaches for my waistband. A determined look passes over her face, making that crinkle in her brow appear and I'm suddenly worried I'll come before I'm even inside her.

I pull her hand away—ignoring the little frustrated growl she releases—and step closer, moving over her.

The lamp on my nightstand provides the only light in the room, making a dusk-like glow around her as I press her back into the mattress.

"Your bed is so comfortable," she moans as I settle my weight between her thighs.

"Sleep here forever, then," I whisper, pressing a soft kiss to the skin beneath her ear. I can feel the goose bumps ripple across her arm where I rub up and down her skin.

My hand trails up her shoulder and pulls the thin strap of her bra down until the soft, scanty fabric reveals her small breasts to me. I suck in a breath at her perfect, pinked skin, dragging my fingers across her little pink nipples.

"S-so good," Sadie whispers, her hands stretching up into my hair and pulling gently. I smile, obliging her silent demand and pressing my mouth to lick gently across her nipple.

She cries out louder than I'm expecting, and my hand closes over her mouth as I look at her, grinning wildly.

I hover over her and lean in toward her ear.

"The entire hockey team is in my kitchen," I whisper. My hand trails along her side to tuck against the soft fabric of her thong and tug it down over her hips. "So maybe I should let you scream as loud as you want, Gray. Then there'll be no mistaking who exactly you belong to."

She shoves my hand off her mouth but grips it in her own like a lifeline. "Oh God," she whimpers. "Rhys."

"Fuck, I love that."

She says my name again as I press my fingers against her, finding her hot and wet. I glide into her easily, still as shocked by how perfect she feels as I was the first time kneeling beneath her in the showers.

She comes, a keening sound bursting from her lips before she's sucking on air, pulling my hand to her mouth to bite on my fingers.

I want to be inside her so desperately I have to close my eyes and focus not to spill in my boxers like a teenager.

I *know* I can love her. I just don't know if she'll let me. But for now, this—her like this for me, soft for *me*—that's enough.

As I slip off my boxers, Sadie slides her bra completely off, leaving her bared beneath me. I lean over her to grab a condom from my nightstand and take a minute just to admire her, the back of my hand coasting over her stomach before I grip her hip.

She's staring too, but there isn't that fervent need in her eyes like there usually is, like she might explode if I make her go any slower.

Her small hand grips my chin lightly—the move so similar to the times she's attempted to take control before. But then her soft mouth parts on a breath and she asks, "Are you sure?"

My chest aches and I copy her move, except my hand caresses and cups her cheek. "I've never been more sure of anything."

I almost say *I love you* but manage to strangle the words in my throat because I know she'll think it's ridiculous.

Sadie smiles at me, her eyes vibrant in a way I rarely get to see, before they haze over at the first push of me inside her.

"Fuck," she gasps, her hands pressing my shoulders for a second. I pause, a mix of apprehension and pride swirling. "God, I really forgot about how big you are. You're going to tear my poor pussy."

I kiss the bridge of her nose, slowly sliding in another inch. "Don't be ridiculous, *kotyonok*. You can take it."

She pulses at my words, moaning as the discomfort disappears and a little writhe of pleasure moves through her body. Another moan pours from her as I press all the way in.

"Seems like your pussy *wants* me," I manage to grunt, but my voice isn't rasping with sex like I intend. It's grappling for some semblance of control as she grips me like a vise.

"*I* want you," she clarifies, and it breaks the leash.

My hips snap, working into a steady, quick pace.

It's almost ridiculous how much such a little thing can move and wiggle around beneath me. She's driving me insane, to the point I snap my hand out and steady her with a light grip on the back of her neck.

She reaches to pull me closer, forcing my weight more heavily onto her. I falter in my perfected pace, barely holding myself up on a knee.

"I'll crush you," I say, chuckling into the mess of her hair tickling my nose and pressing my hand to the mattress to lift myself up.

"I don't care." She smiles with a little giggle. "Please. Harder."

Please. Giggles.

It's never been like this before, so simple and perfect and playful. More than sex; something else is forming between us.

I work my arms around hers like a snake, winding around her waist easily. I lift her off the bed and into my arms, so she feels closer to me without my entire body crushing hers.

The strong muscles of her legs grip my waist in a way that's so comfortingly familiar, I nuzzle into her.

"I'm gonna come," Sadie says, her tone so breathy it's almost a whisper.

"Come," I demand, my hand gentle against the top of her sex between our bodies. "That's my girl. So good, baby."

My words only drive her off the cliff faster, and I'm leaping right behind her, my body frantic with life and feeling and everything I've buried as I catch her mouth and move her hips up and down my length, coming so hard I'm sure I'll black out.

When it crests, I keep her close, and she wraps her arms around my neck, skin damp. Her head falls back against the cradle of my hand, eyes lazy as they take me in. She's sleepy and sated, but I'm still wired—peaceful, but desperate not to take my hands or eyes off her for a second.

This is where she usually disappears, and I'll be damned if I let that happen.

"Shower?" I ask, combing back her hair. She nods and doesn't wiggle or complain even once as I lift her and carry her to the bathroom. She only lets out a hiss of breath as I ease out of her and lean her body against the cool tile wall of the shower, making sure the water is warm enough.

I step under the spray first, pulling Sadie carefully so that she's the one under the water. I use my soap and hands to suds up her body, gently cleaning and slightly playing with the tender space between her legs until she's gripping my shoulders with her hands, digging in her stubby little nails.

I make her come again, slow and soft, and she rests against me as I wash her hair. Her eyes never leave mine, despite the languidness of her body; she seems in awe of me.

It makes my chest throb.

The way I feel about her is real, so deep it feels like a cord looped from inside me to her, tethering me to her. But Sadie's an enigma, all steel walls and eye rolls. I don't know how deep this is for her, and I'll be damned before I scare her off with my level of need for her.

I'll take any bit of her she'll give to me—a dog begging for scraps, until she lets me in. I'm patient.

I can wait.

Once we're lying in the bed together, naked and warm beneath my blankets, I stroke her back even as she faces away from me and scoots closer to the edge.

"I'm not really a cuddler," she argues over her shoulder, biting on her lip.

"Okay," I acquiesce.

But I wake up with her little body pressed to my chest early the next morning, and blissfully cancel every alarm to fall back asleep with her in my arms.

CHAPTER THIRTY-THREE

Sadie

I had the best sleep of my life.

Considering it came right after the best *sex* of my life, I count the entire week as a win. Those are few and far between for me.

There isn't even a bite of anxiety when I wake, because I know exactly who I've wrapped myself around like a monkey.

And I know my brothers are safe.

I didn't intend to spend all night away from them, but I think Ro wanted me to, judging by her continuous stream of all-caps texts to "climb him like a tree." So, when I told her I'd be staying over, I got a stream of ecstatic emojis.

I should probably pull away, but I don't, content to look up at Rhys's soft, sleeping face. He's completely at peace, his forehead relaxed and a contented slip of a smile pulling at his mouth.

It borders on weird, I'm sure, how long I watch him. But it takes all that time to gather the strength to pull myself away. I relieve myself in the bathroom, then search for a toothbrush or mouthwash—anything to help with the grime I feel in my mouth.

I splash my face with water and help myself to a clean shirt from his adjoining closet.

Rhys pushes up on to his elbows when I come back in, a wide, dimpled smile spreading across his face.

"You have no idea how many times I've imagined you in that shirt."

I look down at the gray material, realizing it's almost identical to my usual practice shirt, but with *hockey* printed in big bold letters beneath the university logo.

"This shirt?" I laugh, walking slowly toward him.

He pushes up fully, turning over to prop himself up against the headboard. The sheets pool at his waist, hiding his very naked, very generous lower half.

"Yeah," he says, grasping for me as I crawl across the bed. Ignoring my attempt at being sensual, he sits me on his lap, just the sheet between us. "It's got my last name on it."

My cheeks blaze, satisfaction rolling through me. His hands tighten briefly on my thighs, like he's worried I might bolt at any moment. But I've decided. He's worth any of it—and if he doesn't mind how fucked up and messy my life is, how little time I can afford to lose, then I'm not telling him to go.

"Hey, hotshot."

"Hey, Gray," he says with another grin that I bottle up tight and hold close in my chest. It makes my heart skip and my body warm. I snuggle deeper into him, just breathing in the smell of his skin.

"If I'd known my dick would make you this docile, I would've done that a lot sooner," he teases. "It's like magic."

"Why didn't you?" I try to ask it just as teasingly, but there is a slip of vulnerability in the words.

Rhys angles my head out from my hiding place in his neck and rubs lovingly at my cheek. "Because it was never going to be just sex for me with you. And I knew you weren't ready for that."

My cheeks redden. My eyes burn, and I want to bolt as much as I want to handcuff him to me.

"You think I wasn't ready for your magical dick?"

He laughs, his head tipped back against the headboard, and I can't help latching my mouth to his pulse and laving over it with my tongue. His laugh cuts off into a moan, hands gripping, but not to encourage. To stop me.

"Come on," I whisper, nipping at his ear. I'm addicted to him. I want more—endless more.

"Hold on, Gray," he pleads, groaning as I suck beneath his ear. "Baby, please."

The soft name makes me want to giggle, and twirl my hair, and bask in everything that he is. I manage to only pull back and look at him, my hand splayed across his well-defined stomach, trailing blunt fingernails across his abs.

"What?" I ask.

Rhys's hand tilts my chin so he can meet my eyes. He's still smiling. I smile too.

"I just want to check in. We didn't talk last night after everything."

After he fucked me speechless, he means, in a way that made me regret everything I'd ever wasted on another man because what I had with them wasn't sex—this, it feels like even more. I didn't know it could be like this.

"I'm good," I say, probably sounding too chipper. "I'm—it was amazing."

He smirks, a little bit of arrogance pushing through. "That's not what I meant. But it's good for my ego. I haven't—" His brow furrows, mouth freezing open for a moment. "Did you really never look me up?"

"What? Now that you know my secrets, do I get to know yours?" I say it mostly in jest.

"Actually, yes."

My heart leaps into my throat. "Rhys—"

"I want you to know everything, Sadie."

He tackles me to the mattress with kisses that are cut too short when he stands. I watch him move, mouth watering at the taut shape of his ass—even more at his half-hard cock hanging between his legs. I'm distracted enough that I don't notice that he's got his laptop in hand.

He opens it, sitting next to me and typing a few things before he finds what he's looking for. Then he spins the computer toward me and steps away.

"I'm gonna shower. Just—look at the video."

The screen is paused, but the title reads "Rhys Koteskiy Stretchered Off from Kane Hit (Graphic)" and that is enough for me to feel my stomach fall out of my ass.

For a moment, I just stare, hovering the cursor over the play button until I can force myself to click it.

The video of a hockey game starts up; it's the middle of the period and Rhys looks to be on fire. His face is happy and open, but there's an underlying intensity and focus. The puck drops and they're off, speeding toward the end of the rink after Rhys wins the face-off. He's fast, beautiful, and powerful as his legs push him toward the goal. Another player passes the puck back to him and they're closing in on the boards so fast. But the other team has someone right on top of him, who goes for the hit just as Rhys passes the puck backward.

The hit is hard, like I've seen in hockey many times, but it isn't the hit that does him in—it's his bent posture as he hits the boards full speed, headfirst.

There's a large crack.

He bounces off, slams into the knees of the defenseman face-first, then falls flat on the ice on his stomach.

The silence of the arena is deafening.

But only for a moment, before the entire team starts attacking the player who hit him: Kane, I see in big, bold yellow letters on the back of his jersey.

Toren Kane, I realize.

As in, the guy at my practice.

Oh my God.

I open another tab and search his name and, just like he said, there's a wealth of knowledge there. Headline after headline—kicked out of Boston College, released from his most recent team under unknown circumstances, banned from playing in Harvard's arena. And, most recently, a surprise move to Waterfell University.

Page after page of attempted, *and denied*, interviews about his hit on Rhys.

I shake my head, feeling my fingers go numb as I click back to the main video and search the suggested list for more angles.

I find one dual view where I can see him sprawled on the ice on his stomach, out cold. A medic tries to examine him without moving him, but there's blood on the ice and they can't see where it's coming from.

Then he starts shaking on the ice, little tremors racing through his heavily padded body. A massive goalie decked in blue and gray, who I know easily to be Bennett Reiner, is next to him now, helmet off and face pinched in concern as he starts looking around the crowd for someone, all the while kneeling and holding Rhys's leg.

I see Rhys start to turn over, which is good—it means he's awake. But as soon as he pushes up, he flops backward as if his neck is broken. His helmet is off, blood pouring down his face from a pressure cut.

Terror claws at my throat, tears welling as if he's not in the next room. As if he's not okay now. I suddenly, desperately, need to put my eyes on him to assure myself he *is* still okay.

The camera cuts to the boards where both teams are standing. The coach of the opposing team looks furious, his hand gripping Toren Kane by the neck of his jersey, which is ripped from the fight. The refs come over and there's a lot of silence before a stretcher is wheeled out, several people walking with it across the ice—one of them a tall, well-dressed man crying out for Rhys.

And then the video ends.

I shut the laptop just as Rhys comes back, towel wrapped around his taut, trim waist. His hair is damp, and he shoves it back behind his ears, but a few loose tendrils stubbornly dance in front of his eyes. He tries to grin, but stops when he takes in my face.

"Hey," he coos, rushing toward me and holding my face in his big hands. "You okay?"

"Are you?" I ask, a tremble working down my spine. "God, Rhys—"

"I didn't show you that for you to pity me," he says gruffly, shrugging off my hands where they've absentmindedly started to reach for his cheeks. "I just wanted you to know."

I nod. "I know. But be real—you can't show me that and expect me to shrug it off."

"It was just a hit. Happens all the time. Hockey is a contact sport."

Doesn't matter, I want to say—clearly the hit itself is the smallest part of this problem.

I remember the look of him that first day, slumped against the boards on the ice, the fear and panic blowing his pupils wide. His shaking body, the tremble of his muscles beneath my hands.

"If it was just a hit," I start, "then what happened after?"

CHAPTER THIRTY-FOUR

Sadie

For a moment, I think Rhys will deny me and shut down the conversation.

But he only breathes a little heavier and asks if he can put clothes on. I want to say no, because covering his body feels like a crime. But his skin is also distracting, so he dresses in gray sweatpants and a shirt just like the one I stole and returns to his spot across from me on the bed.

"Everything hurt. But I don't really remember the hit. I remember seeing him coming, then the panic of not being able to see anything. I thought I was dying." He laughs, but there's no humor in it. "And then, I thought I was dying *every night*."

I wonder if I'll pass out from how hard my heart is hammering, like I'm absorbing his anxiety and fear from those days.

"I couldn't sleep. At first, it was just the flashbacks keeping me from even fading off. Then, when I did fall asleep, I'd wake up— or my mom would shake me awake—because I was screaming face down in a pillow and I couldn't breathe." He huffs, closing his eyes tightly and pulling on his shirt. "I really scared her the first month."

God.

"So I just . . . stopped."

"Stopped what?"

"Sleeping."

My chest burns at the nonchalant shrug that accompanies the heartbreaking confession. "F-for how long?"

"I could go about ten days in a row before I passed out some-where, but because I was recovering at home, my mom realized something was wrong. So I got some sleeping pills in addition to the pain pills, and a very irritating therapist."

"Like, for your recovery? A sports therapist?"

He shakes his head. "No. I had one of those, too, but my parents insisted on a therapist who focused on mental health for athletes. I can't imagine how much she cost them, but . . ." He shrugs again, and his fingers start a pattern across my exposed thigh, just brushing up beneath the pooled fabric.

It's distracting, but it's more comforting than anything else.

"Rhys."

"And then, after that . . . I just felt *numb*. Like there was this dark shadow where everything *good* was and I couldn't reach it anymore." He laughs, a real one this time, and raises his eyes to mine. "And *then*." He stretches out the word and kisses my nose. "This little punk figure skater grabbed my wrist and told me not to touch her, and I felt *something*. I was scared I'd never see her again."

"Oh?" I'm dizzy, spinning in the well of his brown eyes. I think I'll drown in his dimples if they grow any deeper. "And then?"

I probably sound like an idiot, but as long as he's looking at me like that, I don't care.

Rhys nuzzles my cheek with his, a slight scrape from the stubble that he hasn't shaved yet, and then his mouth is at my ear.

"And then, she was there with me. Again and again." But he pulls back with a serious look as he keeps his grip on my jaw and draws my eyes to his. "And then, I started to use her like a crutch."

I wince at the harsh truth. "It's okay—"

"It's not," he cuts me off. But he smiles lightly, and continues, "I'm back in therapy. I shouldn't have stopped—and I should not have used you like that."

I want to tell him that I *want* him to use me forever, but I know he's confessing something deep. Showing me that this thing between us isn't just shared pain anymore; it isn't emotional release. It's something real. Something precious.

Rhys kisses my cheek and tangles my hair around his fingers, bracing my head. "Being with you—hell, just being *around* you, was the only time I felt *anything* for a long time."

I open to him, our mouths meeting as he holds me completely at his mercy.

Because of how small I am—even though I'm pretty sure I could kill a guy with my thigh muscles if I really needed to—I've always maintained control when it comes to hookups. Being on top, making it solely about my pleasure, keeping strict boundaries about what they could touch. But with Rhys, I don't need to.

Because I trust him.

I say it aloud as soon as I realize it, basking in the light that ignites in his eyes.

He looks like he wants to say something, but shakes his head and kisses me through endless smiles and laughter, until we tumble back beneath the sheets together.

• • •

We emerge from his room in the midmorning when our stomachs are both growling and we've run out of the expensive protein bars stashed in Rhys's mini fridge.

He goes down before me so that I can freshen up—again, since we've been unable to remove our hands from each other—and call Ro to check on the boys.

She dropped them at school this morning, happy and fed, and I know they both have after-school programs until late. I also know, from the very well-maintained whiteboard calendar above Rhys's desk, that he has to get on a bus in two hours for his away game. It's at Union College tonight, and to complete the little picture of Waterfell Hockey Captain Rhys, I see a printout of the opposing team's stats with scribbled notes about different players.

Smirking, I grab a pen from the holder and scrawl a quick *Good luck, hotshot* with a winky face across the bottom.

I find my leggings from the night before, as well as my bra and underwear, but I *do* wear the shirt with Rhys's name on the back for my trek to the kitchen.

Only, when I step out of his bedroom, there's a shuffling noise. A leggy blonde is bouncing on the balls of her tall-sock-clad feet and shoving a very large black Lab away from one of the bedroom doors. She finally gets the whining animal back, murmuring softly to it before closing the door as quietly as possible. Her hair is in a high, messy bun and a massive threadbare shirt covers her like a dress. It's clear she's trying to leave without getting caught.

"You okay?" I ask, walking toward her.

But I freeze completely when she spins to me, a set of anxious, wide brown eyes locking on to me. Eyes that belong to none other than Paloma Blake.

We gape at each other, frozen and unsure.

She straightens first, pulling her back tight so her posture is more confident.

"Slept over, did you?" I say, sounding snarky, then step past her to lumber down the stairs.

"Seems you did too, huh?" She smiles, stepping with me. "I guess I should just disregard our little conversation, huh?"

My temper flares, but I don't know how amendable the team would be to me pushing their precious puck bunny down the stairs. Or clawing her eyes out—though I don't think my short nails will hold up to her sharp ones.

We've nearly reached the bottom when a booming laugh echoes from nearby and Paloma grabs my arm *tight*.

"Jesus, Blake," I snap, but her other hand slaps over my mouth.

"Can you just . . ." She sighs, and I swear if I didn't know any better, I'd think she was going to cry. "Can you not say anything about me? Just go in there and keep *all* of them distracted?"

I don't want to help her. I can't *stand* her. But she looks remarkably desperate.

"What the hell is your problem?" I whisper, my words barely audible over her firm hand.

Her eyes flare. "God, Sadie, don't be such a bitch."

"Takes one to know one," I say, pulling her hand off. "Now get out of here before I change my mind and decide to announce your presence like we're at medieval court."

She's gone faster than the words come out, but still manages to close the door carefully.

Just as she does, the player I recognize from when he answered the door last night appears around the corner. He looks like a sweeter version of Freddy, like an innocent, handsome boy instead of the cat that caught the canary.

"Hey, sweetheart." He smiles disarmingly. The pet name doesn't seem to be a flirt, more like manners from somewhere south of the Mason-Dixon. "Lost?"

"Looking for your captain, actually."

He laughs and points over his shoulder. "He seems in a good mood. I think this might be his new pregame ritual." I walk past him with a smile, but I know my cheeks are turning bright red and I curse myself again for being so pale.

The kitchen, much like the rest of the house, is fairly spotless. Rhys is standing at the bar top, Freddy sitting on the stool on his farthest side. And there's a magnificent smell permeating the air—bacon grease and maple syrup—all coming from the hulking goalie hunched over the stove with a towel over his shoulder.

Bennett looks at me with a chin lift and not even a slight hint of a smile. Rhys tracks his friend's movement, cutting himself off mid-sentence and smiling at me like we haven't seen each other in weeks.

If I wasn't already blushing, I'm full-on cherry red now.

I walk toward him, letting him decide how to play this because it's his team and we haven't talked about what exactly this is between us. All I know is that he's never going to be *just* my friend—with or without benefits. He's always going to be more.

He loops an arm around me, kisses the top of my head, and continues his game conversation with the boys in the kitchen. He doesn't stop talking, even as he lifts me to sit on the barstool in front of him and rests his arms on the counter, caging me in between them.

I listen, sort of, but perk up fully when a steaming plate of bacon strips, scrambled egg whites, avocado on expensive-looking toasted sourdough, and diced fruit lands in front of me.

"Oh, I don't have to eat first."

Rhys shakes his head. "We have very specific pregame meals, Gray. That's all yours."

My mouth is watering as I look up at Bennett. "Are you sure?"

He grunts and nods, flicking the stove off a little angrily. "There's plenty more if you want. You can have it." He smiles a little brittlely before excusing himself back upstairs.

"He's always like that," Freddy says, stealing a piece of bacon off my plate before Rhys can slap his hand. "It's his headspace before games. Sooo," he drags out, shuffling his shoulder into mine as Rhys heads over to a fancy-looking coffee machine. "What's going on here?"

"Freddy," Rhys warns above the whirl of espresso. "Leave her alone."

"C'mon, Cap. I need the juicy details." His brows wiggle exaggeratedly.

I roll my eyes before returning to chewing and watching Rhys move around the kitchen like a scene from my favorite comfort movie. He plays with a frother for a moment and my eyes light up at his concentrated face; I wish I had my phone to take a picture of it.

"Are you two dating now?" Freddy asks. He whines like a kid when Rhys reprimands him again.

I swallow every hesitation, every moment I've doubted, because I know Rhys wants more. And, for the first time, I do too.

"Yeah," I say, trying to ignore the pinch of discomfort when they both go silent. "I'm his girlfriend."

The word might feel foreign on my tongue, but the sparkling glint in Rhys's eyes and his unabashed smile—with both dimples—make it taste sweeter. He doesn't correct me, which I realize only after I've blurted the title that he absolutely could.

Oh God. My stomach cramps. *Does he want that? Or was last night just a breaking point for him?*

My thoughts start to spiral, ignoring whatever it is Freddy is saying as he stands up from his stool.

"My girlfriend?" Rhys asks, smugly hovering over my shoulder.

I can't look at him, terrified that I've made up everything in my head and that this wasn't what he wanted.

But a green mug of coffee with some sort of slightly misshapen design in the foam slides in front of me.

"What's this?"

"It's . . . ah, latte foam art. It's supposed to be a flower." He says it sheepishly, quiet.

"I love it."

Rhys kisses my neck, tucking my hair up in his hands, and I have the ridiculous urge to cut the brown strands off so he constantly has better access to my skin there.

"I don't think I've ever been happier, Gray," he whispers. Another kiss to the corner of my mouth. "My girl."

Like a balm to a wound I didn't know I carried, Rhys holds me close. And that's more than enough.

CHAPTER THIRTY-FIVE

Sadie

It's my first game, and I'm going specifically as Rhys Koteskiy's *girl-friend*. I'm half thrilled, half terrified.

We're a week into our official relationship—a week in which I've seen him only twice. But sometimes we get little seconds of time between my practices and his. Having him wait a little after his early practices to kiss me before my ice time always puts me in a good mood. In fact, I think my routines are getting higher praise from Coach Kelley the more Rhys's kisses and touches ignite me beforehand.

Still, I'm nervous.

Add to that the pressure from accidentally meeting Rhys's mom when they came into the café.

Rhys was smiling brightly and kissed me chastely on the cheek. The little slip of a woman next to him was beautiful and I was pretty sure she wanted to do a little dance when he kissed me, which made me blush further when she introduced herself as Anna Koteskiy.

I ended up taking my lunch to sit with them, feeling a mixture of anxiety and terror until I was wiping my palms on my jeans from the constant clamminess. Adult female figures in my life have been few and far between, so I wasn't exactly sure how it was best to behave.

Still, as she left, she gave me a tight, squeezing hug, not letting go until I finally relaxed.

Into my ear, she said she was proud of me. And then she was gone.

It's been three days since that interaction, and I haven't seen Rhys on his own since. The Wolves played against Colgate last night and won in the first overtime, but from what I read online, it was a pretty rough game for Waterfell and they ultimately "played like shit."

Tonight, they play Boston College, and it's supposed to be pretty important.

My brothers are coming to the game too. Rhys secured them spots and told me that they'd sit with his mom so I could spend time with Ro. I can't help but still be slightly wary of his family, and I haven't officially met his dad yet, despite the times I saw him at Oliver and Liam's summer practices.

Still, I find myself changing my outfit three times before sitting down in front of the standing mirror in Ro's room to do my makeup.

She finishes much more quickly and helps do my hair into two short, loose braids with thin blue ribbons tying them off. I feel a little funny, but . . . pretty, for the first time in a while. I wonder if Rhys will think I'm pretty like this.

My chest squeezes at the thought and makes me slightly nauseous.

As I pull on my white sneakers, Ro rounds the doorway from her closet and I pause.

"What are you wearing?" I ask, eyebrows skyrocketing at the vintage patchwork-style jacket she's sliding on: black denim with the back cut out, some sort of Waterfell University shirt stitched into its place. The sleeve is bedazzled with blue lettering spelling "Wolves" down one sleeve, with stars blazing up the other.

"What are *you* wearing?" she asks back, her arms crossing at my black jeans and white top. "I thought you were going to wear the dress."

I ignore her question. I *was* going to wear the silk dress until it didn't fit over my ass; I can already hear Coach Kelley in my ear about the weigh-in before the next comp—which is in Denver for an entire four days, so I know I'll be opting out, again.

"Did you make that?" I ask her instead of explaining.

"Yes." She grabs something off her desk, tossing it so quickly I barely have time to reach my hands out. "I made you one too."

I expect a copy of hers, but I shouldn't because this is Ro—she has more creativity and brains in her pinky that I have in my whole body.

It's a vintage bomber with a navy-and-teal-striped collar and cuffs. A large Waterfell Wolves logo is emblazoned on one side, off-set with a patch of denim, while the other side hosts a large 51 in a pearlescent white with navy stitching.

Rhys Koteskiy's number.

"I was gonna put his name on the back, too, but I didn't have enough time." She shrugs. "Not to mention I'm pretty sure I'd mis-spell it, even if I was copying it letter for letter."

Part of me wants to snip at her for meddling, for thinking this was something either of us would want. But I bite my tongue be-cause my eyes are burning with tears at the gentle thoughtfulness of my friend.

"You didn't want to stitch a number into yours?" I ask, turning back to the mirror and picking up the maroon lipstick lying on the desk.

Ro smirks, cheeks flushing. "I did," she replies, showing her sleeve where a small 27 is stitched into the star closest to her hand.

I don't have to pull up the roster to guess that number 27 is the only player she semi-knows on the team.

"For your favorite student, huh?" I laugh. "You and Freddy seem to be getting along."

"We're friends. I wanna surprise him with his test score." She smiles, and this time there's real excitement in her gaze—something that's been missing from her since the breakup. And even before, really. "He passed the midterm."

"He'll be excited to know he doesn't have a suspension coming. And maybe to shut everyone up about exactly how dumb—"

My comment makes her bristle, her face going tight as she pulls her hair from beneath the jacket.

"He's not dumb," she huffs. "He's actually really smart. I mean, look at him play—he reads every move so well. He and Rhys are, like, perfect together."

I nod, admonished, but my brow furrows. "You've seen them play?"

"I've gone to a game or two."

That's news to me, but I can't say I'm surprised I *didn't* know. With everything going on around me—skating, my distraction of Rhys, the boys, the custody case, my father—I haven't really been paying attention to what's going on with Ro lately.

"So you understand hockey now?"

She nods. "I read a few books about it at work before I went to a game. Wanted to fully understand it."

I laugh lightly, not mocking but more impressed as she wraps an arm across my back. "I've been watching Oliver play for years now and I'm still learning."

But I know Ro learned it all. She could probably coach a team if she wanted to, because she doesn't do anything halfway.

Just as we finish getting ready, there's a flurry of knocks on Ro's bedroom door, accompanied by high-pitched giggling that could only be from Liam.

Ro opens the door with a grin, shouting "Boo!" to start up another round of six-year-old giggles. She chases after him as he runs, and Oliver is left standing by the kitchenette.

"You look cool," he says.

It makes me pause for a moment, because it's the equivalent of an *I love you* and extreme approval wrapped into three words.

"Yeah?"

He nods. "Rhys'll like it."

Oliver and Liam are everything to me. But with Oliver, anything other than anger is hard to come by. Even if I know he doesn't blame me, sometimes it's hard to know if I'm doing the right thing. So I squeeze his shoulder and thank him as we all head outside.

• • •

The concourse around the arena is busy—hockey is one of the top-performing sports around here. It's Saturday, too, which means we avoid the disapproving stares from our RA with my little brothers trailing us out of the dorms.

We used to get fined for it, until Ro worked some kind of magic. Since then, I haven't heard a peep.

Rhys's mom is standing just inside the complex as we enter, a tall suit-clad man with a broad smile next to her. I know he isn't Rhys's dad, and that alone makes me pause, gripping Liam's hand in mine a little tighter.

"Oh, beautiful," she says, her hand reaching out to caress the sleeve of my jacket. "Did you make these?"

"My roommate did," I answer, a little short in my response as my eyes flicker back to the man behind her. "This is Ro."

They shake hands, and I can feel Liam trying to maneuver from my grip to go to her . . . but I won't let him go.

Thankfully, I don't have to ask about the man because Ro introduces herself to him, probably assuming it's Rhys's father.

"Adam," he says, smiling.

"Are you a coach?" I ask, brows dipping.

"Lawyer." He smiles, all calm and collected. Meanwhile, my heart rate skyrockets, and I start to feel the panic building.

A *lawyer*? Why did she bring him here? Is this . . . Is it Liam and Oliver? Are they going to take them from me?

My grip on Liam tightens, and even Oliver steps back. The man seems a little surprised at our joint reaction, but I barely notice, too busy trying to find an exit route and hoping Ro will do something insane and distract them.

"Oh," Anna says, her face dropping into pure devastation. I'm too busy panicking to be embarrassed by my reaction, but she puts her hand out toward the lawyer. "No, this is a family friend—Adam Reiner. Bennett's father."

It doesn't calm me—nothing does until Ro presses a hand to my shoulder and catches my eyes.

"They're not trying to take them from you," she whispers. But I know Mrs. Koteskiy can hear her words by the shuddering noise that comes from her.

"No, Sadie, God—I'm so sorry. No, my husband had to go to a press event and his flight back was delayed. Mr. Reiner just offered to accompany us today. Only if that's all right with you."

He's not here to take them. No one is going to take them.

Oliver keeps holding on to me, even as I release Liam so he can run to Anna Koteskiy's side and begin babbling to her about his morning. But Bennett's father—I can now easily see the resemblance in the coif of sun-kissed brown hair and strong features, not to mention the height—steps over to us.

"I'll grab us some drinks," Ro says, and excuses herself.

He smiles at her, something I've never really seen from his stoic son, but then looks down at Oliver and me.

"If you need anything—"

"We don't," I cut him off. "I mean, I have a lawyer. I have the custody papers and everything. I'm just in a waiting period."

The trial date is set for January, but my lawyer hopes we can convince my dad to sign away his rights instead. Then all I'll need to prove is that I can provide for them and house them—take care of them.

Mr. Reiner smiles again, and it's so perfect it looks like a mask. "All right."

Mrs. Koteskiy surprises my brothers with Wolves jerseys. Liam is swimming in his, but they're both happy as I leave them with the two very well put together adults.

"Do you think she hates me?" I ask, following Ro to our seats a few rows above the glass close to the goal.

Ro shoves me gently with her shoulder, but her face is open and bright. "Don't be ridiculous. All that woman wants to do is scoop you *all* up and take you home in her pocket."

"She thinks I can't take care of them—"

"No. She thinks the same thing we *all* do. That you shouldn't have to." She stops for a moment, setting a hand on my shoulder and playing with the end of my braid. "*Both* of your parents are still alive, and you're a talented figure skater and smart girl who spends the majority of her time balancing multiple jobs, keeping her brothers fed and on a schedule. You haven't done something for just you since Liam showed up."

She's right. I hate how much she's right.

"Well, except for Rhys. That was definitely for you. And you deserve it; you deserve him."

I blush again, settling into our spot and watching as the teams come out for warm-ups. We're on the home ice side, so we have a clear view as Bennett leads from the tunnel, settling his water bottle on the net and heading to a corner to stretch.

The boys look like they're running on ice, something I've always thought looks powerful but choppy. And annoying, considering the state it leaves the ice in when I have to skate behind them.

I spot Rhys easily, his hair flowing from the breeze created by how quickly he skates. He makes a loop with Matt Fredderic on his heels before they come to a stop and start a stretching routine as some of the other guys work on dribbling and taking practice shots at an empty net.

Then, as they line up to take shots on Bennett in the goal, Rhys spots me and smiles. He elbows Freddy, who glints up at us with a big grin and winks. After they take their shots, they make their way over to the glass on our side of the arena.

A girl seated in front of us goes bug-eyed at their approach, squealing to her friend about how hot they are, and it makes me smile, albeit a bit smugly.

Freddy taps on the glass above them, completely focused on Ro, who glitters under his attention before making some ridiculous face at him that has Freddy laughing loud enough to hear through the plexiglass.

Rhys only smiles at me and waves—which I happily do back.

"Get it together, son," an older gentleman to our right yells toward Rhys. "Don't let that Kane fucker get in your head. Eye on the prize."

I can see the way Rhys ignores him, but I *know* he can hear it.

My hackles are raised, ready to bite the guy's head off no matter how good his intentions are, but then another asshole a few seats past Ro and down at the glass—and decked in Boston College maroon—starts shouting at the pair.

"Hey, look at that. Their captain managed to get himself back on the ice," he yells. "How many hits does it take for you to toughen up, pussy?"

"Let's see you take one, asshole," I snap, standing and whirling toward him so hard one of my braids slaps me in the mouth.

The boys around him make a collective "*ooh*" as if they're watching a 2000s rap battle begin.

My eyes flick back to Rhys, who seems like he's torn between a swell of pride and wanting me to stop engaging with them. I shoot him a quick wink to show I'm fine, but cross my arms and meet the smirk of the heckler with one of my own.

"Is that your boyfriend, huh? Poor girl seems upset," he says. He walks up the steps and scoots past the empty seats to lean over a seated Ro and whisper to me. "Does the brain damage hurt his ability to fuck? I'll volunteer if you need—"

I kick him in the balls, swift and hard, and then watch with a satisfied smile as he trips over Ro's feet and falls on his ass. He stands slowly and ambles back down, embarrassed.

Rhys taps on the glass with his glove, waiting until the guy meets his eyes. My boyfriend is smiling, his eyes dark. "Look at her again, see what happens." The threat is clear, menacing despite the dimpled fake smile stretching his cheeks. He smacks the glass hard with the end of his stick, making the guy jump back as a roar of laughter from the audience they've drawn echoes around them.

I catch Rhys's eye again before he leaves the ice, getting a little wink from him that fills every empty piece of my soul.

CHAPTER THIRTY-SIX

Sadie

I can tell Ro is annoyed—more annoyed than I've seen her in a while.

It's the end of the second period and the Wolves are up by two. Boston College fans who made the short trip to our arena are very loud in their grumbling, but Waterfell is louder. We've been shouting sieve chants all night, singing songs and listening to some of the more intoxicated fans call out players by name and bang on the glass.

And of course, I've been watching Rhys.

He skates like he was born with blades attached to his feet, like he's got more coordination on ice than running or walking on land. His ability to read every other player—in maroon and in blue—is borderline magical.

He's just as I imagined: the boy with the blues turns gold under the arena lights and the cheers of adoring fans. His face-offs are at 100 percent tonight, and he might as well be glowing. I can see him years from now, playing professionally and lighting up the jumbotron and the screens of phones everywhere with his dimpled smile beneath his visor.

Rhys scored twice—once during the first period, skating through his team at the other end of the rink to high five and humbly angling his stick in the air in celebration. Then, again in the second period, on our side of the ice—the same celebration, only he pointed his stick right at me.

And I turned into a gooey mess.

Overall, it's been an incredible night.

Though, watching Ro fight the trio of girls in front of us would also be incredible.

Freddy scored just before the buzzer ending the second period, skating in a lunge and playing his stick like an air guitar, which got laughs out of both Ro and me—only after she finished screaming like a banshee for him.

But then, the pretty black-haired girl in a Waterfell jersey in front of us says, "God, he's so hot."

"Have you seen his OnlyFans?" the blonde next to her asks. If she thinks she is whispering, it's not even close. "If you think he's droolworthy now . . ."

"Oh my God, Ericka." The boy on her left with strawberry curls, also decked in a jersey—and a pair of black leather lugged Converse that I've been drooling over since I spotted them—sighs. "That was a *rumor*. The guy doesn't even show his face."

"*Oh my God*, Ron," Ericka mocks, rolling her eyes and flicking a piece of popcorn at him. "His *ex* was the one who told everyone. It has to be him."

The other girl pipes up with, "I don't think so. He denied it—and, I mean, he has a reputation on campus, sure, but that doesn't mean he's selling sex."

"He could if he wanted to. I mean, good *God,* he's mouthwatering. And I've heard he's not only generous, but *hu*—"

"Stop it!" Ro squeals, jerking forward between their seats so her head is level with theirs, a mop of curls cascading like water around them. "He's not a fucking object. Shut the hell up and stop spreading rumors you know *nothing* about."

She stands then, grumbling about getting something to drink, and takes off before I can ask if she wants company.

Ro looks a little worse for wear when she comes back, but it melts away as the third period starts up.

The Waterfell boys are dominating, the clock is dwindling, and I'm . . .

I'm very aroused.

Rhys is clearly one of their best players, and I can see many of the hits hammered toward him—but his teammates on every line do a good job of protecting him.

It's actually Kane who they continue to target the most. Whether because his skill and size give an advantage to Waterfell, or because of some sort of bad blood between the teams, it's surprising, considering he used to play for Boston College.

They seem to hate him.

His new team doesn't seem to like him either, but I don't blame them. Part of me wants to confront him, but the other part just hopes he leaves the team before the year is up.

I haven't told Rhys about our standoff at practice—not because I'm hiding it, but because every small piece of time I have with Rhys, I want to use for other things.

"Have you seen where they sat the boys?" Ro asks, gulping down another hard cider.

"Yeah." I nod, pointing toward where the home and away benches are. Just beyond the end of the Wolves bench, pressed right up against the glass, sit Oliver and Liam, with Rhys's mom and Bennett's father to their right. Considering the wealth of attention most of the players have given them, I'd say it's a win for them. Even this far away, Liam is beaming.

And Oliver looks refreshed and happy.

There's a loud crash, followed by the roar of the crowd as a fight breaks out on the ice and everyone shoots up to stand.

I try to decipher what happened, at first only able to spot Toren Kane locked in a brawl with one of the larger BC players.

But then I see Rhys, sprawled on his back, not moving—his chest or his head.

I'm on the stairs before I can blink, heart in my throat as I press my hands to the glass and bang on it. Rhys is nowhere close enough, but Bennett hears, turning to look over at me through his cage; I can't see his expression, but he turns away and skates toward his captain.

Fuck, it doesn't look like he's even breathing.

There are trainers already around him, quicker than I've seen in most games, and I know it's because of his history. Because he's likely already on their watch list.

Bennett is skating back toward his net, slow and graceful for all his hulking size. But he passes right by the net and stops next to me.

I feel like a child staring up at him through the glass, he's so massive. He pulls his helmet off and shakes out the sweat-wet curls, brow furrowing.

"He's okay," he says. "Sit down."

"Ben—"

"If he sees you panicking, it's gonna make him feel worse. Sit. Down."

I do as he says, nearly tripping up the stairs while I try to walk with my head half-turned back to the ice.

He does get up, and he's met with a round of cheers from everyone in the arena, both teams slapping their sticks against the ice. Still, they force him off and through the tunnel.

Considering I don't think I'll be able to breathe properly until I lay my eyes on him, I tell Ro where I'll meet her afterward. Thanks to my figure-skating competition knowledge, I know the paths of the arena well. I don't care if they won't let me see him; I just want to be close.

I pace the alcove near the locker room hallway for a minute before a hand on my shoulder makes me jolt.

I glance up to see a disheveled-looking man towering over me. It's only after I flinch backward into the wall that I realize exactly who I'm looking at.

They are copies of one another, Rhys and his father. And though I've met the man in passing, I've never seen him up close. Rhys has the same chocolate eyes that give a boyish hint even to his father's slightly aged face. He looks young and handsome, disarming in the same way Rhys is. Strong jaw, plush lips, same dark hair.

"Sorry," he says, followed by a word I don't recognize but sounds like a harsh language—Russian or Polish? "Are you here for my son?"

"Yeah, I—" I clear my stuck throat, my heart still racing. "I just want to know he's okay."

The smile he gives me is gentle and warm, and achingly familiar, except he only has one dimple.

"Come, *dochka*," he beckons with that same word, putting a firm hand between my shoulders. He guides me around the loop and through the pungent locker rooms to a smaller room fitted with a medical table and supplies.

Rhys is there, shirtless and sweating with his thick hockey pants still on. The trainer has a hand on his head, using a small flashlight to check his pupils, while Rhys recites the months of the year in reverse order.

"One moment," his father whispers to me, stepping toward his son.

Rhys pauses after June, which seems to alarm the trainer until he peeks at Mr. Koteskiy hovering over his shoulder, spotting his player's distraction.

"Rhys." His father sighs. "All right?"

"Fine." He sighs back and they sound as similar as they look, minus the slight hint of an accent from his father. "You just got back?"

"Yeah—walked into the rink to see my son on his back on the ice. What the hell kind of welcome back is that, eh?"

Rhys chuckles, just a light huff. "Just got the breath knocked from me. Is Mom freaked out?"

"*Nyet*, but there is someone I found a little flustered out there." He steps back, revealing me where I'm hovering in the doorway.

"Gray," Rhys says, a giant smile growing across his face. The trainers go back to their other tasks now that their center is cleared, so it's just the three of us. "Come here."

Two words are all it takes for me to rush to him, letting his arms wrap around me and his sweaty head press against my chest.

"You smell awful," I say snarkily, with a little huff of misplaced anger. My heart still won't stop racing.

"I'll give you two a minute," his father says, before he leaves us in the training room alone.

CHAPTER THIRTY-SEVEN

Rhys

She's perfect.

I can feel a little hint of anger rolling off her and it's intoxicating. She's intoxicating.

Sadie Gray is my fucking *girlfriend* now. I want to shout it so that my dad, the trainers—hell, the whole building—can hear me.

I open my mouth, desperate to find some reason to refer to her as *my girlfriend,* but she smacks me in the chest. Once, twice, before I grip her wrists in one hand and use the other to angle her chin away from where she's hiding from me.

"I'm starting to think I can't do this," she mumbles, closing her eyes. My stomach drops out of my ass, and I can't stop myself from tightening my hold on her wrists.

It's hockey, that dark, mocking voice that I'm realizing is a version of my own taunts. *Hockey makes you something useless and pathetic. She can see what you were before, and she doesn't want this thing you are now. The thing you'll be forever.*

But I've been through this before, and as much as I want to use her to push away the darkness, I want to love her more. So I close my eyes and remind myself that I'm okay. I'm healing.

"Sadie." I breathe, my hand tucking into her hair.

Her eyes blink open, swimming with tears, and I take in the sight like a hit to the gut. A hit she makes good on.

"You *scared* me," she cries, angry and sad, and so beautiful it hurts. "You were just lying there and I-I couldn't tell if you were okay or alive—"

She smacks me again, just a little flick of her palm to my chest.

I huff a laugh and draw her closer, kissing her cheek.

"I was just doing my Darth Vader impression. Trying to do his death justice."

She laughs, the sound almost jarring against the red splotches of her cheeks, tears still free-flowing. "I thought you weren't breathing."

"Dedicated to the role," I say with a smirk.

She shoves me off her completely, her brow furrowing as she looks me over again. I take the moment to examine her back, eyes widening and smile broadening at the 51 over the right breast of her oversized bomber.

"You look so fucking perfect, Gray. I like the jacket."

She furrows the divot between her brows further. "Ro made it."

"I want you in my jersey, too."

She ignores me, still examining every piece of my exposed skin, then flickering her gaze between my eyes. "You're okay?"

I whisper, "I'm perfect, baby."

The soft name does her in.

Her body slams onto mine, knocking me flat on the table as she climbs me. She's layering kisses on me between laughs and sobs, and I think I could stay like this forever, with the comforting weight of her on top of me.

• • •

I feel like I did before last spring, the Hockey House packed with people—half of whom I've never seen in my life—and then the circle of us: Freddy, Bennett, Holden, and me, along with most of our second line; Caleb, Sanders, and Hathaway, a freshman who's become a regular.

Sadie and Ro stopped by the dorms to get ready while we attended the postgame meetings and showered, but they should be here by now—even if it had been like pulling teeth to get them to agree to come. My parents nearly got on their knees to beg Sadie to let Liam and Oliver have a slumber party at their house, and she only agreed after coaxing from Ro and me.

She trusted them.

Something I plan to reward her for later.

Despite the win, and the fact that he only let in two goals, Bennett looks pissed.

He sips on a beer—quite a rare sight for the meticulous goalie—but he's distracted, more frustrated than usual.

A few of the football players we hang out with come to join us by the campfire, followed by Ro and Sadie—still in their homemade jackets, but now decked in scarves and hats, too.

I stand so quickly that there's a little chuckle from Holden. Paloma plants herself in his lap and tries to distract him from the conversation he was having with Freddy. But she doesn't need to, because Freddy's already up and getting laughs from Ro, who plays self-consciously with her straightened hair.

"Hey." I smile, grabbing Sadie and yanking her close to me. I plant a kiss on her forehead and rub my hands up and down her arms. "Ro, your hair looks pretty."

She flushes, but I can tell by the squeeze of Sadie's hand and her smiling nod that I did right with the compliment. Freddy tucks Ro up under his arm and yells something about beer pong, and she gives him another startlingly bright grin.

I would worry, but Freddy has assured me he's purely in friend mode with Ro. Still, it makes me slightly nervous because she

looks at him with stars in her eyes, romantic and gooey. Even if
Bennett and I warned him, Ro might still get hurt by the flirty
forward.

"Wanna play?" I ask before kissing Sadie again. She shakes her
head.

"Just wanna be around you, actually." Her hands snake up over
my shoulders and grip the muscles there, eliciting a quiet groan as
she presses. "Can we go to your room?"

"Already?" I tease, pulling back and flicking her nose. "I'm not
that kind of man, Gray."

She laughs, husky and sexy, and my jeans feel tight.

"A bathroom, then," she teases back.

I grip her chin with a growl and lean down to kiss her softly.
"Whatever my girlfriend wants, she gets."

And then I embarrass her, tossing her up and over my shoulder
as she squeals in protest—but it's lighthearted and full of giggles.

"Sorry, guys—raincheck on the beer pong. Have to go take care
of my very needy girlfriend," I announce, beaming with pride.

Cheers and laughter erupt around us as I offer a quick salute to
my team and take my light little prize, with her soft fists against my
back, through the back door and up to my room.

I set her down and move to click the door closed, and she's already stripping off her jacket when I turn back to her. Before I can
reach for her, she shoves me against the door and sinks to her knees.

"Oh, *fuck*," I breathe out, releasing the door handle and gently
scooping her hair up off her face and neck. "Sadie."

"Yes, Captain?" she says, her hands eager and swift as they undo
my belt and pull my shorts and boxers down in one fell swoop. I
can't even attempt another word before her lips—dark cherry-red
and freshly bitten—are pressed to the crown of my dick. Her mouth
opens then, tongue licking lightly before she wraps her small hand
around my cock, tapping me on her tongue.

I'm going to come, and my girl has barely done a thing.

My hands grip into her hair, massaging the base of her neck and down to her shoulders as Sadie takes her time exploring me with her mouth.

She is perfect, and I want her to know how deeply my feelings run. I'd put a ring on her finger if it wouldn't terrify her. I know she won't run from me now, but I'm prepared for the strength it'll take in the future.

"You're so beautiful," I say, pressing my finger to her cheek tenderly. "So fucking perfect. God, seeing you like this—"

She moans, and the reverberations travel up my cock like a shiver. I barely grab ahold of my slipping control as she rests her hands on her knees and looks up at me, my cock halfway out of her mouth.

She's giving me control. Our push and pull, she's letting me have this moment.

"That's my girl," I whisper, thrusting slow and gentle into her mouth. She squirms beneath the praise, like she wants to touch herself but won't. Unless . . .

"Are you wet for me, baby?" I ask, and Sadie keens, rocking slightly and taking me deeper. "Do you need me?"

She pulls off to gasp, "Want you," before sucking me right back in with an intoxicating noise.

"Touch yourself, Gray. Take what you need."

Her hand dives into the band of her jeans, shoving down. I hate that I can't see what she's doing up close, but her movements give me enough to imagine. And when it comes to Sadie Gray, I have an incredible imagination.

She rocks back and forth, grinding on her hand.

Sadie moans again, her eyes shuttering with relief before blinking up at me, wicked delight stretching her mouth in a smile around my dick.

I barely have time to warn her, trying to pull myself back, but she shoves up higher on her knees and grabs my ass, pulling me far into her throat. Stars shoot behind my eyes, and I feel lost between needing to throw my head back but desperate to keep my gaze on her as I come.

Holding back for even a second seems too long, so when I reach for her and nearly trip out of my pants, we both dissolve into laughter. I manage to take off everything but my shirt and then grab for her hips and roll her jeans down her thighs. I try not to get too distracted by the expanse of her skin beneath my hands. It's when she takes off her shirt, revealing *no fucking bra*, that I can't stop myself from grabbing her up in my arms and tossing her little muscled body onto the bed.

I press her back and try to eat her out, but Sadie begs and yanks on my arms until I pull back.

"This was supposed to be a treat," she says.

I laugh. "You're always a treat, baby."

"A reward," she groans. "For winning—though I'm thinking 'for being alive' might be a better incentive for you, Captain." Her foot connects with my chest and I wrap a hand around her ankle, raising an eyebrow.

"Don't be a brat." I chuckle. "Just tell me what you want. I'll give you anything."

Sadie shakes her head and sighs into the mattress, lolling from side to side. "You're too good to me. Stop it. I was trying to be sexy and . . . and I had this whole plan. And your stupid ass is ruining it."

The way she's whining sounds too much like her sex-kitten voice and I'm rock hard again.

"Want to start over?"

She huffs and crosses her arms, pouting like a grumpy teen—but eventually nods.

"All right. What do you want me to do, Gray?"

She lifts herself up off the mattress, her hair cascading around her in little waves that show it was braided earlier. Her hands press to my chest and push me back, to which I easily comply, stretching out beneath her as she straddles my hips. There is only a slip of silk fabric keeping the heat of her from directly pressing to my very hard cock.

Her eyes are dark beneath the smoky eyeshadow, darker as she takes me in, completely at her mercy.

"All right, hotshot." She smirks and my hips pulse upwards. "Easy." She giggles.

But Sadie turns slightly serious as she reverses our usual stance and grips my chin in her little hand.

"I want to make you feel good, because you always make me feel good. And you're not going to control it, okay? You're just going to lie back." She leans forward, pressing her bare chest to mine. "Relax," she drags out, nipping and licking my ear. "And let me take care of you."

I shudder violently as she tongues my neck, then bites down on my collarbone until I hiss.

As she draws back, she squeezes the muscles in my shoulders as best she can—her hands are too small, even if they're strong, to really do much. But it feels heavenly.

Everything she does feels heavenly, because it's her.

Sadie pushes her satin thong to the side before sliding on top of me, warm and wet and endlessly ready for me.

"God, *Rhys*," she groans. I thrust up again at the noise. "You're so fucking perfect."

Her praise feels like standing in the sun, warming me everywhere.

She rides me slowly, gripping me between her legs like a vise while praise pours from her lips like water. It doesn't matter how small she looks right now, perched on top of me like this; she could easily kill me if she wanted and I'd say thank you as I bled out beneath her.

She comes, and it's just like every time I've seen it before—like she's a little surprised, like it catches the careful, controlled girl totally off guard. It's impossible not to follow after her.

My orgasm is powerful, making me almost lightheaded as I slowly punch my hips unsteadily, abdomen clenching while Sadie slowly rides me through it.

And then her lips spread into a little sleepy smile, and she looks down at me. I'm overwhelmed with *that* feeling again—the desire to keep her here, protected and safe and mine—until I'm biting down on my tongue, desperate to shove the *I love you, I love you, I love you* back down my throat.

I'm not sure how much longer I can hold it back, but I'm desperate to keep her. And this—Sadie melting into my arms and kissing my shoulders, caressing me with gentle strokes and touches that I copy until we're lying with our heads near the footboard, whispering quiet secrets into the glittering dark—this is more than enough.

CHAPTER THIRTY-EIGHT

Rhys

We won. Again.

Fucking finally.

The team is riding the high of gaining back our winning streak, Gym Class Heroes blaring louder than usual as I walk through the tunnel into the dressing room. I smile brightly as my team smacks my back, Freddy and Dougherty skipping around and singing with a few of the more outgoing underclassmen.

Every single one of them deserves this win. It finally pushes our points high enough that we don't have to worry as much before the Cornell game next weekend. Harvard—one of our top competitors this year—still looms on the horizon, but for tonight, a win is a win.

"A motherfucking Reiner *shutout!*" Freddy shouts, whistles blaring all around as he takes the sacred knot of rope, looped from cut strands of conference-winning nets, and hands it to Bennett, declaring him our player of the game. Everyone cheers as Bennett, still in his thick leg pads but stripped down to a long-sleeve compression shirt up top, stands and accepts it with a nod.

I know better than to expect any sort of speech, and he doesn't offer anything other than, "Couldn't have done it without my defensemen and this entire team. Go Wolves." He lifts the long drape of rope before sitting back against his cubby.

Coach Harris smiles, because he knows his star goalie in the same way I do, appreciates his quirks and rituals. He's built trust with all of us, but I know personally how much he's worked with Bennett.

Coach nods at all of us once, and leaves with a quick, "Enjoy your evening, boys. Don't be stupid," tossed over his shoulder.

But it's Toren Kane, sitting sullenly in the corner with his arms crossed over his chest, sweat dripping from his wet black hair, that he pats on the shoulder as he goes.

Something pulls tight in my chest at the sight.

Freddy is already announcing the party at "the hockey dorms"—which will be massive, as our Halloween parties always are. And if the large bags of face paint that currently sit on our kitchen counter are anything to go off, he will be forcing any unprepared underclassmen into designated costumes.

We, as a team, usually go all out.

But, considering *my girlfriend* bailed on said party just before the second period via text, I have other plans in mind.

My girlfriend. Two weeks later, it still tastes just as fucking sweet.

Last night, with my face buried between her thighs, I got her to agree to attend one of my parents' schmoozy galas.

I shower quickly and change into gray sweatpants and a neon-orange shirt that says *I'm Only Here for the Boos* with a ghost sporting heart eyes—a gift from Freddy in our freshman year when I said I was too busy to dress up before we went downtown. It was definitely part of the reason he wormed his way into my heart as one of my best friends. Since then, the cheesy shirts for every major holiday have become a strange tradition between the two of us.

I'm gone before Freddy can try to stop me, only telling Bennett where I'm going. I know the drive like the back of my hand now, as I spend any of my minimal free time with Sadie—and being with her often means running her brothers around, getting them dinner or picking them up from practices.

Still, I've yet to have a run-in with her dad. Which, I'm sure, is a very purposeful thing on her end.

If I'm involved in the plans, we never end up at her house for the night. She avoids it—even if it means I end the night helping her tuck in sleepy kids on an air mattress on her dorm room floor. Sometimes I can convince them to sleep at the Hockey House, where Liam and Oliver get showered with endless attention by whatever players are there, who will play games with them until Sadie turns on her stern voice and forces everyone to their respective beds.

Beds I purchased impulsively one day and put in the unused room at the end of the hall.

I know she's home tonight because there's only a handful of reasons she would cancel. Ro, our new loyal fan, attended the game, but she gave me a quick shake of her head to tell me Sadie wouldn't be showing.

The street the Browns live on is dark, with no real decoration, all porch lights off except theirs. I knock in a pattern before stepping back so Sadie can see me in the peephole before she answers.

"Holy shit," I mutter, smiling broadly as I take in her appearance at the front door.

She's dressed in a brown, fuzzy onesie—complete with a floppy hood—with a big plastic pumpkin-shaped bowl full of candy hefted on her waist, and a tiny Darth Vader hanging on to her leg.

"What are you doing here?" she asks, but there's nothing but joy on her face, hidden lightly beneath my favorite little furrowed-brow expression.

"Who are you supposed to be?" I ask, ignoring her question completely because it's ridiculous—where else would I be but with her?

Sadie smirks, but it's Liam who shouts, "A Wookiee!" as he leaps for me.

I pick him up and follow Sadie into the house, then shut and lock the door behind me. This is the farthest I've been into her home, which is small and cold. It feels like there isn't any heat on—and maybe there isn't.

There's a set of stairs that look a little worse for wear. Directly to the right is a small, blue-tiled kitchen with cookies in a pan on the stovetop, which explains the sugary smell. To my left, I spot Oliver perched on a stained floral couch. The only light comes from a lamp on the side table and the flickering TV.

"Hey, bud."

"Koteskiy." He nods before shifting his attention back to the screen.

My eyebrows shoot to my hairline. Sadie covers her mouth to keep a laugh from bursting, turning toward the kitchen. I follow with Liam still on my hip as he tells me about trick-or-treating in the "rich-people neighborhood" and that Sadie won't let him have any more candy tonight.

I reach for a cookie off the tray, but Liam slaps my hand and screeches, "We have to sing first!"

"Sing what?"

" 'Happy Birthday'!"

"Is it your birthday, bud?" My eyes dance as I look between him and a blushing Sadie.

He laughs, bright and loud, like I've told some ridiculous joke. "No, it's Sissy's. She's . . . um . . ." He leans into his sister and loudly whispers, "How old are you again?"

"Twenty-two."

"Twenty-two," he shouts to me immediately.

My heart drops, eyebrows furrowing as I look at her again. "I . . . I had no idea."

Sadie shakes her head and crosses her arms. "Obviously, because I didn't tell you, hotshot." She shoves a sugar cookie into her mouth before Liam can stop her, smiling wickedly at him as she chews.

It might be ridiculous, but I'm slightly hurt that she didn't tell me.

Liam climbs down from my arms and demands that I get his brother so we can sing and Sadie can make her birthday wish. I take a cookie, imprinted with a little orange pumpkin, and head into the living room.

I lean over the back of the couch. *Halloween 3* is playing on the TV with that same stupid song that plagued my nightmares as a kid.

"How was your game?" I ask Oliver, remembering he had one this afternoon.

He doesn't look at me. "We won."

"Score anything?" I smirk, jostling his shoulder. He shifts to stand, coming around the back of the couch and stopping in front of me, closer than he's ever been to me. Hell, closer than I've seen him get to anyone besides Sadie and Liam.

He scratches the back of his neck before dropping his voice to a whisper.

"My therapist said Sadie probably has trauma with her birthday because when she was around my age something happened with our mom." He shrugs. "I always thought it was because Dad gets really, *really* drunk on holidays. On Christmas, he's sad. On Halloween, he's usually angry. But I don't know."

I still as I look at him, stomach sick, the leftover taste of the cookie souring on my tongue.

"But that's probably why she didn't tell you. And . . . I don't want you to be mad at her."

I try to swallow past the lump forming in my throat.

"I'm not mad at Sadie," I tell him quietly. There's a hesitancy to his stance, in every line of his face, like he wants to say more but he doesn't know how. So I take a guess. "I'm not gonna leave her, Oliver. Never, okay? She may ask me to go one day, but I will *never* be the one to leave. Not her, or your brother, or *you*. Tell me you understand that."

His cheeks blush as he angles his eyes down to the ground. "I understand."

"Good," I say, and for a moment I feel like crying. I want to wrap this kid in my arms, because his shoulders look heavy with the weight he carries—but I know he's a bit like Bennett, and he doesn't really like touch.

So I pat his shoulder once and direct us toward the kitchen, following behind him.

We sing "Happy Birthday" at the top of our lungs, and clap as Liam adds his own little verse at the end that seems completely made up on the spot, adding lots of silly noises with his mouth until he's laughing at his own joke so hard he can't keep it going.

I kiss Sadie on the temple when she reaches for another cookie and she sinks into my touch for a moment.

I'm completely in love with her.

CHAPTER THIRTY-NINE

Rhys

We're lying in her bed, just breathing each other in, and I can tell she's trying to read me.

I'm doing the same to her.

It's icy cold in this house, which Sadie explained was because their house was quite old and led to an astronomical gas bill last year; they planned to avoid using the heater this winter until they absolutely had to.

I plan on solving that problem as soon as possible.

After tucking Liam in with two extra blankets and three bedtime stories, and making Oliver swear he'd go to sleep after one more hour of scary movies, Sadie led me to her room.

It was hard—seeing the pretty blue sheets and little figure-skating trophies and medals, photos from competitions and of baby versions of Liam and Oliver—to pretend I hadn't been imagining her in this room every time I called her from the road. That my fantasies when in a hotel shower or bed at an away game weren't of me pleasuring her for hours, taking her slowly from behind while gray cat eyes looked at me over one delicate, freckled shoulder.

But that isn't what I want now.

I brush my hand through her hair where her head rests on my

chest while my other arm is wrapped around her, skating circles on her back beneath her oversized, threadbare shirt.

"Why didn't you tell me about your birthday?"

She shrugs mildly. "It never came up."

Liar. I kiss her forehead again. "Oliver thinks it has to do with your mom."

Silence.

"You never talk about her."

I can't say I wasn't expecting it, but knowing it's coming doesn't make it hurt any less as she sits up and pulls her body away from me.

"There's nothing to talk about," she snaps, whispered venom echoing in the dark of her childhood bedroom.

"Sadie—"

"Drop it, Rhys."

If she expects me to slink back and let her work whatever she's feeling out on my body—like I'm sure many boys before me have— she's about to try something new.

I sit up and lean back to relax against the headboard.

"I won't. What happened on Halloween?" When she doesn't speak, I continue. "I'm not here *just* for happy Sadie in my bed. I'm here for my frustrated, angry Gray. For my scared *kotyonok.*"

"That fucking word again," she huffs beneath her breath. She keeps asking me what it means, so I know she hasn't looked it up yet. If she knew the translation, she'd probably slap me. "I'm not scared of you, Rhys."

I wonder if she knows she's worked herself nearly into a fetal position, arms protectively wrapped around herself.

"What happened on your birthday?" I ask again. My voice stays just as gentle and soft.

She eyes me like I'm a stranger in her bed, and though the look burns, I endure it.

"My mom left when I was probably Liam's age. And then she came back. Got pregnant with Oliver, and for maybe a year . . . it was amazing. And then she just started to disappear."

"What do you mean?"

She shrugs. "She started having these, like, manic episodes. She would decide in the morning to go on a trip—it didn't matter if I had a skating competition or practice or school, she would just . . . leave. Like, gone—sometimes for weeks, sometimes for a day or two. Every now and then, she'd take me or Oliver with her.

"And then one day, Dad came home and Oliver was in his crib alone. He took Oliver to the hospital, panicked. When he called the school, he found out I hadn't been in class for three days."

My brow furrows and I resist the urge to reach for her. "Why did it take him so long to realize?"

"He played hockey back then. Nothing like your dad, but he played in a minor league and he was traveling for away games."

"And . . . Oliver?" I don't want to voice the implication.

She does. "He'd been alone in his crib for days. She left him a bottle, some cut up food, but that was it." A few tears escape her eyes, though she doesn't stop staring a hole in the sheets between us. "Oliver had to be hospitalized for days, and they were worried it would mess him up. I don't know how he's alive.

"Child Protective Services got called, but my dad and his coach helped smooth it all over. And I didn't want to lose Oliver, so I told them what I was supposed to. But they made my mom go to therapy. Me too, for a while. And things were okay for a month? I don't remember. I just remember waking up one day and my dad was crying, holding Oliver on the couch, and he told me she wasn't coming home. That we had to take care of each other now."

I take a shuddering breath, because I can *feel* that the situation with her mom isn't getting better. And I can bet this isn't the worst of the memories trapped in her beautiful mind, tormenting her.

I wonder if she's ever spoken about all this out loud. Can she feel the way she trembles so hard through some of the words that the bed shakes?

"Then, when I was twelve, I think? Maybe thirteen? She came home. It was . . . the best day ever. She picked me up from school in this shiny, red convertible and took me to the mall to try on Halloween costumes. She wanted us to match and have a party, just the two of us. We got a cake, balloons—everything.

"And when we got home, she sent the nanny home, got Oliver in his costume, and told me to go upstairs to get ready. She was going to grab some candles for my cake."

A sob wells in her throat, but I watch her strangle it down before she lifts her burning, smoky eyes to me and finishes, "I sat outside on the curb with a three-year-old Oliver until my neighbors called my dad."

"Gray," I choke out, wishing desperately I could hold her. Hell, my arms rise, like I might try, but she flinches.

I think it would hurt less if she hit me.

"When my mom left Oliver the last time, something in me knew she wasn't coming back."

She says it matter-of-factly, as if it hadn't altered her world.

"She didn't just leave Ollie, Gray," I whisper, gentle but imploring all the same. "She left you, too."

But she shakes her head. "She left me when I was much younger. She came back to have Oliver, then left him, too."

She'd been abandoned by her mom twice. *Twice.*

"And your dad?"

"He started drinking, more than he already was. Showed up to a game or two drunk and, eventually, they fired him. But that's about when Coach Kelley started helping, creating a scholarship program for me to keep skating. Oliver started hockey because the ice rink was my safe haven, so it became his, too."

I don't want to ask it, but I have to.

"Liam?"

"Um." She huffs out a breath and bites her lip. "Yeah. I don't know much. But I came downstairs one morning for school and there was a baby on the floor, next to my passed-out dad."

I swallow. "How old were you?"

"Sixteen. It was . . . scary, for a while. But I started working around then and my mom started paying child support after my dad took her to court. So he was at least sober enough to get something done." She laughs at this, but there's no humor in it.

I picture her as a sixteen-year-old girl, less angry, caring for children, budgeting, cleaning up her father even when he didn't deserve it. Protecting her brothers. Keeping them close, because there wasn't one adult in her life she could trust.

And no one was taking care of her.

No one had been taking care of her for years. That was her normal.

My chest squeezes tight again.

Not anymore.

"Can I hold you?" I ask before I can stop myself. "Please."

I wait for the rejection, for the wall of frustration—and I'm prepared to fight for her. I always will.

But she only nods, exhausted as she slinks toward me and tucks herself back into my side.

It isn't until she's fast asleep, drained but so beautiful, that I whisper, "I'll never leave you. Happy birthday, Sadie."

I swear she smiles in her sleep, but I'm borderline delusional when it comes to this girl.

"I love you," I mouth, pressing the words into the skin of her forehead, hoping that somehow, she hears them. Somehow, she knows.

· · ·

I jolt awake.

The clock on her bedside table is blinking 3:47 a.m. in a bright red font. My brow furrows as I rub my eyes a moment, trying to figure out what woke me. Did I have another nightmare? I haven't had one in months, but sleeping somewhere foreign I absolutely could—

There's a noise of shuffling, but it makes Sadie shift and curl tighter against me.

She's barely opening her eyes when I press her back into the mattress.

"Stay asleep, baby. I'm just gonna check on the boys. I think Oliver stayed up longer than he promised."

Her body rolls pliantly to the other side of the bed, and I slide on my sweatpants before heading out of the room.

Liam is fast asleep, not moving an inch as I shut his door. But Oliver is awake, standing at the top of the stairs, listening.

"Hey, bud," I whisper, worried about the angry look on his face. "What's up? Can't sleep?"

His brow furrows. "You didn't hear that?"

"I did. Did it wake you?"

He snorts. "Dad always wakes me and Sadie. Liam will sleep through anything." He eyes me up and down again. "Surprised Sadie's asleep though."

"I tried to keep her from waking up." But now I feel ridiculous. I've never had to handle an alcoholic, except in the context of drunken college or high school friends. Not an adult. "Does he . . . is he violent?"

"Not usually. But Halloween makes him angry." Oliver shrugs his shoulders and crosses his arms. "Usually he just breaks a few things and then passes out on the couch. But . . ."

"What is it?"

Oliver has that same look again, like he's not sure if what he's saying is allowed or right—like someone will be upset with him. A little like confusion mixed with anger.

"You can tell me anything, remember?" I try to remind him of my words from earlier. *I won't leave you.*

"It's Sadie's purse. I know it's downstairs still. She usually remembers to hide it, but . . ."

"I distracted her."

He nods.

Fuck. "Does he steal from her?"

"All the time. And . . . I know she just saved up enough for her tournament in December. I'm scared he'll—"

I raise my hand to stop the slight panic I can hear creeping into his voice. "I'll get it, okay?"

"What if he fights with you?"

I smile, all disarming charm. "C'mon, Ollie—look at me."

"I just don't want this to be why you leave."

Another punch to the stomach. Another reason I'm planning to never let these kids out of my sight again. I'd marry Sadie tomorrow if it meant it got them out of this damn house.

Who am I kidding? I'd marry Sadie tomorrow. Period. No stipulations.

"Let me deal with it, okay?"

CHAPTER FORTY

Sadie

I wake up to yelling.

My body jolts like I've been electrocuted. One of my biggest fears from being in this house is of Oliver's anger driving him to confrontation. Of waking up to screams and a fight between a drunken man and a child.

I have to get them out of here.

I'm flying down the stairs, two at a time, seeing Oliver at the base, angled in the kitchen. He tries to stop me, but I push past him to find my dad with a broken beer bottle held like a weapon over his head. And Rhys, palms up, arms outstretched, trying to calm him down.

My dad's gaze shifts to me and he drops his stance.

"Sade," he cries, dissolving into tears almost immediately.

I don't want Rhys to see this part. Where my dad apologizes, and cries, and begs me to help him. I don't want Rhys to know that sometimes Dad tells me he hates me because I look *just like her.* I don't want Rhys to see the way that, when I get close enough to help him, he pats my head gently or shoves my face away so hard that he once nearly broke my jaw on the cabinet.

I hate this.

"You need to go," I snap, stepping between them.

Rhys's voice turns almost desperate. "Sadie, stop."

"I can handle him. I always do—and never with your help. Now, go."

Oliver looks distraught for a moment before he storms off as I get to my dad and try to pry the bottle from his hand. He pulls it back and hurls it at the wall, screaming something about this all being my fault, before he's blubbering again.

There's glass everywhere and Rhys still. Won't. Leave.

"Sadie, be careful," he begs.

"Go. Please, Rhys. I don't need your help!"

"Please, baby. There's glass *everywhere*. Just . . . just let me help."

I whirl on him. "Stop it! I don't need you to fix me, Rhys. I don't need to be *fixed*. I have everything under control. Oliver gets to his practices and *I* make sure he has new skates and gear when he needs them. *I* do that! Liam learned how to read because I taught him— before he ever got to fucking school, because I was nineteen and I honestly had no *clue* what he was supposed to know. I didn't need your help then, and I don't need it now."

I wait for him to leave. To tell me that he knew I was like this, worthless, terrible. A bitch, too angry and unlovable.

But he only stands there, quiet and solemn.

My breath is stuttering and I'm pretty sure I'm crying, which is embarrassing, but I keep my face furious, arms crossed. I want him to leave, I need him to—

He grabs the tiny broom and pan hanging off the wall, and starts to sweep up the glass, on his knees in front of me.

"Rhys," I nearly shout it this time, my fury only ratcheting higher.

He shakes his head before finally looking up at me, all dark chocolate eyes and a stern expression I rarely see from him. "No. I'm not going fucking anywhere. Not now, not ever. We're going to talk about it once this is dealt with. Now . . ." He shudders out a breath and rolls his massive, muscular shoulders. "I'm going to clean this glass up, because if you cut your fucking foot in here—even a goddamn nick—I don't think I will be able to hold back from kicking his face in, okay?"

Every word sounds calm, almost serene, but I can see his own fury beneath the surface. Like he's holding it back because he *knows* I can't handle it.

"Okay," I say, surprising myself.

My dad is nearly passed out already, leaning against the wall behind me, now silent but for snores. I grab his ever-thinning frame and walk him into the living room, mindful of the glass, before tossing him onto the recliner and hoping he stays passed out.

"Rhys—"

He holds a hand up to me and looks over his shoulder. "Go upstairs, Sadie. Wait for me there. I need a minute."

• • •

My skin feels like it's going to start melting off, and I'm quite sure I'm on the verge of a psychotic break when Rhys finally comes upstairs.

He closes the door behind himself, then turns completely toward it and rests his forehead against the wood. He takes several long breaths before he turns around and walks the space of my room, avoiding my eyes. He places something on the desk—my purse, I realize, and my stomach clenches.

"Are you leaving?"

That makes him look up, then away again. I feel that panicked breathing rise, like I'm drowning and kicking for the surface. I want to grab on to his wrist and beg him to stay, so I cross my arms to hold myself back.

"I don't know what I'm going to have to do to prove to you and Oliver that I'm not leaving—and honestly, I don't care what it is, I'll do it."

"Wait . . ." I stall, stunned and lost for words. "Then . . . then why won't you look at me?"

Loathing, self-hatred. If you feed them enough, they grow like irremovable vines. Mine grew thorns and wrapped around me as a kid, and no one has ever bothered to try to get in. Until now.

"Because, Sadie," he grits out, in a harsher voice than I've ever heard him use—especially with me. "If I look at you, I'm going to see that fear I *clearly* saw when you walked into the kitchen. I can't get Oliver's face out of my brain, and now yours. And if I see that, I don't think I'll be able to stop myself from confronting *him*."

I don't say anything. I barely breathe, as if any noise might ruin this moment.

You ruin everything. Look at him—the golden boy who's never angry, suddenly furious. You take everything good and ruin it. Oliver's next, already so jaded. Liam won't be far behind.

I close my eyes.

"Look at me," he commands, and I do, instantly. He's pacing at the foot of my bed, aglow in the muted light of my bedside lamp. He looks larger than life, he always has. Like what I imagine the children of ancient gods might have looked like, great in some way that marked them as different from mere mortals.

"I thought you were broken like me," I whisper, the words pouring out. "But you're not. You're . . . Rhys, you're amazing. You're everything to the people around you, even the ones who don't know you. Out there? On campus or on the ice? You're a shooting star. Fucking golden. And you might've been hurting when you met me, but . . . you're getting better. And my life is going to be like this for a long time.

"Like—I'm in the middle of trying to win custody of the boys, trying to graduate early this semester so I can get a job and prove to a bunch of adults that I'm enough to take care of Oliver and Liam, like I already have been. And I—" My voice chokes off, because I realize I might've been about to say something insane. "I care about you enough to see that you're on your way to this massive, loud, amazing life. I—"

Rhys raises his hand to stop me, and I fall silent. Partially because I don't *want* to say what I was about to say. I selfishly *want* him, always, no matter that I'll always be pulling him down or holding him back.

"I'm gonna say something now, Gray. And I need you to hear me. Really hear me, okay?"

I nod.

"I love you," he says, and he's smiling—both dimples glinting. As if I didn't just spill the mess of my life, first about my mother, then my drunk father trying to attack him—and now with my speech about how terrible it is for him to have me in his life.

My anger has never worked on Rhys; neither have my efforts to shove him away.

So I listen, my heart hammering so fast I'm sure it'll sprout wings and soar from my chest.

"I love you. I love everything about you. I love your anger and your snark. I love the way you skate—like you're full of fire. It makes me remember when I fell in love with hockey. I love how you take care of your brothers, how you protect and love Ro. I love the way you get that frustrated-confused look on your face—the same one you have right now—with the little divot between your brows."

I laugh with him now. My eyes never leave his face, even as he tilts his head back and smiles again.

"And nothing—no dark part of you, or your life—will ever change that. So, like I told Oliver, if you don't want me anymore, that's something I'll have to deal with. But there will *never* be a day that I do not want you."

He's at the side of the bed now, towering over me where I sit with my fingers twisting around the blankets. He leans down and grasps my chin gently. "Tell me you understand."

"I do."

Rhys nods. "Good."

My mouth opens like I might say it back, but I just gape like a fish out of water.

He uses the moment to kiss my bottom lip, sucking it softly between his lips and teeth. Our foreheads press together as he sits on the bed, enveloping me in the comfort of his warmth.

"You don't need to say anything right now, okay? I can love you enough for the both of us."

"For now," I blurt.

He smiles, and I can see the glimmer in his warm eyes. That he understands the words I've given are a promise.

"For now, *kotyonok*."

"You ever gonna tell me what that word means?"

"Maybe one day," he says before pushing me back into the mattress and pressing *I love you* into every inch of my skin while he makes love to me, soft and sweet and slow.

After, he asks for my little Bluetooth speaker and sets it on the bed between us. The big window over my bed leaks moonlight over his naked skin like it's bathing him in the glow.

While he fumbles for his phone, I lean forward and kiss and nip at his neck again.

Two clicks, then music plays. A song I know well, but not one from my playlists.

Brandi Carlile's voice is soft, the pluck of the guitar strings slow and gentle, as Rhys Koteskiy plays "Heaven" through the speakers in my room.

"It's my song for you." My automatic response is to stop him there. Convince him that he shouldn't have a song for me. Especially not this one.

But his face is so open, every muscle relaxed, and I *do* believe him. That he loves me.

There's a boyish innocence on his face, as if he didn't just fuck me slow into the mattress with his hand over my mouth to keep me quiet, before he asks, "Do you have one for us?"

"Only a million," I want to say.

Rhys Koteskiy could never be confined to just one song—he's a symphony, a never-ending playlist that I want to repeat forever.

"I'll think of one," I say, curling against his skin.

He's burned into me, I think, like a brand.

I'll never recover from him.

CHAPTER FORTY-ONE

Sadie

I look beautiful.

Ro found the dress, though she refused to tell me where, and it fits like a glove. Black silk down to my ankles with a single slit to mid-thigh. Just enough to be sexy without being indecent.

While I did my makeup, my best friend did my hair, slicking it all back into a bun and letting two tendrils hang from the front and frame my face. I still sport my usual dark-cherry lips and smoky eyes, but it's more regal. Less "competition Sadie." More like Rhys's Gray.

Rhys's. His.

I've never belonged to anyone, or anywhere.

It's a warm feeling when I thought it would be suffocating.

Ro offered to pick up the boys after they carpool home from practice—something I'm quite sure Rhys's parents had a hand in organizing. For now, we're at the Hockey House, so it feels a bit like prom when I descend the stairs to a room full of tuxedo-clad boys.

Rhys, Freddy, and Bennett—the latter two going solo—look mouthwatering.

Bennett resembles his father even more now. His height and width are just as daunting, but he's in a crisp black tux, sans tie. His unruly golden-brown curls are only somewhat smoothed, but his face is clean-shaven, which somehow makes him more intimidating.

Freddy is in a blue suit with his hair combed back, his shirt open just enough for a glint of the metal he usually wears.

Maybe I'm biased, but Rhys looks like the cover model of a magazine, or some celebrity on the red carpet. His hair is cut shorter, not as shaggy as it's been, and he's put something in it to keep it tamed. His tux is black, simple, with a crisp, perfect bow tie at the center of his collar.

A bow tie I decided to fix anyway, even knowing nothing about it. I just shift it this way and that, because this moment feels like a dream and I want it to stay that way.

He grasps my wrists, stopping me for a gentle kiss. His eyes smolder as he pulls away and takes me in.

"You're so goddamn perfect, Gray." He smiles. "And I'm so fucking lucky."

I almost say it, tell him the words that have been hanging on the tip of my tongue for five days, ever since Halloween. But we're surrounded by friends, and if I know Rhys, the moment those words leave my mouth, we won't be leaving his room for a while.

So instead, I kiss his hand. I'm softer in my affection, and I see the way it makes his cheeks blush.

He might be a solid ice captain when in a pair of skates, the Waterfell Wolves' fearless leader. But for me, he'll always be soft.

Rhys's parents planned to meet us at the entrance, but they're already swarmed in the corner when we get there. It's a fundraiser for the First Line Foundation—which I recently realized is not just a volunteer opportunity for Max Koteskiy, but is *his* charity. He started it, funds it, and everything, so that all kids get a chance to skate.

Anna, Rhys's mother, looks dazzling in her deep green dress. I've heard his teammates tease Rhys about how beautiful his mother is, and they are not wrong. She's gorgeous, clearly fit, and always bright-eyed. But it's easy to be around her; she makes everyone smile, and I think that's the real reason everyone finds themselves drawn to her.

This is only my fourth or fifth time around them, and without the buffer of Oliver and Liam occupying their attention, I'm nervous. I'm learning to trust Anna. Slowly. Max too.

Eventually, after a few spins on the checkered dance floor—where I was pleasantly surprised by Rhys's waltzing ability—we make our way to them.

The photographers jump at the chance for photos of the great Maximillian Koteskiy with his up-and-coming hockey-star son, Rhys Maximillian Koteskiy. They don't bother with Anna until Max makes a fuss and starts shouting about her architectural achievements, which he says matter much more than a washed-up NHL player.

And I see it then: the reason Rhys loves me the way he does. The reason he cares for the boys and wants to keep us close. It's because he's seen this his whole life. Has been surrounded by love.

Loving me, loving my brothers—it's easy for him.

My chest tightens, and keeps squeezing until I'm almost sure I'll die.

So, when they finish posing for photos, I drag Rhys into the conference center's carpeted hallway and down toward the staff entrances. I shove him into an empty conference hall that's vast, dark, and full of tables and chairs in disarray.

He laughs even as I feebly pin him to the wall. His eyes smoldering down at me, half-lidded and all warm chocolate, heating me with his gaze.

"Can't even make it through a few hours, huh? Need me that badly, *kotyonok*?"

He doesn't use the word often, but it never fails to light me up when he speaks Russian.

"I love you."

It isn't exactly how I planned it in my head—no beautiful speech to match the one he gave that I replay in my head almost constantly. So I keep going.

"And I'm sorry that I didn't—"

He shuts me up with a kiss, gripping my hips in hands that nearly span my entire waist, hefting me up so I can wrap my legs around him. It causes the silk of my dress to slip all the way up my legs and bunch at my waist, which seems to be his goal.

"No apologies, Gray." He kisses down my neck. "Never apologies with you. I love you so much. I love you."

Rhys never stops saying it as he lays me across one of the cloth-covered tables, the glow of moonlight illuminating my skin. His bow tie disappears along with his suit jacket before he latches his mouth to my collarbone and gently slides the thin straps of my dress down my arms until my breasts are bared to him.

My breath stutters out of me as his hand drifts to my center. He hisses when he finds only bare skin.

"All night?" he asks, pressing firmly against my clit, then drifting his fingers lightly down my lips before circling back in a cruel little pattern.

"No panty lines," I barely eke out, followed by a desperate, loud moan as his fingers enter me.

I try to calm myself down and keep from coming, because I *know* Rhys is about to sink to his knees and lick me until I'm a shaking mess, but nothing I do is working.

I'm already on the precipice, just from looking at him in the dark shadows of the room. Golden boy Rhys Koteskiy has disappeared, and in his place is the darkness that I know thrums in his veins. Maybe it scared him before, but this unleashed version of him— I love him just as much as the shining star.

He gives me that dark, teasing look, like he knows exactly how close I am.

"Say it again," he demands.

"I love you."

"Good girl," he says, sinking to his knees. He teases my slit with his tongue, not bothering to remove the two fingers he has stilled inside me. It takes barely two minutes with his lips around my clit, sucking and tonguing in rapid succession, before I go off like a bomb.

I clench around his fingers even as he moves his lips away. He appears over me again to kiss me, and the taste of myself on his lips, in his mouth, is so erotic I pulse again.

Rhys undoes his belt and pants, pulling himself free before fishing a condom out of his pocket and sliding it on. I lie like a boneless mass of muscle just watching him.

I think I'd do anything he wanted right now.

"God," he grinds out, sliding slowly into me as my still-pulsing pussy clenches up around him. It doesn't matter that I've barely come down from my orgasm; I can feel that my heartbeat has taken up residence in my center, like it's begging for more.

"The first time I saw you like this, I thought you were too fucking small for me."

I whine, high and loud, as he inches forward again, still holding back.

"But you fit me like a fucking glove, baby," he coos before slamming in to the hilt. My back bows, breasts heaving as he starts to fuck me, hard and insistent.

It always feels like the first time with Rhys, and I wonder if, years from now, when we have kids and a yard and a dog, I'll still feel this way.

He doesn't let up, doesn't pause; he continues to thrust and works me through another orgasm before he's pinching my nipple with one hand and holding my chin with the other.

"Give me one more, *kotyonok*." His voice is hoarse now, his temples shining with a light sheen of sweat.

"Rhys—I-I can't," I cry.

"You can. Say it again, and come for me."

He plays his fingers across my clit, waiting until the words, "I love you," pour from my lips before pressing on me. Like striking a match, I lose myself again.

He follows me, telling me he loves me; murmurs a constant stream of praise as he discards the condom and cleans me up, putting my straps back over my shoulders and helping me up. And he never stops kissing me. I straighten my dress as he tosses the tablecloth we used into the corner trash can.

I can't stop smiling at him, but I finally turn to grab my phone while he gets redressed.

I have five missed calls from an unknown number with a local area code.

Just as I unlock the phone, it starts buzzing again.

"Hello?"

"Is this Sadie Brown?"

Rhys's eyes flicker to me in mild concern and I know he can hear every word in the quiet of the room.

"Yeah, who is this?"

"I'm Samantha, a nurse at Greenwood General." My stomach drops at the mention of the hospital one town over from Waterfell. "We've been trying to reach you. Your father was brought in about an hour ago after a drunk driving accident."

My eyes burn, but I try to keep it together until she finishes.

"But, um, your brothers, I think? Liam and Oliver? They were in the car with him. And you're listed after your father as next of kin."

"Oh my God," I cry, already running barefoot for the door and into the bright, loud hallway. "Are they okay? Are they—"

I can't breathe, I can barely hear what she says. My vision grays out for a moment, and I stumble into the wall.

Rhys is there, like he always is. His hand wraps around mine and he gently pries the phone from my grip, taking over.

And I still can't breathe.

. . .

The room is cold; I know because Rhys's mom is wrapping her husband's jacket around her arms as we listen to the doctor speak about my father. But I can't feel anything, just numbness.

And embarrassment.

Rhys's mother and father took me straight back, but I didn't see where Rhys went. He might've told me, but I can't remember. I feel like I'm watching everything from far away.

My father is in a four-point restraint. I'd heard the nurse warning the Koteskiys about that before we came in, but it's a bit worse to see than I thought. He's still flailing and yelling at the nurse, who ignores him and finishes her dosages and notes before leaving with a sympathetic smile.

No, not sympathetic. Pitying.

"Sadie," Dad saws out, chest heaving. His gray, reddened eyes are a mockery of my own. "God, Sade, please get me out of here. They're trying to take the boys. C'mon, sweetheart."

I can't look at him. I feel a bit like I'm dying.

He switches like a trapdoor. "Don't be a fucking brat, Sadie. I need you."

Anna Koteskiy suddenly stands in front of me, arms crossed. She's a small woman, but still taller than me, and she covers me completely; intentionally.

"Calm yourself down if you want to speak to her," she demands, keeping her voice semi-quiet but firm. "You need to calm down either way."

"You're the people trying to take my kids."

He's turning manic, but I don't say anything. No one is trying to take anyone. Doesn't he realize he's already fucked us up enough? That no family like the Koteskiys would want us?

"Stay away from my fucking kids," he shouts, tearing at the restraints, kicking against the bed. "Sade and I take care of them just fine."

A fire seems to light within Anna, her slight form expanding in the room as she continues to stand in front of me, her beautiful gown brushing the harsh hospital flooring.

"Your child is taking care of your children. Sadie should not be responsible for those little boys, all while going to school, working, and taking care of her alcoholic father."

I stand in shock, floored by the overwhelming wave of emotions that roll through me. Anger, fear, and confusion all muddled under the weight of shame and embarrassment. I can't recall a time that some-one has stood up for me like this—and not just someone, a mother.

"You fucking bitch," my dad shouts. He spits at her, and my stom-ach drops.

"That's enough."

Max Koteskiy abruptly steps forward, his face a hard mask of anger. He looks so much like Rhys; if not for the slight lines of age and the gray strands in Max Koteskiy's darker hair, they could pass for twins.

He grabs his wife in a gentle grip, pulling her slightly behind him. When she begins to protest that she's fine, he brushes a hand along her cheek and whispers, "I know you are, Trouble. But let me handle this, okay? For my own *stupid male pride*."

I can tell it's some sort of inside joke between them, just from the way it softens her.

"Why don't you take Sadie to see her brothers?" he suggests, all while his eyes never leave my father.

She nods, albeit slightly reluctantly, and he turns to grant her a private smile.

"I love you so much it hurts, *rybochka*."

His voice is soft, but his intention is clear. Protection.

The words echo in my head. Affection, open and honest and deep—it's what Rhys would be like as a father or husband. If this were something I could have. It's something I don't know; something I've never witnessed before seeing his parents.

Growing up, I didn't have time for friends.

The girls I skated with were competitors, and according to Coach Kelley, I wasn't allowed to skate or play with them. At school, I was too concerned with keeping my secret. So I never saw what real parents and real love looked like.

"Come on, Sadie girl," Anna coos, her tone suddenly gentle—gentler than the firmness of her beautifully round features as she pulls my nearly catatonic body into the hallway. "Rhys and Freddy are with your brothers in the waiting room."

Freddy?

"Freddy's here?"

Another wave of embarrassment flushes my skin, an itch starting down my spine that I know I won't be able to scratch away.

They see it, they know now—everyone knows. My father called her a bitch. Spat at her. I know they won't want their family near mine—especially Rhys.

I try to repeat his words from Halloween again, but all I hear is my father's shouting. My coach's honesty. I'll never be like these people, just like I'll never skate like any of the girls I looked up to. I'm destined to be just *this*.

My terror.

I hate how much I have to resist the urge to call Kelley, to ask him for help. Because Rhys loves me, but he thinks I can be better, can heal.

Will he love me when he realizes that this thing I am is all I will ever be?

We turn the corner into another room, almost like a conference room, but I don't question Anna as she leads me through it.

The view is a shot to the gut.

Freddy has Liam perched on his knees as my youngest brother giggles and plays a game on an iPad that definitely isn't ours. And Rhys . . .

Rhys is holding my twelve-year-old brother in a tight hug, sitting on the large ledge of the hospital window so that Oliver can stand between his legs and keep his head against Rhys's chest. Rhys is whispering into his ear at a constant rate, and the nod of my brother's head without leaving the embrace, fists tugging at his suit jacket, tells me everything.

Oliver hates being touched, and yet he's wrapped completely in Rhys's arms.

The door closes softly behind us, but it still pulls their attention. Liam notices first with a shout of, "Sissy!" and an unceremonious leap from Freddy's lap that leaves the man holding himself in pain.

I scoop him up quickly, the practiced expression of serenity slipping easily into place as my brothers both look at me. Liam is still bright-eyed and somehow okay, but Oliver's eyes are red, cheeks puffy as he looks toward me without leaving the bubble of safety around Rhys.

And I don't blame him—I've been there. I know how warm and comforting it is.

"Hey, bug." I smirk, kissing his cheek hard. "Did they get you all checked out?"

Liam smiles and lifts his elbow, where a bright orange Bluey Band-Aid gleams. It makes my chest ache.

"He's all right, just scratched up his elbow a bit—right, little man?" Freddy says, standing and messing with Liam's mop of hair. The Water-fell playboy is still dressed to the nines, looking more like he should be on the cover of *GQ* than in a hospital boardroom. But beneath the smile he offers my brother, there's a sympathetic look in his eyes.

"Freddy said I'm the same age he was when he started playing hockey," Liam says, skipping to a new subject just as quickly as usual. "He says I'm gonna be even bigger than him one day."

"I did not!"

My brother dissolves into a fit of laughter, but my eyes never leave the window, watching Oliver and Rhys with a desperate ache gnawing at my chest.

CHAPTER FORTY-TWO

Rhys

I'm careful in every movement, stepping slowly toward Sadie despite the clog of fear in my chest. I can't swallow around the rock lodged in my throat at the sight of her like this.

Hours ago, I had her in my arms. Why does it feel like she is suddenly completely out of reach?

Staying calm, I reach my hand out to her, because I just want to hold her.

Her father scared her, almost hurt her brothers, and I can sense her racing thoughts from across the space. If I can just talk to her, just calm her and reassure her that I'm here, then she won't leave, she won't panic and pack up her smile and her snark and her brothers and everything that I love, to take it away from me.

God, even in my head, I'm a fucking control freak.

Sadie doesn't move toward me, but she doesn't move away either.

My mom took Liam and Oliver, along with Freddy, to get some food from whatever might be open at this hour in the cafeteria, both to distract the boys, who looked a little worse for wear, and to give Sadie and me some time.

"Rhys," Sadie starts, her eyes empty in a way I haven't seen since summer, really. Since "Fast Car" skates in the early morning, when I could feel her hopelessness through her movements.

I wish I'd known then what I know now.

"Sadie," I say back, but cross my arms to prepare myself. *Push me out again, love. Go ahead, try to make me think that you would be better off without me.*

It doesn't matter what she says right now; I'm not letting go.

"We need to stop this. I need to leave you alone and you need to—"

"No." I stop her. "I'll let you say whatever it is that you need to right now, to get it all out. But I will tell you right now what it is I need, so there's no confusion. I need you. Now, you can decide what *you* need."

I can see the anger blanket her as she dons her trusty shield. I prepare myself for the hit of her best weapon.

"You're a fucking hockey player who has enough bullshit in his life to deal with without adding a fucked-up family of three into the mix. That is the stupidest shit I can think of. God, Rhys, barely a few months ago you were too panicked to fucking skate—what makes you think you could help any of us when you can barely help yourself?"

It stings, but I can take it. Because I know she doesn't mean it. I can see it in the sobs wracking her body, the tears running down her cheeks, the way her hand moves to almost cup her mouth.

As if she's in shock about what she just said.

"Finished?" I ask, breathing slow, staying calm in spite of my own urge to panic.

"I-I—"

"I know. You shouldn't have said it. But it's okay, Sadie. I know you're scared and angry and hurt. But I told you, I'm not leaving—"

"I know," she cuts me off, and a niggle of fear roots itself in my chest. Her anger, I can take. I'm ready for it. This . . . whatever this is, it scares me. "But I think . . . I think we need to slow down."

"Gray—"

"Hear me out, please." I nod and bite down hard enough on my tongue to taste blood. "You and your parents are incredible. But I need to make sure Liam and Oliver are safe. And *you*, you're supposed to be my college boyfriend; the hockey hotshot of Waterfell University, currently being scouted by at least three NHL teams."

I smile despite her words, because the girl can grumble about hockey players and ruined ice all she wants, but I know my girl keeps tabs on me.

I bet she could name the teams.

"And that's who you should be right now. Not taking care of me or my brothers, or worrying about me. You should be *thriving* and showing those scouts why they should pick you. Right?"

I don't want to agree, but I'll listen. So I shrug.

Her eyes roll, but I can tell this is getting harder for her. "Rhys, please."

"What do you want me to say? I'm not going to agree with you. I can do both."

"You shouldn't have to."

"Neither should you!" I say as I finally break. "You should be enjoying your life—not worrying if you can feed two growing boys or wondering how you're going to pay bills on a house you don't even live in all the time. You shouldn't have to do it at all, and you *definitely* shouldn't have to do it alone."

She sighs, but I can see her soaking in my words, working them through that big brain in her beautiful head.

Please. I want to beg, but I don't want to be a manipulator. If she wants me, she has to *want* me.

"I don't know what to do, Rhys. I just . . . I need us to slow down, okay?"

"We're not breaking up."

I don't even attempt to make it sound like a question. But she shakes her head.

"No. I don't want to break up. I just . . . I don't know. I *can't* love you how you want me to right now. There's nothing left in me."

"All right," I agree, because what else can I do? I step toward her, hold her face in my hands and let her nuzzle into my palms, eyes closed. "But here's the deal, Gray. You're going to let my parents help, okay? My dad will help with the custody and lawyer stuff. My parents and Bennett and Freddy and Ro—and me—we are all going to help you, okay? If you need some space and some time, need to move a little slower, fine. I'll give you that. But you will not be alone. Okay?"

"Okay," she agrees, tears finally falling from her beautiful eyes.

I trace my thumb along the cluster of freckles beneath the corner of one of her cat eyes before kissing her forehead solidly.

"I'll be here for whatever you need." *Even if it's not me.*

CHAPTER FORTY-THREE

Rhys

Liam is already grinning, his face pressed against the screen door, when I pull up. Just like he has been every time I've showed up.

Sadie's car died on her way home last night, and Ro called Freddy to get a hold of me at the house to go get her—because she wouldn't ask for my help.

I'd found her on the side of the street, walking home. I took a solid minute to stew in my anger and breathe so that I didn't make her own anger—which covered her fear—worse.

I'd calmly stopped my car on the side of the road and walked by her for a little, just keeping watch over her, until she finally turned toward me. I would've walked beside her for miles, but I was glad she gave up the defensiveness sooner rather than later.

Sadie didn't speak, only ducked her head like a reprimanded child and slunk behind me back to my car. I hated how she was shivering, so I got a blanket from the trunk of my car—a blanket I'd planned to call our drive-in blanket, big enough for the two of us and her brothers—to wrap her in.

We didn't speak, but I turned on one of her playlists and let the soothing sounds of Damien Rice echo in the space between us. The space that I hated the existence of.

But she didn't push my hand off her thigh when I settled it there. She sat in the quiet of the cabin of my car until the entire playlist finished, letting me trace patterns on her thigh even as she stared at her darkened childhood home like it was the thing that tortured her each and every day. Like she wanted to burn it down.

Eventually, she got out and I walked her to the door, forcing my way in so I could make sure the heat was on inside before offering to get the boys from Ms. B's next door. I did it partially so she could rest and stay warm, but mostly so I could hear from Liam and Oliver exactly how things were going.

Even if we haven't spoken about last night, Sadie's right behind her brother now, with a gray Waterfell Wolves toque pulled down on her head and a thick gray scarf looped so it covers her nearly to her eyes. She's looking at me with a gentle expression. Like she knew I would show. Like she trusts me.

That's enough.

Oliver looks angrier than I've seen him, shuffling past his sister and me so that I don't really know who he's mad at most, his hockey bag swinging wildly off his side.

Liam is in another Star Wars costume, but with a thick coat over the top that makes him look like a big blue marshmallow. Sadie yanks his scrambling body back as he howls at me; she shoves a little wool cap over his curls before releasing him into the snow, and he slams into my legs in a hug.

"Missed you," he mumbles.

"Missed you too, bud." I ruffle his hat before bending down to fix it. I stand back up, straightening my dark navy dress coat and smiling at Sadie.

She is layered in black, but still, she is everything bright in my life. I love her, I'd do anything for her.

And right now that means giving her support, but also the space to work out her own feelings.

I wanted to connect her with my therapist, but Dr. Bard said that was a decision that Sadie needed to make on her own.

I hope she does. I just want her to feel good again.

Happy.

"Hey, Gray," I say, my hand scratching at the back of my neck to distract myself from reaching for her.

"Hotshot." She smiles and my knees wobble. A good mood today, then. She walks right up to me and fiddles with my collar. "You look good."

My cheeks heat as a smile grows under her attention and the familiarity of the teasing nickname. "Yeah . . . I, uh—we've got a home game today. We usually dress nice."

Her eyebrows dip and she lets go of me, ducking her head a bit as she says, "Oh. I, um—I can't go. I have a group project due for my final and we agreed to meet near the rink where Oliver's practice is. And Liam—"

The kid pokes his head out of the car, where he's already strapped himself into his car seat that I definitely hadn't purchased before the gala when I first realized being with Sadie meant being responsible enough to handle her brothers. My dad and I spent the entire morning trying to get the car seat installed properly. The thing is like a fucking spaceship.

"I wanna watch Rhys!"

Sadie's exhausted. It's easy to see in her eyes and her posture, and I can tell this will help her. Even if she won't ask.

"My parents have seats, and they wanted to invite Liam if you needed some help."

She bites her lip. "They wouldn't mind?"

"No." I smile sadly at her. "They'd love it. They love your brothers."

"Yeah." She nods.

"*They love you too; you just need to let them in*," I want to say, but keep it quiet.

"What are you doing after your game?"

I smile again because I can tell she's stalling. To be honest, I'd happily be late to my game for a few more moments with her.

"What time are you done?" I ask, being a little bolder and pulling her hat from her shining hair, tucking a few strands back and smoothing them before putting it back on. "I'll be there to pick you guys up."

"Rhys—"

"Quiet. That one's non-negotiable."

She nods again, cheeks pink—whether from the weather or me, I'll never know.

We all pile into my mom's kid-friendly SUV.

The drive to the local rink is twenty minutes of ABBA, with Liam scream-singing at the top of his lungs. It's ridiculous, and loud, and yet I can see it soften both Oliver and Sadie.

When I pull into the parking lot, before Oliver can slam out of the car, I pause and look at Sadie.

"I just want you to know that taking care of your brothers by yourself is very brave. You're so strong and smart, and I hope I can be half as incredible one day."

I say it in front of her brothers because I need them to understand how amazing their big sister is—and how nothing that's coming will change that. That no one wants to take them from her, nor her from them.

"I'm here for all of you, okay? I love you." My eyes flick to the rearview mirror and lock with Oliver's. "I love all of you."

Liam giggles. "I love you too, Rhys."

I unlock the doors and Oliver waits a bit before getting half out of the car. He turns back to me, because he's on my side of the car, and nods. "Love you."

My heart clenches because I know how rare those words are from him, even to his own family.

He shuts the door and starts toward the ice plex entrance.

Sadie hesitates, but turns and kisses me on the cheek. For a moment I think about trying to catch her lips with my own, but I stay still as she leans her mouth to my ear.

"Love you," she repeats. "And thank you, hotshot. Now go kick their asses."

•   •   •

We do.

It's an overtime game, and we don't play well enough for our up-coming schedule, but I'm fucking beaming as I shower afterward because that last goal was mine.

That, and because I know my girl saw it; Ro stood right at the glass, decked in our colors, videoing with her phone nearly con-stantly. And when we came off to celebrate in the dressing room, Sadie's text was the first thing I saw:

> *You're golden, hotshot. Can't wait to watch you on my television soon.*

I pick up her and Oliver with Liam fast asleep in the car seat— he'd been asleep in my father's arms for half the game. The ride back to their place is nearly silent.

I carry Liam in, laying him on the sofa and hating how cold it feels in the house. But I can tell Sadie thinks I'm hovering, so I walk back out the front door, praying she'll follow.

She does.

Sadie stands in front of her house, backpack hanging from one shoulder. I want to ask to stay over tonight, just to make sure they're okay, but I hold back. Only if she wants me to.

"I, um, I have a competition next week." Her hand plays with a lock of hair and she looks more nervous than I think I've seen her before. "It's three days, in New Hampshire. I missed the last one 'cause it was all the way in Colorado. And I was going to back out to take care of the boys, but . . ."

My chest squeezes. She's asking for help.

"My parents would love it if the boys stayed with them for a few days, Sadie."

"Really?" she asks, but I'm already striding to her.

I take her head in my hands and kiss her forehead hard before tucking her whole body into a tight hug that I need just as desperately as she does—even if she won't ask for it. She sinks into my arms, tension melting away.

"I'm so proud of you," I whisper. "I know it takes a lot for you to ask for help. But I'm so proud."

CHAPTER FORTY-FOUR

Rhys

It takes one sentence out of my mouth to convince my parents to let me bring the boys to Sadie's competition. Even more, they decide they want to be there as well.

My mom, most of all. Something about Sadie turns her fierce in her protectiveness, stronger than it was over me as a child. She doesn't tell me anything about it, but I can see the way she feels written across her face and in her frequent—beyond the normal amount—questions about my girlfriend.

So, Thursday, the day of Sadie's long program for the competition, we leave before the sun is up. While the boys sleep in the car my dad ordered, I chat quietly with my parents.

The rink is slightly crowded, but the majority of people in the ice plex are coaches and teams. There are a few news crews and reporters preparing for the streams, and a rather small live audience.

Which means we get good seats.

"I've never got to do this before," Liam says, kicking his feet back and forth in the seat next to me. My mom sits on his other side, only because Oliver opted to sit between my father and me.

"What?"

"He means see Sadie skate," Oliver says, eyes scanning the far boards as he searches for his sister. I'm doing the same, but neither of us has spotted her yet. "We never get to. Not like this."

Another lump forms in my throat, and my mom clearly picks up on it as she jumps in with, "Well, then this will be a first for all of us. And we have to cheer really loud for her, okay?"

Liam howls and elbows me in the side. "I'm gonna be the loudest one so Sissy knows it's me."

The competition is slow as they move through each group. But about an hour in, Sadie appears in the warm-up skate with her group block.

She's wearing a Waterfell zip-up over her dress, so I can only see a bit of black fabric beneath it. Her legs are in black mesh instead of the tan of her competitors. Her hair is braided tight against her head and pulled back into an equally tight and shiny bun, not a strand out of place.

She isn't smiling—none of them are as they take to the ice and skate. She throws a few jumps, spins a bit, but I can tell by the lines of her tight-clad legs that she's waiting. She's holding it all back right now.

I spot Victoria skating around as well, looking just as focused and determined. I see their coach too, his arms crossed as he stands at the boards and watches. I keep my eye on him for a few minutes and realize he's *only* watching Sadie.

Judging by the jackets, half his team is out on the ice, and yet he's focused solely on her. Correcting her, calling her over repeatedly.

I wait. And still, he never does it for another skater. Luc's words haunt me again. *"Kelley's not normal. And if you don't know what's going on in that fucking rink . . ."*

I cross my arms, heat licking the back of my neck as Coach Kelley speaks harshly to Sadie. I see her roll her eyes, and it almost makes me smile, until I see him grip the sleeve of her jacket and twist it until it works like a leash.

What the fuck?

Standing before I can think twice about it, I excuse myself for the bathroom and instead head straight to the side entrance where the teams are. I wait for someone to stop me, but then realize wearing my Waterfell athletics jacket is working in my favor.

Sadie spots me before I make it to the boards, her eyes shooting wide as she jerks back from Kelley and skates briskly toward the gate.

There's a mix of apprehension and excitement across her face, like she might want to smack me, but she also can't believe I'm here.

Because no one ever has been before.

I wait for her coach to spot me and kick me out, but another one of his skaters is too busy arguing with him at the gate—or maybe they're just talking, but he's spitting his words.

"What the hell are you doing here?" Sadie asks. Her cheeks are flushed as she pulls me along into a spot against the wall, away from the clamor of skaters and the smell of fresh ice and hairspray. "Where are my brothers?"

I smile and put my hands on her shoulders, spinning her so I can point to the group of my family and hers on the far right.

"They wanted to see their *sissy* skate." I pause, dipping my head into her neck to breathe in her perfume against her skin. "And so did I."

"You've seen me skate a thousand times," she murmurs, but softens under my hands, relaxing slightly.

"Not like this."

"You never know. I might suck," she retorts, turning to gaze up at me, eyes more intense with the darkened shadow and glitter. Her lips are still the same signature dark-cherry color, more matte and looking fiercer now against her very pale skin.

I raise my hand almost subconsciously, finding my favorite little patch of freckles beneath her eye and letting my palm graze her face just slightly.

"You'll be the best one out there," I whisper. "Okay?"

"You're not allowed to be back here," her coach scolds as he approaches from behind, standing so close that, if Sadie stepped back, she'd bump into his chest. "You're third, my terror."

He bites out the nickname, and fury—white-hot and terrifying—crawls up my spine at the sound of it. At the implication. His hand wraps around her neck before coasting down her spine and pressing into the center until she straightens, shoulders back.

She tries to hide it, but I see the wince. My eyes shoot to her coach's with a threat pooling in my mouth. I pull Sadie into my arms, but before I can say a word, he storms off. A legion of skaters exit the ice behind him, the warm-up likely over.

"Stop," she whispers, and for a moment I think I've held her too tightly, that I've *hurt* her. My arms drop from her as if I've touched a burning stove.

It only takes a moment for me to realize she's warning me off her coach.

"He can't touch you like that, Gray," I whisper, albeit a bit harshly.

Her back is up, again, the divot between her brows that I love so much taunting me as she crosses her arms. "You don't know him. He cares about me. He wants me to do well, work hard."

"You work harder than most of the athletes I know, Gray. And I know a fucking lot."

"He just doesn't want me distracted. He's focused."

"*You* are focused. No one is more determined than you."

What I want to say is that if what her coach had the balls to do in front of me is only the tip of the iceberg, then it can only mean how he treats her behind closed doors is worse. And sure, I didn't *ever* figure skate, but I grew up in a rink. I went to a goddamn private hockey academy with some of the strictest coaching staff I've ever experienced.

And not one of them ever manhandled me like that.

But she's about to skate, and the last thing I want is to pull her down. Never again.

So I swallow my words for another time and press a firm kiss to her forehead before tilting her chin up.

"You're a killer, Gray. Say it."

"I'm a killer," she mutters, rolling her eyes even as I mentally bottle up her slipping smile.

"Good girl." I smirk. "I'd kiss you, but I don't want to mess up your lipstick." After I say it, she presses a dark red kiss mark into my palm, so I can hold it. "I'm proud of you, and so are your brothers. Now, go show them their sissy is a badass."

By the time I'm back to my seat with hot chocolates for the boys, she's next.

Without the jacket, Sadie is dressed in a strappy black mesh dress that matches the thin black of her tights. Long mesh sleeves sit just on the cusp of her shoulders. Strategic panels of thick black fabric cover some of her torso, while the other see-through sections display the hard lines of her stomach and waistline.

She takes her place at the center of the ice, poised and beautiful, before the speakers begin blasting Metallica's "Enter Sandman," which sends a vibrating laugh through both my father and me.

And just like the first time I saw her skate while hiding in the tunnel, Sadie Brown skates like she's on fire. Pure passion, pure unrelenting strength. Her movements are hard and fast, her spins so quick she turns into a blur. She takes every jump with jarring speed, but lands them. Every. Single. One.

My fingers feel like they're melded into the chair from keeping myself seated when I want to jump up every time and scream, "That's my girl," at the top of my lungs.

Liam cheers just as loudly as he promised. Oliver grins happily, watching his sister with wonder in his eyes. *Me too, bud.*

By the end of her program, my cheeks hurt from my uncontrollable beaming smile. I'm so goddamn proud of her, so lucky to call her *mine.*

So lucky that she calls me hers.

Sadie bows and looks over at us, winking at her brothers and blowing a snarky little kiss that I know is all mine. I clench my hand a little tighter where her dark lipstick mark still lies.

It doesn't matter how much distance there is between us right now; as long as she'll have me, I'll be right here. Waiting and cheering from the bleachers, if that's what she needs.

• • •

Another anxiety disappears overnight.

Kane isn't just opting out of the Harvard game—Freddy apparently did some digging, as he hurries to inform me when I enter the Hockey House.

Toren Kane isn't allowed to play at Harvard.

It took some intense scouring of the internet to find a video, as it seems someone tried to have it covered up. But there is a quick clip of the incident, shot on a shaking cellphone.

An opposing player says something taunting, spitting in his face. Kane grasps the kid's cage and flings him away like an irritating insect before entering some trance, clearly visible with his helmet discarded. There's a girl, a redheaded Harvard student by the sweater she wears, sitting two rows from the glass, staring at him in the same wonder-filled way.

His teammate yanks on the collar of his jersey, pulling him out of the staring contest, and suddenly, he jerks forward and slams his glove against the glass.

"Get the fuck out of here!" he screams, and the already-pale girl goes nearly white. She stands and stumbles up the stairs to the exit, the boy next to her following blindly.

Still, Kane continues to whale on the glass for a moment before it shatters under his blows and the video cuts off.

"At least we won't have to deal with him tomorrow," Freddy says.

It's a small gift, but I'll happily take it.

CHAPTER FORTY-FIVE

Sadie

It doesn't matter how many times I've been here in the past few weeks—the Koteskiy household always looks like a dream house.

And lately, I've been here a lot. Even without Rhys.

Today, they're letting me use Anna's office for a meeting with my attorney, who seems a bit more motivated since Max Koteskiy and Adam Reiner got involved. Bennett's father had apparently offered to help more directly, but admitted that it wasn't his area of expertise.

I have practice in an hour by the time the meeting finishes. I plan to get there early anyway—mostly to avoid standing awkwardly in the Koteskiy house with just Anna, since my brothers are off with Max at a First Line Foundation event. Rhys is traveling to the Harvard game.

But just as I'm sliding on my thick jacket, Anna descends the stairs.

"Sadie." She smiles. "How did it go?"

"Great. I think I'll be good until the hearing in January. Thanks for letting me use your office. I'm gonna head—"

"Do you have a minute, love?"

I do, but I wish I didn't. She frightens me, and maybe if I looked a little deeper—or went to much-needed therapy—I would realize why.

She sits on a barstool at the kitchen counter and taps the one beside her for me to follow.

"You know I was thirty-three years old and pregnant when I met Max?"

I don't move, just sit quietly. Just looking at her feels like too much.

"With Rhys?"

"No." She smiles, shaking her head and scooting just a bit closer to my hunched form. "It was before Rhys, and the father was my ex-husband, who I was trying to escape. I was absolutely terrified. And when hiding from someone, running into the arms of an up-and-coming twenty-four-year-old hockey star is not a good start."

"I didn't know he's younger than you." The words slip free, and my cheeks heat at how rude that might've sounded. "Sorry, I just mean—"

"No, Sadie girl, I take that as a compliment." She sighs. "Max was so mature for his age, but he should've been out gallivanting around and being messy in his rookie years, not taking care of a woman pregnant with someone else's baby. But he did. Because . . . well, that's Maximillian. He was so handsome, so sure—and the peek of his accent came out whenever he called me *rybochka*, which I believed to be something sweet until he told me at our wedding it meant little fish!"

I can't help but laugh.

"He didn't."

"Oh, he did—and even worse, he'd been calling me *rybochka* in bed for years!" She laughs as I blush, remembering how much Rhys had stressed that his mother has no filter.

"He was there for me for a long time, through my miscarriage, through my difficult pregnancy with Rhys . . . He played professional hockey and I was always, *always* who he put first."

Her eyes close for a moment, before clear peace seems to spread across her features.

"But, what I want to tell you is I was running from someone who hurt me, and as much as I begged Max to leave me alone, knowing how much shit I was pulling into his very public life, he never let it go. I was a secret for a long time, but only because I begged to be—I was still hiding and refused to tell him anything despite how much Max wanted to handle my problems for me.

"Rhys is a lot like his father; physically, I made a mini Max, but mentally, too. He's strong and very capable and he loves with every cell in his body."

"But I—"

She holds up a hand. "My son has more protectiveness packed into his body than he knows what to do with. It makes him a good hockey player, it makes him a good friend, and it makes him a good son. But with you? I know . . . he wants to protect you more than anything."

"Why are you telling me all this?"

Anna sighs deeply, running a soft hand over my cheek and tucking my hair around my ear.

"Because I wish there had been someone there to tell me it was okay to ask for help, and that I wasn't weak or a burden for accepting it."

She starts to stand, to allow me to leave for my practice, before I stop her.

"Do you know any Russian?"

"Only a little. Not as much as Rhys or Max; language was never my specialty."

"Do you know what *kotyonok* means?"

She laughs, smiling wider than I'm sure I've ever seen. "It means kitten, my love."

My skin flushes. I have the urge to call Rhys and threaten him as much as tell him I love him.

But it can wait. Still, I've had enough space. The second he gets back, I'll tell him.

. . .

Practice is brutal.

My ankle is throbbing—I'm almost positive I've sprained it, but Coach Kelley won't let up for a fucking second. I try to put pressure on it again, my head spinning as I look at the stadium clock and see we are well past my two-hour mark.

He's refused every water break I've asked for, ignored my complaints, and now, I'm pretty sure he's injured me.

"I can't."

"You can. Do the fucking jump again."

I limp-skate toward where he's blocking my exit to the tunnels. Once I'm close enough to see the fury in his eyes, I try to skirt past him again.

He grabs my wrist, *again*.

"Is this about the boy? The pathetic hockey player?"

"This is about you *hurting* me. My ankle is killing me. Please, I need just a few minutes."

I don't sound angry, I realize. I sound like I'm about to cry.

"Don't be a baby, my terror. Stop being lazy and do the jump again. We will do it till it's perfect."

"You're going to make me seriously hurt myself."

He grips me tighter on my wrist before shifting his hold up my arm and leering over me. "Not if you do it right. Again."

I can't take it anymore. I don't *need* this.

"No."

"Try again." He grasps my arm somehow harder, twisting enough that there's a sharp pain and suddenly I'm worried that he might break it. My stomach drops as I realize exactly how much danger I could be in. I've trusted him for years. Now . . .

A terrified sound rumbles out of me before I gather the breath to scream.

But I don't have to.

Someone grabs Kelley from behind, yanking him off me and slamming one fist into his face. My coach goes down, out cold.

Toren Kane.

His eyes are bright embers of gold, just as unsettling and intoxicating as the last time I saw him.

"W-what are you doing here?"

"Coaches like that will never fucking stop."

I wrap my arms around myself, still feeling shaken and scared. "Thank you," I manage to mutter.

He scoffs, "Yeah, well. You can pay me back by telling someone how your own *coach* has been overtraining you to the point of injury."

"He . . . He only trains me hard because he believes in me—"

An unsettling laugh bubbles from his mouth. "Yeah. Heard that one before."

He flickers his eyes down at my unconscious coach before looking up at me with a half-smile that's so fake I'm sure I could peel it off.

"Oh, and tell your little boyfriend we're fucking even."

I don't have a single sound left in me that's not a sob or scream so I nod jerkily. I nearly trip in my skates over the mats as I rush to leave.

CHAPTER FORTY-SIX

Rhys

I'm not sure what makes me turn away from the road leading to the Hockey House. Possibly the weight of our Harvard loss, or the desire to avoid my teammates' frustrations and sorrows.

But either way, I find myself pulling into my parents' driveway thirty minutes after the bus drops us at the arena.

My heart squeezes lightly, the weight of the team's loss lifting from my shoulders at the knowledge that Sadie is here.

When I come in through the garage, I hear the cackling laughter of kids in the distance—Liam and Oliver.

In the living room, however, I find only Adam Reiner and Sadie's brothers playing Xbox—no sign of Sadie or my parents.

Just as I open my mouth to ask about their absence, a figure descends the stairs and turns for the front door. A tall figure I recognize.

"Kane," I bark out.

My shout gathers the attention of the boys, and Liam yells for me immediately. Oliver looks apprehensively at the other very large hockey player in the foyer.

"Talk to your girlfriend, Koteskiy. Not me," Kane says without moving.

My heart rate skyrockets and fear wars with my anger—no matter how irrational—as I look at Toren Kane in my house, talking about my girl.

Oliver steps up beside me. "Who is that? Is he why Sadie was crying?"

I look down at him as my throat closes up. "Sadie was crying? Is she okay?"

Oliver crosses his arms, glaring at Kane. His fury is almost palpable.

"Your mom took her upstairs and then your dad brought that asshole in here." I don't bother to chide him on his foul language. His anger melts a little, a slight helplessness entering his tone. "Can you just see if she's okay? Does she need us?" The anxious tone of his voice makes me feel a little lightheaded.

I blow out a breath and nod to Oliver. "You're a good brother. Let me just see what's going on."

I walk into the foyer with clenched fists, about to start a real fucking fight with the asshole, but his gaze darts over my shoulder.

"Rhys," my dad calls.

A wicked little smile takes over Kane's face and he chuckles. "Better answer to your daddy, Cap." His hand pats my chest condescendingly, shoving a little roughly. "And tell your girl I'll skate with her anytime."

"You motherfu—"

"Stop it," my dad snaps, grabbing me by the shoulder.

Kane slips out the front door without another word, and I hear what sounds like a motorcycle take off.

"What the fuck? Why was Toren Kane in our house?" I round on my father.

He holds his hands up in surrender, but I can hear my heartbeat in my ears, anxiety and frustration starting to ratchet higher.

"Calm down, Rhys. Please. Sadie really needs you right now. Do your exercises."

I start counting immediately, desperate to bring myself down from the impending panic attack. When I can breathe normally again, my dad beckons me up the stairs and toward my room.

The door opens and my mom comes out, leaving it ajar behind her.

"Rhys," she whispers, eyes red like she's been crying. She tries to stop me from entering the room, but I move around her.

I open the door gently and step in quietly, taking note of Sadie's sleeping form.

Except I've slept next to the girl for months, seen exactly how she sleeps. And this isn't it. She's pretending.

Her eyes look swollen shut, her face is pink, and her ankle is elevated with ice and a wrap around it.

I leave quietly, trying desperately to hold on to the shredded threads of my temper.

"I'm gonna kill him," I rasp. Tears burn in my eyes as I turn back to my mom and reach for her.

"Oh Rhys, honey." She envelops me in her arms. "No, it's okay. She twisted her ankle skating and she couldn't get home. Toren followed her here to make sure she didn't crash. She was . . . upset."

"About what? If he so much as—"

"She wouldn't say," my mom says, her eyes darting to my father in the same way they have been darting almost constantly.

My dad steps forward. "How much do you know about the figure skating coach she trains under?"

I shrug, a little uncomfortably. Is this something I should've paid attention to? Why are they asking me that?

"Sadie's never complained or anything. But . . . I saw him get physical with her at the competition."

My dad nods as if this is something he expected, then shares a knowing look with my mom. I comb and pull at my hair again, because my hands are still shaking, and if I don't do something with my hands, I'm scared my whole body will start trembling.

"Know anything about him as a skater? Alexan Kelchevsky?"

"Kelchevsky? He goes by Kelley. Is he Russian?" My dad nods. I shake my head, but I'm starting to feel sick. "What is this about? You're freaking me out—both of you."

"You need to see this, then."

CHAPTER FORTY-SEVEN

Sadie

I'm not sure when I drifted into actual sleep, sometime after Rhys initially checked on me. So when I wake up, I have no concept of what time it is.

"Hey."

My head spins.

Rhys is there, sitting in the plush loveseat catty-corner to the bed. His hair is messy, like he's been running his hands through it for hours, and he's dressed in gray joggers and his Waterfell Hockey shirt.

"What time is it?" My voice sounds groggy and foreign.

He hands me a water bottle, opening it for me as he does.

"Six a.m. You managed to sleep through the night."

Yet he doesn't look like he slept a wink. He looks exhausted, like he got back from his game already tired and still didn't sleep. Like he's been sitting there, watching over me, all night.

"How was your game?"

For some reason, the question seems to upset him. "I don't want to talk about my game. What happened to your foot?"

Oh.

"I sprained it, I think. While skating."

The stern face I rarely see from him is back in full force as he stands and crosses his arms. Like this, he towers over me. He's so strong—so handsome. I'm almost too distracted by his beauty to realize exactly what he's angry about.

"Overtraining, you mean. You sprained it because you were overtraining."

Shit. Shit. Shit.

My heart hammers against my rib cage. "No. Why would you—"

"Please, Sadie," he whispers. And then, something changes as he watches me. He blows out a breath and tucks his messy hair behind his ears. "Take your time. My bathroom's right there if you want to shower. But meet me in my mom's office when you're done."

He bends and kisses my forehead hard before leaving.

. . .

It's quiet in Anna Koteskiy's office.

Rhys and his father are standing and talking quietly when I enter. Anna is sitting, and she's pulled up a chair by her computer for me.

"What's wrong?" I ask before I can think twice about it. "Did I do something—"

"You're not in trouble, Sadie girl," Anna whispers, beckoning me again. I sit, back straight and stiff as I look only at her.

"We just want to ask you about your coach."

"Coach Kelley?" She nods. "Oh, well, he's been my coach since I was like, eleven, maybe? He followed me here. Um, he's helped me with my brothers before, but . . ." I take another breath because I don't know what they expect me to say here.

Though it's clear they're waiting on something.

Rhys breaks first. "He's never hurt you? Overtrained you?"

I'm careful as I choose my words. "Everything he does is because he believes in me. He can be tough, but it's only because he loves me."

My words make Rhys huff out an angry sound, his arms coming around my form to wake the monitor. On it, pulled wide, is a video—a competition video from years ago. It's four hours long, but paused somewhere in the middle.

I knew this recording was out there somewhere, but it wasn't taken at some major competition. I never thought Rhys would find it.

But there it is, replaying in my mind like an endless nightmare loop, until Rhys unpauses the video and I'm actually seeing it all over again. I'm fifteen, dressed in a black-and-red number and finishing a routine I still know like the back of my hand. I'd fallen during the combination that was going to secure first place and a shot at Olympic qualifiers for me, but I hadn't been able to shake the anxiety, so the rest of my movements and spins were jerky, robotic, with no feeling.

It's clear how anxious I am as I skate off, red-faced and teary-eyed, toward my fuming coach. His hand grips the back of my neck, hard—even on the camera you can see it as he berates me, whispering into my ear.

I hate that now. I wait for my past self to pull back, to slap him or push away or throw a tantrum. Instead, I burrow into him, holding on for dear life like he's my anchor despite the white-knuckled grip he has on me beneath the warm-up jacket he's put over my shoulders. I can practically hear his words in my ears still.

You look heavy, lost your rotation.

Weak ankles aren't something I can fix, terror. You must train harder.

It was always to be helpful, to push me . . . I thought. Unlike the other girls in my group, I didn't have parents to watch and cheer for me, or a retired skating family to coach me. I'd been alone until Coach Kelley found me.

"That looks normal to you?" Rhys asks, his arms crossed, anger clear across his face.

There are no words when I open my mouth, but I gauge his parents' reactions as I wait.

"He's been my coach since I was eleven." It isn't the right thing to say, but it's all that comes out. "He's—he loves me, but he pushes me. That isn't bad."

Lies lies lies.

A hand falls to my shoulder so suddenly that I flinch. I watch Mr. Koteskiy pull back with a somber look on his face, apologies in his eyes. But it's Anna who wraps me up from behind, her chin settling over the top of my head as she holds me close.

"You've done nothing wrong," she whispers into my hair. "Nothing, okay? But you deserve better than this."

"I don't—"

"Sadie," Rhys begs. He's still fuming, but his fierce expression softens as he looks at me. "You've got to report him."

I can't speak, my tongue heavy in my mouth. I want to assure them, to tell Rhys that I'm *fine*. But I can't find the words.

The tears come easily then, and Anna Koteskiy holds me until they stop.

• • •

Rhys follows me upstairs after I tuck my brothers into their temporary rooms.

"I'm not sure where I'm supposed to go," I admit, the hopeless, lost feeling in my stomach climbing up until it tightens my throat. "I don't—"

"Come here, Gray," he whispers, opening his arms so I can crawl into the safe, warm space of his embrace. He holds me there, murmuring soft words into my hair and littering kisses along my scalp and forehead.

"I'm sorry I pushed you away," I murmur into the fabric of his shirt.

"I was never going anywhere, anyway." He chuckles, the words serious even as he tries to pull a smile from me.

It works, like it always does.

I pull back just slightly, keeping my fists balled in the fabric of his shirt at his waist. Like I'm holding tight, just in case. But if there's anything this man has shown me, it's that he's not leaving.

Guilt tries to take root, and he must see it cross my face because he's gripping my chin and angling my gaze to his before the first tear can fly free.

"I will spend every day forever reminding you how amazing and special you are. How lucky I am to have someone so brave and smart and talented and beautiful love me. I see the way you love your brothers. I know how special your kind of love is."

He tucks my hair behind my ears and cradles my entire face in his massive palms.

"You are worth it. And if I have to fight the little demons in your mind that convince you otherwise every day for the rest of our lives? I'll happily do it. Do you understand?"

He waits for an answer.

"I love you," I say instead. "I trust you. And I'm sorry I didn't show you that sooner."

He kisses me, soft and sweet.

"We have all the time in the world for you to make it up to me." He smirks, all boyish, and it makes my heart flip and my entire body turn to mush in his arms.

I love Rhys Koteskiy. And I'm learning that I do deserve him.

I'm never letting go of his hand again.

CHAPTER FORTY-EIGHT

Sadie

It's the last Learn to Skate of the season, and I really shouldn't be here.

In fact, the handsome coach currently out setting up cones on the ice *specifically* told me not to come. To save my strength for my last practice before the Christmas Gala. But I made a promise to these kids that I would be here, and I intend to be—even if he doesn't let me step a toe pick onto the ice.

Logically, I should stay silent over here, waiting to sneak on as the kids finish tying up their shoes and putting on gloves in the slightly warmer concession area before heading down the ramp. And yet, as Rhys bends over at the waist to grab a stray mini cone left over from the hockey kids earlier, I can't help the loud wolf whistle I release. Because I want to mess with him.

With everything that's happened, Rhys has treated me like glass. I want to rile him up a bit.

He jerks upright, head shooting over his shoulder with narrowed eyes and a furrowed brow that would be intimidating if it weren't for the blush coloring his cheeks.

For all that he is the hockey hotshot, the brilliant golden boy Rhys Koteskiy blushes more often than I'd thought possible. And when I'm the cause of it, it feels like I'm flying.

He spots me quickly, eyebrows shooting up as I lean over the ledge of the bench area with a little smirk, eyes dancing at his flustered expression.

"Hey, hotshot."

It's only a moment before he's abandoned his entire task, skating over to me quickly, stepping off the ice seamlessly, grabbing me around the waist, and lifting me off my feet.

"Pretty sure I told you not to be walking around on it."

"On what?" I ask, relaxing into his easy way of carrying me back into the locker room I've just come from.

He levels me with a dark, disapproving stare. "Sadie."

"Real name?" I question, my hands delving into the curls at the base of his neck. "Damn, I must be in trouble." No part of my voice sounds even a little sad about being in trouble with Rhys. Mostly because I know that his kind of trouble is something I like.

And because I know for a fact that my ankle got approved for skating this morning, in my early practice at the university rink.

"Be serious about this, please," he begs, letting me down as I start to squirm. Even though he lets my feet touch the ground, he backs me up against the wall so I lean on it. "I saw how swollen that thing was. He nearly fucking broke it—"

I put my hand to his chest, seeing that there's a tinge of hurt in Rhys's eyes, not determination or anger. Hurt and fear, I realize.

"Hey, Rhys," I coo gently. "It's okay. It was barely a sprain. Team doctor gave me the go-ahead to get back on the ice."

The tension he's wearing like a coat starts to slide off him, just a slight hesitance as he reaches for me again; this time his hand combing through my loose hair, tucking it back behind my ear. My eyes shutter closed at the soft, intimate motion, before his hand trails to grip my chin and tilt my eyeline to his.

"Really?" he whispers. "You're okay?"

"I promise."

There's a smile now working its way across his lips so beautifully I can't help but reach out for him and press my lips to his. Once, twice—the second one lingering like a gentle caress.

A pinch of anxiety threatens to burst my perfect little bubble as I spot my bag in the corner with my skates propped up against it. It's not anxiety about skating, but it's the fear that maybe I was only so good because of Coach Kelley. What if I am truly nothing without him?

What if he was right?

"I'm so proud of you," Rhys whispers into my hair with a happy, pleased expression.

His eyes are the warmest brown I've ever seen, a smile stretching his lips and letting both his dimples gleam brightly. Rhys is handsome, yes, but he is also everything warm and good and kindhearted, and I never want to let go of his hand.

"I love you."

I don't think I'll ever get over the way he relaxes, melts completely into goo in my hands when I'm the one to say it first. It's like every line of stress and anxiety melts away. And I know Rhys has heard the phrase "I love you" a good amount from his parents. I know that they love him, that they both show and tell him so.

Which, somehow, makes the value he clearly places in my words mean more.

Because I eat up every scrap of his affection like a starving animal, and though I try not to let it interfere with my relationship with him, sometimes I do try to use sex with Rhys to drown out the worst of my feelings, the most overwhelming.

But I'm getting better, each and every day. I am.

So, instead of sinking against his body for the little time we have, to selfishly calm my nerves, I push away from him with a gentle smile.

"Come with me."

He shoots me a puzzled look as I head over and grab my bag and skates in one hand. "We've got our last class."

I smile. "I know. I arranged a little surprise for them."

It was the last official finals day Friday, so it was hard to swing it, but as we head back out into the cold of the rink, most of the Waterfell Wolves hockey team is present, wearing their skates and warmup jackets with the Waterfell logo emblazoned on the pockets.

Rhys looks around, eyes wide as Freddy passes by us with two giggling kids holding on to the end of his stick as he gently pulls them along. Bennett, still just as hulkingly tall without the goalie gear, quietly kneels to help a little girl re-lace one of her skates while she uses his shoulder for balance.

Surprisingly, even Toren showed, which is unexpected, considering how much he's kept his distance. I tried to say a quick "thank you" to him once, but he brushed it off, basically pretended it never happened.

I try, but I cannot figure him out. Toren is harsh, doesn't get along with a single one of his teammates . . . and yet he saved me that day. Not only that, but he called out my overtraining far before—like he knew the signs of it. Like he'd experienced it.

He's standing on the ice in a corner now, dressed in all black with his arms crossed tightly, as Holden skates in circles around him while holding up one of our usual students, the kid who skates more like Liam, a little behind the rest of the class.

"You organized this?"

I nod, lifting a shoulder toward his coach, who is speaking to a few of the parents just by the open entrance at the boards. "He helped. You said that . . ."

My voice trails off, feeling stuck in my throat slightly. "You mentioned that you hadn't felt close with them all, not like last year, really. And I think working with the First Line Foundation and being on the ice when you're not playing hockey is what helped you get back.

I thought it would be something good for the team, for you to spend non-practice time with them. And," I say with a shrug, "it's something that helped you. Maybe it would be good for them too. Make them remember being this age."

He crushes me into his side with a hard-pressed kiss to the top of my head, before nearly shoving me onto the bench in his excitement, kneeling to help me put on my skates. I laugh a little at how ridiculous it is, knowing I'll probably need to re-lace them the way that I like before I can properly skate, and definitely before I show him my new routine later.

But for now, they'll work.

He takes my hand in his, and we step onto the ice together.

From now until . . . forever.

CHAPTER FORTY-NINE

Three Weeks Later

Sadie

"Today was great, Sadie," the woman says over the screen. I nod gently and burrow a little deeper into the blanket.

"Yeah, I think so too."

She smiles warmly, "Okay. Good. Today's our last session before the holidays, and you don't have another session until January. Anything else we should talk about before then?"

"I don't think so."

"If you think of anything else, remember you have my number now, okay?"

"Okay."

"Oh, and Sadie?" she manages to say before either of us end the call. "You're gonna do amazing tonight, okay?"

I thank her again before we hang up, then lie on the big sofa in Anna Koteskiy's office while I decompress.

I started therapy two days after reporting Coach Kelley to the athletic director. When I showed up for practice for the Christmas Gala, he was in his car in the parking lot ready to try to ambush me, to talk.

Thankfully, I brought backup.

Max Koteskiy walked me from his car to the ice rink entrance, but we only made it halfway before he started to argue with my coach stalking behind us. It had taken me a full minute to realize they weren't arguing in English, but Russian. I knew my coach had been born there, before being adopted and brought to America, but I'd never heard him speak the language before.

His face paled over whatever it was Mr. Koteskiy spouted, and I haven't heard from or seen him since.

I teased Rhys's dad for his savior complex. He didn't deny it once.

It was Anna Koteskiy who connected me with my new therapist, and I like her a lot. We have a lot to go through. Some days I like therapy, while some days I hate it and I sit sullenly instead of really trying—but my therapist says that's normal. And it's okay.

Whatever I'm feeling right now is okay.

Today, we really talked mostly about the holidays and Christmas— so, inevitably, we talked about my dad.

My dad is in rehab, but it hasn't changed my plans for getting custody. Mainly because we've done this song and dance before with court-mandated rehab. It never sticks.

There's a knock on the door, and I sit up slowly as Rhys pops his head in, a warm and gentle look on his face as he takes me in.

"Hey," he says, coming in and shutting the door behind him. "You all right?"

"Yeah. Today was good."

He sits next to me, and I curl up in his lap like a cat. His hand starts smoothing through my hair and up and down my back. This has become our post-therapy routine—for both of our sessions. My therapy is on Thursdays and his is every other Wednesday.

Sometimes we talk about our sessions with each other; sometimes we don't.

But we always make a point to tell each other when we see a "good" change. To praise each other where we can.

My brothers have also started therapy, thanks to the Koteskiys. I want to say I owe them everything, but I'm learning that it's okay to ask for help and accept it without constantly worrying about how to repay people.

We've stayed with them all of winter break, which started as a necessity during a snowstorm, and then continued at their insistence. The boys are happy, and I see them falling a little more in love with Anna and Max every day. It heals a deep wound in me every time Oliver lets Anna hug him, or decides to lie on the sofa a little closer to Max while they watch hockey on the "biggest TV in the whole world," according to Liam.

Liam is also thriving. He settled in overnight as if this place was a new home. Rhys and his parents spoil them, but they deserve it.

"What time do you need to be at the rink?" Rhys asks, kissing my forehead and cheeks.

I smile and yawn, a little exhausted emotionally and physically.

"In two hours?"

"Great." He smiles, picking me up bridal style and carrying me out of the room. "Let's take a nap."

Singles skating got a new coach overnight—and I'm suspicious of how much Koteskiy family funding helped pull that off, even if none of the three of them will admit it.

Coach Amber is nice, but firm in a way I identify as a healthy strictness, like a real coach. No manipulation or isolation or brutality. I'm learning that wasn't my fault either—I was too young, with no adults around me to keep it from happening or notice that it wasn't okay.

She also let me choreograph my entire Christmas Gala routine, which I'm performing tonight. It's to Pink Floyd's "Wish You Were Here." Coach Kelley would never let me pick something so lyrical, swearing my strength was only in my ferocity, but Coach Amber encourages me to try new things all the time, even when I fail.

I'm tired but I don't sleep, even though Rhys crashes the moment his head hits the pillow. Daylight peeks through the closed blinds in his room, dancing across his handsome face as I stare at him, a little in awe.

I've watched him grow, change since that day on the ice this past summer. I've seen his body shift and fill out again now that anxiety doesn't stifle his usual massive appetite.

He is beautiful.

In his easy love for my brothers, his support of everything I do. His gentleness with my heart, but stubbornness against my anger. He cut through the vines of my fury and self-hatred like it was the only thing he was meant for.

It's taken me this long, but I know who he is now.

Rhys Koteskiy is pure gold. I know it. And soon the entire world will too.

So I soak up these moments, just the two of us between the dark-blue sheets of his bed. Under the fading light of day, safe and warm in the comfort of his arms, falling asleep to the sound of his steady, strong heartbeat.

EPILOGUE

Three Years Later

Rhys

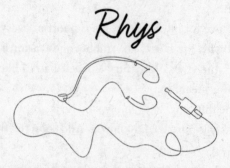

If I thought the press would be bad when I officially joined the NHL, it doesn't compare in the slightest to when my father and I are in the same vicinity.

His fame will never wear off. He still holds the record for most Stanley Cup wins. And while this is my third year with the New York Rangers, the rumors of a trade are endless, which means I'm constantly hounded by sports broadcasters.

Yet, somehow, my dad has managed to keep Waterfell's local rink and the First Line Foundation it houses away from the press.

Entering my hometown rink feels like a little slice of privacy.

Privacy and utter happiness, thanks to the girl dressed in my old Waterfell University sweatshirt and leggings, looking more like a sleepy college student than the current head coach for the new figure skating division of my family's charity.

Sadie Brown will always be the only thing I want to look at, shining and blazing like fire on ice. She's always been beautiful, but I think my attraction to her grows with every day.

She cut her hair recently and didn't tell me beforehand, just showed up at my apartment with her dark, shiny locks in a blunt chop that dusted her shoulders, skin pink from the New York winter winds. I nearly attacked her in the hallway.

I've turned into an animal when it comes to her, with no signs of stopping.

While I should be in my apartment, sleeping as much as possible before my next string of three away games—this time to Montreal and Florida in the same week—I took the train straight here. Because, even if it means a few days of minor exhaustion, I'll do anything for just an hour with Sadie.

I hang back near the cluster of parents waiting for their children to be dismissed, watching her.

I could watch her every minute and it still wouldn't be enough.

"Was that good?" a reluctant little voice asks.

"Great, Tiff." Sadie nods at the slender young girl dressed in all pinks and golds. "You'll be spinning even faster in no time."

The words of praise practically set the girl aglow as she darts off for another lap.

A loud thump followed by a frustrated little scream draws the entire rink's attention to the shorter girl in a pair of older, tan skates and a big T-shirt. It's the girl Sadie talks about, complains about, and defends in the same breath. Looks like her mini-me if you ask me, but I keep my mouth shut.

The girl fights tooth and nail against Sadie's corrections, but dresses like her, and—no matter how reluctantly—does everything she's asked. I can tell she's just like my pretty girlfriend. A little prickly, but soft underneath; just needs the right care and attention. The right type of guidance.

And as much as she might not see it, Sadie offers that guidance.

"Everly," Sadie snaps at the little spitfire. "You don't have to make a scene every time you *don't* do what I say." She crosses her arms and skates a little closer to the girl. "Now, try it again. You're so close."

"This is bullshit."

"Language," Sadie chides, like she doesn't have the mouth of a sailor most of the time. I can see the threat of a smirk from here. "Please."

"Whatever."

Eventually, Sadie sighs and cups her hands around her mouth. "Okay, circle up."

She dismisses them, ignorant as usual of the way her little protégés watch her with stars in their eyes. They all exit quickly, and Sadie starts to gather her mini cones and erase the whiteboard marker from the ice.

I'm smiling and probably looking obviously lovesick as I lean against the open board entry and wait for her to notice me.

When she does, her eyes shoot wide, a smile quickly following as she races toward me. She tosses everything over the threshold before grabbing my jacket and jerking me almost onto the ice. I hold on tight to the glass on the side, letting her devour my mouth for a moment before I reach for her waist and pick her up.

"I missed you," she murmurs into my neck as I carry her to the bleachers.

"I missed you more, Gray." I kiss the top of her head. "Where's your bag?"

She points to it, and I scoop it up. I undo her skates and massage her feet before slipping them into her sneakers. All the while, she keeps staring at me like I might disappear.

The distance isn't too much, but it's enough that it's been hard— especially my first year.

I wanted her to come with me to New York when the Rangers drafted me, but I knew she wouldn't leave Oliver and Liam behind. I also knew she wanted to take care of them and was too scared to rely completely on my parents.

My rookie year had been tough and a learning process, especially about how little free time I would have during the season, but it also came with a lot of rewards. Not only did we make it to the playoffs, though we got knocked out in the first round, but I made friends. One opened up to me about his own struggles with an injury and mental health.

We even co-wrote an article for *Sports Illustrated* about men's mental health and how to ask for help when you need it. I'd almost say that was more successful than any of my plays during that first year, garnering worldwide media attention, interviews, TikTok fan accounts—the works.

It also gained enough traction to leave me with a jealous Sadie ready to pounce and devour me every time I picked her up from the train station, met her after games that she could come to, or came home to where she'd moved into my old room at my parents' house.

It had calmed my protective instincts over not being near her enough, settling some strange primal part of me, to know she was falling asleep each night in *my* bed.

She ended up graduating late, finishing the next fall after the other seniors graduated in the spring. It helped her complete her degree with more pride in herself and her work, and to have another round of competitive skating without the pressure of her abusive former coach.

"I can't believe you're here. I thought you only had like two days before you travel."

I wince, pressing a few circles into her legging-clad calves. "I do. But I'd rather be here than there."

Sadie took the job my dad offered when she graduated. He

wanted her to help him open up an entire sector of the First Line Foundation dedicated to figure skaters in need.

While it would be nice to have her closer to me, work somewhere where we could live together, she is happy now, helping and still doing what she loves.

And that is worth so much more.

"Did you drive?"

She shakes her head. "Your dad picked me up this morning before our meeting with the trust executives. So I'm all yours."

We drive back to her new apartment in a beautiful development slightly outside Waterfell, on the road leading into Boston. It's only a few minutes' walk to the train there, where our small university town is starting to really grow.

We don't make it into the house; Sadie climbs over the console of my rented car and into my lap, hands tangling in my hair and lips pressed hard to mine. It's borderline freezing outside, but I'm sweating, panting beneath her by the time she releases me.

"Let's go inside, hotshot," she murmurs, laying her head on my chest underneath my chin. I squeeze her a little tighter and smile. "I need more of you."

"Okay, Gray."

Sadie

I wake up to a loud bang and turn over to cold sheets.

Both prick my irritation. But mostly, I'm annoyed at the lack of 6′3″ muscle that should be naked and curled around me, asleep.

Instead of shouting for Rhys, I roll out of bed and into my tiny bathroom, slipping on one of his old T-shirts, which I practically live in now, and a pair of long pajama pants because it's *freezing*.

Born and raised in the Northeast, and still, I'll never get used to how cold it can feel.

After brushing my teeth and combing through my shortened hair, I bump up the heat a little as I pad toward the kitchen, pausing when I hear a familiar giggle.

I hover just around the corner, peering in to see Rhys in sweatpants and a navy Rangers sweatshirt that's big enough for the broadness of his shoulders. He sets plates on my little breakfast table, right outside the green-tiled kitchen, which sold me on the entire apartment.

He looks larger than life, just like I've always thought he would. The NHL has beefed him up even more, his body in peak condition, and my mouth waters even though I still feel the ache from the multiple times he took me last night.

But with him, it'll never be enough. I'll crave every part of him, inside and out, forever.

Oliver, fifteen and so tall he towers over me now, sits on one of the chairs, shaking his head at nine-year-old Liam, who is grabbing pancakes with his bare hands and ripping into them like a dog with a steak.

Liam laughs and looks up at Rhys, making sure the guy he idolizes more than anyone is still watching. Rhys laughs wholeheartedly, mussing my brother's auburn curls playfully.

It doesn't matter that Liam doesn't play hockey anymore—now fully obsessed with Marvel comics and art, spending most of his time drawing his own superhero stories in endless art pads provided by Anna Koteskiy—he still looks at Rhys like he put the stars in the sky.

My therapist believes the hero-worship comes from Rhys's treatment of me in front of the boys, the way he cares for me. For Liam, he's the first male role model he ever had; the first adult man to take care of him. To say *I love you* to him.

Oliver is different. He *loves* Rhys, and since Oliver is still playing hockey, he sees him as someone to look up to, someone to aspire to be like. But it's the older Koteskiys who've made him feel safe for the first time in his life.

Which I've had to learn doesn't mean I did a bad job with them. I did the best I could; I protected them. But Oliver was too old, and he understood everything, which meant that he wanted to protect *me*. So he always lived on edge, ready to fight for me.

My father went to jail over another drunk driving incident—and a backlog of warrants that I had no clue about—and he gave up the remaining threads of his custody easily. I was appointed my brothers' primary guardian, with Anna and Max at my side.

From there, after several months of discussions—and a promise that no matter what, I would always be their real guardian—Anna and Max Koteskiy adopted my brothers.

It's been a journey for the three of us, and therapy has made it better.

But now, I get to be their sister. Love them, lift them up, watch them grow up—and not worry about where their next meal comes from or how I'll pay for our rent.

Now, Oliver gets to go to private hockey academies and training camps, if he wants. Now, Liam gets to see his grades and art projects displayed on a fridge that doesn't contain beer bottles and empty promises.

Now, I can watch them flourish and know that when I sleep at night, they're happy.

That *I* did it. I got them out.

I lean against the entryway arch, relaxed while I watch my brothers ask question after question about Rhys's games, which they watch religiously on TV, decked out in his jersey, which has been a top seller everywhere. The boys nearly rival Rhys's dad in their energy level on the couch, when he's not traveling to Rhys's games.

"Pancakes today, huh?" I ask, smiling as I come up behind Oliver and comb my hands through his shaggy dark hair.

"Means it's gonna be a good day," Rhys answers, leaning over to kiss my cheek. "Right, boys?"

"Yep," Liam sings, taking a gargantuan bite of pancakes dripping with syrup and bopping in his seat like he's dancing to music. "Gonna be a good day 'cause Rhys is asking you to marry—"

Rhys's hand plops over Liam's mouth while I feel a thud of Oliver kicking Liam under the table. Liam looks thoroughly embarrassed and apologetic as he swallows and ducks his head.

"Sorry."

A smile slips across my face, happiness bubbling in my stomach until I'm practically giggling. I watch Rhys anxiously rub the back of his neck but fight a laugh himself.

"Let me get your pancakes," he mumbles, turning toward the alcove of the little kitchen.

I follow behind him and quietly and quickly slip my arms around his trim waist, my face pressing into the middle of his back so I can inhale his clean summer-rain scent.

"Rhys is going to do what?" I ask, pressing kisses between words.

I'm almost certain I know, but I'm bursting with a desperate need for him to say it *now*. I don't want to wait. I want to be *his* Gray forever.

He sighs and slumps forward before turning around in my arms, tilting my chin up in a light grasp.

"Marry me," he says with pink cheeks and a little tremor in his hand. He's nervous.

It makes me feel warm—so warm I'm sure my cheeks are flushed darker than his—but I pull his hand up to my lips and kiss his palm.

"Yes, hotshot," I say into his skin, like telling a secret. "Forever, yes."

He shouts, "She said yes!" at the top of his lungs before hoisting me into the air with a yelp. And while Oliver smiles and claps, and Liam howls like a little wolf, I stare right down into the eyes of my golden boy, whose sad eyes aren't sad anymore.

And if I have anything to do with it, they never will be again.

ACKNOWLEDGMENTS

Every time I start to write, I think of a million people out there that have a favorite book, well-loved and tabbed on top of their bedside table. Or maybe in perfect condition, placed on a special shelf and admired.

When I was scared to pick up my metaphorical pen and continue on, I kept hearing the same words: "Every book is someone's favorite book." And if this book brings someone comfort, becomes just one someone's favorite, then it's worth the fear, isn't it?

Heck, I'm just happy (and still a little shocked) this thing—that started as a few swirling thoughts about a boy healing and a girl desperate to heal too but unsure how—exists beyond my Notes app.

To my dad, the best man I've ever known: I don't think I'll ever meet someone like you again. Maybe one day the wound won't ache so much and I'll be able to talk about you without my throat closing up. But for now, I love you. I miss you. I see little pieces of you in Max Koteskiy and hold this book a little closer to my heart just for that.

To my family, who have watched me stumble through careers like sampling ice cream flavors, writing little manuscripts in my spare time: thank you for never once doubting me. Your endless faith in my ability to write (since I was a little middle schooler writing fan fiction like it was my job) has made taking this leap possible.

Isabella: I could write books and books for you, and it would never be enough. Thank you for suffering alongside me, for holding me on the hard days when grief fights to win. For being my forever reading buddy and for late night FaceTime sessions that keep me sane being so far away from you.

To Austin, who believed in me when I didn't, took me on walks or to pretty places when I couldn't get past my grief or fear into creativity: your steady love has kept me warm like my favorite cardigan. I love you, unconditionally, forever.

To Caitlin, from fan-note to becoming my personal knight in shining armor, bodyguard, and the best agent I could ask for. I am thankful every day that you picked up my book and made this entire thing possible. You have changed my life, and I will be forever grateful to you for that. Here's to many more years of *Twilight* kismet moments.

To Suzannah, thank you for being my amazing UK warrior. Your smile is infectious, and with you and Caitlin at my side, I feel invincible.

To Jenna, my pen pal, secret personal assistant, cheerleader, lion tamer, and quite literally any other thing I could ask of you: thank you for existing. You know *Unsteady* better than I do; this book (and my sanity and mental health) wouldn't exist without you.

To every person who read the indie version of *Unsteady*, who made TikToks, Reels, and posts about this book to tell their friends (and their friends' friends) to read, thank you. This is all because of you. You championed *Unsteady* from day one, and that is something I will truly never forget.

To all my beta readers for *Unsteady*: words fall short of describing how much your feedback and help meant to me. You helped to shape this book into what it is today, and I cannot thank you enough. Thank you, forever.

To you, readers, who make the world more magical just by existing and giving time to beautiful stories: read what you love. Keep doing it.

And lastly, to myself: I finally did it. I wrote a whole book and put it out in the world. For that, I'm proud of *me*.

ABOUT THE AUTHOR

PEYTON CORINNE is a writer of romances with imperfect characters, angst, and lots of heart. She grew up on swoony vampire books and endless fan fiction and has wanted to be an author since she was very young. When she's not writing, she's probably at home making another cup of coffee, rewatching *Twilight*, or frantically reading through her own never-ending TBR. Visit PeytonCorinne.com and follow @peytoncorinneauthor on Instagram and @peytoncorinne on TikTok for more.